# THE SHADOW HEALER

# THE SHADOW HEALER

HEART & HAND – BOOK FOUR

## NICOLE E. KELLEHER

jewel lake books

Jewell Lake Books LLC
www.jewellakebooks.com



Cover Design by Kanaxa
Mapwork by Nicole E. Kelleher

**The Shadow Healer, Heart & Hand: Book Four**/Nicole E. Kelleher   – 1st ed.
ISBN 979-8-9857041-7-4

Dedication

In memory of my companion and muse:
Tully.

# The Prophecies

*Recitation to the Goddess as recited by the Fanm
to her followers in The Southron Isles*

After blood and storm
And scorched flesh and bone
Banished from her dark lands
Into the cold sea
Betrayed by love, by family
Gentle hands and grace brought breath
And yet our Goddess heals
And waits.

*Lost Translation from the Exiflos
The Mother's Library, The Fenrhi Temple, Naca'an, Nifolhad*

Duty and shield to cast out blind obeisance
Truth and healing be a warrior's protection
One saved by four
Five control the sixth
But first and last, there will be blood.

# The Known Realms

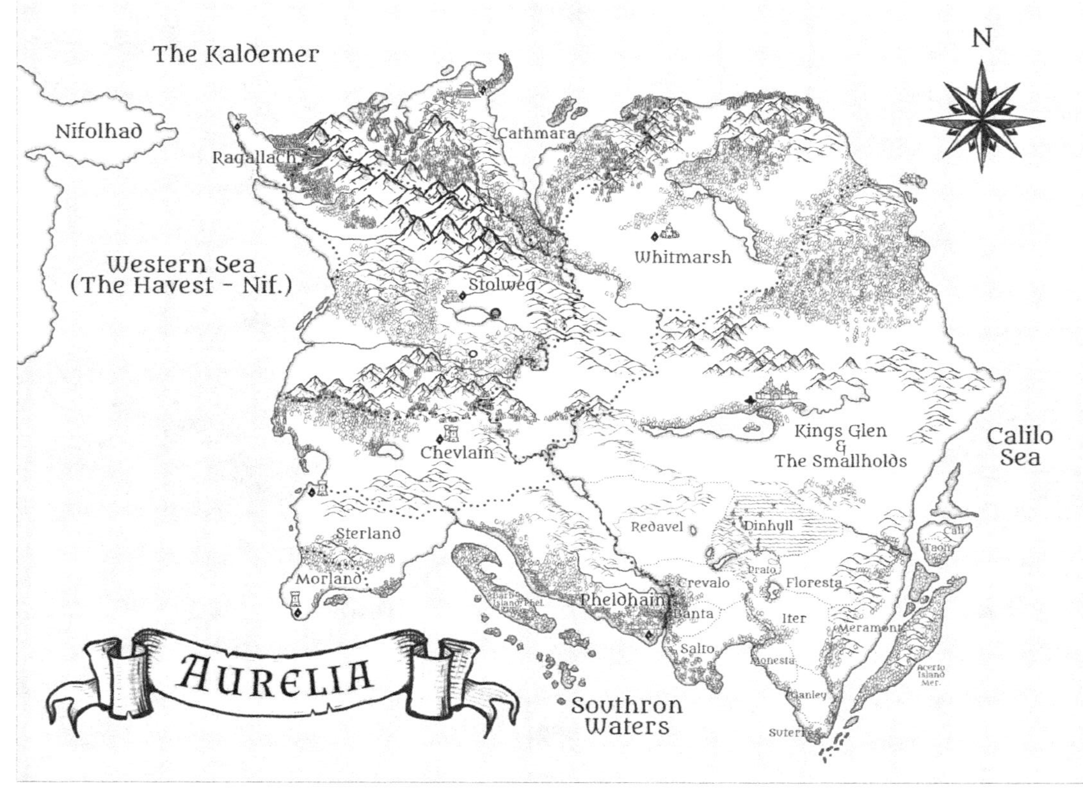

N
The Kaldemer
Nifolhad
Western Sea
(The Havest - Nif.)
Cathmara
Ragallach
Whitmarsh
Stolweg
Chevlain
Kings Glen
&
The Smallholds
Calilo
Sea
Sterland
Morland
Redavel
Dinhyll
Drato
Crevalo
Floresta
Pheldhain
Banta
Iter
Meramont
Salto
Monesta
Stanley
Cull
Taon
Acerto
Island
Mer.
Suteri
Aurelia
Southron
Waters

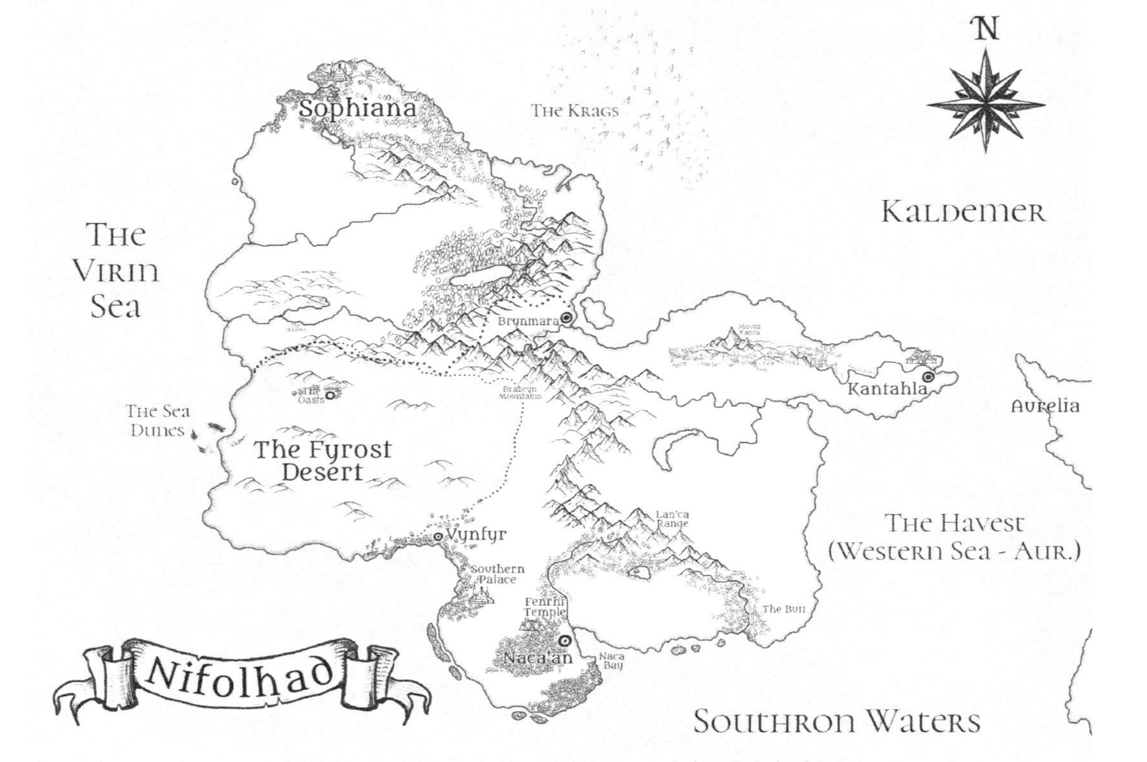

N
Sophiana
The Krags
Kaldemer
The Virin Sea
Brunmara
Mount Verra
Kantahla
Aurelia
The Sea Dunes
The Oasis
Brabryn Mountains
The Fyrost Desert
Lan'ca Range
The Havest
(Western Sea - Aur.)
Vynfyr
Southern Palace
Fenrhi Temple
The Bull
Naca'an
Naca Bay
Southron Waters
Nifolhad

# Prologue

## The Beach in the Territory of Pheldhain, Aurelia

Another wave rushed in, and the inverted skiff under which she was hiding sank deeper into the soupy sand. Murel frantically dug under the boat's edge, but the liquid slurry kept filling the void. She refused to cry. She wouldn't give her brother and cousin the satisfaction. They already viewed her as an annoying girl, tagging along behind them on their misadventures. Slowing them down.

With the next wave, the boat wallowed deeper, closing off her sole light source, a crack in the hull. Damaged beyond repair, the beached vessel had been a fort, a pirate ship, even a chariot. Now, the waterlogged planking would be Murel's tomb. With the thought came the image of her parents' grief, and the floodgates of her tears opened.

Along with the next influx of water, panic welled in her chest. She gulped at the air in the dark space, completely disoriented as to which direction she faced. She drew her knees under her, squatting and pressing her shoulders and back to the bottom of the boat. Her legs trembled with effort as she tried to stand and lever the heavy skiff up.

It lifted! A mere inch. A sliver of daylight. But it was enough, and Murel screamed for all her worth, "Help!" The tide pulled back into the sea, taking Murel's new scarf with it. "Help!" she screamed again.

Another wave swept up and over the vessel's hull, and this time, Murel's feet sunk along with the boat, casting her back into darkness. Then, Murel just screamed.

...

Jesper held out his hand to Tomas while Marten sneered at him, and Tomas wished, not for the first time, that Warin could have pulled his nose out of his journal for once and joined them in their game of hunter-hider on the beach. Warin was nearly as tall as Marten and better able to control his brother's rougher side.

"I won, runtling," Marten jeered.

Back on his feet, Tomas started brushing the sand from his breeches. Jesper tried to help, and Marten hooted at them. Tomas shoved ineffectually at his friend and stalked away, burning with embarrassment. Though he was Jesper's age, he was nowhere near as big as his friend or his friend's cousins.

"That's right, blondie. Run away. Take your skin and bones and go play with my chubby cousin, Murel. You can cry together about how you'll never be as good as I am!"

"You didn't win, Marten," Jesper taunted as Tomas stormed away. "You never found Murel—my sister is always best at this game."

Tomas didn't need to look back to know that Jesper was sprawled on the ground. He passed by the rocky outcropping that marked the path back up the cliff, passing Warin, where he was engrossed in making notes in his journal.

"I don't know why you bother with my brother. It always ends the same way," Warin noted as Tomas continued down the beach.

"Someone has to watch out for your cousin, and that never seems to be you."

"Jesper can handle himself."

"I'm not talking about Jesper," Tomas shot back, woefully aware that Jesper was much stronger than his own puny frame. But he could help Murel, step in and take the occasional shove or swat when her always-on-target barbs hit too closely to Marten's pride. She could turn her cousin's words against him faster than Warin's father could turn the wheel of his fleetest ship. Even if she didn't know it, Tomas counted her as his closest friend, more so than Jesper. Something in his gut told him she felt the same.

He put Warin behind him and walked up the beach, skirting the tide as it rushed in. His parents were traveling to Kings Glen, and Tomas was summering with Warin and Marten's family in Pheldhain. Another wave crashed in, splashing over his boots. The wind had kicked up, and seafoam flew across the normally balmy beach. There must be a storm somewhere to the south, but all Tomas could see was a pale-blue sky with high, wispy clouds. Over the constant crashing of surf, the wind screamed. Lost in thought, he almost missed the scrap of turquoise silk as it washed back into the sea.

He might be small of stature, but he was quick, and darted out his hand to snag the cloth. Soaking wet, he recognized Murel's new scarf immediately—it was her favorite color.

A sudden sense of dread gripped him, and he stared out at the waves. Murel was a skilled swimmer, but the sea was rougher than usual. Besides, she was too smart to venture out alone.

Was she still playing the game? She could tuck herself away in the unlikeliest of places—it was this ability that made her so good. He scanned the beach. There was nothing in view except the old derelict boat he'd already passed by. Upside down and buried under the sand halfway to its keel, it didn't offer much coverage. He started toward the cliffs, but something in his gut clenched. She wouldn't.

She would. He dashed back to the skiff and pounded on the hull. "Murel! Murel! Are you under there? Murel!" He went to the bow, the end closest to the cliffs, and began clawing at the wet sand, digging it out in great scoops with his forearms. But the waves kept erasing his progress. He speared his fingers down searching for the edge of the boat's prow. More seawater washed over the hull, softening the sand, and his fingertips found the edge. He pulled up with all his strength, but the boat refused to budge.

He searched the beach, vaguely aware that someone was running toward him. Nearby, he espied a long piece of driftwood. "I'm coming back, Murel. I'll get you out of there, I promise." He sprinted to the log, dragging it back and trying to jam it in the space he'd dug out.

"What are you doing?" Warin demanded.

"Murel is trapped under there!"

Warin frowned. "Are you sure? How do you know?"

"I found this in the waves!" He brandished her scarf.

Warin took his time weighing the facts. "But you don't know for sure," he stalled, scanning the beach.

Tomas grabbed Warin's tunic. "I. Just. Know!"

Warin nodded, then rushed off to the cliff.

"There's no time," Tomas yelled, believing Warin was going for help. Instead, he bent over to pick up a large boulder. Larger than anything Tomas could imagine even Marten picking up.

Warin duckwalked back to the boat. "Good idea with the log, but we need a fulcrum." He dropped the boulder. Tomas dug out more of the sand as Warin levered the driftwood into place. "I'll push, and you grab Murel. I'm afraid the log might snap, so be fast!" He pressed down with all his might on the log's end. The boat remained stuck.

Tomas stood and helped. Slowly, the seal of sand and water started to give, and the prow of the skiff lifted.

"I've got it now...grab Murel!"

Tomas dove back down, reaching his hands under the boat and coming up with nothing but wet sand. He wasn't wrong—he knew she was there. "Murel!" he called, shoveling more sand to the side and reaching farther under the boat. Behind him, Warin continued to apply pressure to the log. "Higher!"

"It'll snap!"

Tomas's fingers brushed against something smooth and cool. "She's here! I have her wrist! A little higher and I can pull her out. I'm small, I can shimmy under." He heard Warin grunt with effort, and the skiff lifted another inch. Far enough for him to grab Murel's upper arm. He pulled her, but she was too heavy, nearly buried in the wet sand. Suddenly, the boat lifted higher, and the log groaned with the pressure of the weight it carried. Then he was shoved aside, as Marten grabbed Murel's arms and yanked. She came free with a squelching sound, clearing the skiff's edge just as the log snapped.

She wasn't moving.

Warin rolled her to her side, vigorously rubbing her back. "Come on, Murel. Breathe!"

Tomas sat back on his haunches, staring at her blue lips and willing her to take a breath. After what seemed like forever, she coughed and gagged.

A slurry of saltwater and sand gushed out of her mouth, and she drew in a ragged breath. Her eyes fluttered open, and her gaze landed on Tomas. He crawled forward to push her hair back.

"You sniveling coward!" Marten yelled, kicking him away with his boot. "Why didn't you come find us for help! She could have died!" He drew his foot back again to kick Tomas in the stomach when Jesper tackled him from the side, sending Marten crashing into the sand.

"Marten!" Warin yelled. "He found her, you idiot!"

"I'll smash you next, little brother."

"Like hell you will!" Warin shouted, crowding Marten.

Tomas crawled to Murel and cradled her in his lap. "Stop it!" he yelled. "Murel needs help. Not that any of you ever cared about her." As one, they turned to Murel as her eyes rolled back in her head.

His accusations shook Marten out of his rage. He stared down at his cousin, curled up and defenseless, and then he scooped her into his arms. "This isn't over, weakling," he spat at Tomas.

Tomas clambered to his feet and squared off against Marten. "Anytime, you big oaf!"

Marten grunted a laugh, then strode away with Murel in his arms. Jesper hurried ahead of him to alert his aunt and uncle.

When Warin placed his hand on Tomas's shoulder, he shrugged it off.

"You saved her life, Tomas."

"No, Marten was right. I should have gone for help."

"Maybe. But you trusted your gut today—she's alive because of it."

"What's your secret, Warin?"

"What do you mean?"

"How were you able to carry that boulder? Marten could never lift something that heavy."

"Sure, he could."

Tomas waited.

"I don't always have my nose in a book. I work. On ships, with the farmers and herders, everywhere I can. And I lift things."

"Things?"

"Heavy things. All right, I practice. Marten may pick on you and Jesper—"

"And Murel."

"Yeah, well, that ends today. Look, Tomas," he said soberly, "you stay with us for a couple months each summer—imagine living with him every day of your life. Last time he pushed me, I pushed back. I don't like violence; I'm not a brute. And I'm not saying that Marten is, either, but he respects strength."

"Great."

Warin laughed. "You stood up to him. He's eighteen years old and four times bigger than you, and you called him an oaf."

"A big oaf," Tomas corrected.

"You might not have noticed it, because you were more worried about Murel, but there was a grudging respect in his regard."

"But I'll never be as strong as him, or you, or Jesper."

"You're joking? Have you seen your older brothers? Your dad?" Warin asked. "You're what, twelve, thirteen?"

"Fourteen," Tomas said flatly.

"Sorry. But it doesn't matter. Your brothers are in their twenties. I remember when they used to be small like you. My mother calls you the late bloomers. Give it a few years."

"A few years is too long. Can I join you?" Tomas asked. "When you go to work, I mean."

"Why?"

"Because your cousin is my best friend," he confessed. "Next time she needs my help, I want to be able to do something about it."

Warin studied him for a long moment. Then he nodded. "Meet me in the stables before the sun rises. Tomorrow is mucking day."

# CHAPTER ONE

# State of Affairs

## Kings Glen, Aurelia

Praying for the musicians to bring an end to their tune, Murel tried her best to divide her attention between her current dance partner and keeping a sharp eye on her brother, Jesper—Jess for short. But by the look Lord Galerin was giving her, she was doing a poor job of the former. He spun her around once more for good measure, and she completely lost sight of Jess, then craned her neck to try to find him through the crush of dancers.

"Are you unwell, Lady Murel?" Galerin inquired when the music finished.

The step she took away from him was not only required for her to search where she'd last spotted her brother across the room, but to also give her bosom a break from Galerin's poorly hidden ogling. There'd been a time when she'd adopted the more conservative styles of court, but then asked herself why she should do so. She preferred the more comfortable—but more revealing—styles from Pheldhain, where she'd been born and raised. Besides, other men were able to converse with her without staring at her décolletage, even if she was curvier than most of the ladies at court.

"M'lady?" he repeated.

She turned so as to only offer him her profile. "Am I...?"

"Feeling unwell?" He tried to come around to face her again, his eyes once more dipping toward her ample cleavage.

"No, quite the opposite," she answered, sidestepping him again. "Please forgive me. I was a bit distracted."

Galerin frowned as if he didn't really trust her to be telling the truth. Then his eyes followed her gaze to where she finally located her brother. Thankfully, Jess was having a conversation with one of the King's Royal Guards—Ailwen, a thoughtful, soft-spoken man. She hadn't heard that Ailwen had arrived from Ragallach, where he'd been assigned to safeguard the coastal territory until the king and queen appointed a new lord to the region. As her brother was in safe and secure environs—crowds made him nervous and could trigger one of his attacks—she leveled her attention fully on Lord Galerin of the Smallhold of Salto. Salto was situated on the southern shore of Aurelia and was a neighbor of her own family's Pheldhain. The crease between his brows impressed the sincerity of his concern, and Murel did her best to appear as if all were right in the world. She pasted on a smile and commended him on his dancing—he was nimble of foot. "And how do your parents fare?" she asked.

Galerin launched into an account of how taxed his family's resources were of late. "We've always had the means to keep our own people fed and happy. This unfortunate migration of people from Dinhyll…" he droned on.

Murel listened as if rapt—at least he'd stopped staring at her breasts— and offered her sympathies at his family's plight. Of the even greater flow of families into Pheldhain, from Dinhyll as well as Salto, she made no comment. As a daughter of Pheldhain, she could never imagine complaining about the burden these economic refugees caused. No, Pheldhain would do what it always did—her uncle, Lord Marin, would absorb any seeking help into his territory, and then give them aid by way of shelter and work until they were back on their feet. 'Twas always the Pheldhainian way, as much as it was to neither complain nor boast.

"…my father had to station men at the border crossing to try to impede the flow of Dinhyllians, but you know how good they are at finding another way in, usually through Iter or Crevalo."

Murel's smile dimmed. A celebration honoring her homecoming from Nifolhad, as well as the safe return of her brother to Aurelian shores, was not the place to bandy opposing viewpoints with her recent dance partner, but she would have to speak with the queen. Lord Galerin was on *The List*, after all, that all important catalogue of eligible bachelors that Queen Juliana and King Godwin had put together when they got it into their royal brains to play matchmakers. First Lady Anna of Stolweg and the Queen's own nephew, Lord Larkin. Then, there was the marriage of Anna's sister and Murel's friend, Lady Claire of Chevlain, to Lord Trian. And lastly, Lord Warin, her cousin and heir to Pheldhain, to Princess Anwyl of Sophiana.

Beside her, Galerin continued his litany of complaints against the migrants from Dinhyll. If this was the caliber of remaining suitable men on the infamous list, then Murel would rather remain unwed for the rest of her days.

"What is Lord Marin's secret?" Galerin asked in earnest. "I have heard no complaints from Pheldhain during the Royal Council meetings. Tell me, how do you keep them out?"

"We don't."

Galerin opened his mouth to add more, then shut it when her words infiltrated his mind. Of course, he couldn't conceive that she was serious. Celebration or no, it was time to set him straight. His eyes flicked to hers, down to her chest, then, as he dragged them back up, he had the temerity to insist, "You must mean that you don't have a problem. Salto is udderly overrun."

"Utterly," she corrected under her breath, then lifted her chin. "Not overrun at all—we keep our borders open. Pheldhain will always welcome new ideas and cultures into her bosom. It is at the heart of our territory's prosperity. This is true for Salto, as well, yes? Your family has reaped the benefits of our seafaring ways for generations. We ship your products to all the known kingdoms."

He moved, unwittingly blocking her view of Jesper.

"Considering Pheldhain's great maritime traditions," Murel added, "we can do naught but open our arms to new peoples."

"But surely, those coming from Dinhyll have nothing to offer that is of val—"

"We've welcomed peoples from Chevlain and Ragallach when they fled their territories," she interrupted. "We will continue to give succor to any Aurelian who needs it. We've even received a few Saltoan refugees."

Galerin bristled. He opened his mouth to refute her claim, but she laid a gentle hand on his arm. "Galerin, your father is a smart man. He knows that these migrations are cyclical. With fewer people to tend, Dinhyll will recover. Her people will move back when prosperity reclaims the smallhold."

"But some will stay," he intoned.

Really, it was too much. Murel's patience was already thin with worrying for her brother. "Please, Galerin, convey to your father that if he provides temporary shelter and food to these refugees, my uncle will gladly send as many ships as necessary to Salto's ports to ferry them to Pheldhain." Though it was petty of her, she slid her hand up his arm and, with delicate fingers, lifted his chin and forced him to look at her face. "I see someone trying to get my attention. Enjoy your evening, Galerin." She doubted that he got the hint and, not waiting for his reply, went in search of Jesper.

Not for the first time, she wished her father had put off this visit to court. She and Lord Tomas, a Royal Guard and the fifth-born son of the Smallhold of Floresta, had spent nearly a year in Nifolhad. Much of their time there was spent in the Princedom of Sophiana, where the healers of the Sylvan Caste from the Fenrhi Temple had helped to bring her brother back from despondency. While in Sophiana, she had renewed her acquaintance with Tomas. Uncommonly attractive, he'd never once expressed any interest in her above his brotherly affection. Their connection went back as far as being children, but Murel wasn't too proud to admit that she had yearned for more from time to time.

Time? More like timing. It had never been right. Besides, Tomas seemed immune to her charms, and she was more than happy to keep their relationship platonic. It was wholly true that, without his companionship, her brother would never have survived his ordeal. And Murel would do nothing to risk Jesper falling back into a fugue.

For the last nine years, the envoys King Godwin had sent to maintain peaceful relations with Nifolhad had disappeared without a trace. Jesper had volunteered to try to find his fellow Aurelians and had sailed to Sophiana, an independent princedom occupying the northwest corner of Nifolhad. A storm had pushed his ship too close to Brynmara, a northern port under Steward King Diarmait's thumb. His ship had been captured by Diarmait's fleet and, like the diplomats before him, Jess had fallen victim to his stable of torturers.

When Princess Aghna re-emerged as Nifolhad's rightful ruler and laid siege to the steward king's stronghold, Diarmait's prisoners in other liberated cities had been set free. Jesper, the only Aurelian envoy to have survived his grueling incarceration, had been discovered in a tiny cell, deep in the dungeons of Brynmara Fortress. Murel and Tomas had been sent by their king and queen to see Jesper through his recovery. For seven months, Jess uttered not a single word. It was another three before he recognized her and Tomas.

He was back to his full strength, but his hand had been so badly damaged, the Sylvan healing women had had no choice but to remove it. The left side of his beautiful visage bore the marks from someone's cruel blade, and his body was covered in scars, burn marks, and brands. Jess held himself proudly, but his confidence was a façade. When surrounded by nobles and friends, each exclaiming their happiness and relief at his return, Jesper closed himself off, most times by falling silent until the uncomfortableness of the moment had his former acquaintances seeking excuses to leave his company. Those who continued the one-sided conversation soon found themselves with no audience, for her brother would simply walk away.

But these breaches of decorum were easily excused. The same was not true when the turmoil warring in his mind grew too great to contain, leading to his inevitable lashing out. Jess wasn't himself during those feral moments, and when once she failed to hide the bruise he'd given her during one of his breakdowns, and he discovered what he'd done, he'd decamped. Thankfully, her cousin Warin and his wife, Anwyl, had managed to track and find him where he'd hidden himself in the wilderness. Princess Anwyl, having been trained in the healing arts of the Sylvan, spent several weeks with Jess. She taught him how to recognize the warning signs and how to remove himself from situations that triggered his violent episodes. But more importantly, she, having witnessed the devastating results of Diarmait's torturers, was the one person who finally made him comprehend that what he did during these detached states was not his fault.

Anwyl had explained to Murel that the few survivors of Diarmait's torturers lived each day wishing they were dead. Murel could not refute this, seeing as how her own cousin Marten, also a victim of Diarmait, had sacrificed his own life rather than live as a shell of a man. Jess's recovery would last the rest of his days. But he now had the tools to survive, the most important being knowing there were always loved ones nearby who could offer him an escape.

Murel espied him now, across the ballroom, and she could see the telltale signs that his inner panic was growing. He nodded a little too quickly, and his good arm repeatedly crossed over his torso to where his sword once hung on the opposite hip.

Queen Juliana arrived at Murel's side. "He's been holding up so well, my dear. But I think—" She stopped speaking, and Murel turned to see that which had captured the queen's attention. Damn, didn't they realize they were crowding him? Her brother began backing away, accidentally jostling Lady Caroline. Those before him encroached even more into his space.

"Fools," the queen hissed, and Murel was swift to assist her brother, not even taking her leave of the queen. She gauged the distance, measuring it against the wildness growing in his eyes. She wouldn't make it in time, and he would never forgive himself if he exposed his family to ridicule or—worse for any Pheldhainian—pity.

Murel sought the queen's eye, and she nodded, then made some imperceptible signal to King Godwin. He rose to speak. Several of the nobles surrounding her brother eased back to attend the king. But not enough.

Jess's body seized in an unnatural stance, a sure sign that he was an instant away from one of his attacks, and there was nothing Murel could do but helplessly watch the scene unfold. Her brother gulped, as if unable to draw air into his lungs, and he reached for his once-long locks, to begin the ripping—but they had cut his hair short, making that sort of self-harm impossible.

When his mouth opened in a silent scream, the agony and fear in his eyes not yet reaching his features, Murel broke into a run. And those seeking his story, crowding him, begging him to divulge the horrid details of his incarceration, clueless of the torture they reawakened, pressed him further. She could no longer see him, blocked by the broad shoulders of a very large and tall blond noble, one who amazingly managed to shoulder some of the others back. Murel slowed her pace, relief and gratitude flooding her as Tomas led her brother away, all the while talking as if there were nothing amiss. Slowly, the tension in Jess's shoulders uncoiled.

He was nodding at something Tomas was saying. And a moment before they exited the hall, she caught Tomas's eye. He tilted his chin to her, communicating with a look that he had everything in hand. And as Queen Juliana reached her side, Murel reflected on how fortunate she and her brother were to have such a good friend.

"He's better," she breathed, more to reassure herself than to inform the queen.

"Yes," Juliana agreed. "But not completely healed."

"My queen," Murel started, "Jess will be—"

"Let me stop you there," Queen Juliana gently ordered. "We have nothing but respect for the incredible sacrifices Pheldhain has made in support of our kingdom. First Marten, and now Jesper. We are indebted to you for the loyalty shown to us by Lord Marin and his family. And to you. Whatever succor you require, we will humbly give. Now, go. Find your brother and see to his comfort. He's played his part at court admirably and long enough."

"But the rumors will—"

"Nonsense," the queen interrupted. "We will find some other fancy to occupy the wagging tongues."

Murel wasn't sure what to say. The queen had tacitly given her brother leave to return home, and Murel permission to go with him. She would be packed and ready to leave by first light. She curtsied to the queen, then rushed off to find Tomas and Jess.

# CHAPTER TWO

# Shoulders

*Lord Marin's Palace, Pheldhain, Aurelia*

The gentle breeze of dusk had given way to gusting winds, and Murel pulled her cloak tighter. She was helpless to give her brother what he needed to heal because she had no idea what it was.

Far below her, he paced the beach, seemingly heedless of the crashing waves and the ominous rumblings coming from the skies far out to sea. It was strange that after these increasingly frequent tempests, Jesper's turmoil would ease. She stared out into the dark night, praying for the mother of all storms, one that might bring a sense of tranquility to Jess's fractured mind. At least enough of it to last him through the coming weeks.

She and Jess were sojourning at their aunt and uncle's palace. Her friends Lady Claire and Lord Trian from Chevlain would be arriving on the morrow, along with Claire's sister, Lady Anna, and Lord Larkin from Stolweg. They were bringing with them several of the great Chevlain steeds that they bred, along with the dainty, but deceptively hardy, horses from a small band of Nifolhadian steeds hailing from the vast Fyrost Desert and now residing in Stolweg. A few of the horses would be given as wedding gifts to Princess Anwyl and Murel's cousin, Warin.

The gathering had an ulterior goal—a meeting of minds. The three couples had been marked by fate for a greater purpose and had been tasked by Queen Juliana to determine the identities of the other three couples hinted to in an obscure prophecy.

Murel was eternally grateful that fate had passed her by—she was neither a trained warrior, nor gifted with sight, and her life would not be filled with intrigue, plots, and danger. That sort of thing happened to other people, not to her. One day, she would marry, though those plans had been put on hold whilst she cared for her brother.

Murel had enjoyed her time at court, waiting in attendance to the Queen, and would no doubt be called upon to do so again. Except for a stolen kiss here and there, Kings Glen had been unexciting. Invariably, any eligible noble she found interesting ended up treating her more like a little sister than a grown woman ready to settle down and start a family. It had been quite perplexing at the time. And then, when Jess's issues manifested themselves, the lack of amorous attention focused on her became a boon.

Down on the beach, her brother stared at the violent skies to the south. He turned, walking toward the palace, disappearing into the morass of the night-blooming lunastra trees. Murel would wait on the terrace; Jess, not wanting her to worry, always made sure to check in before heading to his chamber. She sent up a silent prayer that he made it to her before the storm rolled inland. Judging by the lightning streaking down from above the Southron Sea, the rain would begin at any moment. Confirming her estimate, not ten minutes had passed by before the wind kicked up, swirling and spiraling around the terrace. Murel grabbed her wine goblet just before it was blown off the ledge.

"You don't have to wait up," came the soft voice of her brother. "Warin knows of my nocturnal wanderings. He asked the guards to keep an eye out for me. Come on, Sis. I'll walk you to your chamber."

"Jess," Murel said, pausing once they entered the palace through the arched entryway. "You'll be surrounded by friends this week. People who have all experienced their own tragedies."

"I'll be in excellent company then," he said dryly.

"I only meant that they will all understand. You won't need to pretend that you are not suffering. They won't take offense if you get up and leave. Or you could give me a signal, and I could distract—" She stopped talking upon seeing his rueful smile.

"Your shoulders must be incredibly strong to take on so much. You should be at court, not here, acting nursemaid to your big brother."

"Reverse our roles, Jess," she countered. "Go ahead. Do it."

"I refuse to." He'd blanched. "I would kill every person in Nifolhad if they took you."

"Oh, Jess, I didn't mean then, but now," she corrected immediately. "What wouldn't you do for me if I needed help?" She didn't expect an answer. "You are my brother, Jesper. Always. What you are not is a burden. And if you forget that fact, I'll tell every person you know all your childhood secrets."

"Why do I always forget that you fight dirty?" he asked, gifting her with a lopsided grin, one made even more crooked by the ragged scars on his cheek.

"Perhaps you are unable to contemplate my amazing mind? Or is it my engaging personality? Or maybe my—"

"Thanks, Sis," he interrupted when they reached her room. And this time when she hugged him, he didn't stiffen up like a tree. "See you in the morning."

"Good night, Jess. Come get me if you need anything."

He nodded and went on his way. Her brother was naught but eleven months older than she, yet he'd lived a lifetime. If caught off guard, when he wasn't trying to keep up his defenses, the pain of those lost years shone from his eyes. A handful of time in the span of his life that affected him as if decades had gone by.

She peeled off her robe and slid under the blankets. Within minutes of her head hitting the pillow, Murel was fast asleep.

. . .

"It was his idea," a woman's voice said. "And I happen to agree."

"Well, not really, Claire," a male voice that Murel recognized argued...Tomas. "It was something Trian told me about...when he lost his memory of you, and Warin told him he was going to Nifolhad to find and bring it back. Of course, what Warin meant was that you were what Trian was truly missing, not his memory, and he sailed off to find you."

Murel paused outside the room. She'd gotten up early, hoping to eat before everyone else. Ever since she had shed her childhood weight, it was her habit to eat little in the morning. It was easier to break her fast alone than to be asked to defend her healthy, if not meager, selection of a bit of fruit and cheese. Anything more, and her curvaceous figure might revert to its formerly pudgy ways. She took a deep breath and smoothed her hands down her gown.

"Tomas. Claire," she greeted as she swept into the dining room reserved for family. Then she smiled at her brother, who was sitting near the broad opening to the terrace with its expansive view of the Southron Waters. He wasn't usually one to rise so early, and Murel did a double take at his bleak expression. "When did you all arrive?" she asked, shooting sideways glances at Jesper.

Jess gave her the briefest of nods by way of greeting, then resumed his study of the calm sea as if it held the answers to all of life's mysteries.

"Minutes after the storm broke," Claire answered. "Trian and Anwyl were here a moment ago, but they went to the stables. Anna and Lark are still sleeping—they stayed up later to make sure the horses were bedded down for the night. I swear, they all consider me helpless because I'm with child again. I'm only four months along, for goodness' sake. Perfectly strong enough to fetch water for the horses." She gave Tomas a scorching look, telling Murel that he was in league with Trian, Claire's husband, and not likely going to let Claire lift a finger in her condition. *Men*, Murel thought, throwing a knowing smirk at Claire.

"All right," Jess announced to the room. Claire, seated next to him, reached out to touch his hand, and amazingly, instead of flinching, he squeezed her fingers in return.

"You're sure?" she asked.

"Yes. I'll do it."

"Do what precisely?" Murel immediately asked as Tomas handed her a folded letter. The royal seal's wax glimmered in the sunlight. Murel always hated breaking the seals—they were so pretty—and slid a knife under the wax to pry it from the parchment. If it cracked, she could try to melt it back together later. Fixing things seemed to be her forte. This seal came free without even a chip, and she read the short missive. "Again? I feel like I just got home."

"Both of us," Tomas stated.

"Am I wrong to believe that there is more to this than is written?" she wondered aloud.

"No, you are not wrong," Claire replied. "Queen Aghna is worried about our mutual friend, Lady Madyan, and she requested our assistance. I can't go, for obvious reasons."

"I'm all for helping," Murel started, "but what can Tomas and I do that she and King Ranulf haven't already tried?"

Lady Madyan was once Queen Aghna's protector when she was in hiding in the Fenrhi Temple during the years before Aghna became the rightful ruler of Nifolhad. But few at the time realized that Madyan, an Umbren master in the arts of stealth and combat, was a leader in her own right. The people of the Fyrost Desert called her the Malikáfyr, or Fire Queen. After a few years of living with Claire and then traveling with Princess Aghna and Lord Warin across Aurelia, Madyan's people had finally called her home.

It was in this very room they had arrived, two Fyrjian warriors from the arid heart of Nifolhad, the Fyrost Desert. What stood out most in Murel's recollection was Madyan's response to the appearance of her brethren. Her normal stoicism, as she rose from her seat to hug Princess Anwyl and then Lord Warin, was filled with emotion. The fiercest woman Murel had ever met, rivaling even Lady Anna in her expertise in fighting, had tears in her eyes. She gave no explanation as to why she was leaving. She simply packed her belongings and boarded the skiff waiting to take her to the Nifolhadian ship moored at Pheldhain's Barb Island.

King Ranulf, the princess's brother, had later written to say that accounts of Madyan's return, landing in Vynfyr, the port city near the southwest edge of the Fyrost, had reached Queen Aghna. But Madyan had spared no time to visit her longtime friend and companion, and had disappeared into her desert with her escort. Over a year had passed, and there was still no word from her.

"Aghna believes that if a foreign diplomat applies for an audience with the Fyrjians, they will not be turned away as her own emissaries have been," Claire supplied as the memories came and went from Murel's mind.

"Especially if said Aurelian diplomats arrive with a gift of specially bred Fyrjian horses," Tomas added.

"Maybe," Murel allowed. "Madyan and I did become friends when we were in Cathmara together, and again here in Pheldhain." Her brother had taken to looking out the window again. "Jess," she asked softly, kneeling before him where he sat in silent reflection, "what did you agree to do?"

He focused on her in a way that he hadn't done since coming back to Aurelia. There was fear in his eyes, and pain. But more importantly, she recognized the stirrings of hope. "I'm going with you."

Murel was shaking her head, even before she got back to her feet. "You can't. I mean, you can. But Jess, *you can't.*"

"It's all right, Sis. Tomas and Claire know everything. I asked for Claire's help this morning."

Murel trusted Claire but wished she hadn't interfered. Few in the realm knew about Claire's extraordinary gift of sight or could even dream of the other powers she possessed. Murel knew. She'd witnessed the miracles Claire had performed firsthand. Like Princess Anwyl, Claire had been trained in the Fenrhi arts. But not one or two areas—all of them. She'd been marked with the six designs and colors of each of Nifolhad's Fenrhi castes—Sylvan healers, Umbren defenders, the duty-bound Earth Caste, the fearsome powers of the Kena, the secretive Blood Caste, and, finally, the caste of one, the Mother. Each caste, represented by its unique color, had been indelibly marked upon her skin, in accordance with the traditions of the sect of women called the Fenrhi.

Even now, Murel could see the designs—moss vines and indigo swirls peeking from Claire's hairline and interlacing with the shades of dust and charcoal as they trailed down her neck and under her collar, only to reappear from under the cuffs of her sleeves, where they decorated her hands and fingers. And underneath the colors, the latticework of the honeycomb, inked in amber and amplifying the runic powers of the designs marked on her body. The rich color of honey, signifying the unifying power of the Fenrhi mother. Claire shared little of what was done to her in Nifolhad. From surviving its vast cities to seeking refuge in the Fenrhi Temple, and even traversing the Fyrost Desert, she had returned to Aurelia a changed woman.

"Before you ask," Claire started, "I wasn't able to *see* Jesper's future. Nothing of the like has ever happened to me, except with Trian and my children. But it is not the same—with Jesper, I sense naught but a void. One fact is true, however; if he wants to heal both his mind and heart, he needs to find his answers in Nifolhad."

"I know you don't like it, Murel," Jess said with unexpected vehemence, "but the more I think about it, the more I'm convinced that this is my path. The things that happened to me in that prison...locking away those memories isn't helping. I must confront them."

"But..."

"Will you help me?" he asked.

"You know I will," Murel conceded. The entire room seemed to sigh in relief. "How else can I keep an eye on you if you don't come with Tomas and me?"

He chuckled at that, then turned to discuss the arrangements with the others. As she stood there, staring longingly at the buffet of delicacies, Tomas joined her. She ignored the sweet pastries; the days of loading her plate with the honeyed palm cakes famous in Pheldhain were over. Beside her, Tomas scooped up a spoonful of raspberries—her favorites—and, instead of putting it on his plate, set the serving on hers. Funny that he remembered such a trivial thing as her penchant for the fruit.

"I'll help you with Jesper," Tomas promised.

"Thank you. He trusts you more than anyone else," she admitted.

"Except you," he replied, as Warin joined them in the dining room.

"I hear you're off to play diplomats again," Warin noted as he piled palm cakes onto his plate and pinned Tomas with a look that Murel couldn't translate.

She narrowed her eyes at her cousin. "It's not exactly playtime, Warin. We work hard at what we do, and we make an excellent team. Don't we, Tomas?"

Surprise flashed in his eyes, and he averted them to inspect the breakfast offerings.

"What was that look, Tomas?"

He shrugged, smiling good-naturedly, and then nodded to her and to Warin. "I promised Trian I would help him with the horses," he said, changing the subject.

"Warin?" she demanded.

"Don't ask me what goes on in blondie's head," he said, using the childhood nickname they had for Tomas. Tomas never took offense. For in a sea of dark-haired Pheldhainians, his towheaded curls had stood out like a beacon. With age, the color had deepened to a pale gold.

Tomas shifted under her scrutiny as Warin stepped away. "Let's all meet together later to discuss the plans," he suggested.

"It's a date," she said, and he blinked as she popped a plump raspberry into her mouth. He turned to leave, but stopped before he reached the door, and then spun back to her. "I forgot to give this to you." He placed a piece of cloth in her hand before disappearing through the doorway.

Murel set her plate of berries on the table and sat to eat her quick meal. She opened the fabric to find a perfectly formed wax seal nestled inside. It must've come from the missive Tomas had received from the king and queen. She stared at the raspberries he'd put on her plate and wondered, as she often did, why there'd never been a spark between them.

"It's for the best, I suppose," she said to herself as she finished breaking her fast, before making her way to the stables to see for herself the horses they would be transporting to the Fyrost Desert. Besides, she didn't think she could bear one more complication. She rolled her neck to release the tension that always coiled there. An unbidden image of Tomas's wide shoulders and lean waist as he left the hall came suddenly to mind. "Definitely for the best," she repeated and grinned.

· · ·

Tomas detested being late. It put him in a bad mood. As did the letter he'd, a moment ago, read from his mother. Being the youngest of five sons had its benefits, but so too were there negatives. Like this very moment. He'd enjoyed relative freedom to do what he wanted, but with his older siblings married and well into establishing their own broods, his mother decided it was time to make a project of the baby of the family—and of course she would name the one person Tomas couldn't have, along with other less inviting alternatives. He stuffed the unwanted letter into his pocket as he entered the library where Warin and the princess, Trian and Claire, and

Lark and Anna all waited with Murel. Jesper hadn't been invited to this council, and he wondered at the import.

"Bad news?" Murel asked as she stepped over to him, pointing to where he had stowed the missive from his mother.

If she only knew. "A bit of unwanted motherly advice," he groused.

She swatted at his chest. "You be nice to your mother. She's the sweetest woman alive. How such a tiny woman managed to have such enormous boys is one of the realm's biggest mysteries."

"I used to be smaller, remember?" His breath nearly caught when she smoothed his tunic, lightly brushing the fabric on his chest. He resisted the urge to flex his muscles.

"Oh, I remember, all right. And now you're bigger than your older brothers." She gave him one last pat on his chest and then stepped away with the hint of a smile. Why was he always drawn to staring at her lips? And, as she sashayed away, her hips, too, and her fine—

No more of that! He poured himself some wine from the sideboard, and then took the sole remaining seat, the one next to Murel's. He nodded to the others already chatting at the table.

"Glad you could join us," Warin jibed. When Tomas scowled at his friend, Warin added, "Everything all right in Floresta?"

"Just perfect," Tomas stated a little too curtly, drawing seven pairs of eyes. "Which means my mother is bored."

"Ah," Trian commented in his usual curt but insightful way. That *ah* held a wealth of meaning. Everyone save Princess Anwyl nodded in commiseration.

"What?" she asked.

Warin grinned. "Simply put, the mothers of Floresta pride themselves on being matchmakers, and Tomas's siblings are all dutifully settled." He turned to Tomas. "I'm guessing this next mission is looking a bit more attractive now."

Tomas could feel the heat rising in his face.

"Oh no," Warin said, noting how Tomas darted a look at Anwyl. He laughed heartily. "Go ahead and ask her."

"Warin," Murel admonished. "Leave Tomas alone."

His friends waited expectantly, and Tomas gave an exasperated sigh. "My mother was wondering, Princess Anwyl, if you know of any more wayward Nifolhadian princesses needing rescuing." The others burst out laughing. Everyone except, at least at first, Murel.

When the ribbing finally ceased, Claire brought the group back to the matter at hand. "I'm afraid that after what we tell you, your mother will be disappointed. I doubt there will be time for you to woo any wayward Nifolhadajanas," she started, but quickly grew serious. "What we are about to share with you is known only to this group, the king and queen, and a few others. Before we begin, we must ask you to make an oath, one that is held higher than your oath to king and country."

"What do you need us to do?" Murel asked, already agreeing to make the oath.

"Wait, Murel," Tomas cautioned. "It's always best to hear the details before giving your word and being bound to a promise you would've rather not made." He snuck a glance at Warin. "Will this oath contradict the vows we've already made to the king and queen?"

"Possibly. There's no way of knowing, Tomas," Warin said.

"But I *do* know," Claire averred. "This oath that we will ask you to take is one meant to protect this realm and that of Nifolhad. And in protecting the two, you are keeping your oath as a Royal Guard. But I cannot say if it will contradict any other promises you may have made." Claire smiled thoughtfully at him, then added, "Your past oaths will be tested in the coming months, Tomas, but your honor will not be tarnished."

Anna spoke next. "Will you swear to guard the secret close to your heart, protect it with your lives, and not speak of it to another living soul?"

"With one condition," he stated, taking the dagger Claire held out to him. Holding it by the blade, pommel up, Tomas promised, "I swear, by this blade and on all that I love and hold dear, and with my life, will protect this secret and not repeat to another man or woman, unless abstaining from doing so means risking Murel's life." Then he kissed the center where the quillon married grip to blade. He handed the weapon to Murel.

"Tomas is right. On these missions, we've always protected one another. Even with Diarmait's power waning, Nifolhad is a dangerous place. And if we are to enter the Fyrost Desert, then I will use every weapon I have to keep us safe, including information. So, I vow the same." She repeated his prior words, substituting his name for hers, and then returned the dagger.

"Before Anwyl and Warin can begin," Claire stated, "you both must see something. Please stand." She walked over to them and set one hand each over their hearts. "Close your eyes." They did. And Tomas wondered what she was doing, for when she finished, he felt no different. "All right," Claire said.

Tomas turned to Murel, and she to him, as they opened their eyes. She wore the same confused expression that he was sure was on his face. Then he regarded Lark, his former mentor in the Royal Guards—there was something about his friend that he couldn't quite define.

Murel was looking back and forth between Warin and Princess Anwyl and frowning. "They're glowing!" she shouted, pointing at Claire and Trian. She lowered her voice. "You...you're all glowing."

"Indeed, you are," Tomas agreed. It was most noticeable around Claire and Trian, a soft amber shimmering around their silhouettes.

"The color of honey," Murel whispered. "Like the Fenrhi Mother. And you, cousin," she said to Warin, "there's a blue sheen surrounding you and the princess. Like the sky. No! Like the Kena."

"I see," Tomas said, staring at Lark and Anna. "It's not that yours is a dimmer light; it's that it's the muted color of dust. Earth Caste!"

Murel sat and promptly tipped her goblet to her lips. Tomas stopped himself from drinking down his wine in one gulp. Princess Anwyl set a large, folded fan on the table. She then unfurled its pieces, forming a six-petaled flower.

"Always in sixes," Murel stated. "Our crest with the flower. The new crest of Sophiana. The six Fenrhi castes."

"The six of you," Tomas added.

"We are only three, actually," Warin corrected. "Three couples. For it is Anna, Claire, and Anwyl who were fated and then made whole by, well..."

"You," Princess Anwyl finished sweetly, and Warin lifted her hand to his lips and pressed a kiss there.

"With the exception of Anwyl and Warin, who noticed first, we detected our auras only recently," Claire explained.

"Wait!" Tomas demanded. "We're not glowing, are we?" Murel suddenly appeared as stricken as he felt. Thus far in his life, he'd been ordinary compared to his friends. In fact, he and Murel had confided their relief to one another on this point on more than one occasion. Everyone in the room, save Murel, burst out laughing.

Murel cleared her throat. "It's not *that* amusing," she censured. "He's right to ask. There's something about the number six, and if we're not emanating a Fenrhi glow, then we should ask if you know who the other three pairs are. And more, other than finding Madyan, what else have you cooked up for us on this mission?"

Claire gave Murel an appreciative half smile, then nodded to Anwyl. "First, Anwyl needs to go over a few basics with you. Details we've cobbled together from the Fenrhi, ancient scrolls in Kings Glen, Warin's notes from when he visited the Southron Isles, and finally, a few barely discernable etchings on the henge stones at Stolweg. Princess?"

"Right. First, this parchment fan is an *exiflos*. The women of the Fenrhi Temple in Nifolhad use them much like other scholars use scrolls and now books. This one describes the six Fenrhi castes. What do you know of their system for compartmentalizing their members?"

"Only the basics," Murel admitted. "What each caste means, historically and currently, and that members are marked by a specific color representing their individual castes."

"And some members can be marked with more than one color, as was done to Claire," Tomas added.

"The distinction between the old and new is an important one to note," Anwyl stated, then pointed to the first page of the exiflos. "The amount of information we have is both overwhelming and a mere drop in the ocean. I encourage everyone here to interject their thoughts and impressions as we go over each of the castes." She turned to Warin.

"I'll take notes," Warin stated, pulling out a journal. "I think you should start with The Mother."

The way the princess smiled at him had something in Tomas's gut clenching, but before he could ponder it, she began anew.

"The Fenrhi Mother is a caste of one and is signified by an amber or honey hue. She represents, and is meant to maintain, the unity and harmony between the castes. Ni'mala is the current Fenrhi Mother and, until recently, was focused solely on the acquisition of power. Only time will tell if she'll be able to regain the trust of her brethren."

"Ni'mala was first marked with Kena Caste, and then later, as Mother," Claire stated. "But, like the Mothers of old, I was marked for all of the castes. At the time, the Fenrhi Artists hoped I would replace Ni'mala."

"There are four Fenrhi Artists, two of which I count as friends," Anwyl said. "Most of their designs are Fenrhi symbols, but sometimes—as in Claire's case—a greater power takes over, and their designs flow from heart to hand, their minds barely conscious of what they are doing until they finish."

The princess smiled at Claire. "Anna knows this already, and Warin, of course. I'm marked as well, Claire." She drew up the folds of her gown to reveal that her thighs had been marked in moss green and a purple so dark it was nearly black.

"Sylvan and Umbren trained," Tomas marveled. "And they marked you? But you're not Fenrhi."

"No, and my markings are different than those of the Fenrhi women, as are Claire's."

"What is it, Murel?" Warin asked.

"I...well..." she started. "These glows that you have don't match."

"Keep going with that!" Warin encouraged.

"Of course!" the princess exclaimed at the same time.

"Claire's glow makes sense," Murel continued. "But why is your glow the blue of the Kena Caste when you are marked for Sylvan and Umbren? And why is Anna Earth Caste? Shouldn't she be Umbren and Sylvan? She's a warrior and a healer."

"Are you gifted with sight, like Claire?" Tomas asked the princess. "Can you influence and control other people as the Kena do?"

"No," Anwyl stated, "but the true foundation of the Kena Caste is not control, as it was under recent leadership, but the search for truth and knowledge. What I see is potential, and possibilities." She turned to Warin. "Maybe the colors predate the Fenrhi, as do the markings, when the artists are entranced."

"Separate from the Fenrhi," Warin wrote in his journal. "No, adopted by the Fenrhi and assigned to give some order to the caste system. We'll have to write to Ni'mala about this."

"If we already know this, then why the need to take an oath?" Tomas asked.

"There's a larger mystery to unravel," Anwyl explained. "And we believe some of the answers may lie in the Fyrost Desert."

"And perhaps the identity of the three missing couples," Tomas guessed. "You're missing the green of the Sylvan, the shadow colors of the Umbren, and…"

"The red of Blood Caste," Murel finished.

Anwyl nodded and opened another fan. "This exiflos tells of the legend of the Sky Goddess. She was—perhaps still is—worshipped by the Fyrjians in the desert. Because there is so much to discuss, I'll paraphrase what I know. But when you sail to Naca Bay, I recommend that you have Captain Grieg tell you the story in its entirety—he's quite poetic.

"Here's the short of it: Nifolhad was once ruled by powerful beings, gods and goddesses. The most powerful of all was the Sky Goddess. And in Nifolhad, she loved the Fyrost Desert the most. Some say that the sands reflected her own beauty back up at her, and that the heat warmed her heart and made her love the people of Nifolhad.

"One day, she met a man in her desert, a man from faraway lands. He wooed her, and she fell in love. This man loved his home, a land filled with forests and woods and rich, loamy earth. When he came to Nifolhad, he was seduced by the Goddess of the Woods. As gods and goddesses covet power, she lamented to him that her trees would not grow in the desert." Anwyl paused to take a sip of wine. "To make a long story short, the man intentionally broke the heart of the Sky Goddess. Her tears of grief wet the sands, and the forests thrived, so much so that their branches grew to pierce the Sky Goddess's heart."

Anwyl pointed to the last petal of the exiflos. "She was enraged and called upon her brother, the Wind God, and together they razed the trees from the desert. She was determined to excise the people from the land below. Her brother took pity on them and flung them to the five corners of Nifolhad. When, in her rage, she threatened to kill the man who'd courted her and to destroy the Goddess of the Forests, the Wind God blew his sister into the Virin Sea to extinguish her wrath."

Warin pulled out a scroll, unrolling it to show them a depiction of a multi-armed woman. In each hand, she held a different gem: sapphire, onyx, diamond, amber, and emerald. In the center of the woman's stomach, a great ruby. "This is from the library in Sophiana." He next opened a well-worn journal and turned to a page that was dog-eared from frequent visits. A similar image appeared, albeit with six arms. Only five circles, though, had symbols with colors matching those on the parchment from Sophiana. "This is a drawing I made when, years ago, I visited the Southron Isles. The original was painted on a wall, an altar in someone's home. I drew the extra arm by mistake."

Tomas reached out and placed his fingers on each circle, then rested the heel of his hand on the red mark. "I've seen this symbol before."

"Where?" Claire demanded.

"My mother bought some goods, jewelry and fabric, imported from the Southron Isles. It's a repetitive motif. And it's on the henge at Stolweg, isn't it?" he asked Anna, and she nodded.

"And here, on my blade," Claire added. "Queen Juliana assumed it was a partial rune, worn away by time. I saw this same symbol carved on some ruins at an oasis in the Fyrost Desert."

"And here," Warin remarked casually, pulling the collar of his chemise and tunic to the side.

Tomas squinted his eyes at the spot above Warin's heart. "I always believed that to be a bruise, or a birthmark. But it's the same shape. Have you always had it?"

"No," he said. "It was a gift from a woman born in the Southron Isles. Grieg said that I was goddess-marked."

"You think this goddess the Southron Isles folk worship is the same Sky Goddess of ancient Nifolhad," Murel said. "And how does this fit in with the Fenrhi?"

"We don't know that it does," Anwyl replied.

"Or the Fenrhi don't realize," Tomas guessed. "But I would wager that Madyan and her merry band of Fyrjian warriors know more. And if they find out that the Sky Goddess now resides with the Southron Islers, what then?"

"Not resides," Warin rectified. "Held captive by their queen, Fanm Larenne."

"Thus, the oath," Tomas ended.

Murel sighed and shook her head. "Right. Let me get this straight. We are sailing to Nifolhad to: one, find Madyan for Queen Aghna; two, confirm the Sky Goddess is the same goddess now worshipped in the Southron Isles; and three, uncover the identities of the missing three couples—"

"Perhaps not all of them," Claire interjected with a smile. "Even determining the identity of the fourth couple would be a step in the right direction."

"And four," Tomas added, "don't forget helping your brother."

"At least the third goal is easy," Warin said, then added with a grin, "simply look for people who are glowing!"

"And we haven't even discussed the prophecy yet," Anwyl reminded the others.

Beside him, Murel slumped. "What prophecy?" Tomas asked.

# Siblings

Tomas greeted Captain Grieg where he stood at the helm. They were aboard Pheldhain's newest ship, *Moon Caster*, on loan to them from Warin. She was a lithe vessel—one made solely for speed—and modeled after Lord Ronan of Meramont's more agile coastal fleet.

And speak of the devil, Tomas watched as Ronan strode across the deck to join him where Grieg was putting *Moon Caster* through her paces as she crossed the Western Sea, riding high on the water and scorching her way across the waves. It wasn't that Tomas didn't like Ronan; he simply didn't know him well enough. Ronan had once been a Royal Guard but had given it up to return home to the Smallhold of Meramont well before Tomas had joined the elite group of warriors. Ronan's father's untimely death had made his departure from the Guard necessary. Under Ronan's management, and with his mother's aid, his smallhold had thrived. They were the largest producer of two of the most coveted crops in the realm— the royal pomerois and the beneficial pihaberries. Tomas had sampled enough of Meramont's brandy to know that the man had a way with the fruit of his orchards that no one in the realm could rival.

"She's a nimble thing, isn't she?" Ronan called out by way of greeting. "Fortunate for me that I get to stand in for Warin on this voyage."

"Aye, she is," Grieg concurred. "I'd wager she's the fastest ship in the known realms. She won't hold much contrab—er, cargo, though."

Tomas smirked. Captain Grieg had been born in the Southron Isles and was an anomaly. Southron Islers did not mix with Aurelians and Nifolhadajans alike. They were a secretive nation, one that King Godwin now had an eye on. For generations, the Islers had harried the southern coasts of Aurelia, finally stopping when Warin's ancestors treated with them. And while Warin's family had *mostly* moved away from smuggling, the Islers kept to their not-so-aboveboard ways. Ronan caught Tomas's eye and was no doubt thinking the same.

"This ship will outrun anything that floats," Ronan boasted. "And maybe even those storms your goddess keeps sending north." When Grieg's hand on the wheel slipped, and he paled, Ronan quickly added, "Her blessings upon us."

"It's not wise to tempt fate where the Goddess is concerned," Grieg warned, glancing over his shoulder to the southeast and making a complicated motion with his hand, invoking some prayer or another. They'd left the Southron Waters without incident. Moreover, the skies had been fair, and the winds steady. The new ship design would see them to Naca Bay on the southeast coast of Nifolhad at least a week faster than if they'd taken one of Pheldhain's other trading ships.

Tomas had once considered Grieg superstitious. Events over the last two years, including a better understanding of the gifts possessed by the Fenrhi women, the wondrous properties of the pihaberries—a fruit that could protect a person from being manipulated by those same Fenrhi—and the sea tempests that defied explanation, had Tomas opening his mind to things he once deemed fantastical. And he would never forget seeing his colorful, glowing friends. Though they were quiet about it, they formed a triangle of strength and support upon which the king and queen had come to rely.

His friends had sworn him to secrecy about the prophecy, and he hadn't repeated it to anyone, but the words were forever etched into his brain.

> *Duty and shield to cast out blind obeisance*
> *Truth and healing will protect the warriors*
> *The fourth shall save the fifth*
> *All must survive to control the sixth*
> *But first and last, there will be blood.*

While Ronan and Grieg waxed poetic about the ship, Tomas rubbed his temples. He'd spent the morning attempting to suss out the meaning behind the latter half of the prophecy, and his skull was throbbing. He'd never been very good at solving riddles. Now, give him a quarterstaff, and he would take care of all your problems. Why in all the realms had his friends enlisted his help in their quest?

"Are you not feeling well, Tomas?" Murel asked, coming up behind him.

"If he's sick, it's not from my brandy—it's hangover-proof," Ronan tossed to them, then began conferring with Grieg in earnest.

Murel smiled. "Headache?" she guessed, and he nodded. "I know the feeling. I've been trying to figure out who the other three couples are since we left Aurelia. But when I remember that I'm not numbered amongst those in the prophecy, I breathe a sigh of relief. I don't know about you, but I'm not one for adventuring and battle."

"Agreed. Except for the battle part." She laughed, as he'd intended. Murel was beautiful, especially when she laughed. It was the kind of sound that made a man want to spout witty bon mots merely to hear it again. Titillating conversation, like solving riddles, was also not in his wheelhouse. Oh, he did all right at court, thanks mainly to his physique. But he wasn't quick with his words like Warin and Lark. Or Ronan, for that matter. Then there was the oath—words sworn to Warin, years ago. He frowned.

"You really do have a headache, don't you?" Murel worried, seeing his pained expression. "Here, give me your hand. I would like to try something that the princess taught me."

He presented his right hand to her, happy to have something to take his mind off the conundrum his friends had laid on their shoulders. "I'm willing to try anything." She turned his hand up at the wrist, then proceeded to pinch and knead the few soft spots in the pad and webbing of his palm. "Sorry about the callouses. Your cure probably won't work on me."

"Let me concentrate," she shushed, and then bit her lip in the most endearing way. He turned to stare at the waves before he embarrassed himself. Making good on his vow to Warin, he'd been treating Murel like a sister for so long that she would never see him as anything but a brother.

But he wasn't her brother. He swallowed at the thought. Then he swallowed again at the exquisite relief that worked its way up his neck and cranium. And his hand had never felt so wonderful. Every tensed muscle seemed to melt away, one after the next.

"There," Murel announced, releasing her hold. "Any better?"

He blinked a few times, then felt his grin spreading.

"Good. I'll let Anwyl know it worked. There's but one problem, as far as I can tell."

"What's that?" he asked.

"I can't perform it on myself."

"Then you'll have to teach me, and next time your head hurts, I'll take care of you."

"It's a deal."

"What's a deal?" Ronan asked, joining them.

"You wouldn't be interested," Murel teased. "Seeing how the brandy you make on Acerto Island seems to be your cure-all."

"You would be surprised at the things I find interesting, Lady Murel. For example, the way you massaged the pressure points on Tomas's hand to relieve his tension has roots in more than one culture of the known realms."

"I didn't know that you were learned in the Fenrhi healing arts. Have you hired a Sylvan woman to tutor you?" Murel teased.

Ronan looked confused for a moment, then frowned. His features cleared, and he quickly replied, "Princess Anwyl showed me."

"I didn't realize she had—" Murel started.

"I understand that she is quite learned in all functions of the body," Ronan added, cutting her off and winking.

Tomas straightened to his full height, a warning gesture Ronan chose to ignore.

"The feet, for instance. Did you know that it's believed that the nerves there have a direct connection to one's midsection?"

There was nothing Tomas could do. Ronan hadn't crossed any lines, though he had pitched his voice in a seductive timbre. And yes, he'd alluded to the training that the princess was rumored to have had, training of a most private nature that all Sophianan nobles were given. Sure, Tomas couldn't bandy glib words, but he understood subtext. Nuances that Murel, an intelligent and well-versed lady in the queen's court, would not miss.

"The feet and the stomach?" she asked. "Surely you need no such remedy, Ronan, considering the quality of your...bottle. I'm starting to believe that the reputation of your juice may be exaggerated."

Tomas had to hand it to Murel. She could spar with the best of them. Ronan bowed and conceded the win to her. She'd called his bluff, and to go any further in a conversation that had nothing to do with brandy would cross the line of civility.

Ronan turned to include Grieg. "The smaller cargo area isn't the only thing that's wrong with this vessel," he complained. "Her speed is to be lamented, for *Moon Caster* will deprive me a full week of repartee with the fair Lady Murel. I suspect there is much she could teach me."

"About what?" Jesper demanded, coming late to the conversation, but instantly seizing its tone.

"About feet," Ronan answered, never without a quick rejoinder. "And how I should be schooled in not putting mine in my mouth."

Everyone was silent for a moment, then they all burst out laughing. Jesper finally loosened up and smiled.

"Do I hear the horses neighing? I think I'll check on them," Murel said, deftly removing herself from the conversation. "Would you like to join me, Jesper?"

"In a few minutes. I need some advice from Tomas."

Murel leveled a shrewd look on her brother. "All right. I'll see you in a moment then." The four men bowed to her as she took her leave of them.

Jesper drifted away from Ronan and Grieg, and Tomas followed him to where he stopped some yards away, leaning against the rail and staring out at the swells of the Western Sea.

Tomas set his forearms on the rail and was caught up by the hypnotic rising and falling of the water. It was an overcast day, and the waves below them were dark and forbidding. He grew up on the coast but hadn't felt the call of the sea as his older siblings had. To be sure, he could sail, it was in his blood, but he preferred dry land and his Chevlain steed under him rather than a wood-planked deck. Jesper, as usual, was taking his time, formulating his query with care and consideration. When he finally spoke, it was not what Tomas expected.

"Can we trust Ronan?" he asked.

"Ronan? Yes, of course. Why do you ask?"

"Murel." He paused for a moment, then gave Tomas the hard look of a brother bent on protecting his younger sister's honor. "He's a smooth one, isn't he? There were rumors. And I was there at court during his time in the Royal Guard. It was before your arrival, but I remember his rivalry with Lark and Warin. Ronan was a bit too committed to winning their little game of hearts. There was some talk then that if he hadn't returned to Meramont on his own, he would have been expelled by the king and queen."

Tomas had not heard any of this. "It's been at least ten years, Jesper. I'm sure time has tempered him."

Jesper raised an eyebrow. "He's not married yet."

"I think you can trust him to act honorably where your sister is concerned."

"Thinking isn't the same as knowing," Jesper pointed out.

"Then trust your sister. She's well-equipped, both in wit and weaponry, to protect herself." At his words, Jesper's face fell.

"That used to be *my* job." He clenched his fist and banged it on the rail.

"There's no reason you can't—"

"Can't what?" Jesper hissed. Tomas had never once seen him react in anger to what had happened to him. He'd raged, to be sure, but this was controlled. Tomas didn't interrupt, knowing that it was probably good for his friend.

Jesper unclenched his fist. "I've tried, Tomas. I've never been able to wield a sword properly with my nondominant hand. It's one of the reasons I didn't join the Royal Guard. I'm too damn clumsy. They might as well have taken both hands for all the good that I can do now." He hung his head.

"Let me help you, Jesper. I don't know what you've tried, but some of the tricks that I've learned from Princess Anwyl and Lady Madyan might help. Their techniques seem to stem from attaining balance and fluidity, rather than nimbleness of hand and wrist."

Jesper looked up at him—the doubt was still there, but a spark of interest as well. "I would appreciate that," he finally said, and Tomas knew how badly it hurt for him to ask for help. "I don't know what I would do without you and Murel. You're the brother I never had."

Tomas winced.

"What was that for?" Jesper asked.

"Warin, of course. He made all the Royal Guards swear an oath to treat Murel as if she were their own sister."

Jesper laughed. "Murel is going to have his hide when we get back. Our parents have been pressuring her to settle down. They want grandchildren, and it doesn't appear as if I'll be accommodating them anytime soon. Whenever they remind her of her duty, she claims that no one has shown her any interest." Jesper narrowed his eyes. "See here, Tomas. I would like nothing better than having you as a real brother. And if marrying my sister is the way to do it, then you have my go-ahead to woo her. And as far as Warin's concerned, a brother's blessing trumps a cousin's any day of the week."

"But I swore to him that I—"

"If you are not interested in Murel, that's one thing. But if you are, quit wasting time. You never know what can happen in life. Make the best of it while you can."

"But—"

"Your problem isn't here." —Jesper jabbed him in his chest. —"It's here." He tapped him on the forehead. "For honorable men like you, if it means enough to you in your heart, your head shouldn't get in your way." Jesper turned to walk away, then paused, chuckling at the idea. "Warin really made you all take an oath?"

"He did. But, uh, don't tell your sister, all right?"

"I may be brutally honest, but I'm not cruel, my friend. And look on the bright side. At least we won't have to worry about Ronan; he's never broken his word as far as I've heard."

"Ronan wasn't a Royal Guard at the time, nor was he at court. I doubt Warin got to him." As one, they turned to regard the man in question. At the helm, Grieg lifted a hand in salute. Ronan was nowhere to be seen. Then Grieg laughed and pointed toward the hold.

"I think I'd like another gander at those Fyrjian steeds. Want to join me?" Tomas asked.

"No, you've got this one," Jesper answered. "Do you reckon...I mean, does Murel have feelings for you?"

"Yes," Tomas answered glumly. "Sisterly affection."

"Then I guess we both have things to work on, don't we?"

"Truer words...truer words." Then Tomas went in search of Murel.

# Knocks and Knots

## Naca Bay, the Port City of Naca'an, Nifolhad

The cry of gulls roused Murel, and she drew in a deep breath, and a riot of odors fought for purchase in her nose—the persistent scent of salt air, rotting algae at low tide, smoke and spice and food, and the sweat and breaths and body odor of thousands of people. After weeks on the open sea, it was a welcome assault on her senses. Murel hadn't been to the bustling port city of Naca'an before, and she was looking forward to visiting their famous marketplace. Much of the silks the Pheldhainian women worked into their gowns came from Naca'an's Grand Bazaar.

She hurriedly readied herself, checked that her belongings were packed, then exited her cabin. The passage was narrow, and as she passed her shipmates' doors, one on her left was pulled open, and, not seeing her, Ronan stepped into her path. She lifted her hands to his shoulders to stop herself from crashing into him. The broad expanse of his back was rock solid. He spun around in surprise, and before Murel could ricochet from him, he caught her around her waist and steadied her. Behind her, another door clicked open.

"Mur—Ronan, ah, pardon my interruption," Tomas stammered.

She didn't miss the mischievous gleam in Ronan's eye, and she pushed at his hands in an effort to get him to release her, but Ronan persisted in holding her waist, his palms grazing over the fabric of her tunic. *Strong, large hands,* Murel found herself imagining, and wondering what the sensation would have been had she donned one of her light, silky gowns. She met Tomas's eye precisely as the notion occurred to her, and blushed. Inwardly, she harrumphed.

Tomas's expression turned inscrutable. "I seem to have forgotten something in my cabin," Tomas stated curtly. "Excuse me, m'lady." He ignored Ronan completely and quickly departed, leaving her to wonder why she even felt the need to explain.

Murel pursed her lips together and scowled at Ronan. He finally lifted his hands away and up, as if he needed to fend off her barrage. *Wise man,* she thought. "Ronan, you know we don't suit. Why must you be so immature?"

"Because it's entertaining," he quipped, giving her his conspiring half smile, the one that showed off the darling dimple on his cheek.

"I'm not a pawn in some game, Ronan. I don't play at court, and I don't play here. Do remember that from now on." Murel had been in Ronan's company before, and although the conversation was diverting and he was devilishly attractive, she'd never been seduced by him. She used to rue that fact, but then she came to understand that Ronan was waiting to find a woman who could meet him measure for measure. Not that Murel couldn't hold her own. She simply didn't want to. Not with Ronan. And Ronan knew it.

"My sincere apologies, Lady Murel. I was only having some fun at Tomas's expense. I did not mean to importune you in any way."

"Why?"

"I—" he stammered. "You—" He frowned. "Because I respect you."

"Wait, what? No." Murel sighed, then added, "Why antagonize Tomas? Has he offended you?"

"No. I like Tomas, quite a bit. I wanted to see his reaction. It's—I actually don't know why. We've always played these games as Royal Guards. It's habit, I suppose."

"I say this with all due kindness, Ronan. But isn't it time that you grew up?" He started at her words. "Few in the Guard persist with such waggeries. Even the youngest members eschew the former game of hearts at court. Yes, there are the usual flirtations, but that silly contest with the queen's ladies has seen its day."

"I consider myself schooled again, m'lady," he said, but Murel heard no rancor in his tone. He smiled at her once more, held out his arm, which she took, and led her up to the deck.

So close to him, she couldn't help but note that he smelled of some strange-but-familiar spice. "Why did you wish to see Tomas's reaction? I daresay that you are lucky he didn't knock you on the head. He's more protective of me than my own family." She wondered at his amused smirk but was distracted by her brother, who was watching the crew lower the gangplanks.

. . .

"I'm being ridiculous. Hiding in my room like a jealous fool. Murel is free to make any mistake she wants." The idea of mistakes made with Ronan had him pulling open his door and stepping briskly into the hall. Regrettably, the corridor had been abandoned. He made his way to the deck, and still feeling idiotic, strode over to where Ronan was standing by himself.

"Ronan—"

"I apologize."

"What?"

"That was not worthy behavior on my part, and I'll try to do better in the future."

Tomas laughed so loud that the dock workers looked up from their toils to watch. "Put you in your place, did she?"

"She basically told me to act my age," he confessed. "Truce?"

"Truce," Tomas concurred. "Are your intentions—"

"Let me stop you there, my friend," Ronan interrupted. "I have no intentions where Murel is concerned. We are friends, that is all." Tomas couldn't stop his sigh of relief, and it was Ronan's turn to laugh. "The two of you suit well."

"I'm glad someone thinks so," Tomas confided. "But like you, my intentions are purely brotherly."

"Are you blind, man?" Ronan asked, aggrieved.

"Would that I were. No, I made an oath to Warin, and now, Murel will only ever see me with sisterly eyes."

"The more you act like her brother and protector, the thicker the wool will be that blinds her."

"She's not a sheep, in case you haven't noticed."

"Oh, I've noticed, as have many others. Surely, she's been pursued."

"When she first went to court, perhaps. But then Warin called the wolves to task." Tomas gave Ronan a rueful grin. "With one growl, Warin fashioned us all into lambs with his threats."

"I see your problem. And its solution."

"Oh?"

"Stop acting the lamb and be a wolf."

"That easy?"

Ronan studied Tomas, reached up, and rubbed his knuckles on Tomas's cheek. "Smoother than a babe's bottom."

Tomas rolled his eyes. He took shaving seriously.

"Try letting a little stubble grow on that cherubic face of yours. Roughen yourself up," Ronan suggested, and Tomas laughed, until he realized the man was being serious. "What have you got to lose?"

Tomas massaged his chin between his thumb and fingers. "Not a damn thing at the moment," he said to himself as Ronan left him to join the others. He gave Murel an appraising gaze, and feeling the weight of it, she turned his way. She waved him over, then was distracted by something her brother was saying. As Tomas walked toward them, he reflected on the number of years he'd known Murel. A memory of chasing minks on a terrace in Pheldhain, wearing nothing but nappies, came to mind. His family and Murel's were longtime allies, and as children, he and Murel spent weeks, months even, in one another's family's care.

She was giving him a wry look as he approached. "Why the grin, Tomas?"

"I was reminiscing about the minks," he said, leaning in and whispering, "and you and I in our birthday suits trying to catch them." Her eyes widened, and she blushed furiously. "When we were children," he added, trying to minimize her distress. "In Pheldhain."

She smiled up at him with relief in her eyes. "As I recall, I was chasing you, trying to warn you that the little beasts bite. But you didn't listen."

"And we both got bit," Tomas finished, taking heart that he'd caused color to blush the apples of her cheeks.

Murel took her brother's arm in hers and then led the group to the gangplank. Ronan fell in next to Tomas and lifted his eyebrow knowingly. The man had been right. As long as Tomas acted like a protective brother, Murel would never see him as anything but.

It was early, and the dock was already bustling, forcing them to weave and wend their way through the increasingly crowded pier. Tomas couldn't make out what she and her brother were discussing over the din of shouting and singing and signal whistling. Boom arms hung over the rails of many of the ships at port, either lading or unloading the goods that had been brought to the busy trading city. More than once, Tomas found himself inspecting the rigging under which they walked, making sure the heavy pallets were secure.

Ronan was several yards portside and so not at risk of being injured by the potential peril from above. Tomas had never been a superstitious man, but upon noticing Ronan's tense countenance, he moved faster to catch up to Murel and Jesper. That was when he became aware of how far away they were. Ronan was moving faster, cutting through the crowd, and pointing up.

One of the wood pallets was cracking down the center. He tried yelling out to Murel and Jesper, but the dockers had already noticed the impending crash and were shouting to one another to lower the cargo back to the dock. In the din, the sailors couldn't hear, and continued hauling on the ropes to bring the load to the ship's deck. Murel and Jesper had stopped directly beneath, and Jesper was arguing with a man who had grabbed his sister, trying to pull her to safety. Tomas started knocking people out of his way to get to his friends. Ronan, on the outskirts, had a clearer path. He barreled into Jesper, knocking him aside and grabbing Murel by the waist as he dove past her. Tomas reached the spot as the wood pallet began to give way, and he knocked the dock workers from underneath the deadly cargo. Heavy oaken barrels slipped free, smashing and cracking open, drenching everyone in the vicinity with wine.

The silence following the crash was deafening. Tomas hauled himself up. The men he'd knocked out of the way had slipped into the gathering crowd of onlookers. Jesper was hale, pushing himself to his feet one-handed. Murel was nowhere to be seen, and Tomas sought out Ronan. That was when Tomas saw a slim wrist and delicate hand pushing at Ronan's shoulder. He rushed to them.

"Get off her, Ronan!"

"Tomas," came her muffled cry. "He's hurt. Help me to roll him over." Jesper arrived, and they managed to move the tall man off Murel. She sat up immediately and began palpating his head. She listened to his breathing, then sat back. "He's knocked out, is all. Thank goodness. If he hadn't barreled through those men, we might be dead!"

The captain of the offending ship hurried over to them with a medical kit and a bucket of water. Murel took a clean rag from him to wipe the dark-red wine from Ronan's brow; they were all relieved to see he wasn't bleeding. She pressed gently on the growing goose egg near his temple, and Ronan groaned.

"We off-loaded that cargo last night," the captain groused. "I can't fathom why it was bein' laded again."

"The culprits from your crew have decamped," Tomas said.

"My crew? I'm sorry, m'lord, but my crew, except for me and a few others, are on leave until tomorrow."

"But the men who were trying to warn Lady Murel and Lord Jesper—"

"I've never laid eyes on them before this morning."

"It's all right," Murel interjected. "Thank you for your help. Ah, here comes our good Captain Grieg with his men." She gave Tomas a quick signal, one that indicated they should hold their tongues, when the others were distracted by the newcomers. Jesper was scowling at the shattered barrels. Ronan groaned again, then blinked open his eyes. "A hard knock," Murel said softly. "I imagine your skull is thick enough to withstand any real damage. Can you stand?"

"Why?" he asked. "It's so comfortable here with you."

"If you hadn't saved us, I would knock you on the head again for such sass," she quipped.

Tomas stuck out his hand, and Ronan took it with a grin—one that quickly turned to a grimace instead.

Grieg finished speaking to the captain of the ship that was being laded, and sent one of his men with two from the other crew to try to track down the missing dockworkers. Ronan was still a little unsteady, so Grieg tucked his shoulder under his arm and helped to prop him up. Jesper took the other side, and Tomas helped Murel up from the dock. She brushed off her tunic, amazingly free of wine stains, thanks to how thoroughly Ronan had covered her.

With his hand draped loosely on the pommel of his sword, Tomas led the way to the inn where they would sojourn before traveling to the Palace of Queen Aghna and Prince Ranulf. They skirted the marketplace. When Murel ignored the vibrant wares being offered in the Grand Bazaar, a place she'd been longing to visit, he knew the accident was not some simple affair. The grim line in which she set her lips did nothing to dampen her beauty. In truth, the fire in her eyes only made her that much lovelier. She caught up to his side when they marched up the broad alley leading to their accommodations, her generous hips swaying with determination.

"Can you forgive me, Murel?" he begged.

"Not here," she hushed, putting him off and pulling ahead of him.

He redoubled his pace to keep up with her, pressing forward so that he was an inch or two in the lead. "Murel, you have to slow down," he ordered, though gently. She gave an exasperated sigh, one he'd never dreamed he'd be the cause of, opened her mouth to say something, then peered around him to where Grieg and Jesper struggled to keep pace. Ronan was flagging between them, if not looking a tad green.

"Oh, for goodness' sake," she hissed, perturbed. "Let him sit there for a moment." They lowered Ronan to a step, and Murel leaned over him, resting her hand on his shoulder. "Head between your knees," she said soothingly. "It'll pass in a moment."

Her demeanor had switched so swiftly from annoyance with him to kindness for Ronan that Tomas was momentarily stunned. Indeed, it took him a moment to realize that she was demanding something of him. He'd been distracted—again—and he scanned the wide alley for any threat. Except for two women coming back from the market and two young boys playing with a ball, they were alone.

"Tomas," Murel repeated.

He held up his hand. He'd heard what she asked already and set his sights on the boys. "Do you live nearby?"

Their eyes widened as they took in his height, and then the length of the sword resting in its scabbard. "Yes, sir," the braver of the two ventured.

"Excellent," Tomas said. "What is your name?"

"It's Baqi, m'lord."

"Think you can run home and bring back some water?"

"Right away!"

Tomas turned to address the other youth.

"I'm Aggy, sir," the boy offered, standing at attention as if he were a soldier.

"Great. Do you know of the Stone Hearth Inn, Aggy?"

The boy nodded.

"We need you to take a message to the innkeeper, asking him to return here with a cart."

"Yes, sir!" the boy said after taking in the group, and eager for an adventure, pivoted around and tore down the alley.

Tomas was surprised to see Baqi still standing before him. "Is there something a matter?"

"No, sir. Well, yes. Your friends are blocking my door."

"Ah, good. Murel, if you could move for a moment, this lad'll retrieve some water for Ronan." He ignored the look she was giving him, unable to discern its nature. The boy slipped inside, returning a moment later with empty hands.

"Mum says to come in off the street," he said, holding open the door and pressing himself against the thick planking.

When Murel moved to step inside, Tomas reached for her arm to stay her. "Grieg."

The captain was quick to enter, climbing the steps that led to one of the upper floors of the two-storied building that leaned over the street. "It's clear," he called down.

"Can you manage the steps?" Tomas asked Ronan, and he nodded. Jesper held out his good hand to help him up. The two entered, then Murel. Tomas scanned the alley in both directions and, confirming the way was clear, backed in through the entranceway.

"You can see the street from the front window," Baqi offered. "When Aggy comes back, I'll run down and let him know you're here." He bounded up the steps, and Tomas closed the door to the street, throwing the bolt in place. He didn't know what threats lurked without, but better safe than sorry. When he turned, he came face-to-face with Murel—she was standing on the first step, staring at him with narrowed eyes.

"Why did you—" she started.

"Are you ready to forgive—" he asked at the same time. "You go first."

"I only wanted to know why you apologized. You go ahead," she ordered.

For the first time since the accident, Tomas wanted to smile, but he checked himself. "I should've seen what was happening."

"How? Even I didn't realize at first, and I was there!" Anger and disappointment sparked in her eyes.

"Still, I'm sorry. I—"

"You keep that up, Tomas, and I'll grow as mad at you as I am with my brother! At least you and Ronan saw what was happening. He got there first for one reason and one reason alone—he was closer."

"Seeing is not the same as protecting, Murel. I wouldn't have made it to you in time. Hold on, you're not annoyed with me?" She rolled her eyes at him. "What did Jesper do wrong?"

"He didn't do anything. He merely stood—"

The scraping of furniture being moved across the floor above had Murel peering up the stairs. She met his eyes, and he saw the mix of pain and guilt in them, and he understood. Tending to her brother was taking a toll on her, whether she wanted to admit it or not. Tomas did the only thing he could—he took her wrist and tugged her so that she was standing on the landing and not the step. Then, he drew her into his arms and held her.

She didn't try to move away, and as he counted the heartbeats between them, he felt the tension slipping from her shoulders until she sagged against him. "Framk yoo," came a muffled voice, followed by a sniffle. She sighed, then stepped back.

"Anytime," he promised, reluctantly letting her go.

She patted her cheeks and blinked her dewy eyes until they were clear.

"No one will ever know," he assured her.

"Never know what?" she demanded.

"That you were overcome with emotions and needed rescuing," he said, straight-faced. Her lips twitched. When Tomas held up his arm and flexed his bicep, she burst out laughing.

"What would I ever do without you, Tomas?" she asked, shaking her head and climbing the steps. "Do you agree we should wait to discuss the accident until we are at the inn?" When he didn't answer, she stopped. "What is it? Do you need a hug as well?" She held up her arm and made to flex her muscle as he had done.

Tomas grinned. Perhaps it was time for him to follow Ronan's advice. He climbed the stairs, took her hand in his, and, stepping past her, tugged her up behind him. "I would happily receive any embrace you are willing to gift me, Murel." He felt her hesitate on the step and let go of her hand. It took every bit of willpower he possessed to not turn around to gauge her reaction.

. . .

Kantapan Castle, Mount Kanta
*Last Refuge of the Self-Proclaimed King of Nifolhad*

Diarmait allowed himself to be propped up in his bed. He pushed ineffectually at the hands trying to open his mouth to pour some new tincture or potion down his throat.

"You must drink this, m'lord."

"Your king!" he croaked. "Your king! Guards! Arrest these assassins!" But no one rushed into his chambers. "Where's Phelan, that coward?"

His physicians gave each other wary looks. "He's gone, my l—king."

"Gone where?"

"He passed two moons ago, my liege. He did not survive the journey here. Please, this tincture will relieve you of your pain."

Diarmait, in a fit of rage, regained enough strength to sweep his arm at the man trying to spoon-feed him the noxious syrup. He grinned, revealing his stained teeth, and the oily medicine splashed in the man's face and down the front of his tunic. Diarmait laughed then, thick and mucous-laden, and the motion wracked his body with pain. He welcomed it, for it proved he was still alive.

"Look what you've done now, my liege," the older physician tutted as if Diarmait was a toddler. "Calm yourself. You're only causing more damage."

"Do not speak to me as if you are my better," Diarmait managed between croaks that were quickly becoming gasps for air. "Get out! The both of you! If you return, I will have you killed."

The men gathered their medicaments and beat a hasty retreat.

Alone and awake, Diarmait finally lay back on his cushions, taking stock of his aches and pains. He lifted his arm and stared at the poultices and bandages, and he ripped them away. Raw and oozing ulcers, some of them putrefying, covered the exposed flesh.

"And how will you have them killed? There's no one left to do your bidding."

A tall figure stood at the threshold of his chamber, and Diarmait focused his rheumy eyes on the man. "Bowen? My son returns to haunt me."

"Not Bowen," the man said, approaching. "I'm one of your many bastards. Danold, remember? You and Bowen once sent me to Sophiana to impersonate the prince."

"Danold," Diarmait rasped. "Yes, the resemblance is striking. I want you to call my guards. Those charlatans are trying to kill me, and I want them tortured and beheaded."

"This chamber reeks of death," Danold noted, ignoring Diarmait completely. He walked to the broad window and yanked back the thick tapestries keeping out the light.

"Keep those closed!" Diarmait ordered.

"I learned a thing or two after being kept in captivity by King Ranulf," Danold stated. "More pertinent to your situation, Father, is that fresh air is good for your health." He proceeded to open the shutters to the broad balcony, allowing the bright light of day to flood the chamber. Then, he went about dousing the myriad incense pots and lamps spewing their fetid fumes.

Diarmait glared at him for a moment, then gazed out the window. Mount Kanta was the highest point in all of Nifolhad. His balcony boasted an immaculate view of the rich river basin, the Brynmara Range, and beyond it, the tumultuous skies above the Fyrost Desert. As a child, Diarmait had summered here with his older brother, the late King Cedric. Those were the golden times of his youth, well before their views on how the kingdom should be run had ruined the brotherly love they'd shared. It wasn't that Diarmait regretted the fratricide, it was nostalgia for simpler days that had him missing his brother. Days when he could hunt, and ride, and bed the many beautiful maidens willing to give themselves to him. He got many with child, each one hoping he would do the honorable thing and wed them. Not a chance—only Lady Ulicia of Ragallach had been able to force him into marriage. It was that union, ordered by his brother, King Cedric, which had sealed his brother's fate. Lady Ulicia had borne Diarmait his one legitimate son, Bowen, at least until he discovered that she had also given him Roger, birthed in Aurelia and kept hidden from him until he turned up on Nifolhad's shores.

Both were gone now—Roger murdered by his wife, Lady Aubrianne of Stolweg, and Bowen by King Ranulf's insufferable sister, Princess Anwyl. "I detest every last one," he spat.

"Who?" Danold asked.

"Women."

"All of us? Really?" a woman asked, entering the chamber with a tray.

"Before you get any ideas," Danold said, setting a chaise longue near the balcony, "that's Princess Mirra…one of your legitimate daughters."

Diarmait sneered, but she only lifted an amused brow. Then she set down her tray, and he smelled the delicious aroma of beef. "Broth," she explained. "Ready, Danold?"

"As I ever will be," Danold answered, looking at Diarmait as if taking his measure. He approached and reached out his arms.

"What do you think you are doing?" Diarmait shouted.

"He's moving you to the chaise," Mirra answered. "Your bedding appears to be liquifying. And the smell—you've lost your nose, but trust me, it's eye-watering."

Diarmait glared at her. "You wouldn't talk to me like that if I were stronger."

"If you were stronger, I wouldn't be here!" she snapped back.

"Mirra," Danold calmed. Before Diarmait could sputter another word, his son plucked his frail body from the bed and carried him to the chaise. "Comfortable?" he asked, after setting him down.

"You're not afraid of me in the least, are you?"

"What can you do?" Danold asked flatly.

"I could regain my strength."

Behind them, Mirra snorted. "And then what?" she asked. "Danold and I are your only children who haven't abandoned you. Would you hurt us for our loyal service?" She didn't wait for an answer. "Brother, help me with this screen. The servants will be here soon, and they must not see him in his current state."

They moved the large privacy screen to the chaise. Danold carried the table with the tray of broth over and then pulled up a chair to sit next to him. "Can you feed yourself?"

Diarmait took a broth-filled spoon from his son with a trembling grip. By the time it reached his lips, the liquid had sloshed everywhere down his front.

"Let me," Danold said.

Diarmait scowled, but dutifully sipped the broth, surprised at how hungry he was. Behind the partition, Mirra was instructing the servants to burn the bedding, including the mattress. The sound of scrub brushes and sloshing water could be heard above the muffled gagging noises as his deathbed was deconstructed.

"When is the last time you ate?" Danold asked, giving him the last of the broth.

"Judging by the filthy bedpans stacked next to your sleeping platform, weeks," Mirra answered for him. "No wonder they were burning so much incense." She gazed out the broad arch that opened to the balcony and beyond. "Another desert storm is brewing."

"I don't want that grit blowing in here!" Diarmait coughed out.

"It'll be weeks before any dust will reach the castle," she countered. "And we'll close your window before it arrives. Now let's sit here quietly and enjoy the view while they finish restoring your chamber."

"I don't want you here!" Diarmait shouted.

"Hush, Father. You don't want the servants to hear." She stepped out onto the balcony and sat on the tiled floor, her back straight and her legs crisscrossed in front of her. He stared at the back of her head, wondering why she was sitting so still, until he felt his mind tire, and he let his eyes drift closed.

Diarmait woke to a coughing fit. He had fallen asleep. Mirra, hearing him, turned. The partition had been removed, and his chamber had been returned to its former stature of a royal apartment. Gone were the noxious incense pots and the spoiled bedding and cushions. A warm fire burned in the clean hearth. On the table next to him, a neatly folded pile of clothing waited.

"Time to tend to these ulcers," Mirra said, "but first a bath and change of clothes." She reached out to take his arm, and her sleeve exposed her wrist and the green Fenrhi markings of the Sylvan Caste.

"Don't touch me!" Diarmait cried fearfully.

"Father," Danold soothed, "Mirra would never hurt you. She's trained as a healer."

"Her kind is the reason I'm dying!"

"She's no longer Fenrhi," Danold assured him. "She's family."

Mirra held out her hand to him, waiting. "I'm your daughter first. Besides, blood is stronger than any caste. But you know that already, don't you?"

Grudgingly, Diarmait weakly lifted his arm, setting his wrist in her warm hand. She began her examination of his wounds, as outside, the western sky had taken on a surreal orange glow, unnatural for even a sunset. "You're wrong about that storm, Daughter. The dust will reach us much sooner than a week."

"Will the wind carry it this far?" she asked, pausing to take the bowl of hot water from her brother.

"Of course," he replied. "The dust from the Fyrost touches all the known realms. He says it's the blood of the earth."

"Who says that?" Danold asked, but Diarmait ignored him.

# Sobering Truths

At the Stone Hearth Inn, Murel finished freshening up. They would rest at the inn long enough so that a proper escort from the palace could meet them. The sojourn would give Ronan enough time to recover from his head injury whilst Captain Grieg refitted the ship. There was a knock on her door—hers was the largest apartment, situated between that of Tomas and her brother—signaling the arrival of the meal she had ordered. The innkeeper was early.

Caution flared as she reached for the latch. "Who is it?"

"It's me. Tomas." Murel wasted no time and let him in, closing the door behind them.

"I must be running behind," she worried.

"I'm early," Tomas stated at the same moment.

Murel grinned. "We keep doing that, don't we? Talking at the same time."

He flashed a smile at her. "Like an old married couple." He laughed, then crossed the room to peer at the courtyard below her window.

Murel swallowed. That wasn't exactly how she'd been thinking about it—more like siblings—but now that he'd said it, the idea took on a life of its own in her brain. Friends. Confidants. Possibly parents. Oh gracious, lovers as well.

She stared at his broad back, the way his strong hands braced on either side of the open window, and almost sighed upon seeing the flex of his shoulder muscles under the lightweight shirt he wore. Her gaze drifted lower, to his trim waist and taut... No. This was Tomas. Her friend and trusted companion. He only saw her as a sister...

But she wasn't his sister, she reminded herself.

She looked away, afraid that perhaps a blush bloomed on her cheeks. "Shall we sit?" she asked, hating how her voice betrayed her nerves. She discreetly coughed, then added, "Can I get you a glass of wine?"

"Let me pour it for you," Tomas offered instead, and she knew, without a doubt, that he had noticed her sudden discomfiture. "As I was saying—"

"You're here early because…" she prompted, taking a seat on one of the benches at the compact dining table that had been placed in her large sitting room. They'd done it again, talked at the same time. Tomas chuckled, then set two goblets of wine on the table before throwing one leg over to straddle the bench and sit facing her. She took a sip of wine to hide her nervousness, glancing away to avoid drooling over how his breeches stretched over his muscled thighs. Good gravy, her friends would tan her sideways if they knew that Murel had succumbed to acting like a lovestruck girl in front of a Royal Aurelian Guard. Especially Tomas, considering his reputation at court. She'd heard the stories, though it'd been a while, two years perhaps, since the ladies at court shared any gossip concerning him. And the stories they had shared…well, goodness. She took another sip and stared up at the ceiling to avoid looking down.

"Is something wrong?" he asked, glancing above where they sat.

"N-nothing," she stammered. "I…I'm fine." She gave herself a good chastising for letting her thoughts wander.

"If you're sure…" Tomas said, not sounding convinced.

Having reined in her salacious imaginings, she regarded him expectantly.

"I hoped that we could talk before the others arrive," he began. "Ronan is still a bit addled. And Jesper is being his quiet self, as usual. If we share what we saw, then we'll be able to draw more out of the others."

Murel nodded and pursed her lips together to make a conscious effort at breaking their habit of starting and finishing each other's sentences. Tomas must've had the same idea, and an awkward silence grew between them.

"I don't mind it, Murel," he stated. "It's what makes us a good team and one of the reasons the queen and king assigned us to be ambassadors to Nifolhad. Together. We're of like purpose."

She let out a relieved breath and smiled. "You're right, of course. We *are* a good team. As for the attack—can we agree to call it that?"

"Yes."

"I didn't see anything amiss, at least at first. And then, no matter how many times I tried to head west toward the marketplace, we continued along the pier, pushed toward the ship side. It quickly became clear to me that we were being...how to explain..."

"Herded?"

"Exactly! That's when I noticed that the same three men were constantly blocking our path. In rotation."

"Four men."

"Four! No wonder." She waited a moment, reluctant to share what was bothering her.

"And Jesper was oblivious to the danger," Tomas said for her.

She nodded painfully, and he took her hand in concern. His long, capable fingers enveloped her feminine counterparts in warmth.

"You're not betraying him, Murel. Jesper is so caught up in his own pain, he can't see anything else."

She blinked at her welling tears.

"Say it, Murel. Say it out loud." He waited. "It's all right. You can tell me. You need to say it."

"I...I'm...so angry with him," she whispered, then reiterated a bit more forcefully, "I'm so angry, Tomas." She leaned back, surprised at the feeling that a weight had been lifted off her chest. And the world around her hadn't ended at her admission. "Heavens, but that felt good. I'm not a horrible person, am I?"

"You're a kind and loving sister. And it's natural to feel the way you are feeling. Think back to before Jess was taken...a time when he annoyed you. What would you have done?"

"You are so right! I would never have let him get away with it. I mean, I know he was hurt...is hurting...the torture alone. He'll never fully recover. And his hand. He'll never..." Tomas simply stared at her. Expectant. "What?"

"So, you gave yourself a break. But you haven't admitted why you're mad at him."

"Why are you so damn intuitive?" she demanded. His eyes widened, and he drew back, his warm fingers leaving hers. The sudden loss of his touch stung. "I didn't mean to swear at you. I'm sorry if—"

"No. It's not that, Murel. It's only that no one has ever said that to me." He pulled a wry face. "Lark, Warin, and especially Trian, sure. But me? Intuitive?"

Something important was at war in her friend's heart. And then she understood, as he understood her. Every comment she'd ever heard about Tomas was about his physical prowess, his handsomeness, his weapons skills, but never his intellect. She'd been as guilty of pigeonholing him as everyone else. She reached out for his hand, drawing him back. "Yes, you." There was a knock at the door, and she reluctantly let go so that Tomas could see who it was.

"Am I late?" Jesper asked, seeing Tomas. Murel stood and folded her arms across her chest. He strode into the room, and then poured himself a goblet of wine. "Can I get—?" he started, then espied the two cups on the table. He darted his eyes first to Murel, and then hastily to Tomas.

Murel began tapping her toe and watched as her brother took in her impatience with him. He knew his time was up, and he tried pivoting. "Was I interrupting something here?"

"I'll ask the innkeeper to hold our meal a bit longer," Tomas said, then wisely left the room, but not before fisting his hands in front of himself in a signal for her to remain strong. Good thing Jess didn't see the exchange, for he would have bolted as well.

"Sit down, Jesper."

"Now look here, Murel. You don't need to talk to me that way. This has been a rough beginning to my return here, and I—"

"I would appreciate it if you let me finish without any interruptions." She softened but a fraction. "Please, sit down."

"I'll stand," he said, walking to the window and staring blandly at the scene below.

"I can converse with your back as easily as I can with your face."

"Get on with it," he said. "The faster you finish telling me that I'll be all right, that time will help heal me, the faster we can eat."

"Right at this moment, I couldn't care less if you feel better or not!"

He spun around. "That was unkindly said, Murel. I'm trying. I'm here, am I not?"

"We're *all* trying, Jesper. And you are not here. Not completely, anyway."

"That's low, Sis. I'm sorry to have been such a burden."

"You know I'm not talking about your hand!" she scoffed. "And yes, you have been a burden. One that I'll gladly take on for the rest of my life if necessary. But that's just it, isn't it?"

"You don't need to be cruel, Murel. I'm leaving." She moved to block his path to the door. "Fine. I hereby release you of all responsibility for my well-being."

"How dare you!" she yelled. "How dare you stand there and dismiss me. So help me, Jesper, if you don't sit yourself down this instant, I will scream."

"We wouldn't want that, would we?" he countered, sounding bored.

Murel closed her eyes.

"What are you doing?"

She ignored him.

"Murel?"

When she had her anger under control, she opened her eyes and stared him down. "I will be here for you as long as it takes. As I said before, for my entire life, if need be. But, if you don't put in some effort, my life will be over before I have a chance to live it."

"What are you saying?" he demanded.

"I'm saying that it's been long enough, Jesper. Even if you never again feel whole, even if you continue on as if you are a ghost, even if you don't care enough about me and your friends, I will not permit you to put us in danger again."

"Danger? Murel, I have no—"

"We almost died, Jesper. *I* almost died. You might not care about yourself, but I never imagined you would try to bring me down with you." He finally sat. "I refuse to coddle you a moment longer. It's more than not helping; it's making you worse."

"I do care, Murel. I helped carry Ronan off the docks."

"Ronan wouldn't have been injured if you had been awake, Jess. I tried to tell you about the men. You ignored me. You let them push us into their trap. You didn't even try to break free."

"I didn't realize two men were a problem. Not with Ronan and Tomas keeping guard."

"You saw two men, and you did nothing?" she accused.

He had no answer.

"Point in fact, there were four," she corrected. "I myself detected three." She sat on the bench next to him, touching her fingers to his arm. "You may have lost this hand, Jess, but you haven't lost your eyes. It's been two years. Don't you think it's time to open them?"

All the pain in the world was in his gaze, and she breathed a sigh of relief. At least he was feeling something. "There you are." She drew him into her arms, and as he let his tears flow, she held him.

It took him a moment, but he eventually lifted his arms to hold her back. "I'm sorry, Murel," he said, pulling away. "You are more dear to me than anyone else in the whole of the known realms."

"All that I ask is that you try, Jess."

He nodded. "I can't promise you that I'll ever get over what was done to me, but I'll do better by you."

"It's a beginning." And it was leagues farther than they'd come before. He was giving her a look, one that was reminiscent of when he was preparing to give her brotherly advice...a look she hadn't seen in years.

"So, do I have to ask?" he started.

"Ask what?" she replied, completely baffled by the change of subject.

"Come on, Sis. You? Tomas?"

"What? No. It's not like that."

"Try not to sound so forlorn next time you say that." He chuckled. "Do you want me to say something to him?"

"No! I mean, no. How embarrassing."

"But you like him?"

"I'm not sure. I've always liked Tomas. But he's been more like a brother to me." She sighed. "Every man I meet treats me like a little sister. Well, maybe not Ronan. But he and I agree that we're not a good match. I'm not...I don't know...enough for him?"

"What are you talking about? Enough for Ronan? Murel, you are one of the queen's favorite ladies at court. And from what I know of Queen Juliana, she doesn't surround herself with sycophants and vapid women.

She befriends intelligent and generous ladies. Don't ever sell yourself short like that again."

"I only meant that he needs a woman who is not so... Someone who is more like him. Not a woman you come to like, as if she's your sister."

Jesper looked guiltily away.

"What was that? Jesper?"

He scrubbed his good hand over his stubbled jaw.

"What do you know?"

"All right. But it wasn't me. Though, had I been here when you were first introduced at court, I might have done the same thing."

"What, pray tell?"

"I was gone, and well, you see, Warin got it in his head to...well, protect you."

"What. Did. He. Do?"

"First, you have to see it from his perspective. I mean, he and Lark at court, before they were married. And the ladies...the games and flirtations..."

"Spit it out, Jesper!"

"He secured the promise of all the nobles and Royal Guards at court that they would treat you honorably...as if you were their sister. He made them take an oath." He said it all in a rush, and when he finished, he took a big breath and let it go, like a giant hurdle had been cleared. "I just found out. And I would've told you...eventually. Are you going to be all right about this? Murel?"

She turned on the bench, too stunned to speak. She opened her mouth to reply, then promptly shut it as, unbidden, each and every interaction with the noblemen at court unspooled in her mind until she was left with a tangled knot of memories. "An oath?"

Jesper nodded.

"An oath," she repeated, more to herself. "But Ronan?"

"Never took it, from what I gleaned."

"An oath." She stared at the door. Her thoughts were awhirl. "Oh. My. Heavens! I'm going to kill him! When I get back, Warin is as good as skewered. Jesper! You have no idea! What a terrible thing for someone to do to another."

"His intentions were noble, Murel. And I might've done the same. I suppose without the threat of dismemberment or worse."

"What could be worse than dismemberment?"

"Castration," Jess squeaked.

Murel picked up her cup and drained the wine. She poured another. Drained it again. When she reached for the bottle, her brother pulled it away. There was a tap at the door, and he went to answer it. The innkeeper came in, followed by two serving girls carrying the evening meal. While he instructed the servers on where to set the overladen platters, Murel managed to grab one of the fresh jugs of wine they'd brought with them and poured a third goblet to the brim and took a hefty gulp. This time, she didn't drain the cup but hooked the jug's handle with the crook of her finger and went to the window to peer at the lengthening shadows. In the background, she heard her brother thank the innkeeper and the serving girls. Then the door clicked shut.

"I promise to not murder Warin," she said when her brother came to stand next to her. She took another sip of wine. "Tomas and Ronan will be coming soon and—oh no! What am I going to say to Tomas?"

"Nothing," Jesper counseled. "You don't have to say a word. Besides—" There was a light rap on the door, and Ronan poked in his head. He entered, followed by Tomas.

Murel could feel the heat rising in her cheeks, and she downed the rest of her cup, then poured herself another. She gave her brother a look that was meant to infer that she would be fine, but whatever he read in her expression had him grimacing. He managed to wrest the jug from her hand before greeting their friends. Murel turned away to compose herself.

When she sensed someone standing next to her, she assumed it was Tomas. Masking her turmoil, she started to tell him that her conversation with Jesper had gone better than she'd anticipated. Instead, Ronan stood before her, smiling that deliciously wicked half-smile of his. Murel took another sip of wine, trying and failing to smother a giggle. How was she already drunk?

"Are you?" Ronan asked, lifting an amused eyebrow.

"Oh dear, I said that out loud." In her mind, it wasn't funny at all, but her heart found it hilarious, so she giggled some more. Ronan was staring at her, as if daring her to make some decision. "Oh, what the hell." She took another sip.

"Indeed," Ronan stated. Taking a drink from his own cup that she hadn't erenow noticed. "Some advice?"

"Why not?" She snorted, setting her empty cup on the window ledge. Ronan set his next to hers.

"Drink as much water as you drink wine. And eat. You'll thank me in the morning." He tilted his head to his cup, picked up hers, and stepped away.

When Tomas joined her, she picked up the goblet and took another drink, nearly choking when she discovered it was only water. Across the room, Ronan saluted her. It was an evening of revelations.

"Are you all right?" Tomas asked, studying her with no small amount of concern.

"I find myself truly ravenous," she managed, though there might have been a little slurring. She lifted Ronan's cup to her lips and finished off the water. And then she smiled at him, as if all was right in the world when, in reality, she felt like everything was crashing down around her. She patted his front, noticing again how hard his muscles were. She wondered suddenly if she scratched his bare chest, would her nails even leave a mark? Realizing that she had been resting her hand on his chest a moment too long, she pivoted and glided—gracefully, she prayed—to the table.

Three very handsome men—yes, Jess was as handsome a man as any, even with his scars—surrounded her. So much masculinity. It wasn't fair, really.

"What's not fair?" Ronan asked, sitting and returning her goblet to her. He broke off a generous hunk of bread from the steaming loaf, setting it on her plate.

She reached for her cup and took a ladylike sip of...wine. She followed it up with a wink to Ronan and a dainty bite of bread. Despite her slightly incapacitated brain, she caught the nod her brother gave Ronan, who was currently loading her plate with food. She sighed. "I'm not helpless, you know," she stated to the room. "I might not be able to wield a sword like Lady Anna, or a staff like Princess Anwyl, and please don't even compare me to Lady Claire, because, frankly, there should be laws against a woman being so talented. I am quite…" She frowned, having lost her train of thought.

"You are quite what?" Ronan prompted. He grunted, and at the same time, the table shifted, rattling the utensils and sloshing their drinks. "What I mean to say is that you are quite accomplished in your own right. Isn't she, Tomas?"

Murel dearly wanted to hear his answer and focused in on his beatific face with all his curly, blond locks. He had scarcely taken a bite and stared uncomfortably at the group whilst he hurriedly chewed and swallowed his mouthful.

"And beautiful, too," Ronan added, at the exact moment Tomas opened his mouth to speak. "I have always enjoyed conversing with you. You have an astute mind and a keen grasp on politics. It's no wonder the king and queen have entrusted you with the ambassadorship with Nifolhad. A better Aurelian representative than you does not exist. And Tomas, as well." He lifted his cup to salute them, and Murel struggled to find the sarcasm in his statement. Finding him sincere, she lifted her cup in turn, took a sip, and found that her wine had changed into water again.

She tried for another jug, but Ronan pulled it away to refill his cup at the same moment, setting it out of her reach. "Eat first," he ordered under his breath. As her tablemates fell in on their plates, Ronan provided a running commentary about *Moon Caster*, and by the end of it, Murel discovered that she had finished most of her food. Ronan smiled at her, then proceeded to refill her cup with wine. He shifted suddenly, as if his leg jerked back, and then he shrugged at Jesper.

"Ronan!" she said a little too enthusiastically. "How is your head?"

"It's better than yours will be tomorrow," Jesper answered for him.

"If your sister is determined to get soused, nothing I can do will stop her," Ronan said, leaning back when she picked up her cup with a flourish, sloshing some of her wine in an arc across the platters. "So, if you please, stop kicking me under the table. As for my head," he continued, "it's sore. But your sister is an accomplished healer, so I expect that I will be quickly on the mend."

"Oh, that's right, I wanted to ask after your poor head." She made what she hoped was an exasperated sound when she found Tomas looking back and forth between her, Ronan, and Jesper. "What?" she asked, but then found herself distracted by Ronan when he swiveled on the bench to regard her. "Oh, yes, your head." She held up two fingers and asked him to count them.

"Two."

"Are you sure?" she asked, staring at what appeared to be four. She reached for her cup, and then finished her wine. "I meant to ask, how is your head?"

"Tomas," Ronan suggested, "perhaps you could take Murel into the courtyard for some fresh air. Jesper and I will straighten up here."

"I don't need help," Murel stated, getting up from the bench and swaying but a little. She felt fine; in fact, she felt like dancing or laughing or both. But Tomas was at her side, looking unsure. She patted his arm reassuringly and led him toward the door.

. . .

"We'll talk about this tomorrow, Ronan," Tomas called back, finally finding his voice for the first time during their meal. "And you, too, Jess." The door closed behind him, blocking his view of a grinning Ronan and a scowling Jesper. Tucked next to him was Murel, a petite-but-amply curved woman who had consumed the equivalent of two bottles of wine in the space of two hours. The effects she was feeling now were a scintilla of what was to come on the morrow. At least Ronan had plied her with water and had been insistent on making her eat.

He held her a little closer to his side as they navigated the staircase that led to the common room. She fit perfectly against him, as he always knew she would. Waving off the innkeeper, Tomas steered her toward the entrance and into the courtyard. It was a cool night, and Murel drew in a deep breath, swelling the very bosom that he was astutely avoiding looking at.

"Come on," she begged, taking his hand and dragging him to the right. "I want to see the horses."

"Then you're going in the wrong direction," he said, pulling her to a stop.

"Oh, that won't do. Please, lead the way, good sir." She bowed low to him, rolling her wrist in an elegant fashion. It wasn't until she stood straight that she teetered.

Tomas stepped in as she fell forward and into him. He froze when he realized that her hands were roaming over his chest.

"I could've gotten a black eye," she stated. "Your chest is every bit as hard as Ronan's. Instead, I find that I am perfectly comfortable." And as if to prove her point, she laid her cheek against him and snuggled. "A better pillow I have never had." She started shaking.

He clamped down the yearning he felt in his heart from having her so near. "What is so amusing?" he asked, upon realizing that she was laughing.

She pulled back but wrapped her fingers around his left bicep and squeezed. She skirted her other hand down his chest to his stomach and drummed her fingers there, giggling. "Imagine, muscles as hard as rocks being the most comfortable cushion I ever wanted to lay myself upon." She grinned up at him, her gaze wavering, her lips slightly parted as she stared at his mouth. The tip of her tongue moistened her lip, and Tomas pulled her tighter. She closed her eyes in anticipation. He was so close to kissing her. He wanted nothing more in the world.

But not like this.

Instead, he placed a chaste kiss on the top of her head. Before he let her go, he tightened his hold for a mere second, memorizing what she felt like against him. Then he released her, swinging her around and next to him. "The stable is this way."

"The stable?" she asked, sounding slightly dazed.

"Murel, you are very drunk. I'm taking you back to your room. Where you will go to bed."

"I will?"

"Most definitely." He spun them around, steered them through the busy common room, then up the stairs to her quarters. They arrived as Ronan and Jesper were leaving. Ronan frowned as if disappointed. Jesper looked relieved. Murel kissed her brother's cheek, then held out her hand to Ronan, who bussed it with a kiss.

"You need rest, Ronan," she chided. "You are much too pale again. Let me help you to bed, make sure you have enough of the tincture I made."

"I'll see to it," her brother offered, letting a flagging Ronan lean on him. "Oh, no. We left some wine in there!"

"I'll get it," Tomas promised. He turned to go into her room, but almost toppled over her where she stood in the middle of the hallway, frowning and tracking their friends down the corridor.

"He covers it well," she said, "but his injury is hurting more than he's admitting." She made the diagnosis so soberly that it was if she hadn't had a drop of wine all night. Then, she pivoted on her heel and entered her room. "I really need to pee."

Tomas followed her, scanning the room for the wine. Seeing that she had closed the door between her sleeping chamber and the parlor, he sat down and poured himself a cup. He waited, trying to not envision her undressing and slipping into her sleeping gown. He finished his wine, paced for a moment, then tapped softly on her door. "Murel?"

"Tomas! Help!"

He threw open the door and crashed into the room, then burst out laughing. In her attempt to remove her gown, she managed to trap herself in her skirts and sleeves, all of which were now wrapped around her shoulders and head. "Aren't you supposed to step out of your gown?" he asked, pulling the fabric back down.

"I forgot," came her muffled voice. "Thank goodness you're still here. I was suffuficationing. No, that's not right. I was suffusenation…"

"Lift your arms," he ordered, then proceeded to loosen the laces more. She extricated herself from her sleeves, then drew the fabric off her shoulders, shimmying until the gown lay in a cloud around her ankles. She took his hand and stepped out from the middle. Her shift was cream-colored and, though it covered her completely, accentuated her curvy figure.

"Good thing you've experience disrobing women," she said, then slapped her hand over her mouth.

"Enough to know that you should've removed your shoes first." He backed her to her bed, lifted her by her waist, and set her on the high platform. "Foot, please."

She obediently lifted her foot, and he unlaced the short boot, drawing it off. She kept her foot aloft, waiting. After a moment, he drew down her stocking. "Foot," he said again, and repeated the process. When she kept her naked foot lifted, he took it in his hands, marveling at the feel of delicate bones under silky skin. He pressed his thumbs into the arch, and she sighed.

"I'm very ticklish," she whispered as he gently massaged her foot.

"You are?"

"I thought I was."

Tomas cleared his throat, then let her foot go. After making sure she had water and picking up her gown and draping it over a chair, he turned to say goodnight. But she wasn't on the bed, she was standing near the open door to the parlor. The light from the hearth cast her form in silhouette, and she was even curvier than he'd imagined. Softer, somehow. He swallowed.

"I have to lock the door behind you," she whispered.

"Of course," he managed, following her into the parlor.

He stopped at the door, opened it a crack, and checked to make sure the hall was deserted. "Sleep well, Mur—"

She was right there. A breath of separation. The heat in her gaze matched the yearning hammering away in his heart. Damn it—she might never remember, and he was a bastard for taking advantage—but he was going to kiss her. Before he could, she stood on tiptoe and kissed him instead.

Softly at first, then with more insistence, until he responded in kind. She tasted of honey and wine, and he kept his hands pressed against the doorframe to stop himself from pulling her closer. She tilted her head, giving his mouth more access to her own. When his tongue brushed her lips, she groaned, then echoed the action. She pressed the length of her luscious figure against his, and he thought, one hand, just one hand, and slid it to the small of her back. Her lips parted again, and her teeth, and he delved his tongue into her mouth. He kissed her thoroughly, keeping his hand glued in place, thrilling when her tongue began its dance with his.

She growled, and then slid her hands down from where she'd placed them on his chest. He removed his hand from where it rested and peered down at her. She was panting, her chest falling and rising, her nipples taut and straining against the linen of her shift.

What should he say? What *could* he say?

She placed her fingers on his lips, and heaven help him, he kissed them. Kissed her palm. The inside of her wrist. She stared up at him. Raw hunger lit the dark fire of her Pheldhainian blue eyes. She opened her door, clearly wanting him to leave. He backed out of her chamber, then turned to walk to his room next door.

"Tomas."

He spun around upon hearing her whisper his name.

"I'm not so drunk as everyone imagines." She lifted her hand to her thoroughly ravished lips to cover her smile, then shut the door, throwing the latch in place. He fixed his gaze on the wood planking. After heaving a great breath, Tomas retired to his room and the promise of a restless night. Now that he'd had a taste of Murel, he was doomed to break his oath to her cousin. But the punishment would be worth it and more if he could only kiss her one more time.

# CHAPTER SIX

# Breaking Bread

"Morning," Murel grumbled, sounding nothing like her usual bright-eyed self and avoiding making eye contact with him.

Hell, Tomas didn't know what he would say to her, anyway. Not after her sober announcement following their kiss. His night was not the restless sleep he had anticipated—it'd been a thousandfold worse. Anything would've been more welcome than the deep, dream-filled slumber he'd had. Every fantasy he'd had of Murel, all rolled up in one night. Intensely graphic dreams that, when he woke, he'd had to—

Better to not go there. He rubbed the back of his neck, trying to erase the images of her naked limbs and curves. Eating was safer, and reaching for one of the boules of bread set in the center of the table, he froze mid-reach. Two perfect bread globes sat before him, appearing for all the world like Murel's bottom when she'd bent herself over in one of the many positions they'd tried in his dreams.

He had to get ahold of himself. So, he grabbed the loaf and cut it into thick slabs, taking a sizeable chunk for himself. He looked up in time to see that Murel had been staring at him. She flicked a look to her brother, who, thankfully, was oblivious to the uncomfortable undercurrents in the parlor. Without taking his eyes off his plate, Jesper pushed the jam and butter toward Tomas. Well, perhaps not so oblivious after all. Tomas hated to say it, but even Ronan's japing would've been welcome.

"How's your head, Sis?"

"Fine, Brother," Murel mumbled, then took a sip of tea.

Tomas noticed a soaked tisane sitting on the table. No doubt some herbal remedy that she'd concocted to counteract the aftereffects of imbibing too much. She drank more of her tea, selected a piece of fruit to eat, then stared at the bread. After plucking one of the smaller pieces from the basket, she cleared her throat and slanted a look to the butter and jam. Without saying a word, he pushed them across the table.

"If you'll both excuse me, I'll see what's keeping Ronan," Jesper stated, then got up from the bench. At the door, he paused. "I'm not one for lively conversation, but even spending time with Ronan has to be better than this. You two need to work out whatever this"—he waved his good hand in the air—"is."

Tomas stared at the door that shut behind Jesper. Finally, he turned back to the table. Murel was massaging her temples. Tomas took a piece of bread and spread some butter across it. He handed it to her. "Food helps. Jam doesn't."

"Thank you." She sighed. "I owe you an apology."

"Not necessary. You weren't yourself."

"I took advantage of my intoxication and—"

"Besides," he continued at the same time. "I'm the one who should apologize. I should have been... I shouldn't have taken advantage of your state. I wasn't—"

"You're sorry?"

"Yes."

She frowned at him.

"Wait. No. I mean, yes?"

She sighed again, and then rose from the table, leveling him with an unreadable look. "If anyone needs me, tell them I've gone back to bed." She took a step, stopped, grabbed the piece of bread he'd prepared for her, and returned to her sleeping quarters, closing the door behind her.

For the first time in his life, Tomas felt out of his depth with a woman. Was he sorry that he'd kissed her? Not one bit. That he was breaking an oath? Maybe. Could he leave Murel alone, in her room, believing that he regretted that moment of intimacy? Hell, no.

He got up and strode to her door, barely stopping himself from pounding on it. Instead, he rapped softly.

"Go away, please."

"Murel, I'm counting to ten, and then I'm coming in. So, you had better—"

"Fine. Come in."

He entered and found her curled up on her side, the blankets pulled up over her shoulder. The window was wide open, allowing fresh air to circulate in the small room. "It's too cold in here," he said, walking over to the small hearth and stoking the embers. "I thought Naca'an was supposed to be warm, like Pheldhain."

"Even Pheldhain can have cold days."

A breeze gusted through the room, and Tomas lifted his brow.

"Fine," she repeated.

"You keep saying that."

"What?"

"Fine," he supplied, closing the window's shutter so that all but a small crack remained. "But you're not, are you?"

"I feel terrible, if that's what you need to hear. Happy?"

He ignored her, poured some water on a cloth, and then sat on the edge of her bed. Gently, he wiped her brow. "It could be much worse, you know. If Ronan hadn't plied you with water and food, you probably wouldn't have made it through the night without losing everything that you ate—"

"Please stop," she begged.

"For the record, I'm not sorry."

"About almost making me lose my tea and that bite of bread. Very kind of you," she groused.

"No. About kissing you."

"I knew what I was doing," Murel whispered to him. "I wanted to get drunk...for courage."

"You're braver than me, then." He brushed her hair back, letting his fingers trail along her scalp. Something between a moan and a sigh escaped her lips. She rolled onto her back, scooting over to make room for him. Her eyes were shut, her long lashes only slightly darker than the deep shadows bruising the skin under her eyes. Gently, he ran his fingers through her hair, fanning the tresses out onto her pillow. He pressed his fingertips along her temples and behind her ears. This time, she did moan. He made small circles along one side, and she turned her face away from him so that he could reach behind her neck. Her dark, sable hair was finer and silkier than even the fur of the fisher minks that made up Pheldhain's crest. And when he heard a soft snore, he dipped down to kiss her temple. She smiled in her sleep, and he pulled up the blankets higher on her shoulder.

He had just sat back down to finish breaking his fast when Jesper returned. He looked at the closed door, then at Tomas. "Do I need to have a conversation with you?" he asked, sounding like it was the last thing in the world he wanted to do.

"No," Tomas said. "But I'm officially letting you know that I think I'm in love with your sister and that my intentions are honorable."

"Think?"

"Am."

"She was really drunk last night..."

"She was," Tomas granted. Jesper stared at him. He stared back.

"Promise me this won't be awkward."

"I can't do that." He ripped off a piece of the crusty slice of boule with his teeth, chewing thoughtfully. "I haven't told her of my regard...yet. But I believe she's aware of it."

"You may be the one person who knows Murel better than I do," Jesper added. "Once she decides her course, she doesn't deviate."

"Noted. And whatever happens, I'll take it slow."

"That'll drive her crazy."

Tomas smiled.

"As long as you keep me out of it." Jesper sat down, took a slice of bread, and slathered it with butter. "It goes without saying what I'll do to you if she gets hurt."

"It does." He nodded toward the door behind which Murel was napping. "She went back to bed."

"That's for the best."

"Remind me to thank Ronan for helping her last night. How is he, by the way?"

"Unusually quiet. Murel will need to check on him when she wakes."

"There's something I need to take care of, Jess. Will you stay here... keep watch over her while I'm gone?"

Jesper set down his cup with a thud.

"We haven't yet discussed what happened the other day...as a group, and—"

"Yes."

"Yes?"

"Do what you need to. I'll keep her safe."

"Just like that?"

"Exactly like that."

Then Tomas recalled how he'd returned to find Murel drinking and Jess stewing. "To your sister." He lifted his cup.

"My sister," Jess echoed, clunking his cup against Tomas's.

Grinning, Tomas left his friend. With luck, he'd be back before Murel woke from her nap. After securing directions from the innkeeper, he headed toward the market.

. . .

Murel stretched, enjoying the cocoon of warmth the blankets provided. She opened her eyes, drew a deep breath, and tried to determine the time: noon, maybe a little later. She took stock—the dull throbbing in her brain was gone. The light didn't hurt her eyes, either. Her stomach growled, but from hunger, not queasiness. She rolled to her side. Someone had placed a cup with wildflowers at her bedside. There was fresh water as well, and she sat up and drank it down. Tomas.

Leaving the warmth of the blankets, she slipped her feet into her shoes, shook out her wrinkled skirt, and addressed the call of nature. After washing her hands, and rinsing her mouth with more fresh water, she opened her door and entered her parlor, a much less groggy version of her earlier self. Her brother was there, as was Ronan, reclining near the hearth.

"Ronan!" She rushed to his side. "You look terrible. Why didn't anyone wake me? Jesper, grab a blanket from my bed." She held Ronan's head in her hands, turning him toward the light. He furrowed his brow. "No jesting this time...how many fingers?"

"Three."

"Hmm. Your pupils are the same size."

"Is that good?" he grumbled.

"Yes." She sat back, studying the bruising that was filling in under one eye. "Does it hurt more today than yesterday?"

"It feels like someone is using my skull as an anvil. But I really don't remember much from the last few days. Only hazy images."

Murel felt the solid bone under his swollen contusion. "I'm sorry, Ronan, but this pain you're feeling now is part of the healing process."

"Then next time, don't start with 'I'm sorry.' You scared the wits out of me—I thought I was dying!"

She patted his arm. "I'll give you something for the pain. And no wine. If I hadn't been in such a state last night, I would've stopped you from drinking."

"You were in a state?" he asked, attempting to wink and flinching for the effort.

"Never you mind that. Why don't you lie back? That's it." She tucked a pillow under him. "I'll return in a moment. Don't fall asleep on me."

"That has never been a problem of mine when a beautiful woman is present," he flirted.

"Ahem." Tomas had entered the chamber's parlor with a cloth-covered crate in his hands. He set it on the table. "Is he going to make it?" he asked, taking in Ronan's condition.

"Yes, of course he is," she said. "Pour him some water, please, Tomas. Jess, don't just stand there...cover him with that blanket. And someone stoke the hearth."

"She's feeling better," Jesper said in an aside to Tomas.

"I heard that." In her room, she searched for her case with the medicaments that she kept with her when traveling and pulled out a bundle of pre-measured herbs drawn tight inside a neat linen pouch. Going back into the sitting room, she ordered Ronan to tuck the tisane between his teeth and left cheek. "And don't worry about falling asleep. If you do, we'll remove it if you start choking."

"What is it?" he asked. "It tastes like mint."

"That's to cover the more bitter herbs. There's meadowsweet, cowslip, and wormwood to help with the pain. Trust me, you'll start feeling better by this evening." She patted his shoulder, and then walked over to where Tomas was unpacking the crate.

"The innkeeper said this was the perfect thing to eat after drinking too much," he explained.

"He knows that I…"

"No, he believes it's for Ronan." He pulled out a crock, opened the lid, and the most delicious-smelling steam wafted across the table. "Good, it's still hot." Behind them, Ronan edged down lower on the banquette.

"It smells wonderful. What is it?"

"Fish stew." —She made a face.— "I know, I wouldn't think to eat fish after being in my cups, but the innkeeper swears by it." He tore off a chunk of bread, placed it in the center of a carved wooden bowl, then used a ladle he'd procured from the innkeeper to spoon the stew over the bread. He prepared three bowls.

Murel watched with a smile as he opened a small packet of fresh herbs and then sprinkled them over each serving. He cut up more bread, then motioned for Murel and Jesper to sit. Near the hearth, Ronan began to snore. Her brother and Tomas seemed to be waiting for her to try it first, so she dipped a piece of bread into the stew, making sure to scoop up some of the small white clumps. She took a bite, and bright, savory flavors exploded in her mouth. "So good!" she pronounced, taking another bite and closing her eyes to enjoy the tasty food.

Halfway through their meal, Tomas tipped his chin over to Ronan. "Can he travel?"

"Not for a few days. It's at least a week to Aghna's palace." She returned to eating her stew, examining the chunks of fish as if they would somehow provide them with the answers to their troubles. She pushed them around her bowl.

"Uh-oh," Jesper said. "She has an idea."

Murel loved her brother, but really hated it when he said things like that, as if what she had to say lacked merit. Lately, she'd been letting the comments go unchecked. But not this time. Not when they were a man down.

"I've found that your sister's ideas all have merit," Tomas stated, countering her brother's comment. "Her excellent mind has gotten us out of more scrapes than I can count. All with grace, dignity, and preservation for any party involved. In fact, Jess, if you—"

"Yield! I yield." Her brother took another bite of his stew. "Murel knows that I'm teasing her. It's a brother-sister thing, right, Murel?"

Murel wanted to get up and hug Tomas. Instead, she stared down at her soup and avoided her brother's question. Tomas ladled stew into another bowl, then took it over to where Ronan was dozing.

"Murel?" Jess asked. "You know I'm joking?"

"Sure, Jess. Don't worry about it."

"Now hold on," he insisted. "Why didn't you say anything before?"

"I…"

"Poor Jess," he whined sarcastically. "So delicate."

"If you think I've… Fine, I'll tell you. You used to tease me all the time when we were kids. And then you stopped. You listened to me. Asked for my opinions. But since we got you back, you've, well, reverted to your fifteen-year-old self. So, I held my tongue and tried my best to ignore your cuts."

Murel glanced over to Tomas, who was handing Ronan chunks of bread so that he could dip it into the stew. The two were studiously avoiding listening to them. She lowered her voice. "You've been a real pain, Jess. But I love you. And that means I'm going to stop coddling you. I've done everything I can to help you heal. But there's nothing more I can do." She said it gently. "I should have stopped months ago."

"You don't know—"

"No, I don't. I can't imagine it either. What you went through. You are one of the strongest and bravest men I've ever known. Princess Anwyl told me the stories. No one survives what you did and—"

"Not that," Jess interrupted. "I mean to say, you don't know how relieved I am to hear that you won't care anymore. Bad choice of words," he added hastily when she narrowed her eyes at him. "I see you trying, over and over. It's too much pressure knowing that I'm failing you in some way."

"But you're not," Murel insisted.

"It's okay, Sis." He took another bite of his stew, chewing thoughtfully. "I'll never be the same person that I was before. Never. And not because of this stump. Since our conversation last night, I've been thinking hard about my life. I have to find my place. In my own way." He lowered his arm to hold down the loaf of bread with his forearm, then awkwardly cut another slice.

Murel placed her hand on the stub of his wrist. For once, her brother didn't pull away as if burned. "You are more than this, Jess," she finally choked out.

"You have to let go," he whispered, and he wasn't talking about his arm. "My life may depend upon it."

She brushed away the tear that ran down her cheek. Jess set down the knife, and then squeezed her hand. He didn't promise her that he would be all right. And though it was the hardest thing she'd ever done, she nodded, and then she let him go.

"Thanks, Sis." He looked toward the hearth. "Ronan's awake. You should lay out your plan." He rose from the table and walked away from her.

Murel sat for a moment, feeling the weight of someone's notice. And knowing it was Tomas, and that he was concerned for her, she felt a tiny bit better. He hadn't finished his stew. She scraped away the congealing remains, ladled a fresh, albeit not as hot, scoop into his bowl, then picked up the last of the bread. Rising from the table, she carried it over to him. He accepted it, making room for her on the cushioned bench and giving her the closest seat to the fire.

Jesper pulled up a low stool. "All right, Murel, spell it out for us."

Murel took a deep breath and then started. "They were waiting for us to make port."

"Which means they knew we were coming," Tomas added. "Someone in Aurelia sent word ahead of us."

After giving everyone a moment to let the implications sink in, Murel continued, "The list of people who knew we were coming is short, and the attack was well coordinated. Because of this, it's clear that whoever came after us has people ensconced in Aurelia—Kings Glen, Pheldhain, or Meramont."

"Or all three," Tomas put in.

Ronan frowned as if trying to recall something, but then his expression cleared, and he stared at the fire.

"A week's ride to the palace," she continued. "Our messenger should be there in three days. Then another week to return and provide an escort."

"That sounds about right. We shouldn't try to get there without one," Jess counseled.

"Agreed," Murel said. "But ten days, sitting here, not doing anything."

"You want to set a trap," Tomas guessed.

She nodded.

"Where? How?"

"At the market in four days. It'll give Ronan enough time to heal. We'll need Grieg, and though I don't want them placed in danger, the boys who helped us earlier would make excellent lookouts." Murel began outlining her plan. "They need to believe our numbers are reduced."

She turned to Ronan. "The day after tomorrow, you should be feeling a little more like yourself. If you are up to it, you should go back to the ship and begin preparations for your voyage back to Aurelia. If whoever was behind the attack assumes that you and Grieg and the crew are occupied with refitting the ship, they—"

"They'll likely pounce on the opportunity for another try at us," her brother finished.

Tomas stared at her, a frown forming on his brow.

She would have to choose her words carefully. "Exactly," Murel said. "We'll go to the market. Give them a chance ripe for the picking. And in return, we'll—"

"No," Tomas said flatly. The others swiveled their heads to regard him. "You will not be the bait. Not you, Murel. No."

"Not only me." She stood up and paced. "All three of us. What do you suppose will happen to me if I stay back here alone whilst you and Jess go to the market? You know it, and I know it, Tomas. They separated us on purpose."

"They? Who do you think *they* are?" Jess demanded.

"There are several suspects," Murel replied.

"We can certainly rule out Queen Aghna and King Ranulf," Tomas stated.

She nodded. At least he was listening again. And he'd stopped pacing.

"Short list: former-Steward-King-now-under-siege Diarmait; the rogue Fenrhi women. Maybe both, though why those women would willingly pair up with Diarmait again, I cannot fathom. And, least likely, the Fyrjians."

"I don't like it," Tomas stated. "I don't like you being on your own."

"I won't be. You'll be there, next to me. Grieg and his men will be in the market, not on the ship. And Jess will be there. All that I ask is that you listen to the full plan before deciding."

"I'll hear you out," Tomas said. "As long as you listen to me when I point out the flaws in your scheme. And you'll have to promise me, right now, in front of your brother and Ronan, that you will agree to a vote at the end of your presentation."

"But what if there is a tie?"

"We'll invite Grieg. That'll make five votes; majority wins. And our captain should be here anyway; he'll have a part to play as well."

"How soon can he get here?" Murel asked.

"I've already asked him to join us for dinner this evening."

"Fine," Murel said. "In the meantime, I'm going to my room to prepare. Ronan, I want you to stay near that fire and rest. Jess, you're in charge of Ronan."

"No orders for me?" Tomas asked, and she heard the humor in his tone and was thankful he was trying to diffuse the tension.

"Let me mull it over," she replied with a half-smile, then added a wink to leave him wondering. Alone in her sleeping chamber, Murel sat on her bed and ran through her plan. She imagined every conceivable argument that Tomas might have and how to counter it. In the end, she determined that she could count on Grieg's support. And probably Ronan's, too. Five years ago, her brother would've been an absolute no, but now, Murel hadn't any idea. But his vote didn't matter if she could gain the majority. In the end, her biggest argument would be that they simply had no other choice than to try.

· · ·

Hours later, she exited her room. Ronan was on his side, facing the fire and quietly snoring. Tomas squatted before the hearth, adding another log and stoking the embers underneath.

Their supper had yet to be delivered, and Grieg and Jess were nowhere in sight. Tomas reached for yet another log, and she felt a blush stealing up her neck and cheeks as she admired the way his shoulder and back muscles bunched and flexed. One really ought not objectify a person this way, then immediately forgot her admonition as he rose to his full height and stretched at his waist, first to the left, then to the right.

Murel caught herself before revealing her inspection with some involuntary noise. But when Tomas leaned over Ronan, pulling a blanket up over the other man's shoulder, she sighed at his thoughtfulness. Tomas must've heard it because he straightened, homing in on the soft noise. The toastiness of the parlor became uncomfortably warm.

Murel, never one to be skittish, especially around Tomas, found herself unable to calm her hands. She smoothed a nonexistent crease from her skirts, and when she looked back up at him, he was still studying her. Lit from behind by the merrily burning flames, the fire burnished each curled tendril of his blond hair, setting them alight with orange and red and gold. He regarded her, and she felt as if he could see through her façade and straight into her soul.

This was her friend, her confidante. The man who had helped her to save her brother. The angel who draped a blanket over a wounded friend. But there was nothing angelic about the way he watched her now.

She had to move, and she stepped to the left, toward the table. Stopped. Turned around. She must look ridiculous pacing, so she strode to the window and the view of the courtyard below. At least it would be cooler than the heat that seemed to be radiating more from Tomas than the hearth. As she stood there, she pressed her palm against the mullioned glass and watched the condensation form around her fingers. The courtyard below, mottled and distorted by the thick glass, was indistinct in the waning light. The door to the inn opened to issue some traveler from her depths, and yellow swathes of light fell against the cobbled ground, interrupted only by the shadows of the passersby.

Her eyes were drawn to the spot where she had stood with Tomas the previous night. She crossed her arm over her chest, holding her shoulder, and the memory of where he had touched her came unbidden to her mind. As the inn's door closed, the shadows of the growing night once again enrobed the courtyard, and her own reflection stared back at her.

She felt the heat of him as he came to stand behind her, placing his hand over hers where it remained against the glass. And she had the wild notion that his touch would set her afire. The idea of it stirred her, and she held her breath, fearful he would do nothing. His fingers inched up until they covered her hand, but his touch was surprisingly cool compared to her feverish thoughts.

Gathering her courage, she lifted her eyes to his, but he was engrossed in the spot where their hands met. She took the moment to catalogue his features: the strength of his jaw, often-times tense with concern for her or their friends; the lushness of his mouth, one more prone to an engaging grin than a frown; the line of his nose and flare of his nostrils, an indication of his nobility and strength of resolve. All these aspects were a summation of the man himself, of his innate goodness.

She felt him go still, felt the swing of his regard, yet she would not meet his eyes. For this, she wanted to see clearly when she added them to her catalogue of his makeup. She slid her hand out from under his and slowly spun around. Finally, she gazed up and into his eyes and memorized the hue, the shape, and the warmth and humor twinkling therein. And the hunger.

He rested his hand upon her shoulder, and he shifted them so they were no longer standing at the window, but next to it. If not for the solid wall behind her, Murel might've melted to the floor. When he tilted his head and moved a fraction closer, she exhaled, and her lips parted. But he focused his attention to where Ronan still slumbered peacefully across the room. Murel, too, turned, exposing her ear and the length of her neck to him.

She felt the tip of his finger as he gently traced the shell of her ear, tucking a wayward tress behind her lobe. She sucked in her breath and closed her eyes when she felt his warm exhale on her neck.

"Your skin is so soft," he whispered. "Ever since our kiss last night, I can't stop fantasizing about how you taste." He paused, and Murel held her breath. "May I?"

The idea that Tomas wanted to taste her sent shivers through her body. She wanted him to kiss her everywhere, but she could never say such a thing out loud. He continued caressing her neck and ear, waiting for her reply. She swallowed. "Please," she said, finally letting go of the breath she'd been holding.

"You'll have to keep a lookout," he whispered, and she opened her eyes to stare across the room at Ronan. There was something wicked about the suggestion, and heat speared straight to her stomach and, heaven help her, lower.

He nuzzled her neck then, applying soft kisses behind her ear and sending little puffs of air over her skin. "Sweeter than I dreamed of…"

The hair on her arms stood up, and she stretched the column of her neck. He next applied soft kisses to her jaw, nearly reaching the corner of her mouth, and her lips opened as she gave a soft gasp. His arms bracketed her against the wall, and as the tip of his tongue traced a lazy trail back to her ear, Murel moaned.

Across the room, Ronan shifted, but resumed snoring. Tomas touched her chin, turning her face to his, and dipped lower to set a sweet kiss against her lips. He broke away, and Murel couldn't help but lean forward, following him. But he gently cupped her chin, directing her awareness back toward the hearth. "Stop me if he wakes," he ordered, tracing her ear with his tongue.

Murel moaned again as exquisite gooseflesh flushed over her. There was a gentle scrape of teeth, followed by a nip to her earlobe. His broad hand settled on her waist, and through the thin layer of her gown, she felt the heat and pressure of each of his long, splayed fingers. When he took her lobe between his lips and sucked, she whimpered.

He alternated kissing, nipping and sucking the sensitive areas of her neck and ear as she tried to keep her awareness on Ronan's consciousness. When Tomas began tracing circles on her ribs, reaching higher until he was a hair from touching the underside of her breast, Murel's eyes fluttered in anticipation. He immediately withdrew, and she snapped her attention back to across the room. She thrilled inside when he rewarded her obedience with searing kisses trailed down her neck.

Again, he moved his hand, inching higher, and her breath came in shallow pants. Murel heard a growl, and realized it came from her. Tomas was set on torture, and she was aflame, wondering how far he would go. She was bad. So bad. And this was so good.

He spent long minutes kissing and laving the hollow above her collarbone, and making delicate swirls with his talented fingers, but never connecting with her breast. Her nipple ached to be touched, and she felt it gather and harden. And when she leaned forward to try to engage him for more, he gently but forcefully pushed her back against the wall. He stopped paying tribute to her with his mouth and rested his forehead on the wall above her shoulder. Murel sighed. Was it relief or disappointment?

She wasn't a stranger to arousal. She'd had dreams and had woken deep in the night, panting for more and having to pleasure herself lest she be unable to fall back asleep. She turned her face, her lips meeting that dimple below the apple of his neck, and she pressed an open-mouthed kiss to the spot where his pulse beat.

He brushed his lips across hers in a feathery touch. Then, he suddenly straightened, stepped back and walked to the hearth. He muttered something that she couldn't make out to a half-awake Ronan.

Inside, Murel moaned her frustration—why couldn't Ronan stay asleep? Smoothing her bodice and skirts with shaking hands, she focused on calming her racing heart. Tomas, thankfully, blocked Ronan's view of her, and he winked at her as she hastily retreated to her sleeping chamber, closing the door silently behind her.

She fell back on her bed, every inch of her body craving to be touched. Damn. How had she allowed this? There was no way she could concentrate on her plan, all roiled up inside like this. She was an instrument strung too tight, so taut that she wanted to scream. Hunger. Want. Desire. Her body was aquiver, and Tomas had been the one to pluck her strings. The need for release was so great that she jumped from her bed, ready to kick both men out of her parlor if only to have privacy to shout out her frustration.

She reached for the door handle, but stopped, picturing Tomas's bent head, envisioning him cupping her. He must have been able to see down her bodice. Would that he had lifted her so that he could kiss the swell of her breast. Murel groaned softly and turned to lean against the door. She reached up and touched her ear where Tomas had stroked her with his tongue and lips and teeth, then trailed her fingers down, recalling the path his mouth had taken. With her other hand, she cupped her breast—it was *his* strong fingers that were holding her.

She tweaked her nipple—as she had craved him to do—then rolled the nub between her finger and thumb. She let her other hand drift lower and lower until her fingers, pleat by pleat, rucked up the skirt of her gown. She touched herself, imagining it was Tomas. In the other room, she heard someone leave the parlor. There was a soft rap on her door, and she froze.

"Murel."

It was the very object of her passion.

"Ronan has gone to his chamber to change. The innkeeper will bring our meal soon. Murel?"

Though his words were not romantic, the timbre of his voice resonated through her. "Thank you, Tomas," she answered. "I'll be out in a few minutes." She took a moment to fall back into her fantasy...yes, there it was, that warm tingling. She needed to hear him say her name again. "Tomas?" she called out.

"Yes."

She ignored him. Waited.

"Murel?"

There it was. Her name on his tongue. His very talented tongue. She stroked, bringing herself the pleasure she so desperately craved, all the while knowing that only the wood of the door separated them.

"Murel?"

"Never mind," she managed to eke out. "I'll come and join you in a few minutes." She was so close to release, mere moments away, and she would be there.

"All right. Let me know if you need me to lend a hand."

Oh, heavens! His strong hands. His long fingers. Murel bit down on the heel of her hand as she pushed herself over the brink, sliding to the floor as her thigh muscles quivered.

She took a few minutes to catch her breath, then stood and straightened her gown. Fortunately, her skirts were unwrinkled. She tucked up a few stray tendrils of hair, washed her hands and splashed cool water on her face.

Standing before the looking glass, she patted her skin dry. A healthy flush stained her cheeks, and her eyes were bright and clear. Previously befuddled by Tomas's kisses, she was now as sharp as the hidden dagger in her boot...every detail of her plan crisp in her mind. She marched toward her door, refreshed—physically *and* mentally.

$\bullet \bullet \bullet$

Tomas waited near the hearth, staring into the flames, giving Jess, Grieg, and a returning Ronan the merest acknowledgment when they entered the parlor. He had never imagined that Murel would be so responsive. He'd been ready to spend himself upon hearing her little moans and whimpers. Hell, he'd had to take his time folding the blanket he'd pulled off Ronan to hide his arousal. Thankfully, Ronan seemed none the wiser.

When Tomas had tapped on her door, she hadn't sounded angry. Perhaps a little intense. He'd only meant to kiss her neck, and he nearly fondled her breast, all with a man sleeping across the room. But her reactions were so erotic, he couldn't help himself. That line of thought had him shifting uncomfortably where he stood.

"Is Murel still in her room?" Ronan asked, coming up behind him with the others and slapping him on the shoulder. "Probably perfecting her plan."

Tomas inwardly groaned. If Murel was as frustrated as he was at this very moment, her pitch was sure to suffer. And if it did, then she would be angry with him, no doubt about it.

"Gentlemen, shall we eat first, and then discuss my trap?" Murel all but chirped as she exited her sleeping chamber.

In fact, Tomas realized, she *was* chipper. More, she was radiant. She glowed with, dare he imagine it, satisfaction? As if…

"Please sit then," she directed, walking over to a side table where wine and goblets had been set. "I'll pour the wine. And don't wait for me. Dig in."

Tomas approached her, his outward intention being to assist her with the wine. A couple of feet separated them as she handed him two of the cups she had poured. She grinned up at him, her eyes alit with mischief. Her cheeks glowed, and she lifted her eyebrow and the corner of her lip. Tomas swallowed. Hard. She took the other two cups and sashayed to the table. Ronan gazed up at her, and then leaned back in his chair, crossing his arms, and smiling appreciatively. Murel answered his leer with a haughty scowl and took her place at the head of the table.

Jess seemed oblivious to her mood, joining Grieg in piling sliced beef onto their plates. Ronan, nearest to the platter, lifted it up and presented it to Murel.

"Oh, thank you, Ronan. I'm utterly famished!" She loaded her plate with two slices of rare beef, piling mushrooms, turnips, and roasted carrots on top.

"Don't forget to save room for dessert," Ronan reminded, setting the platter on the table so that it was between him and Tomas.

Murel, reaching for a second helping of bread, paused. "Perhaps one slice will suffice. For now." She then dug into her meal with the gusto of any one of the men sitting with her.

"Aren't you hungry?" Ronan asked Tomas upon noting that he hadn't taken a bite.

Tomas glared at his friend, picked up his fork, and stabbed a piece of meat. He managed to clean his plate, and when dessert turned out to be a cobbler with fresh cream, had two helpings. More wine was poured, and they cleared the table. Grieg reached into his satchel and then handed Murel a roll of parchment. "This is as accurate as I could make, given the short notice, but it should suffice for what you have in mind."

"Thank you, Grieg," she said, unrolling what appeared to be a diagram of the marketplace, remarkably detailed, despite Grieg's protest otherwise. "I appreciate your help."

"*Hmph,*" the ship's captain commented.

Tomas and the others sat rapt as Murel outlined the overall plan. Once done, she went back over the information, incorporating more details, using the map to point out potential escape routes and danger areas. She answered every query and concern, asking questions of her own before elucidating her points. Tomas was impressed.

"You don't have enough men," Grieg stated, surprising everyone.

"But the plan involves some of *Moon Caster's* crew. With all of us, plus Baqi and his friend as lookouts, we'll be fourteen. If we station the crew here, here"—she pointed to the alleys and lanes leading from the marketplace—"and here..."

Grieg leaned forward. "Aye. But this is no lane or alley. Nor is this." He pointed to the north and south routes leading to the square. "These are roads, and broad ones at that. You would need two men at least to cover them."

"But surely they're the least likely place for an attack."

Grieg grumbled something in his throat.

"Perhaps we can have the boys posted near those two spots," Murel said, frowning. "Or—"

"It's a thorough plan, Murel," Jess said. "We understand enough of it to take a vote. You've answered all our questions and provided good counterarguments to almost every concern."

"Almost?" she asked. "What am I missing?"

"A good reason," her brother stated baldly. "I want to find the perpetrators as much as you, but the risk isn't worth it. We don't even know if the attackers are still in Naca'an."

"If they're gone," she reasoned, "then letting this trap play out doesn't hurt anyone."

"And if they are still in the city?" Jess continued. "Let's say this works, and by some miracle, no one gets hurt. What are we going to do with the attackers?"

"Find out who's behind this, then give them to Aghna, of course."

"I vote no. The cost could be too great. We should concentrate on preparing for another attack, not going on the offensive."

"Jess!" Murel cried. "I thought you at least would be on my side. This is our duty, Tomas's and mine. The attack has roots in Aurelia. We are honor-bound to find out the truth." She trained her eyes on each of the other men, one at a time. "I, obviously, vote yes."

"I agree with Murel," Ronan said, sounding surprised at his own words.

"No."

Everyone turned to Grieg.

"I'm sorry, Lady Murel," he said, as she slumped down in her chair.

"I guess that's it then," she conceded. "I'll—"

"Yes," Tomas stated, watching as she rolled up the map to cast aside. "Murel, I vote yes. We all agreed that we would go with the majority. Grieg? Jess? We can't do this without you."

Grieg sighed. "You don't have to ask. You know House Pheldhain will always have my loyalty."

"What changed your mind?" Jesper asked.

"Your sister did. She's right. She and I swore to uphold the ideals of Aurelia in all things whilst here in Nifolhad. We swore to protect Aurelia's reputation, its assets, and its people. If someone here attacks us, it's more than our responsibility to investigate and apprehend the culprits. It's our duty." He brought over another bottle of wine, refilling everyone's cups. "Let's go over this again."

Grieg sat back down. "I might be able to hire a man or two to help on the ship. That would give you another crewman."

Murel nodded, and they huddled together over the table to go over her plan, finetuning each step and making contingencies.

Hours later, Grieg finally returned to the ship. Murel had checked on Ronan again—he seemed to be well on his way to recovery and had headed back to his room to retire early. Jess was sitting near the hearth, staring at the flames. "I should be going," Tomas said, standing at the door. "I would like to walk the square tomorrow with the boys. They're local and might have some additional insight."

"Thank you," Murel stated, glancing her brother's way before pushing at his chest with her hand until he was out of view of Jesper.

"I meant what I said," he explained. "My vote had nothing to do with what is going on between us."

"I know it didn't. You believe in my plan. It means much to me." Behind her, a chair leg scraped the floor, followed by the clang of metal as Jesper stoked the fire and added more fuel. "And this has nothing to do with your vote." She stood on tiptoes and pressed a sweet kiss to his lips. As she pulled back, she gave a little sigh. Her eyes were veiled by the shadows of the corridor, but he could see the heat in her expression.

Before he could do or say anything, a determined look stole across her features. "There's something I need to talk to Jess about. Good night to you, Tomas." She turned, closing the door behind her.

# As Plans Go

Murel vowed to one day revisit the marketplace when they could do so without fear of an attack. Her outward role was to play a noblewoman more interested in the beautiful silks and damasks on display than her own surroundings.

Not a difficult task in the least, for the spectrum of pastels and vibrant hues was astounding. She purchased another bolt—this one would be sent back to Princess Anwyl: water silk in the deep fuchsia of ripe raspberries. The vendor thanked her, then pulled out another roll of cloth from under the counter, this one in deep indigo shot through with silver threads.

"A one-of-a-kind weave," he promised. Murel handed the already purchased fabric to Tomas. He gave her a look that told her they should be moving on if they were going to stick to her plan. "Not even our beautiful and benevolent Queen Aghna possesses a gown made with such treasured threads. If I may say, m'lady, the beauty of this cloth is only rivaled by the midnight blue of your eyes."

Murel smiled. "Are all the textile vendors of Naca'an poets?"

"Only the successful ones," he quipped.

"Lady Murel, we must keep moving if we are to see the offerings of the entire market," Tomas insisted. "Perhaps if we return this way," he said to the merchant, leading Murel from under the shade of the canopy. "And if there is room in my arms to hold more goods."

Murel nodded her thanks to the man, and with one last look at the indigo bolt and a sigh, she let Tomas lead her away. He set down their purchases as she took a seat on the broad rim of the massive water fountain that held reign in the center of the square. Feigning regret for having not made the last purchase—well, half-pretending—she spoke quietly to

Tomas, periodically scanning the crowd. "I'm starting to think this effort is for naught. Have you noticed anyone suspicious?"

"The boy in the dark gray shirt is a pickpocket," Tomas noted, nodding to the far left. "He's working with that man in the straw hat with the ripped brim." He swiveled to indicate one of the fabric vendors that he had steered her past. "I skipped that tent—the woman handling the purchases is stealing from her customers."

"That's horrible—cheating people out of their hard-earned coin. How does she do it?"

"She sets their change on the table, then her husband places a bolt of cloth over the coins. Usually something ugly that they won't purchase. When they sweep the fabric away, so too goes some of the change. They're very good at it. One coin here, another there."

"That's amazing," Murel stated.

"I'm surprised they haven't been caught yet."

"No, not the thieves. You." Murel stared across the marketplace. "I can barely make out the crew. If I didn't know where they were positioned, I would never recognize them."

Tomas grinned. "That was the point, wasn't it?" He hefted their goods back into his arms—enough bulky items to appear overloaded, but deceivingly lightweight so that he could throw them at someone, or easily drop the load to reach for his sword.

Murel checked her waist. The pommel of her dagger was barely visible, though it nudged uncomfortably at the underside of her breast. She had chosen to don Fenrhi-style leggings, a long tunic, and the tall, lace-up boots that housed another blade. She was passing-fair with a bow and arrow, and daggers were easily handled—just poke with the sharp end. But at quarterstaffs—Tomas's forte—she was hopeless. Princess Anwyl and Ladies Claire and Anna had all tried to tutor her. Even the missing Madyan had failed to teach her how to do more than poke someone in the stomach with a stout rod. She frowned. This distraction was keeping them from their true purpose in Nifolhad—finding Madyan and the fourth couple.

"Are you disappointed that your plan isn't bearing fruit?" Tomas asked.

"I suppose it was always a possibility." They began walking toward the last stop on their route, a wine vendor situated slightly away from the other booths and near the broad avenue that led deeper into the city of Naca'an and its labyrinth of alleys and walkways. She and Tomas would stop there, take a quick refreshment, then pretend to argue. "I was thinking about Madyan." She stopped speaking when the wine-seller greeted them. It was time to play their roles.

Tomas jostled the tote carrying their purchases and the fabric bolts in his arms, then asked to sample the wine.

"I told you already," Murel said as a taste was poured, "this wine came recommended. You never listen to me." She directed her next words to the seller. "Really, every booth with food or wine, he needs a sample. If you ask me, he's had a free midday meal and evening supper rolled into one."

"I didn't hear anyone ask you, m'lady," Tomas said under his breath, winking at the purveyor. "Besides, a man needs refreshment if he's going to carry all your fripperies."

"Keep that in mind, m'lord, seeing as it will be my coin that may or may not be buying that wine you are tasting." He rolled his eyes and set his cup down a little too forcefully. Then he readjusted the purchases as if they were heavy, allowing a fabric bolt to slip to the side. "Careful!" Murel cried out, catching the red fabric and knocking over his cup so it splashed down the leg of his breeches.

"Now, see here!" he faux-seethed. "You are simply going to have to carry that if you want to keep it. If you recall, I recommended bringing one of the servants with us."

"But you're the one who didn't want to wait! Fine," she said, then turned to leave, tucking the cloth under her arm. It wasn't exactly a good color, too bright of a red, but that was why they had purchased it first, per her plan. Like a flag, it would mark them out to any possible attackers. Murel hadn't added to the others that if she was carrying it and they were separated, it would serve the same purpose. She held it in a way to ensure that she could quickly grab her dagger.

"Well?" she asked when he didn't move to leave. Tomas lifted an eyebrow expectantly and nodded toward the wine. "Fine again," she said with an exasperated sigh. "Two"—Tomas *ahem'd*—"make that thr... four bottles. And please tell me that you can have it delivered to the Stone Hearth Inn."

"Yes, m'lady. For a small fee," he added quickly. Murel paid him, as if impatient to be gone. "Ready?" she asked Tomas, letting the irritation in her voice ring out.

"You know," Tomas said under his breath, as they made their way to the broad avenue, "the wine wasn't half bad and…" he trailed off.

"What is it?" she whispered.

"Just a feeling. Like we're being watched. And not by our own people. Keep alert, Murel," he ordered and moved closer.

She reached across as if to support the fabric with her other hand, but instead set her fingers on the hilt of her dagger. Ahead, Baqi gestured to them. Off to the right, a man who might've been Grieg angled toward their location.

"Two men. Behind us," Tomas cautioned. A large group of people spilled onto the main artery from a smaller side alley. Tomas positioned himself directly behind her.

The crew member stationed at the avenue was struggling to get past someone. But not in their direction. "Tomas, they're taking Baqi!"

She instinctively gave chase as the young man was collared and dragged away. Tomas had dropped their packages and was drawing his sword. He hadn't heard her over the noise of the crowd. But Grieg was shouting at her. And she had made eye contact with Ronan, signaling to him the direction she was going.

She caught a glimpse of the boy being pulled farther up the avenue. If she didn't follow, he would be lost, and it would be her fault. She held onto the bright bolt of fabric, lifting it higher like a banner.

For a minute, after pushing her way through the revelers, she lost sight of Baqi. Then, she saw the man's back as he entered one of the many branches that fed the main avenue. This was *not* part of the plan. She approached the alley with care. Glanced behind her. The avenue rose a little as it traveled farther away from the marketplace and the docks on the opposite end. She could see the throng struggling at the entrance of the avenue. A blond head rose above the others, sword drawn, legs wading through the people. Tomas. Using her wits, Murel tore off a piece of fabric to leave behind as a marker, and then entered the narrow, curved alley.

Though it was still midafternoon, shadows ruled in the angled space. The buildings rose two and three stories above her, leaning over the street like trees in a forest searching for a gap where they could touch the sun. There was a scuffle ahead, and she could make out a large shape looming over a smaller form on the ground. The man had put Baqi in a roughly woven sack and was cinching a rope around the opening, then drawing a blade to stab at the struggling boy. Murel gripped her dagger, and pulling it free, she charged forward.

He whirled in surprise, clearly not expecting her to attack him. But a sly grin spread across his features, so perhaps her ambush didn't matter. He advanced on her, sneering at the blade in her hand. He sheathed his weapon, and this did naught but stoke her anger. When he ran at her, Murel shuffled back and collided with someone behind her.

She heard an *oof* and turned, hoping it was Tomas. Only, it was one of the brutes who had accosted her and her brother when they first arrived. He'd lost his wind when she'd butted him in the chest with the wood stave around which the fabric was wound. Wasting no time, she used the bolt to jab out again, catching him in the throat. He grabbed his neck, choking and falling back. In one motion, she swung around, hurling the bolt at the other man. He ducked just in time, and her cloth went sailing down the narrow alley. All she had now was her knife...a knife her attacker found amusing.

He stalked her, fingers spread wide like talons. "Give me your blade, pretty dove. Maybe I won't dump that sack in the bay." He made a grab for her wrist, but she pulled back, then stabbed out, catching him in the hand. He howled in pain, then bore down on her. Murel backed up, but then her heel hit an uneven cobblestone and she tottered. She flailed her arms to keep her balance, but it was too late.

Her shoulders hit first, stealing her breath and sending spikes of pain down her spine. Strange how everything seemed to slow, giving her time to wonder how hard her skull would hit the cobblestones. When it did, pain cracked through her mind like white hot lightning. The thin slice of dusky sky turned dark as black spots filled the plane of her vision. The last thing she saw before she passed out was a bloody claw reaching for her neck.

• • •

Tomas whirled in the street, frantically searching for Murel. Behind him, Jesper worked his way through the ring of onlookers to where the crew was securing the man who had caused a fistfight near the opening to the avenue. Murel had disappeared. *Think*, he urged his brain. It was no accident that Murel had purchased the bright bolt of fabric. She'd wielded it like a flag bearer, signaling her location as she pursued Baqi and his abductor. At the time, that pennant had acted like a blazing banner waved in front of a bull. The fact that Murel was as smart as she was deliberate stopped him from roaring out his frustration at losing her.

*Think*.

The fabric.

He retraced his steps, checking the alleys and walkways and narrow passages through the crowded-tight-together buildings that ranged the street. Murel wasn't reckless. She would've marked her location.

He espied a flash of color, a strip of bright crimson that had been wedged between the building's stone and its iron corner-guard at the entrance to a tight, dark alley. He gave up one precious second to make sure he had Jesper's eye, then ran up the sharply curved incline. A mere ten paces in, he found her. She was on the ground, and an ogre of a man straddled her, choking the life from her body.

Tomas charged, leapt, and hurtled toward them. The man, taken completely unaware, was caught by Tomas's shoulder and driven backward a full body's length away. Tomas's initial goal was to incapacitate him so that he could get back to Murel. Then he saw the blood on the man's hands, and he grabbed his head on either side and smashed it down onto the hard cobblestones. The sound of pounding feet behind him barely stopped him from doing it again. It didn't matter—one sickening crunch had been enough. He scrambled back to Murel, ready to protect her.

"Murel!" Jess cried. "Tomas, is she..."

Tomas's heart nearly stopped upon seeing the mess of blood on her neck. He searched her tender skin for a wound, but there wasn't one. Gently, he pressed his fingers to her throat. There! A faint pulse.

"She's alive," he breathed. "She's alive, Jess. But I don't know for how long."

To his right, another man struggled to sit. He discovered that his cohort was dead and lying in a widening pool of blood. Catching the murderous intent in Tomas's eye, he began crab-walking backward. Jesper was quick to hit the butt of his sword against the man's temple, knocking him out. Farther down the alley, they heard a noise, and a misshapen form flailed and kicked at the rough sack imprisoning him.

"I'll see to the boy, Tomas; you tend to Murel."

Grieg arrived with two crewmen. "We'll take this one to the ship." The man groaned as they hoisted him between them and, dragging him from the alley, they staggered, pretending drunkenness.

Tomas tucked the bolt of fabric under Murel's head to cushion it. He used some of it to wipe away the blood on her neck and then swore when he saw the bruising on her windpipe.

Two more crewmen arrived, and Jesper ordered them to take the boy home and find a cart for Murel.

"There's not enough time," a female voice exclaimed, dropping down into the alley from a silken rope secured to the rooftop above. She wasn't alone. Two other women slid down with such grace, Tomas thought he might be imagining it. Except he wasn't. These were Fenrhi women, and from the Umbren Caste, judging by the dark color of their garments. The woman walked over to the boy. "Are you injured, Baqi?"

His eyes went wide. "You know my name?"

She ruffled his hair. "Go find your friend, and then run home. Your mother is waiting." He nodded, then sped down the alley. "Dispose of the body," she ordered the two crewmen. "But examine him first. Bring anything you find to the temple." They nodded, already moving to do her bidding.

Jesper stayed Tomas's hand as he reached for his sword. "They're not part of *Moon Caster*'s crew—Grieg must've hired them. They won't answer to us."

The woman issuing orders stepped forward. "Please," she stated simply. "If we are to save her, we must get Lady Murel to the Sylvan. She's lost too much blood already."

"But it's not her bl—" Tomas stared down at Murel's ashen face. The garnet-colored cloth had hidden the signs of her injury. And as he had cracked her attacker's skull against the cobblestones, so too had hers been dashed. The women moved to pick up Murel, but Tomas stepped in. "I'll carry her."

"We're faster."

"I'll keep up."

She took his measure, then directed one of her companions, "Take the Rottu to the temple."

"Yes, Sefrina," one of the women said, moving toward Jesper.

Tomas had no idea what a rottu was but didn't care. He was busy holding up Murel's head while the other woman tightly wound some of the silk around her to slow the bleeding. When she was finished, Tomas picked up Murel, cradling her limp body against his and with the aid of the Umbren woman, used more of the fabric to bind her to him in a tight sling.

"If you think I'm going to let you go without me..." Jesper started.

"Can you climb walls with one hand?" the woman named Sefrina asked unapologetically.

"I will see you to the temple," the other woman promised Jesper. "We will run through the city, and not even the wind will catch us. Come," she urged, pulling him toward the main avenue. "We will race against my sisters."

"Are you ready?" Sefrina asked Tomas.

For answer, he grasped one of the ropes and began scaling the wall. The women were faster, and they helped him up over the edge so that Murel would not be overly jostled.

Sefrina pointed to the west. "Do you know the tale of Princess Claire and the Malikáfyr?"

"Mali...? You mean Lady Madyan." Sefrina's eyes darkened, and Tomas understood. This woman was more than Fenrhi, more than their fabled Umbren warrior caste; she was Fyrjian. "Yes, I know of their nighttime escape from Diarmait's men, taking to the rooftops of Naca'an."

"Then you know that we will fly across this city." She pirouetted, then took off toward the northwest and to the temple where the Sylvan healers waited.

Neither woman looked back to make sure he was keeping pace, and only when they needed to drop to a lower roof, or climb a higher one, did they slow to assist him. When they finally came to a halt, Sefrina pulled open a trapdoor, and then dropped down into the darkness.

"You next," the other Umbren told him. "There's a ladder on the left."

Using the grab bars on the edge of the trapdoor, he carefully eased into the opening. The other woman followed, closing them in the dark space. Below him, came a scrape and a brief hiss, then the sound of squeaking metal as Sefrina lit an oil lamp. The passage down was narrow and steep, and he had to readjust Murel so her knees wouldn't be knocked. Even then, he would have to angle them through to accommodate his own shoulders.

"Watch your head," Sefrina cautioned, taking in his height. "The stairs are even, but the ceiling is not." She took the first few steps at a light pace, then sped up for what seemed like three stories' worth of stairs. Even with the lamp, it was very dark. With Murel secured to his front, Tomas could not see where his feet were landing.

"Slow down; there's a sharp turn before you."

Tomas's hand brushed against the roughly hewn stone of the wall as they descended.

"We're almost to the bottom. Careful now." When they all made it to a tiny vestibule, Sefrina snuffed the lamp's flame. In the absolute darkness, there was a scrape of wood on stone. And then suddenly, the space was filled with the golden russet light of a sunset filtered by long trailing vines of deep green. "Mind the thorns," she said, stepping through. "Quickly now."

Behind him, the other woman closed the door—it'd been painted to resemble the roughly carved stone of Naca'an's massive curtain wall and was covered in the same moss and vines growing there. Sefrina gave a soft chuckle when they heard the snort of a horse.

"Took you long enough," Jesper said, sitting atop one of the Fyrjian horses they'd transported from Aurelia.

"It was the Rottu's idea. Otherwise, we would've been an hour behind you," the other Umbren woman stated, similarly mounted and holding the reins of three more Fyrjian steeds.

Sefrina steadied Tomas as he mounted one of the horses, and then she vaulted onto the back of another. She waited while he checked Murel's pulse again—her heart still beat, but weakly. "Let's see how these Aurelian-

bred fyrjór run. We should arrive at the temple before the night descends."
She flicked her reins, and her mare shot forward.

Tomas followed, moving directly into a fast canter. The breed, while
smaller than the Chevlain steeds the men of the Royal Guard rode, were
equally as fast and as sure-footed. Still, he was relieved to have an extra
horse available in case his mount faltered from the double load.

True to Sefrina's words, they reached the temple in a little more than an
hour. A group of women, clothed in the moss green of the Sylvan Caste,
waited for them. Tomas slid off his horse. He set his lips in a grim line,
discouraging any attempt to remove Murel from his arms.

"This way. Hurry!" one of the women ordered. "My name is Hedra." She
led them through a series of passages and courtyards, and Tomas, in his
haste to see Murel safe, left it to Jesper to memorize the route through the
vast maze-like complex of the Fenrhi Temple.

"How did you know one of us was injured?" he asked as they entered a
hexagon-shaped room with a high, narrow bed set in the center.

"I told them," another woman stated, this one garbed in the honey-hued
robes of the Fenrhi Mother. "I am—"

"Ni'mala...the Mother," Tomas finished. "What did you see?" he asked
the Fenrhi leader—a seer in her own right.

"She will live. But we will need you to trust us to do what is necessary."

"I won't leave her."

"Of course not." She finally seemed to notice Jesper. "I did not see you."

As Tomas carefully eased Murel onto the bed, he realized the Mother's
words held a double meaning. "Jesper is Murel's brother."

Sefrina, with a curious gleam in her eyes, bowed to Ni'mala. "He is the
Rottu, Mother. He cannot be seen." Her statement startled Ni'mala.

Hedra looked up. "Now is not the time. Please, everyone but Tomas
must leave. Jesper, you may wait outside."

Jesper stepped forward as if to argue, but then glanced down at his
sister. He took her limp hand in his and held it to his heart. "You're sure she
will make it?" he asked Ni'mala.

"It is not her time to die," Ni'mala stated.

He bent down and gently kissed his sister's forehead. "Come back, Sis.
I still need you, despite all my protestations."

Sefrina led him from the room. Ni'mala followed, and one of the Sylvan closed the door. Hedra unwrapped the silk bandage and turned Murel to her side. "They did well, binding the wound like this. The bleeding has slowed." Tomas watched as she gently examined the gash on Murel's scalp.

"If you stay, you must wash your hands and help." One of the other Sylvan led Tomas to a large basin with hot, clean water. She gave him a rough cloth, one woven with the stems of fragrant herbs, and instructed him on how to scrub his hands.

"Her skull isn't fractured," Hedra stated, sewing up the two sides of the wound. "But it doesn't mean that what is inside isn't injured."

"Her eyes," Tomas said. "It was dark in the alley, but her pupils were the same size."

Hedra lifted an appraising eyebrow at him.

"Princess Anwyl has been tutoring Murel—she made use of what she learned a few days ago when another of our party was injured."

"I consider the princess a good friend," Hedra said warmly. "It pleases me to know that she continues to share her knowledge." She set to work, applying healing salve to the wound, followed by honey and gauze, and then a new bandage.

When another Sylvan entered, carrying a heavy, carved stone box, Tomas relieved her of the burden—it radiated cold. He set it on a nearby table, then took off the lid.

"Thank you," the Sylvan woman said, reaching into the container and pulling out a chunk of ice. She placed it in an oiled pouch, then hit it repeatedly with a small mallet. "The ice is cut from a glacier in the Brabryn Mountain Range and then brought here by sea. When it arrives at the temple, the blocks are a tenth their original size." She handed the packet of ice to Hedra.

Tomas watched as she gingerly placed the wrapped ice under Murel's head. "Won't that make her worse?"

"It is a delicate balance," Hedra divulged. "The ice will cool the blood and reduce the swelling." She reached down, and with the help of the other woman, lifted one end of the bed. "Tomas, please set that block of wood in the gap." He did and then stood back so she could cover Murel with a blanket. "It is imperative that the moment she regains any sense, we give her fluids. We have already prepared a restorative tea." She pointed to a carafe on the worktable. "Propping her up this way will aid her in swallowing."

"Can I help? I can spoon drops into her mouth. I can..."

Hedra was inspecting Murel's throat. "Perhaps later. For now, another ice wrap is needed," she told the other woman. "Her neck is badly bruised and restricting her breathing. She won't be able to swallow yet." She stopped and stared at Murel's grayish hue.

Ni'mala returned and took in that which had been applied to Murel.

"Is there nothing else to be done?" he asked.

"There is one other thing," Ni'mala stated. Three more women entered the room, one each garbed in a different color: dust, a blend of the darkest hues, and pale blue.

It was the last woman who Tomas recognized: Radha, cousin to Princess Anwyl and King Ranulf, she of the Kena Caste and the Fenrhi Artists. He gave Hedra a hard look as the memory of a conversation with Princess Anwyl came back to him. "You are the Artists, all of you." They nodded. "You can't mean to mark her. Not like Lady Claire. Murel would not want that."

"No one will be marked like Princess Claire again," Radha answered. She closed her eyes for a moment. "At least not in our lifetime. This will be different. A few designs, ones meant to give Murel the strength she needs to heal. The strength of the Earth Caste."

"No," Ni'mala interrupted. "She is a healer. She requires a Sylvan mark. Radha, can you not see it already? Her aura? So nurturing, such strength already."

"She's not like Lady Claire, or even Princess Anwyl," Tomas insisted. "She knows the basics, but she's not a healer."

"Isn't she? Look at what she has done for her brother. He may—"

"Ni'mala, we must decide for Murel," Hedra reminded. She gave Tomas a compassionate look. "She *is* tutored in the healing arts. Probably more than you realize."

"Just as Princess Anwyl is the purest form of the Kena...enlightenment and the sharing of her knowledge, Lady Murel is Sylvan," Ni'mala averred. "She has an innate ability to nurture, and when necessary, the courage to step back and let someone grow or fail on their own. It is she who made her brother truly separate. She must have let him go.”

Tomas sat heavily, remembering the recent arguments between Murel and Jesper, and her resolve to give Jess the support he needed, even if it meant he had to stumble to find his own path. He stared up at Ni’mala.

“You see it, don’t you?” she asked, and he nodded.

She sat next to him. “If you do not allow this, it could change her fate. The Lady Murel that I saw alive had been marked.” She set her hand on his wrist and closed her eyes. “There’s more. You, too, must take part in the rite.”

“Ni’mala, are you sure?” Hedra asked. “We have never marked a…a man.”

“I don’t know why, but I feel the rightness of it,” the eldest of their group stated. “Lord Tomas must be marked for Umbren Caste.”

“Will you do this, Tomas?” Ni’mala asked. “Will you give of yourself to Umbren Caste?”

“No, not to Umbren Caste,” he stated. “But to her, to Murel. I would give her my protection, for that is Umbren, is it not? I will be her shield.”

“And I would be honored to mark you,” Jenai stated. “Come sit over here.”

When Ni’mala departed with Radha to check on Jesper, Hedra sat next to Tomas. “Do you have any questions? About the marking, I mean?”

“Will it hurt her?”

“She won’t feel anything. Do you love her?”

Tomas nodded.

“And does she love you?”

Did she, Tomas wondered? He contemplated what he would do for her and knew that she would do the same. There was passion. Respect. Friendship. Love? “Yes,” he stated. “I believe she loves me, though she hasn’t said the words. Hell, I haven’t either.”

“Then I suggest armbands. Circles are very strong and have great power.”

Tomas swallowed. “It is a Fenrhi rite, Tomas. Not marriage…though both Radha and Jenai have seen your connection. Funny, Jenai has never hinted of possessing any Kena traits.”

"That's because I don't have a speck of Kena in me," Jenai said. "But I do understand the need to protect those I love. And this man has that same desire written all over his face."

The oldest of the Artists stepped forward. "I'm called Gudrun. I think that we will begin with you." She tugged at Tomas's tunic. After he stripped to his waist, she had him sit back down. "I hope you brought enough ink, Jenai," she stated, measuring his upper arm. "The lad is as big as an oak tree!" She turned serious and set about smoothing a thin layer of cream around his arm while Jenai readied her tools. There were several needles in different sizes, each one with a tiny reservoir above a grooved tip.

"I'm happy to see you've finally embraced the new needles from King Ranulf," Hedra stated.

"Bah," Jenai grumbled. "I was the first to try them, and you know it. Now let me get to work while you tend to the lady."

"Do you draw the design first?" Tomas asked.

Gudrun chuckled. "No, my boy. We are the Artists."

Jenai looked up at him, holding the finest needle of the set a hair's breadth above his skin. "Ready?"

He nodded, and she set to work. Precise pin pricks, over and over. At first, he could not discern a pattern, but slowly, the shape of a thin band took form. Dark charcoal, almost black, like coals lit from within by the glowing heart of fire. Across from him, Hedra worked on Murel's bare arm. She'd had to cut off the sleeve of her tunic so as to not disturb her. Gudrun hovered about, checking Murel's neck and head. Ice was removed. More was gently applied. She went back and forth, assisting Hedra and Jenai, even serving warm tea. Hours passed, and Tomas kept his eyes focused on Murel. He had no idea what form the marks on his arm took, and Jenai blocked his view of Hedra's work.

Finally, Jenai stopped, massaging the cramps from her hand. "What's troubling you?" he asked.

"It's missing something. Hedra?"

"Mine, too," Hedra replied.

Gudrun examined them both, then pulled up. "Ah, of course! You need to finish each other's work." Hedra and Jenai switched places and finished the patterns.

When Radha returned alone, she looked at the markings and demanded, "Has anyone else seen this?"

"No, only we three."

"Bind them, quickly. Before anyone else enters." Hedra and Jenai immediately complied. "Tomas, if anyone asks you, tell them your mark is a simple band in black. When Murel wakes, I will try to explain to you both why you must keep them covered."

"You act as if the marks have put us in danger."

"Not here at the temple," she said. "But I sense that elsewhere, you may not be safe."

"What have you done to us, Radha?"

"I haven't—"

Just then, Murel stirred. Tomas was up and immediately at her side. Her eyelids fluttered open, and the whites were stained red with blood, making the deep indigo of her irises glow. She panicked, and he took her hand, "You're all right, Murel. Don't try to speak; your neck is bruised."

She noticed the four women and tightened her fingers on his.

"We're in the Fenrhi temple," he told her. "You're safe. We're all safe. Baqi, too."

"I'm Hedra, of the Sylvan," the woman stated when Murel turned her way. "You are very fortunate that Tomas was able to bring you here in time. You cracked your skull and lost so much blood, and your throat is swollen. But I want you to try to drink something. To restore your fluids."

Tomas used a spoon to trickle some of the tincture that Hedra had handed to him. "Not too fast, m'lady," Hedra cautioned. "Just hold it in your mouth. Let a little at a time go in your throat. Good. Now swallow, softly."

Murel winced when she did, and Tomas's heart hurt for her pain. But she was able to swallow a few more sips, at least before her eyes closed and she passed out again. Before she did, she lifted her hand to his bare chest—he'd forgotten he was shirtless—and a touch of a smile graced her lips.

# CHAPTER EIGHT

# Banded Together

## The Fenrhi Temple, Nifolhad

Her mother's laughter sounded like the tinkling of wind chimes, and its beautiful music married with the deeper chuckles of her father. She ran to the next terrace. Where were they hiding? They were always within hearing, but never within sight. "Mama," she called out, coming upon a private terrace, where two fisher minks paddled and splashed in the water of a large stone pool. Their sleek bodies stopped, and their inky black eyes fixed on her. Their chattering resumed once they deemed her inconsequential.

This wasn't home, but the palace of her uncle, Lord Marin. Except for the musical laughter, the place was deserted. She followed the sounds to the next terrace, and the next, searching for someone to help her find her way out. And then she woke and heard the laughter for what it truly was—wind chimes with their high tinkling notes and deep bass tones. She was in the Fenrhi Temple.

Above her was a beautiful mosaic ceiling, but she was drawn toward the light streaming into the room.

The entire wall of her chamber was open to a lush courtyard, where peacocks strutted and pecked. And sitting on a cushioned window seat was Tomas. She studied him, in quarter-profile, with the afternoon sun haloing his head and setting his blond curls aglow. He was watching the birds...or staring perhaps at nothing at all. Tension cloaked his neck and shoulders, and then, as if perceiving that she was awake, he relaxed. He turned to her, swiveling his whole body on the seat. Silhouetted as he was, she felt rather than saw the initial trepidation in his gaze. And when she smiled at him, he was by her side in a single stride.

"Murel," he whispered, reaching out to cup her cheek. "You're finally back with us. They told me not to worry, and it looks like they were right." He bent down and placed a gentle kiss upon her lips.

He hadn't shaved in days, and she touched the long stubble. Tomas had never worn a beard, no matter the fashion. "How"—she coughed a little to clear the dry rasp from her unused vocal cords—"how many days?"

"I lost count," he responded. "I've been waiting for you. I knew you would come back. But I worried. You simply slept. And slept. Are you in any pain?"

"No. Maybe. My throat is sore." She reached up to touch her neck and felt a pull on her arm. They had changed her into one of her sleeping gowns, and she pulled up the sleeve. "I don't remember hurting my arm."

He took her hand in his, sitting in the comfortable chair that had been set near her bed. "Murel, you lost so much blood. When we got you here, I almost couldn't find your heartbeat. Hedra and her healers—"

"Hedra? That's Anwyl's friend. Was Radha here? And an older woman?" It dawned on her—Hedra was Sylvan and a healer, but she was also one of the Fenrhi Artists. "They marked me, didn't they?"

Tomas nodded. "Just your arm. They said it would give you strength."

"Which caste?" she asked, needing to know.

Tomas rose from his seat and unwound the bandage from her arm. Encircling her bicep were beautiful swirls and eddies of moss-green ink, intertwining in a delicate leaf and flower pattern. Here and there, tiny runes had been hidden in the foliage. Like a signet ring, the vines came around to meet a small circle of dark-gray and green leaves. In the center, a starburst pattern. "Sylvan," she said. "But the charcoal of Umbren, as well. And are those swords and daggers that make up the star?"

"And staffs," Tomas added.

The pattern, if one superimposed the design of the tiny arsenal over her family's crest, would match the outline of the nighttime blooms of the lunastra trees that were featured in its center. "Weapons?" she wondered aloud. A memory teased her mind. Tomas. Shirtless and seated with a woman in Umbren garb. Had there been a bandage on his arm? Floresta's crest was made up of weapons. "What did you let them do to us, Tomas?"

"I did what I had to. To make sure you would survive." He removed his tunic and then pulled his arm from his sleeve. "I would do it again and more," he added, no apology in his tone as he removed his bandage.

The marking that girded him was similar to hers, but instead of flowing vines and delicate leaves, swords and daggers, and spears and quarterstaffs were artfully engaged with one another in a dark-charcoal hue. Only one rune had been marked into the design. The ends of the band clashed together, leaving a small circle where one perfect lunastra bloom in moss-green floated.

"Oh, Tomas." She leaned back, closing her eyes.

She could hear him wrapping his bicep and slipping back into his shirt, and then he gently lifted her arm to rewrap the permanent artwork etched into her skin.

"It was Hedra and Jenai who marked us. Radha said she would explain everything once you woke. She insisted that we not tell anyone else. That it could put us in danger." He held her hand. "Murel?"

She remained quiet for several heartbeats and then opened her eyes. "I need to think, Tomas. But first, I need more rest."

"I understand. I'll be here when you wake."

But he didn't understand, not truly. If the Fenrhi were involved, especially a Kena—even if she was cousin to King Ranulf and Princess Anwyl—then chances were that she and Tomas would be embroiled in more trouble than was healthy. Her skull began to throb. And because those beautiful brown eyes of his were filled with concern, she gave him a tentative smile. But the effort caused her to ache even more, and her jaw tensed as she ground her teeth together.

"Headache?" he asked softly, pouring water from a carafe into a cup. She nodded. "No wonder. Three days with hardly anything to drink except the sips of tea we were able to spoon between your lips and absolutely nothing to eat, I'm surprised you're strong enough to keep your eyes open. Here, this is plain water." He gently cupped her nape, his fingers spread to reach between her shoulders, and assisted her with sitting up a little. Then, he held the glass to her lips, and Murel drank the cool fluid, swallowing carefully.

At least her throat didn't hurt as much. "A little more," she asked as he started to draw away. He helped her to finish off the remains, then set the cup near the carafe. "Tomas, can you do something for me?"

"Anything."

"Can you leave?"

He chuckled. "Do I smell that bad?"

"It's not that... I need to..." She felt herself blush.

"Finally, a little color in your cheeks." He kissed the top of her head. "I'll go fetch someone to help you. I could use a bath and a shave."

"Thank you," Murel said. "I know you did what you believed was necessary. And I probably would have done the same if it were you in this bed."

He smiled at her and went to the room's door.

"Tomas," she called, and he turned. "Maybe don't shave. Not yet."

"Your wish is my command," he answered with a lopsided grin. And then he was gone.

A few minutes later, a young Sylvan woman entered and helped her to make her toilette. No sooner had she left the room when another woman, this one from Earth Caste, entered, carrying a tray. "Just a light broth, m'lady, and some soft bread. If you feel up to it, that is."

As if it had a mind of its own, her stomach answered with a resounding growl. "Perhaps a little," Murel admitted. She waited as the woman ladled a small amount into a wooden bowl, placing it in Murel's hands.

"Just drink from it as you would a cup. It's not too hot."

Murel did as told, finding it much easier to forego the spoon, especially in her weakened state. "This is delicious," she exclaimed.

"Thank you," the woman said. "But I suspect not having had any sustenance in days would make anything taste good."

"No, truly. Could I have more?"

"Of course," she said, and ladled broth into Murel's bowl. "My name is Attaja, m'lady, if you need anything." She straightened the room, placing items on an older tray that Tomas must've eaten from. "Your husband is very attentive. He never left your side."

"My husband? Oh, you mean Tomas. We're not... We're just friends."

Attaja came back to her bedside, her smile was one of a knowing woman. "Not *just* friends, I think. One need not be Kena to see that you love one another."

"Maybe," Murel allowed. "There is something between us. But we've been friends for so long..."

"May I offer you some advice, m'lady?"

Murel nodded, and Attaja sat on the edge of her bed.

"I was once like you. My family was wealthy, and I had many suitors. There was one man who mattered more to me than the others. But I waited, and I paid a price for my fickleness.

"Diarmait came into power, and everything changed. I was given away to another, one who would help my family remain in the steward king's good graces. He was old and cruel, and I pretended to go along with their plans. The night before my wedding, I escaped the inn in Kantahla, where I was staying with my family, and snuck onto a ship to Naca'an. The Fenrhi took me in, but I lost everyone that I loved."

"Things are better now in Nifolhad. Surely your family will welcome you back." When Attaja's eyes grew damp, and she blinked, Murel touched her arm. "I see. They are truly gone. I'm so sorry."

"It's done and past," she said. "And I am through grieving. I only tell you my story so that you open your eyes to opportunities while they are in front of you. Life is too precious to not fully live it." There was a light rap on the door, and Attaja went to answer it.

Murel smiled when her brother stepped into the room.

"Hello there, sleepyhead," he teased, taking her hand as Attaja departed.

"Jess," she said, her voice still gravelly to her ears.

"You scared me, Murel." He closed his eyes and took a deep breath, almost as if he were centering himself. He grew suddenly serious. "You are not to get hurt again. This isn't about me, I know. But at the risk of sounding selfish, I'm telling you that I'm not strong enough without you being in this world, Sis. If you had died..."

"But I didn't die, Jess."

"You put yourself in danger, chasing after the boy. You should've waited for one of us."

"Tomas knew where I went. I left a trail."

"Did he tell you that? Because he told me that he saw you, and then you disappeared. And that he spent what seemed like an eternity searching for you up and down the avenue. It was chance that he noticed the cloth you put on the corner guard." Murel set her hand over his where his grip had tightened to an uncomfortable level. "Another minute, and your neck would've been crushed. As it was, you nearly died from blood loss!"

He must have suddenly realized that he was shouting, and he closed his eyes again. His fingers relaxed. Yes, he *was* centering himself. "Jess?"

"Just don't die on me, all right?"

"I promise," she said.

There was a tap on the door, three short raps, then one more. Her brother leaned over and kissed her forehead. "I have to go now. I'll check on you later."

"Go? Where? You arrived but a few moments ago."

"I'll tell you when I come back." He glanced at the door. "Besides, you need more rest."

"Jess," she said, her tone that of a censuring older sister, even though she was younger than him.

He held up his maimed limb. "Sefrina—she's with the Umbren—offered to teach me, er, train me... Basically, I bet her that she couldn't teach me how to climb a wall. It's a long story, and I'm late. And if there's anything I've learned about the Umbren since coming here, it's not to be late."

"I guess I'll see you later then." Her brother actually wanted to do something, even if it was to win a wager that he would fail.

She sighed. Outside, the shadows had grown long in the courtyard. One of the fabric panels hung for privacy had loosened, billowing like a sail as it caught the early evening breeze. It would deflate, settling softly back to hang straight before filling again in time with the tones and rings of the wind chimes. The very air around her felt alive.

Murel closed her eyes, breathing in and out with the notes of the chimes, letting them lull her back to sleep. Scents of an arid landscape, swirling like a dust devil, filled her waking dream. It was the aroma of a desert she'd yet to visit, and the sense that she was being watched and cared for. She could only guess how much of it was Kena manipulation.

. . .

Murel was still sleeping, but her color was returning, replacing the ashen pallor that had taken over her complexion. Days ago, maybe weeks, a sleeping pallet had been set up for him, one layered with a thick cushion, and set near the window. It was low to the ground, but high enough that Murel's face would be the last thing Tomas gazed upon before falling asleep and the first when waking. And that's what had happened this very morning.

Attaja, the Earth Caste woman who had been bringing their meals, quietly entered the room and nodded to him upon seeing that Murel's eyes were closed. She brought him a cup of steaming tea and a plate of fruit and morning pastries.

"Thank you," he whispered. "I can get her meal when she wakes."

"She may wish to bathe first," Attaja guessed. "I will be nearby to help."

And so, Tomas silently ate his breakfast, and when Murel stirred, he watched her, marveling at how beautiful she was. The moment she became aware of her surroundings, her gaze fell on him, and she smiled. "How do you feel?" he asked.

"Like I should clean my teeth and take a bath."

Tomas chuckled, then searched the corridor for Attaja. True to her word, he found her a few rooms away.

Together, they helped Murel to stand—she insisted on not being carried, but didn't resist him when he held her around the waist with one arm. Slowly, they made their way across the courtyard, stopping to rest and admire the peahens and peacocks as they pecked at the lawn. "It's beautiful here," Murel said. "Is this where your Mother resides?"

"Oh no," Attaja stated. "You are in the section of the temple reserved for people who require our Sylvan healers. No matter their station, all are welcome here. The Sylvan believe that nature soothes the mind and restores the senses. Come, the bathing rooms are not far."

The scent of spring water hit Tomas's nose first, followed by a gentle wave of moist heat. Maneuvering around a wall into a hexagon-shaped room, they discovered a carved stone pool set in the floor of the temple and fed by an underground hot spring.

"I will help the lady from here," Attaja stated, pushing Tomas from the room. Murel smiled at him, and he promised to wait for her in the courtyard.

He went back in the direction they'd come and found a bench. As he watched the birds strolling in the yard, movement from another open room caught his eye. Three windows down from Murel's quarters, a man stood and stretched, greeting the morning—Jesper. Across the courtyard, a woman in gray came out of another opening, and then spread a blanket on the grass. A Sylvan woman followed, carrying a small child in her arms. She lowered the young girl to the blanket, then sat next to her. The stump of the child's knee was wound up in clean, white bandages.

That was when Jesper left his room, striding across the green to where the girl sat. To Tomas's surprise, he also settled on the blanket, handing something to the girl. He was facing the other direction and so didn't notice as Tomas silently rose from the bench to give him some privacy. He headed back into the corridor leading to the baths, but the delighted laughter of the little girl made him pause. She was tossing feed to the elegant birds occupying the courtyard, and they had surrounded the blanket where she sat with Jesper.

"Healing takes many forms," Attaja noted, having come up behind him.

"I wonder that you are not Sylvan," Tomas observed.

"My joy lies in the kitchens," she stated, and laughed, banishing the melancholy in her voice. "It is where I find my own kind of peace."

"So many people have a story," Tomas realized aloud. "Something in their lives that they've survived, that made them stronger and shaped whether they would be a positive or negative force in the world. My own life has been easy in comparison."

Attaja set her hand on his arm. "It is true that some people never experience hardship while others experience nothing but. My trials happened when I was but half this age, and each day of quietude with the Fenrhi is a day erased from my past. Jesper's story was a happy one when he was younger; his struggle is only now beginning." They watched the scene before them a few minutes longer, and then she added, "Lady Murel should be finished."

Would good fortune continue as his companion through life, or like Jesper, would he be changed by some unimaginable evil? He followed Attaja back to the baths, drawing up when he saw Murel, sitting and running a comb through her dark locks. He could count on one hand the number of times he'd seen her with her hair loose—even in the room where she convalesced, she'd worn it in a long braid.

She smiled and reached out with her hand for him to help her up. "Attaja said it would be good for me to sit in the sun. At least my hair will dry faster, and I can braid it properly."

"It's lovely." He kissed her, gently. He pulled her to him, feeling how perfectly their bodies fit together. And a moment later, though it was the last thing in the world he wanted to do, he stepped back before their passion could grow. He took her hand, placing it on his forearm, and walked her back to the courtyard outside her convalescing room. Neither spoke, not wanting to disturb the tableau where Jesper still sat with the young girl.

On the far side of the garden, Tomas found an area where large cushions had been arranged on a thick rug. He steered Murel to a grouping placed under a large palm tree and helped her to sit. He couldn't help being affected by the serenity of the courtyard and stared up into the deep blue sky. Above him, the palm fronds shifted in the breeze, and the bladed leaves shushed against each other, adding rhythm to the tinkling of the many wind chimes.

Murel patted the cushion next to her, then quietly added, "Unless you have somewhere that you need to be."

"Nowhere but here with you," he promised, and settled next to her. The sunlight played across her skin in geometric patterns made by the moving fronds, highlighting the auburn undertones of her nearly black hair. She rested her head on his shoulder. How long they sat there, neither speaking, Tomas couldn't say.

Finally, Murel sighed. "It's too peaceful here. Do you sense it, too?"

It took Tomas a moment to understand her meaning, and when he did, he frowned. "The Kena?"

"Mm-hmm."

"I was so worried about you that I forgot to guard against their manipulations."

Across the lawn, Jesper was returning to his room. He stopped when he saw them sitting together and changed course to join them. "I see that you're finally awake," he noted.

Beside him, Murel bristled. Tomas placed his hand over hers. "Explain, please," he softly ordered.

"Before you think there is some plot happening here, Radha told me what the Kena were going to do, and I agreed with her. Murel needed to rest and recover, and knowing how you both worry about everything, they encouraged your desire for peace and quiet."

"For how long?" Murel demanded.

"As long as it took your body to heal. Or, ten days."

"Ten," Murel squeaked.

"Days!" Tomas interjected. "But Ronan, and the attack, and Grieg and the ship, and—"

"I'll explain everything, if you give me a minute," Jesper complained. "Ronan is fine—he was chasing down another man who had gone after Baqi's friend, but couldn't catch him.

"Later, he and Grieg interrogated the man from the alley. Save a fat coin purse, there was nothing on him to tie him to any place or person." Jesper paused. "He managed to escape the *Moon Caster.*"

"Hired thugs," Murel stated.

"Assassins," Jesper corrected, giving her a shrewd look. "Are you hearing me, Murel? They came damn close to completing the job."

"Where is Ronan now?" Tomas asked.

"Well on his way to Aurelia. Grieg visited you to explain."

"He did?" Tomas asked.

"Seeing as you just woke up, I'm not surprised that your memory is hazy. Radha assured me that it will all come back to you. Maybe not Murel, as her skull was nearly cracked. She also said that your...sleep...was a natural one. When Murel's mind was strong enough, it would wake of its own accord."

"But why was Tomas affected? He wasn't injured."

"Radha said she couldn't tell me, but that you would understand."

Murel frowned and then nodded. The marks banded around their arms were more than mere decorations.

"Uh-huh," Jesper stated. "Do I even want to know what they did to you when they kicked me out of the room?"

"One day," Murel said somberly. "Tell me, Jess, why didn't they try to manipulate you?"

"Oh, they tried," he stated, puffing out his chest. "But according to the Fenrhi here who hail from the Fyrost Desert, I'm the Rottu."

"Sefrina called you that in the alley," Tomas said.

"It's a Fyrjian word," Radha explained to Murel, coming up behind them with Sefrina. "It means severed one."

"That's apt," Jesper commented wryly, holding up his stump. "Am I late for our training, Sefrina?"

"No. But we will be leaving the temple for this next session, and I came to show you the way. It is time for you to lose your bet and climb the wall."

As Jesper followed Sefrina away, Radha turned to them. "He's wrong, you know. About the true meaning of Rottu. But I suspect that he'll learn that soon enough." She motioned to someone approaching behind them. "Ni'mala tells me that you'll be leaving tomorrow. Before you go, we need to talk." Several women wearing the gray garb of Earth Caste appeared, carrying more cushions and a low table. After positioning the table before Tomas and Murel, they artfully arranged the additional cushions, then departed.

Before Tomas could ask who would be joining them, Attaja arrived with another woman, one dressed in the mossy green of a Sylvan healer. The sash wrapped around her waist was intricately embroidered with pearls and gems. The vining design was the Fenrhi's way of indicating that she was of high birth, no matter her station in the temple. Like Attaja, she carried a tray laden with food. After Attaja set down her tray and departed, the woman set out four plates, then took the seat across from Murel. Upon recognizing her, Tomas started to rise to bow, but she lifted her hand to forestall him.

"Playing Sylvan today, my queen?" Radha asked, for the woman was none other than Queen Aghna of Nifolhad. "Should we call you Milla?"

Queen Aghna smiled wistfully. "Sometimes I miss being Milla, the Fenrhi Earth Caste initiate aspiring to be a Sylvan healer. Her persona saved me many times over in those dark years when I was in hiding. Today, I deemed it easier to blend in," she explained. "But, please, let's eat while we talk. Radha, tell us what you have discovered about the meaning of Rottu."

"Sefrina was not very forthcoming, but Fyrjians rarely are," Radha began as she sat next to the Nifolhadian queen. "I asked Ni'mala, and her research found a bit more."

"Is Jess safe with Sefrina?" Murel asked. "He's...different."

"I suppose he is, at least in his mind. But I believe him to be safe," Radha assured her. "Rottu means severed in Fyrjian, yes, but that is its common usage. Severed, not as in broken off, but more so removed, as in no longer present. It is a difficult term to explain."

"Sefrina uses the word as if it's a title," Tomas noted. "Not a description."

"Precisely. Ni'mala wasn't able to read him, nor could I, nor any of my Kena sisters. Per our Fenrhi Mother, the Rottu is here, and he is not. More, in not being here, he creates an empty space. A void."

"Voids can be filled," Murel stated soberly. "He seems to have come to some understanding of himself after spending time with the Umbren. Lady Claire encouraged him to come here. She was unable to read him as well, but said that his path, whether to live or die, was to be followed in Nifolhad. Jess felt the right of it and was less troubled once he decided to join us."

"And when you made the decision to let him go, Murel, you nudged him closer to his path. Yes...he told me about how you've supported him, both of you," Radha explained. "Now, the texts that Ni'mala shared with me indicated that the Rottu was prophesied to heal the Fyrjians. They have been watching for him."

"Could it have been the Fyrjians behind the attacks on us?" Tomas asked. "If they wanted Jess, would they kill to get him?"

"Most definitely," Queen Aghna replied. "But I do not believe it was them. Why not take Jesper when Murel was attacked? It would have been easy with you being distracted. And if you haven't guessed, Sefrina is Fyrjian. She saved Murel by bringing her here."

"I see your point," Murel conceded. "So not the Fyrjians, and we can rule out the Fenrhi, at least those still loyal to Ni'mala."

"It's possible it could be the faction that splintered off when Rhiannon betrayed us," Radha revealed. "But there are other threats in Nifolhad."

"My ignoble uncle escaped our net when we took his stronghold in Kantahla," Aghna related. "He has retreated to his castle on Mount Kanta. We are unable to get to him, but at least he is contained. And we've had word that he is on his deathbed. Still, it's not out of the realm of possibilities that he was behind the attacks. His children are spread across the breadth of the kingdom." Queen Aghna gave Murel a shrewd look. "You've been briefed on the prophecies?"

She nodded, but, like Tomas, did not offer any additional information.

"Then you know 'one' will be saved by the fourth couple?" Radha asked.

"Yes," Tomas replied. "Do you think Jesper is one half of the couple?"

Queen Aghna frowned, and Radha shook her head at him. Murel slumped into the cushions. He stared at her for a moment, the realization dawning on him. "No. Absolutely not. I won't accept it."

"Accepting or not, it is. Nothing you can do will change your fate," Queen Aghna stated. "Trust me. I know this firsthand."

Murel had closed her eyes. Her eyebrows pinched together as if the idea hurt her to contemplate. "I'm sorry, Murel," Tomas begged, taking her hand. "They told me you needed...we needed...to be marked for you to survive."

"It was not your decision that determined this, Tomas," Radha said gently. "You were both already marked." She touched the space above her heart. "Here. The both of you. We saw this to be true the night you arrived here. I wonder that Claire chose not to share this with you."

"Claire doesn't reveal that which is not asked of her," Murel stated, opening her eyes.

This wasn't what they wanted. Ever. He and Murel had discussed it at great length. "It can't be us," he averred. "We were sent here to find the fourth couple."

"And we did," Murel said, placing her hand over his. "Heaven help us, Tomas, but we did. We found each other. It took coming back here to do it." She stared up at him, waiting for his reply.

"I guess we did, didn't we?"

The queen and Radha watched them as if they were the cutest kittens or puppies or whatever they had ever seen. Tomas didn't care. He lifted Murel's hand and kissed her knuckles.

"So, tell us about our marks...all of them," Murel said, pulling up her sleeve to show the band inked around her upper arm. Tomas did the same.

"They're beautiful," Queen Aghna remarked. "So intricate."

"And they connect you to one another," Radha added. "As far as I know, no man has ever been marked by the Fenrhi. But we—the Artists, I mean— we all felt the necessity of it. The circles are powerful. Murel's Sylvan marking was incorporated into your band, and your Umbren markings into hers. You are forever linked together."

"Why weapons, I wonder?" the queen asked. "The designs have never been so literal."

"They are the same weapons that make up the crest of my house, Floresta," Tomas provided. "Did Jenai know this?"

"No. The Artists draw what they feel. And in giving Murel part of your design, she gave her your protection. Just as the Sylvan colors on you will fortify your strength. Together, you are imbued with an innate sense of how to help others."

"That doesn't seem too serious. So why the warning?"

"It is because of the runes," Radha said. "You see, we fall into a sort of trance when we design. Some of us believe that inside every Artist, is a little Kena."

"Or, perhaps," a voice from behind them deduced, "it is the influence of the Mother that guides your hands."

They all turned to see the newcomer who approached their alfresco meal.

"Ni'mala," Queen Aghna greeted.

"My queen," she replied. "Radha."

There was an awkward pause as the three Fenrhi women exchanged a wealth of guarded looks. Finally, Murel scooched to Tomas's side. "Please, sit here beside me."

"Perhaps I should come see you later..."

"But I've already made room for you." Murel then leveled her coolest gaze upon Radha and the queen. "If I can offer you each some advice, as an outsider…"

"Brace yourselves," the queen quipped. "We're in for some Aurelian directness."

Tomas smiled, for it was well-known that Nifolhadians preferred dancing around the point.

"Queen Aghna, Radha—"

"Aghna is fine, for we are friends, yes?"

"Aghna, then. It has been years since Ni'mala was under the influence of Rhiannon." Murel set her hand over Ni'mala's. "Isn't it time for you to let go of your anger and mistrust?"

Radha looked aghast that Murel had spoken so boldly, but for her part, Aghna smiled, as did Ni'mala. "Pray, continue."

"It is so…inefficient. When you need information, you consult with Ni'mala's notes and translations, but not with her directly. The Mother of this temple can provide you with more insight than her documents. It is time to trust her, or the mystery of the prophecy will never be fully solved."

"Thank you, Lady Murel—" Ni'mala began.

"I'm not quite finished. You, Ni'mala, you need to stop hiding that you know much more than you let on."

"I don't…"

"Yes, you do. Because not telling your queen and sisters everything that you know means that they will have to come back to you for more. And that is what you've always wanted, is it not? To be included? To be trusted again?"

"Well, I—"

"To borrow from your own Nifolhadian coinage, it is time to bury the rotten fish and discover what will grow."

"Sylvan, indeed," Radha stated, appraising Murel.

"Good, now that that is settled, tell us what makes showing the marks on our arms so dangerous," Murel demanded, bringing them all back to the point.

Aghna studied Murel's arm, as did Ni'mala. "I've seen some of the symbols before…in the desert. They're Fyrjian runes."

"Unfortunately, I have not been able to discover anything similar in the Temple library," Radha confessed. "But I worry that if the Fyrjians knew of the markings, they would take an unhealthy interest in you."

"Like they do in Jesper?" Tomas asked.

"Yes and no," Radha stated. "I do not feel that they will harm Jesper. They will put the Rottu on his path, but it will be up to your brother to walk it. As for these marks, they are very old. Ni'mala, have you seen anything like this before?"

"Perhaps. And I'm not holding back information, I promise. It's that I only have a wisp of a memory."

Tomas and the others waited, each with similar expectant expressions.

"The markings you now bear..."

"Gave me the strength to heal," Murel finished impatiently.

"Yes, but more." Ni'mala stared off into the distance as if trying to recall something. Then, she homed in on Tomas. "You are physically strong. And now Murel is imbued with some of that strength. You have been *opened* to one another."

"What does that mean?" Murel asked, her voice taking on a panicked edge.

"I sense that you will be challenged in a way that you've never been challenged before, and you'll need Tomas's strength to survive."

"Survive?" Murel demanded. "Again? We did not want this!"

Tomas placed his hand over hers. "Whether we want it or not, we are now part of whatever this prophecy is." He could feel her emotions calm, second by second, breath by breath, as if they were the only two present, the others having faded into the space they occupied. No one spoke, or moved, for that matter, and it seemed to him that everyone around them had frozen in time. And then, Murel's eyes flicked to his. She sensed it as well. That moment where they were so in tune with one another that the others existed just out of step. At the same time, their regard was drawn to Ni'mala.

*You are each other's strength and support, and energy and recovery. Attuned. And because of this, you are open. Be careful. I sense things in this world that seek ones such as you.*

The Fenrhi Mother hadn't spoken aloud, but they both heard her thoughts.

"Ni'mala," Aghna started, breaking whatever spell had been cast over the group. "I would also like to know what you mean by survive."

"The prophecy, of course," she answered. "The fourth couple must save the one."

"So, who is the one? Could it be Jesper, or Madyan?" Tomas asked. "And if the pattern continues, will the one we save be two people? Perhaps the fifth couple?"

"I hadn't considered that," Ni'mala said. "The remaining unclaimed castes are Umbren and Blood Caste. But which one will represent the fifth...the one you need to save?"

"And save from what?" Aghna asked. She reached into her tunic and pulled out a folded bit of parchment. "I received a note from Claire. It arrived only a week before you. The one thing that she is sure of is that if you stay here, in Naca'an, you face mortal danger. Someone has already attempted to assassinate you—they almost succeeded."

"We should keep to our original mission and find Madyan," Tomas stated. "Venture into the Fyrost...I doubt anyone would dare to follow us into that wasteland."

Murel frowned.

"What's bothering you?" he asked.

"We don't as yet know who tried to kill us."

"You," Tomas corrected. "Tried to kill you."

"There's no way to tell if I was—"

"You were."

"—the target," she finished, giving him a scowl—one that he returned. "They could've gone after any of us. I happened to present the best opportunity...going off on my own like I did."

"Your logic is flawed. This was the second attempt on your life. The first was on the docks. Or did you forget that?" He felt his ire growing; hers was an aspect of mounting anger as well. Heavens, but she was gorgeous. Heat flashed in her eyes the moment he had the thought, and he blinked. He leaned back upon realizing how close they'd come to kissing.

Ni'mala, Queen Aghna, and Radha were smiling wistfully. "That's so sweet," Radha noted, uncharacteristically non-cynical.

"Perhaps they should handfast now," Aghna suggested wryly. "Why fight the inevitable?"

Murel's nostrils flared, but she kept her cool. She narrowed her eyes at the group. "We'll need a guide. How soon can you get us ready, Tomas?"

"Right," he said, on the same page as Murel. "A day at most. We already have the horses."

"And you have a guide," Ni'mala stated. "Sefrina approached me this morning. She wants to take your brother to the healing waters in the desert. She believes it will help him."

"What is it, Ni'mala?" Tomas asked, sensing there was more.

"Sefrina is Fenrhi, yet she is also Fyrjian. And for the people of the Fyrost, being Fyrjian will always come first."

"Consider us warned," Tomas stated. "Now then, our plan is settled."

The others rose to leave, but Murel remained seated. "I would like to sit here a bit longer and enjoy the serenity of this courtyard. Will you stay with me, Tomas?"

"Always," he promised as the others departed. He sat and waited until they were alone. "I want to get you away from Naca'an and even from the Fenrhi. Are you sure you're ready to travel?"

She nodded. "I am. Tomas, you may be correct about the target, but whoever is behind the attempts is also targeting you. I was merely easier to reach. And, we come in pairs. We're numbered in the prophecy. Taking out one of us essentially destroys the pair."

"You have a point," he said.

"And though we can probably rule out the Fyrjians, I don't trust that we are entirely safe with them."

Tomas agreed. "They have their own motives for wanting Jess and won't take kindly any interference from us. This Rottu business and whatever is happening with Madyan…it's connected. Who does that leave on our list of suspects?"

"Diarmait, for one," Murel noted.

"And don't forget Marlita's warning about the Southron Islers."

"The Islers!" she exclaimed. "The smell. It reminded me of the time when Grieg's crew celebrated one of their festivals on the beach in Pheldhain. The spices they used and the smoke from the fires and cooking meat."

"What smell?"

Murel frowned. "It's gone. I mean, I can't remember when or where I smelled it. But I know it's important."

"Then it will come back to you," he promised her. "And if the Southron Islers are behind the attacks, the last place they would venture is into the Fyrost Desert."

• • •

## Kantapan Castle, Mount Kanta

"How's the old man?" Danold asked.

Diarmait scowled. "I can hear you, you know." He couldn't understand why his progeny was set on tending to him. He'd never said a kind word to either one. The opposite, in fact. He'd made their lives hell. Mirra was sitting next to him, changing the bandage on his arm.

"The wounds aren't healing, are they?" Danold went on as if Diarmait weren't in the room.

"No," Mirra answered. "But they're not getting worse."

"Nothing in the world can save me from the Sylvan poison I consumed over the years," Diarmait ground out. "I don't know why you bother."

"Penance, perhaps," Danold answered.

"Or revenge," Mirra added, her lips twitching.

"Now *that* is something I can believe!" Diarmait proclaimed, then succumbed to a fit of choking when he tried to laugh. Mirra shifted him so that he sat more upright and then held a glass of wine to his lips. "Thank you," he rasped when the attack was over.

"Thank you?" Mirra chirped. "Careful, Father. I might start wondering if you like me." And this time, she did smirk.

"The shutters are secure, and the fire is stoked," Danold informed him. "The storm will hit sometime during the night, but we'll all be tucked away and sleeping. Goodnight, Father."

Diarmait grunted.

"Try not to die this evening," Mirra goaded, and together, they left the chamber before he could form a retort.

They reminded him of his lost sons, Roger and Bowen. Danold had that same quiet patience and strength that his secondborn had had. And Mirra? Except for being born the wrong sex, she carried herself exactly as Bowen had. Irreverent. Haughty. Proud. Though he was loathe to admit it, he rather liked the pair.

Tucked neatly under thick rugs and his head and shoulders propped up on soft cushions, Diarmait closed his eyes and tried to shut off his mind to the constant pain from the multitude of open sores on his body, including a new one that had formed on his forehead. Soon, the soporific herbs with which Mirra had dosed his wine had his thoughts blurring until he fell into a fitful sleep.

Sometime later, hours, he reckoned, staring at what was left of the logs in the grate, Diarmait woke to his name being called. "Who's there?" he whispered to the room. The only reply came from the wind howling outside the shutters. "Just a dream," he said aloud, closing his eyes to try to find sleep once more.

"*Diarmait,*" the night called. "*I've come for you.*"

This was it then, some fantastical specter to guide him to his death. "Have at it," he dared.

"*Let me in, King of Nowhere.*" A stronger gust buffeted the shutters, causing them to rattle.

"Maybe I don't want to. Maybe I would like to live a few days more."

"*For you to live, first, you must die.*"

"Who are you?"

"*No one. Nothing. Everything. Let me in.*"

The voice compelled him to move, and he was helpless to stop himself from throwing back his blankets.

"Fenrhi witch! Stop this, I cannot walk!"

"*I am no witch! You insult me by presuming that I am female. Let me in.*"

Diarmait's legs swung over the bed, and he pushed himself upright. But he was too weak, and he crumpled to the floor.

*"Let. Me. In."*

Thus compelled, he dragged himself across the floor to the shutters. There, he clawed his way up the wood, ripping his fingernails, until finally, he reached the latch. The wind pounded the panels, and they blew in with such force, they knocked him away like kindling. Diarmait heard several of his ribs crack, and he lay in a twisted heap on the floor.

A gust of wind rushed around him, catching him up in a whirlwind and lifting him from the floor like a broken puppet. It spun around him, picking up speed, drawing more of the night in through the shutters. And with each new blast came the sand.

It ripped away his sleeping clothes and tore at him, scouring and burning away his flesh. Diarmait, held aloft with his arms outstretched and his useless legs dangling, screamed and screamed. On and on it went, until his cries were indistinguishable from the roaring of the wind. Not a single inch of his skin was spared, from his ears to his fingers and toes and even his cock. His body was flayed alive, stripped clean until he had no sense except for the sound of his own impending death. And then it was over, and he was dropped unceremoniously to the floor. He heard pounding and shouting, and then he heard no more.

# CHAPTER NINE

# The Fyrost

"Remind me again why we are crossing the Fyrost on the brink of the summer sandstorms," Murel asked, her voice muffled by the fabric she was constantly readjusting to limit her exposure to the scorching rays of the sun and the occasional gale force winds that seemed to erupt from no discernable direction.

Beside her, Tomas was similarly garbed, but the twinkle in his eyes revealed that he was amused. "We're falling behind again," he said, and they both nudged their Fyrjian mounts into a trot. Ahead of them, the small herd—fleet-footed and broad-chested desert horses to a one, but bred in Aurelia—followed their guide, Sefrina.

Slowing their mounts to a walk as they neared the small herd, they pulled slightly upwind of the dust made by the twenty-eight hooves—forty-four if you counted the mounts with riders. Jesper, riding alongside Sefrina, twisted in his saddle.

"That's about the hundredth time your brother has turned back to check on you," Tomas noted. "Sefrina is good for him. He has more confidence than before. He asked if I would spar with him when we next make camp."

"Hmm," was the only comment Murel was willing to make. Their sand-colored scarves reflected much of the heat away from them, but they were still in the low desert. Above her, the sun beat relentlessly on their heads and shoulders. They might not be melting now, but—

"What's on your mind?"

"The high desert. And our guide."

"Do you not trust her?"

"I would like some answers before I decide."

Tomas waited patiently as she sorted out what was vexing her.

"Claire once told me the story of her Fyrost crossing with Madyan and Aghna. Weeks before they entered the desert, and every day after, Madyan taught them their route, over and over, until they could draw it in the dirt and recite it by rote. We've been here three days, and Sefrina has not provided one hint as to our direction."

"What else?"

She stared at Sefrina's back. "Where are the warnings? The advice as to what to do if a sandstorm hits? Claire told me that Madyan said lashing oneself to their horse was the best chance of surviving getting lost in the desert. And Sefrina is the only person in our group who is riding a mount actually bred in this wasteland."

They let that hang in the heated air between them.

"Anything more that our wise friend told you?" Tomas asked.

"A few things about the constellations—the Weeping Sisters and the Boar's Eye—that I'll point out to you this evening. I think we should keep the fact that we know how to set our compass at night quiet."

"But what motivation would Sefrina have to lead us astray?"

"You know the mantra as well as I do—every person in Nifolhad has their own agenda. Sefrina is no different. She wants something from Jesper. The gift of the horses, my presence and yours, are superfluous to her motives."

"Then we stay together as if tethered. I mean it, Murel. I want more than our markings linking us. If she is planning on ditching us in this wasteland, we need to be prepared."

"Agreed."

"And Jesper?"

"They need him, so he is safe. At least for the time being."

As if sensing she was the topic of conversation, Sefrina nodded to Jess, then wheeled her horse around and rode toward Murel and Tomas. They pulled up as she neared.

"We'll camp in the lee of that rise," she said, pointing northeast.

"I would hazard that it's a two-hour ride," Tomas noted. "It'll still be daylight; why not ride until the evening?"

"The high desert awaits us tomorrow, and we must travel at night," she explained. "We will rest this afternoon."

"Is there water there?" Murel asked.

"If you know where to look for it."

She turned her horse and cantered away, and Murel gave an exasperated sigh. But then Sefrina pivoted her horse, and she swung low and sideways in her saddle, sweeping her hand along the ground, where she expertly grasped at a few, thin blades of green sprouting from the loose sand. Dirt and dust went flying as a bulbous root popped free of the earth. Her horse arced back to them, and she tossed the tuber to Tomas before riding to rejoin Jesper.

Tomas pulled out his dagger and lopped off one tapered end, breaking through the crusty husk. He used his blade to release the chambered membranes inside the root's rind, splitting away two wedges, one each for them both.

"The cells are like orange pulp," he noted, studying his portion. "Only drier."

Murel bit into hers, and juice squirted into her mouth. "I don't think you're supposed to swallow it," she said, when she was unable to chew through the fibrous membrane. "Just mash it between your teeth to drink the liquid."

Tomas tried his. "It's not bad. There's a slight sweetness to it once you get past the minerals."

"It tastes like this desert smells," Murel noted. "Best stow that in your bag. We need to catch up again, and I intend to get more information from Sefrina."

· · ·

"How is it possible that it is even hotter than last week?" Jesper complained, wiping his brow.

Murel craned her neck to gaze up at the blazing sky from under the simple canvas lean-to they'd constructed. The light-hued fabric reflected the sun, shielding them from its burning rays. Sefrina had them situated in the lee of a great dune. "The sun should drop behind the crest in the next hour," Murel judged. "Then we'll have more shade."

Jesper reached up to prod at the sagging canvas, but Sefrina made a noise—between a grumble and a *tsk*—from where she appeared to have been dozing. "The settled sand adds to the canvas's ability to screen out light. Poke it, and the dust will swirl around us and cause us to choke."

Jesper reluctantly settled his hand in his lap. He was restless. Murel couldn't blame him. The great dune that rose up behind them was both unsettling and oppressive. Almost as bad as the steady stream of grit that sieved off its razor-sharp ridge.

"Why don't we check on the horses?" Murel suggested.

"You should rest," Sefrina stated. "Tomas's watch is not yet finished."

"You still haven't explained why we need to be so guarded," Murel stated. "Are there enemies here?"

"The Fyrost itself can be dangerous. Now, rest."

Murel's ire prickled. Sefrina was their guide, and though they followed her lead, she was not their leader. This time, Jesper grumbled, eerily mimicking the noise Sefrina had made. He rose and then held out his hand to Murel. They wrapped their heads and faces in scarves to screen against the flying grit and hurried to the larger lean-to under which the horses rested.

Tomas was standing to one side and turned to them as they approached. "Hell of a place to keep watch. Someone could easily come up behind us from over that ridge."

"I don't like it much either," Murel stated.

"No one would risk it in this heat," her brother noted. "At least according to Sefrina."

Tomas grunted.

"Are you going to make me guess?" Jess asked.

She and Tomas remained silent.

"You don't trust me," Jess accused. "Murel, I would never—"

"Not intentionally," Tomas interrupted.

"You take that back, Tomas," her brother threatened. "You take it back this instant, or I'll—"

"You'll what?"

"I'm not helpless anymore. I could—"

"Stop it!" Murel hissed. "You're friends, remember? Ridiculous, the both of you. It's this desert. Or the heat. It feels like...like..."

"Something is biting at our heels," her brother finished. "Something terrible."

Tomas peered out from under the tarp.

"Admit you feel it, too, Tomas."

He sighed. "I do. And I'm sorry...for what I said. Of course I trust you, Jess."

"Murel?"

"Shut up, brother," Murel said kindly. "It's Sefrina I can't get a read on. What do you talk about when you ride together?"

"Everything and nothing," Jesper replied. "She's hiding something...something big. That feeling we have, being pursued, she has a sense of it as well. It's why she has us bed down in the lee of the dune."

"Why do you say that?" Murel asked.

"Because when I worried about that crest breaking off and avalanching down on us, she mumbled something about it being an added layer of protection. And I've asked her to tell me stories about the Fyrost. She shared the one about the Sky Goddess—Sky—with me, adding in some details I hadn't heard before."

"Tell us," Murel encouraged.

"There's more to it than a man betraying his goddess. For starters, after the Wind God threw his sister, Sky, into the Virin Sea, she disappeared. The Wind God—Wind—had only intended to extinguish her rage. Sefrina said that he went mad, searching for her. And the man—the one who betrayed Sky in the first place—trapped him."

"Trapped him? How?"

"By taking Wind into himself. And thus contained, his powers tore the man apart, but not apart."

"What does that even mean?" Tomas asked.

Jess shrugged. "Long story short, the Fyrjians believe that there's an ancient madman, or spirit, who roams the Fyrost Desert, searching for his lost Forest Goddess. This spirit takes the form of deadly sandstorms. The Fyrjian legend is that as long as he is in this form, he is asleep. It's why they hide from the wind, sheltering as we do now."

"Sefrina told you all of this?" Tomas asked.

"Bits and pieces that I cobbled together. Yes."

"And?" Murel prompted. "Come on, Jess. What else? I know you're holding something back. A sister can always tell."

"They think he is waking."

"He?" Tomas asked.

"The man. The Wind God. Both. And he's seeking a new vessel." Her brother stared up at the steady stream of sand blowing off the ridge and over them. He hunched down. "Fyrjians...they're a tough lot. But Sefrina, she was...afraid."

Murel lowered her voice. "Jess, I don't want you involved in their machinations...this Rottu business...something is really off. We're on our way to an oasis to recharge. If it's the same one that Claire and Queen Aghna visited, I can get us to Sophiana. We could leave."

"If that is indeed our destination," Jess said. "I don't get a sense that they are going to hurt me. It's more like Sefrina wants to keep me safe. But I'm worried about you, Sis. This malevolent spirit, if it even exists, destroys that which it finds. Besides, I'm the Rottu—I can't be seen."

"This is making my skull ache," Tomas put in.

Above them, the sun dropped to the dune's lip, and the afternoon waned. The wind kicked up a notch, screaming angrily as it whipped over the sand in one last attack, and then began to die down. Murel hadn't realized how loud its voice had grown, not until it disappeared. Despite the oppressive heat, she shivered, and Tomas put his arm around her.

"Sefrina is starting to trust me," Jesper stated. "I'll try to get more information from her."

"Ask her if this is related somehow to Madyan," Murel stated.

He nodded. "Go rest," Jess ordered them. "I'll feed the horses, then wake you for our meal. We'll want to eat before this evening's journey."

"What's bothering you?" Murel asked as she walked with Tomas.

"I'm not sure." He stopped and turned to her. "Five couples, all with their own gifts, joining together to battle some great evil. I hope it is not this sandstorm. Because you and I would be alone in our fight."

They were about ten paces from their makeshift shelter and out of view of either Jesper or Sefrina. "If I hadn't been here, in this wasteland, and felt the animosity of this climate...let's just say that my mind is more open today than it was before," Murel allowed. "You'll help me to protect Jesper?"

"He's not my priority," he said, pulling her into his arms. "But yes, you know I will."

Murel gazed up at him. They hadn't shared a moment like this since they'd been in the Fenrhi Temple, and she felt a deep yearning to be kissed by him again. "I'm recovered, you know. Completely. I won't break."

Tomas made some deep noise of appreciation in the back of his throat, one that made her tingle all over. "I do, but I didn't want to rush you—I had this whole plan mapped out to take things slow. And then the marking rite happened. I thought that you might need some space."

"Let's not ever do that...assume things about each other. You and I...we don't need the drama and excitement like our friends. When I remember how long it took for Princess Anwyl and Warin to recognize what they had..."

"Oh, they recognized it, all right," Tomas said with a chuckle. "Neither wanted to be the first one to capitulate to their feelings." He pulled her tighter to him. "But I'm not afraid to admit that I'm falling in love with you. Hell, I'm braver than that. Murel, I love you."

"Oh!" she stammered, feeling suddenly nervous around him, but in a tantalizing way.

He laughed. "Don't worry, I know you love me back."

"I do. Now kiss me, Tomas," she begged.

"As you wish, my love," he murmured, and slanted his lips down to hers. They stood there, in the twilight silence of the desert, and kissed. The heat between them kindled once again, and Murel pressed herself against his broad chest while he ran his hands over her back.

They pulled apart, aware that they could be interrupted at any moment. "I stand by my words about wanting no drama between us," she said, taking his hand and kissing his knuckles. "But I find myself warming to the idea of excitement. Besides, I don't think we'll be able to stop it."

He pulled her roughly to him, splaying his large hand across the small of her back. "I agree," he growled, then crashed his lips against hers in a pulverizing kiss. And Murel did the one thing she could—she dug her fingers into his muscled shoulders and held on for the ride, returning his kiss with equal ardor.

"Well!" Tomas exclaimed after pulling back once more.

"Well, indeed," Murel said with a satisfied grin.

. . .

Murel lagged behind as she rode herd on their small group of both men and beasts. She hadn't been sleeping and had even considered tying herself to her saddle when, earlier, she caught herself nodding off. A few lengths ahead, Tomas twisted in his seat, checking on her. She waved and nudged her horse into a brisk trot to catch up.

Something about this desert. The menace they'd spoken about—an invisible animosity ready to scratch its claws down their backs the closer they rode to sunrise—grew throughout each day, not fading until the sun dipped below the horizon. And the wind, too, gusted with more intensity. Murel attempted to logic it away by pointing out that, as the day warmed, the sands heated and forced the air currents to rise and gain strength. But each morning when they pitched their camp, she found herself sitting so that she faced that flow of pure spite and whatever might come with it. Then Tomas and Jess started doing the same. Only Sefrina was immune.

Or so Murel had believed. Once, she had woken from a fitful sleep to find Sefrina on her knees under the blazing sun, oblivious to its heat and the stinging sands. She was bent over with her hands stretched before her, chanting. Then she would lift up and raise her arms. Murel had searched the skies for the object upon which Sefrina called. Through the haze of dust, she could just make out the waxing moon, standing out in the midafternoon sky.

When Sefrina returned to the tent, her lower arms and hands were raw from the strafing grit borne by the wind. Murel produced a pot of salve, one given to her by Claire before they'd departed Aurelia. The layered perfumes of wildflowers had immediately evoked memories of green fields and trees and even rain. It had been as if their recollections were being eroded by the constant pressure of the oppressive wind and blowing sand. So, each evening, before they began their nighttime trek across the desert, and each morning, as they sheltered at the base of some great dune or rocky outcropping, she removed the jar's stopper and breathed in the healing scents from home.

She itched to take out the balm to revive her senses but was afraid she would drop it in her lassitude, forever losing it to the sands. As she pondered this, her hands loosened on the reins. She imagined the pot tumbling, end over end—

"What happened?" she asked.

"You were listing in your saddle, so I rode back. Caught you just in time, too." He kissed the top of her head.

"We're too heavy for your horse. I should—"

"We're almost there," Tomas assured her. "Besides, it's been naught but an hour. And Sefrina says that we'll finally be able to rest at the oasis."

Murel yawned. "Should I swing my leg over, at least?" Tomas tightened his hold on her in answer, and she tucked in next to him. To the east, the sky was brightening. "It'll be sunrise soon. Will we make it in time?"

"Our intrepid guide thinks so. Though all I can see ahead is the rise of yet another pile of sand."

Murel could scarcely make out Jess and the horses. Sefrina's silhouette disappeared as she rode over the top of the dune. She closed her eyes and, perhaps because she was held in Tomas's arms, she was able to drift back to sleep.

She woke, slowly coming to the realization that she was no longer moving, but on her side on a blanket. The air shimmered around her, and she rolled onto her back and stared up into the thick palm fronds rustling high above her. Murel couldn't remember a time when she had felt this thirsty. She was parched. Her mouth... Her skin... Everything. She sat up, unwound her headscarf, and drew in a deep, cleansing breath. Minerals and moisture were in the air. Someone approached.

"I wanted to wake you when we got here, but Tomas told me to let you sleep," Jess said, looking around. "This oasis is something else...there's peace here." He handed her a cloth bundle and some water. "Fresh dates." He pointed up. "Sefrina bet me that I could climb the tree."

"And?"

"We can add it to the list of best wagers I've ever lost." He grinned. "It's a good thing the sand here is soft. I fell three times to prove her wrong—she still won." He held out his hand. "Come on, I'll take you to the spring so you can wash off the Fyrost. You'll feel much better after."

Jesper was dressed in fresh garments, his dark hair was clean, and even his eyes had lost the perpetual squint that they'd all adopted since entering the desert. She let him pull her up, and then she stretched and twisted at her waist. After taking a long swallow of the water he'd brought her, she ate a couple of the dates and followed him to a hidden break in the scrub palms. Their fronds rubbed her booted legs as they walked along a path paved with large flat stones. "Where are Tomas and Sefrina?"

"Sefrina is sleeping. And Tomas has been on watch. I slept already and am about to relieve him. You take over for me later this afternoon. An easy job, it seems. Sefrina claims we needn't bother." He stopped walking and turned back to her. "Can you feel it, too? Or not feel it."

Murel nodded.

"I didn't realize how physical that horrid pressure felt until it was suddenly gone." He spun her in the opposite direction. "We came over the dune from the east." He pointed. "Now that we're away from the taller palm trees, you can see how high it rises."

"Are those giant steps?" Murel asked.

He nodded, then took her hand to pull her deeper into the palms. "Cut into an ancient curtain wall that curves around the oasis, surrounding and protecting it. There's an old temple built on the opposite side."

"Where are the horses?"

"Near the temple wall—there's a bit of forage for them, and water," Jesper explained. "According to Sefrina, there are several springs and oases in the Fyrost, but only two that were fortified. I got a sense that the other temple must be near the Fyrjians' main encampment—she said our travels would take us there. As for this place, I haven't had a chance to explore, but I'm sure we'll have time tomorrow." He stopped so that Murel could come up beside him. "Here we are."

A large, clear pool lay before her, circular in shape where broad stones had been placed to gird it. The edges were timeworn and smooth. On one side, three sets of garments had been neatly laid out to dry in the sun dappling through the taller palms. Murel immediately dropped down to unlace her high Fenrhi boots. Once removed, she stepped into the pool, dust-encrusted garments and all.

Her brother laughed. "Tomas and I did the same. I'll leave you to it, then."

Murel grinned, then completely submerged herself into the cool water. Near the edge, the smooth stone sloped toward the center, and she pushed off it to dive down, feeling with her hands until the bottom dropped away completely. She wondered how deep it went, but the spring's currents buoyed her and lifted her to the surface. She swam back to the edge, and carefully peeled off her garments one by one, giving each piece several good swishes and wrings to clean them. She would spread them out later. For now, she wanted to enjoy the water, and she pushed from the edge to float on her back.

Something about the minerals in the pool made her skin tingle. Her hair felt as if each strand stood separate from the others on her scalp. She couldn't explain it, but her body's vitality was restored from the enervating effects of the desert. She heard steps then, and she swam in the direction of the noise, resting her arms on the stone edge of the pool as Sefrina arrived. She was barefoot, and she drew to a stop when she saw Murel.

"I came to get my boots," she explained. "And to see if my garments were dry. But I can come back later."

"Not on my account, I hope," Murel replied. "I was finished, anyway."

"You should stay in longer. The Fyrost affected you more than the rest of us, and the pool will heal you."

Before she could leave, Murel asked, "Can you tell me about this place?"

"I should check the horses."

Murel raised her eyebrow, then pushed away from the pool's edge to tread water.

Sefrina was silent for a moment, then sat down. "The oasis was a wedding gift from the Wind God to the Sky Goddess. A place where she could come to rest and commune with him in human form."

"But aren't they brother and sister?"

"They are—were. But not in their human forms." Sefrina dangled her legs in the water. "The oasis is sacred, and not because of the temple built to honor them. This place is said to have given birth to the first woman—made from fire. There is another oasis, one that the Sky Goddess gifted to her brother, which is said to have birthed the first man—made from bone."

"Fyrost," Murel said, swimming to the pool's edge and to where Sefrina sat. "Fire and bone."

"Exactly," Sefrina said.

"How are your arms?"

"The burns were light, and your balm eased the pain." She pushed up her sleeves and twisted her arms back and forth for Murel to see. The rawness was gone, and she appeared to have suffered merely a slight sunburn. "The pool did the rest."

"Amazing. Do you think you could hand me my bag over there?"

Sefrina rose from her spot to retrieve Murel's saddlebag. As she handed it down to Murel, she gasped and dropped the bag. "Who did that to you?"

"Did what?" Murel demanded, suddenly worried that she was aglow and that Sefrina could see it.

"Marked your arm!"

"Oh!" She put her hand over the ink runes.

"You can't... You shouldn't... This changes things. I can't unsee them."

"Changes what?" She pulled herself from the water and quickly donned her clean chemise. "Sefrina, answer me."

"I've told you too much about this place already. I can't unsee them." She turned on her heel and strode away.

"You forgot your boots," Murel tried calling after her, but she was already gone.

"Who forgot their boots?" Tomas asked, coming up behind her from the opposite direction.

"Sefrina did."

"I, uh..." Tomas swallowed. His gaze darted here and there, everywhere but at her.

Murel looked down. Her chemise clung to her and was made translucent by the water from the pool. Rather than trying to hide, she stepped closer and peeked up at him. "Tomas?"

"Murel." He stared up into the palm trees.

She took another step. His proximity emboldened her. She could feel the heat pouring off him, and she wrapped her arms around his shoulders. "Thank you for catching me earlier."

"It was my pleasure."

"And mine...waking up in your lap." She pressed herself against him.

"You'll be the death of me."

"I don't see how."

He took one of her hands and guided it down, pressing her palm where he'd grown rock hard. Then he instantly pushed her away. "I'm sorry, Murel! That was too forward. This place. You."

"What about me?" she said, not trying to hide her disappointment.

"I can barely...I want you so badly, Murel. But then you were hurt, and I wanted to be gentle with you. And now"—his eyes raked over her figure—"with your chemise hinting at what's underneath. Your naked legs. You're stunning."

A delicious warmth spread through her, chasing away her self-doubt and her fear that he didn't find her attractive. She rushed back to him, pressing herself along his body. He circled his arms around her, ran his hands down her back, and cupped her buttocks, squeezing and massaging them. She stood on her toes, sliding her core along his hardness, and he groaned. She needed to feel his skin, and she pulled at his tunic. He lifted his arms, and she dragged the fabric up and away. The broad expanse of his chest, the muscled shoulders, the type of taut stomach that should not be allowed to exist... But for Murel, it was his arms—more precisely, his beautifully carved biceps—that made her whimper when she was alone at night. She ran her hands over them and squeezed...rock-hard muscles. He flexed, slightly, under her fingers, and Murel sighed. "Please, kiss me," she begged.

He hesitated. "Are you—"

"I won't break, I promise."

"I know, but I'm afraid I might." Then he slanted his lips to hers in a devastating kiss that stole away her breath. He stopped suddenly and let her go to retrieve his shirt.

A few seconds later, Sefrina reappeared. "I forgot my boots." She looked back and forth between the two of them. Tomas turned as he shrugged into his shirt, and Sefrina homed in on the very same bicep Murel had been admiring, the one with the dark band. Her frown lines grew even deeper. "I came to show Murel where we put the horses. Come," she all but ordered.

"I can show her," Tomas offered.

"You should get some rest."

"Go, Tomas," Murel whispered when Sefrina moved far enough away to give them some privacy. "I want to learn more about this place, and I have a feeling that Sefrina wants to tell me something. She saw the runes on my arm and seemed disquieted...more so when she noticed yours. She was not so much angry as she was frustrated."

"All right. But be careful. And wake me before you relieve your brother. I would like to join you."

He kissed her, long and hard, and pulling away from him took all her willpower. After making a wry face, letting her know he felt the same, he strode away.

Murel pulled on her leggings and hastily shrugged into her tunic. She pulled on her stockings and boots last, then said, "I'm ready."

# CHAPTER TEN

# The Cleansing

### Kantapan Castle, Mount Kanta, Nifolhad

Shoulder first, Danold charged at the door that refused to open. When the windstorm hit the castle, the fortress had trembled, waking him from his sleep. He dove into his clothing and stumbled into the corridor to find that Mirra had done the same.

"Wait!" Mirra shouted, when he moved to try again.

The roaring in their father's chamber suddenly ceased. So too had Diarmait's screams.

"Father!" she cried out, then pounded on the door with her fists.

The latch gave way. Danold tucked her behind him. "I'll go first. Something's blocking the door." He shoved at it with more force, and it rasped open. "It's sand!"

Piles of it filled the room, covering every surface. "The shutters broke open," Mirra cried. "He's not in his bed."

"He's over here," Danold said. "God's oath! Mirra, don't look."

But his sister stepped around him. "How?"

On the floor, their naked father, curled in a fetal position, was nothing but raw flesh and blood. Unlike his chamber, there was not a speck of sand on his body, nor in the perfectly clean circle surrounding him.

"We have to move him before the servants arrive," Mirra insisted, shoving the door closed and latching it. "He can't be found this way."

Danold carefully stripped the bed of some of the blankets, taking the sand with them. Then he went to pick up his father's lifeless form. "I...I don't know how to... His skin...he was completely flayed."

"I'll help," Mirra said. "Take him by his shoulders, and I'll lift him under his knees." She reached down to carefully straighten his legs and heard a whimper. "Danold! He's still alive. Quickly, we need to get him to his bed."

"There's too much sand in it still."

"Strip it completely, then flip the mattress."

While Danold took care of the bed, taking care to make sure the sand sifted to the side opposite of where his father lay, his sister hurried to the wardrobe to retrieve fresh linen. She tossed the cloths to him and then opened another above their father, letting it float gently onto him. Blood leached through the white linen, staining it crimson.

"Be careful, but do not tarry," she instructed when Danold squatted near his father. "Every motion will be agonizing for him."

He slipped his arms under Diarmait, then lifted him from the floor. As gently as possible, he deposited his now silent father onto the bed.

Mirra merely stood there and stared.

"What do we do?"

"I don't know. I don't know where to start."

"Mirra?" Danold prompted as she continued to gape at what was left of their father. "Mirra!"

Behind them, a servant knocked on the door, and the latch jiggled. "M'lords? M'lady? Do you require assistance?"

"No!" he shouted, then thought better of it. "Wait! A broom. And water. Enough to fill a bath. And clean bedding. Set everything in the corridor, then knock to let me know it's here. Do not enter this room under any circumstances unless we request you to do so."

"Yes, m'lord. Right away!"

"And honey!" Mirra shouted. "Every drop of honey on the mountain!"

Mirra leaned over Diarmait and gently touched her fingers to his neck. "How is he still alive?" she whispered.

"What do we do, Sister?"

"Normally, I would clean his wounds, but that's his entire body. Besides, he's already been scrubbed clean. There's not a speck of dust on him. Even his infected sores have been erased." She looked around the chamber.

"We have to do something," Danold insisted.

"Take the shears from my kit and cut as many long strips of linen as you can. And bring me what's left of the honey. It'll help ward off infection."

Danold watched as she started with their father's face, gently applying a layer of honey to his raw flesh, then winding the linen strips around his skull, face, and then neck. More honey and fresh linen arrived, and she repeated the process over and over again until every square inch of his body was covered. It took hours to complete the task. "We'll have to rotate him so that he doesn't rest too long in one position." She lowered her head so that it was level with Diarmait's chest.

"Is he gone?" Danold asked, mistaking the gesture.

"No," Mirra stated, rising and staring at Danold in disbelief. "He's still breathing." She turned toward Diarmait. "You're a stubborn old man, aren't you?"

She was flagging quickly, Danold observed, and he led her to the chaise he'd already brushed clean—she fell asleep at once. When he went to retrieve the water buckets and broom, one of the servants waited farther down the corridor. "Bring our supper to the chamber. And broth for Lord Diarmait. We'll need two sleeping pallets and blankets, and more wood for the fire. Leave everything outside the door."

Some of the sand that had drifted against the door spilled into the corridor. The servant's eyes widened at the amount. "I'll see to everything. M'lord?"

"Lord Diarmait is resting," Danold stated.

"Yes, but...?"

"Speak."

"The sand, m'lord. If I may be so bold, when you sweep, moisten the sand first. It will control the dust. And I'm sure this was already your intention, but you could simply push the sand over the balcony's edge."

Danold nodded, then shut the door. He surveyed the damage to the chamber. The sun was already beginning its descent, and he had much to do if the room was to be cleaned before Mirra woke.

• • •

# Barb Island, Pheldhain, Aurelia

Captain Grieg boarded the skiff that would see him to the beachhead. After dropping off Lord Ronan in Meramont, he'd set sail for home.

"Home," he said aloud to himself. He was a Southron Isler, but now exiled. Grieg studied the crew members who had joined him on the skiff. They, too, had been banished from their island realm, and he wondered if they thought as he did now—that Pheldhain was now home. For years, it was a condition of his that his crew have no wives or family connections. Nothing that could be used by Fanm Larenne, the leader of the Isles who communed with the Goddess, to control their loyalties.

One of the younger crewman cocked his head at Grieg. "Aye, home, Cap'n." The others nodded.

"Robi is eager to return to shore, Cap'n," one of the sailors japed. "He's got himself a woman he desires to make his wife." Everyone fell silent, trying to gauge how Grieg would take the news that contradicted his orders that they not get involved with Aurelians.

"I myself will be happy to see Marlita again," he admitted. "I suppose you'll want me to preside over the wedding."

The small sail on the skiff caught, easing their need to row, just as Grieg's words eased the tension in the vessel. He never considered marriage, for he loved but one woman his entire life, and she belonged to the Goddess. But now in exile and residing in Pheldhain for what remained of her days, Grieg wondered if Marlita shared his sentiments.

As they sailed toward the short pier, their waiting party stood. He grasped Lord Warin's hand, and his friend pulled him up from the skiff. They embraced, and then Grieg greeted Princess Anwyl.

"Well?" Warin demanded.

"Warin, give the man a moment to catch his breath," the princess chastised, then laughed. "I'm sure he'll tell us everything about Tomas and Murel and Nifolhad."

Warin waved his hand in the air. "I don't care about that," he stated. "I do, of course. But what I really want to know is how *Moon Caster* performed."

"A man after my own heart," Grieg sang. "She's a thing of beauty and the finest vessel I've had the honor of sailing."

Together, they left the bustling marina and mounted the horses that would take them to the castle, where Grieg would brief them on the mission in their private quarters.

No sooner did Grieg dismount than he saw the familiar figure of Marlita. His heart softened as she approached, and he regarded her for the first time through eyes that were open to the possibility of love. She smiled at him in a way that silently communicated that she'd been waiting for him to come to the realization.

Princess Anwyl clapped, and Warin beamed at them both.

"Marlita," he greeted, then kissed her cheeks. "You are looking so well!"

"Being here, closer to the Southron Waters, has been wholly rejuvenating for me."

"I asked Marlita to join us," the princess noted, then gazed around them. "Did Ronan remain on the ship?"

"Ronan?" he asked, confused by her question. "We sailed to Meramont first. Lord Ronan is home. He was needed there."

"That's odd, isn't it?" Warin observed. "It must have been important. He was to sail with you here first, and then captain his own ship back to Meramont. She's currently moored in the marina with a full crew."

"We sailed to Meramont first. Lord Ronan is home. He was needed there," Grieg repeated.

Marlita frowned and asked, "How did Ronan receive word that he was needed in Meramont?"

"We sailed to Meramont first. Lord Ronan is home. He was needed..." Grieg's brow furrowed. "Why are you looking at me as if I grew another head? What's wrong?"

"Your memories, for one thing," the princess explained.

. . .

## Mitra Oasis, The Fyrost Desert, Nifolhad

They'd rested a full day and night, and Murel now followed Sefrina around the pool, taking the sandy path to the temple wall. Reeds grew near the water's edge, and tall grasses with feathery plumes on long stalks brushed her arms. "I'm still surprised at the enormity of this place," Murel stated.

"Like the Fyrost, it shifts and changes at the whim of the desert winds. Different sections are exposed while others are covered by the sands. If pressed, I would say that it is about the same size as the Fenrhi complex."

"That large? And the pool? How deep does it go?"

Sefrina stopped and turned. "No one has tried to find out. Did you?"

"I dove deep, but it went too far down."

Sefrina waited.

"It wasn't that I was afraid," Murel tried to explain. "But it felt wrong, like trespassing."

"Then you understand better than most." She started walking again. "Do you know that you, your brother, and Tomas, are the only non-Fyrjians that have ever visited the Mitra?"

"The Mitra?" Murel prompted.

"The name for this place."

"But that can't be. Queen Aghna and Lady Claire came here with Madyan."

Sefrina laughed. "Not to this place. The Malikáfyr took them to Palamia. It is far from here, and to the northwest. It is also much smaller. Come. There is something I must show you."

Tall palms and twisted trees with smooth, mottled bark ringed the clearing. Sefrina plucked a small green fruit from one and tossed it to Murel. "Olives. Though not ripe yet."

The horses wandered freely, nibbling on the long shoots of grass growing under the shade of the trees. Near one side, a small spring gurgled, coming up from a grouping of rocks and tumbling into a shallow pool spanning about three paces. But it was the stone formation across the clearing that captured Murel's attention.

"Why am I drawn to this wall?" she asked.

"The Temple of the Mitra is a place where love and life and even death exist as one."

"Built for your Sky Goddess," Murel remembered aloud. "And Palamia? A temple for her brother?"

"No. The Wind God's place is where we must take the Rottu. Palamia has no temple, but it is no less sacred."

"Sefrina, why did you bring me here?"

"Because I want you to understand. I want you to really see the temple."

The stone face rose three stories above them. "But it's only a wall. Was the temple destroyed?"

"The wall is the temple. You are not truly looking."

Then, she saw them...carved into the rock were runes. She traced her fingers into the grooves. The Fenrhi markings on her skin blazed hot, and she whipped her arm back.

"The most I can do is lead you to this place. The rest is up to you."

"That's all you're going to say?" Murel demanded, tired of never getting a straight answer from their guide.

"Your answers are before you," Sefrina replied, as if reading her thoughts.

Murel looked back at the etchings, then pulled up her sleeve. The markings from the Artists were the same! "How is this possible? The Artists—" From the corner of her eye, she saw something swing down toward her. *Not again*, she prayed, as pain wracked her skull, and she crumpled to the ground. "Why, Sefrina?"

The Fyrjian woman bent over her. "I was ordered to bring the Rottu to the Temple of Kardia. Not you. Not Tomas. It was decreed that your deaths would be humane—not left to the one whose power is ever growing."

"Please, Sefrina. Don't kill him." Murel tried to get up but grew too dizzy. She fought the urge to pass out.

"I cannot kill him now. Nor you. You both bear the marks of this place." She leaned forward, lifted her hand, and Murel cringed at the imminent blow. Instead, she tipped a waterskin to Murel's lips. "It's mala'eth. The same that I gave to Tomas. And to your brother. It will make you all sleep. When you wake, we will have carried the Rottu far from this place."

Murel tried to resist but was helpless to swallow the drink that Sefrina squeezed into her mouth and down her throat. A thick, pleasant haze filled her brain. She couldn't identify the herbs that had been added to the mead to drug them, and she tried in vain to fight the soporific effects.

"I am sorry that I struck you. But you would have smelled that the mead had been tampered with. I should not say this, but I am happy to not have had to kill you outright. I have grown fond of you. You must trust that you and Tomas can survive what is coming."

Murel grabbed at Sefrina's tunic to stop her from leaving, but her hand dropped uselessly to the ground.

"By the time you wake, we will be long gone with your brother. This is the final race, Murel. Everything depends on riding faster than the wind."

"We?"

"My people. They have been following us since we entered the Fyrost."

"Won't they be angry that we are not dead?" she slurred. "And kill us?"

"I will tell them that you disrespected this place. That you will wake only in time to hear each other's screams as you are consumed by the storm."

Murel's eyes widened in terror.

"Oh, no! It is not true, Murel. You will wake in time, as will Tomas! But it *will* be too late for you to follow us."

"Madyan will be angry with you. She will—"

"The Malikáfyr's life depends on taking the Rottu to Kardia."

Murel tried to focus on reasoning with Sefrina, but her brain grew even foggier.

"Stay here; this temple has life yet; you felt it when you touched the wall. It may help protect you until after the storm passes. Murel, you will have to fight to stay alive; this is the best that I can do for you without betraying my people."

"'It's only a wall," Murel managed, each word sounding warped to her ears.

"You must use your eyes, you *and* Tomas. If anyone can find the door, it will be the two of you."

Murel's head lolled, and Sefrina gently guided her sideways to the ground. She blinked her eyes open just enough to see Sefrina's boots leading the horses away. Then, her mind and body yielded to an unnatural sleep.

# Mitra

Tomas's beard was really growing on Murel. Like now, when his whiskers tickled her chin and nose, and his hairy lips felt soft and velvety. Wait…that wasn't right… She opened her eyes.

*Pfft*, her Fyrjian mare snorted in her face, blowing back her hair with a humid, grass-scented breath.

Murel pushed her horse's muzzle away, then levered herself into a seated position. The ground tilted, and she closed her eyes to steady her brain. When she opened them again, she noted that a waterskin had been left next to her, along with dates. Her belongings—clean clothes, saddle bags, even Tomas's gear—were in a neat pile.

"Tomas!" she cried, her voice dry and hollow. "Where are you?"

It took her three attempts to successfully stand. Using the wall for support, she skirted her way along it to the nearest tree, then flung herself toward its trunk. Then again to the next, and again, until she was at the entrance to the path. When the tree trunks gave way to the squat scrub palms, she halted. No matter, she would crawl if she had to. "Tomas!" she cried out.

"Murel!" Tomas shouted, sounding as frantic as she felt.

"Over here. By the horses!"

He crashed through the foliage, staggering toward her like a drunken bear. One final lurch, and he slammed into the tree to which she clung, causing the unripe olives to break free and pepper down upon them. He pulled her to him, hugging her tightly to his chest. She didn't care that she could hardly breathe, overwhelmed as she was that he was alive and well.

"I woke up and couldn't move, helpless to do naught but stare at the stars as the sky slowly lightened. I was so worried for you, Murel. And then, when I finally could, I crawled to the pool. Our things were gone. I thought you'd been taken, or worse."

"I would never willingly leave you!"

"I know. I know. I kept calling your name. And finally, I heard you." He let her go long enough to take her cheeks in his hands. He searched her eyes, then dipped down to kiss her lips, her nose, her cheeks...everywhere. Then he pressed his forehead to hers and simply breathed. When he drew back, his hand came away with blood on his fingertips. "Oh, Murel, not again."

"I'm all right. I promise." She placed his hand over her heart. She set her own on his chest. *"We're* all right," she stated calmly. When their racing hearts settled, Murel took his arm. "Come on. Sefrina left us some food. Eating should help."

"You can't trust her! She could have poisoned it."

Murel, feeling stronger now, pushed away from the tree. Together, they tottered toward the temple wall and their belongings. "We would be dead already if she wished it. She had orders to kill us. When she saw our markings, she deviated from her plan. The food will be safe."

They sat and ate the dates and drank the water. Tomas reached for his saddlebag, pulled out a package of dried meat, and offered her a piece. "How long do you reckon we were out?"

"Yesterday afternoon, then all night."

"And Jesper?"

"They took him. A group of Fyrjians have been shadowing us across the desert. Sefrina drugged him as well, or he would not have left us."

"Whatever she gave us is wearing off remarkably fast. I'm feeling steadier already. You?"

She nodded.

"At least she left us our horses," Tomas said. "We can track them."

"I'm afraid there won't be time. Sefrina said something was coming." Murel showed him the runes on the wall. "Touch one."

He did, then immediately drew back his hand and grabbed his upper arm.

"They match our markings. I don't know the import, but our guide was unsettled."

"Why would the Fyrjians want to kill us in the first place? Why not just abandon us here?"

"Sefrina said it would be more humane."

"More humane than what?" he asked incredulously.

"Whatever is coming."

"But we don't feel it here, that evil presence that hounded us in the desert." He stared at the wall. "Some temple this is. There's not even an eave to protect us from the sun, let alone a sandstorm."

"This is the Mitra Temple. I think it means haven. Or womb. The wall is but one side of it."

"The rest is buried under the dune?"

"Yes," Murel said. "And we need to find the door."

Tomas hauled himself up, then held out his hand to help her. "It could be buried. Can you read these runes?"

"No."

"Then we should start by finding those that match our markings."

"Agreed. How much time do you reckon we have?"

"It's still morning, judging by the light. I don't want to split up, Murel. But I should get to higher ground and risk a look around."

"I'll stay here with the horses and try to find the door."

"You're sure you're all right?"

"Not even a headache, I promise." She stood on her toes and gave him a quick kiss. "Now go."

She saddled their horses and refilled the waterskins first. A strange, keening whistle knifed through the sky, and Murel had the uncanny feeling that the noise was searching for her. "Hurry back, Tomas," she said to herself, then marched up to the wall to study the designs.

Though the wall was three stories high, the entire façade spanned a mere four or five paces. Her cursory scan revealed no demarcations that would indicate an entrance. She slowed her examination, methodically moving from section to section until she found a similar rune to one on her arm.

"I wonder…" She pressed it, but quickly removed her hand. "Ow." She pressed it again and again, each time feeling a burning sting on the band marked on her arm. "This isn't working."

"Talking to yourself?" Tomas asked, coming up behind her.

She gave him a lopsided grin, but then grew serious at what she saw reflected in his eyes. "How long?"

"Maybe an hour. It's the mother of all sandstorms, Murel. Black as night and moving fast. There's heat lightning, and when it flashed bright, I could see that it was a solid wall of sand. I only watched it for a minute, but it was long enough. Perhaps too long."

"What do you mean?"

"I swear, it sensed me and homed in on our location." He turned to survey the area. "You saddled the horses and loaded our gear, but there's no possible way we can outrun what's coming. And this place—I don't care how sacred it is—it's not going to save us."

"Then we have to find the portal into this temple."

"What if we push—"

"I wouldn't touch that... Doesn't that hurt?" she asked when he touched the circle-shaped rune with a line through its center.

"Not at all. It's remarkably cool to the touch."

"Not for me." She moved a pace or two away. One of the runes was cup-shaped. "I wonder..." She pressed one that was at the same height as the one Tomas had said was cool—it didn't burn her fingers like before. "Tomas, try yours at the same time!"

They each touched their assigned symbols. At first, nothing happened. Then, they both heard it, the slithering of sand being displaced. The sound grew fainter, then trickled down to nothing. The wall remained as it was.

"That was disappointing," Murel lamented.

"Let's try again," Tomas suggested, and they both pressed. "I think mine moved!"

"Mine didn't."

"You have to press hard."

Murel tried again, to no avail.

The sky grew ominously darker. When a strong wind sluiced over them from above the wall, the horses whinnied in panic. Tomas grabbed their leads while Murel tried pressing the design with both hands.

"We'll give it one more try, Murel, and then we have to leave. We may be able to find shelter in the palm trees. Together on three. One..."

"Two."

"Three!" they said in unison.

"It moved, Tomas! It moved a little bit." If there was any shifting of sand to be heard, the loud, howling wind blotted out the sound. Murel looked up—the gusts were now visible, carrying the dust of the desert in the currents. "Again!"

They both pushed. "I'm not strong enough!" She pounded the side of her fist against the immovable object before them.

Tomas reached out his hand. "We have to go, now!" he shouted to be heard above the violent wailing above them.

Murel reached across and clasped her fingers in his. "It's too late. I'm sorry, Tomas." She slapped her other hand over the rune she'd been pressing, and the cold stone flashed hot, sending a current of warmth up her arm and across her body, then down her other arm and into Tomas's hand. Whether from the wind or the energy zinging between them, her hair danced wildly about her head. "Of course! The Artists told us that you would be able to lend me your strength! Can you feel it?"

Tomas nodded. "Once more, then." And holding hands across the span of the wall, they slammed their palms against their respective runes. Like her own hair, Tomas's lifted, standing on end.

"Look!"

A distinct outline of a broad entranceway emerged as sand slipped from its seams. Tomas pushed harder, his muscles straining under his tunic, and the solid rock began to swing in on his side. He continued pushing while the raging wind above them dipped lower, sending grit strafing toward them. The horses bolted into the opening, taking their belongings into the dark void of the temple. Tomas pulled Murel to him and into the gaping maw at the exact moment when the storm-driven sand ripped across them.

Immediately, the air pressure dropped. They stared at the darkening storm outside the entrance. A whirlwind touched down, screaming like some inhuman monster, pulling up several date palms and flinging them to the heavens. The water in the spring was drawn up and out of the basin and dispersed in all directions. Murel squeezed Tomas's hand even tighter, watching the maelstrom, amazed that the havoc seemed unable to penetrate their sanctuary.

No sooner had she imagined it, when a vicious gust caught the branches of an olive tree, causing its wizened limbs to bend and crack. She and Tomas had only enough time to dive sideways and to the ground as the trunk cracked and the tree was flung in their direction.

"We have to close the wall," Tomas yelled.

It was the last thing she wanted to do, to be closed up inside what might end up being a pitch-black tomb. "Just don't let go of me."

"Never."

Together, they pushed the stone portal back into place. On the other side, there was a crash, and splinters of what had been another tree flew fletch-like through the narrowing gap. There was a snick as they sealed themselves in, and the darkness within was so much more permanent than the dense blackness of the possessed storm.

Tomas pulled her into his arms and held her. From somewhere in the dark came the scrape of hooves. "Whoa!" he shouted to the horses. "Hold on to my shoulder, Murel. I need both hands."

She nodded, realizing too late that he couldn't see her. But she took his arm in both her hands and held on as if for dear life. His muscles flexed as he moved his arm to unsheathe his dagger.

"I keep a flint on me." He cracked the two together, and Murel grasped onto the brief spark as if it would be the last light she would ever see. Tomas slowly pulled her away from the door. His foot scuffed, swiping the stone floor back and forth. "I'm going to kneel down."

"Hurry," Murel said, her voice sticking in her throat when the panic that had nothing to do with the storm threatened to overwhelm her. Anything could be lurking in the dark. Or they could take a step and tumble into some bottomless pit. She hated her fear and bit down on the scream that was rising in her throat.

"Just a few more minutes, Murel." He set something down, either the flint or his dagger, and then placed his warm hand on hers where she gripped his shoulder. "I almost have it."

He struck his dagger to his flint, and a spark shot out. He did it a few more times, and then finally, there was a red glow as some kind of fiber caught flame. Tomas bent low and blew softly. The glow grew brighter.

Murel finally let go of his arm to gather small bits of palm fiber to add to the tiny flame that was quickly burning through the fuel.

She moved to his other side and swept her hands over the floor in the meager light, collecting bits of wood shrapnel. She handed the pieces to Tomas, who carefully stacked the kindling over their little fire. When the wood caught and the flames illuminated the dark space, she stepped quickly to the remains of the olive tree, breaking off the smaller branches and passing them to Tomas. They had a merry little fire going, but without proper fuel, it would soon burn out. At least they had an entire tree.

"Keep feeding it, Murel. I'll grab the horses." He whistled to them, and they were rewarded with an answering snort. Like apparitions from the dark, their equine friends emerged, drawn in by the light. "Good boy," Tomas soothed, patting his gelding's haunch. He reached into one of his saddlebags and pulled out a hatchet, then set to work hacking at the smaller branches. He set a few sturdy lengths to the side. "For torches."

After the blaze was large enough so that they could rest and regroup, they sat before the fire and took stock of their immediate surroundings. "This must be an entrance hall," Murel guessed, hugging herself and shivering despite the heat from the fire.

"It is. When I called for the horses, I made out that it opens to a larger space." He took a deep breath and wrapped his arm around her shoulders, pulling her close. "I've never seen anything like that storm—and I've seen Warin get struck by lightning!"

"When those trees were ripped apart and flew at us..." She trembled. "I wasn't hit by anything. And you saved me from the dark, like you did so many years ago." He rubbed her arm and shoulder, warming her. Slowly, her trembling subsided. "What about you?"

"Just some grit in my eyes from the sand... It hit me as we were diving into the temple."

She took his chin in her hand to turn him toward the light. His skin was red where the sand had blasted him, but he was otherwise fine. She leaned forward to kiss him, to reassure herself that they were safe, when she saw something glint behind him. "What's that?" she asked and stood.

Tomas grabbed one of the longer branches he'd set aside and lit the end. He followed her as she walked to the opposite wall. "Is that a brazier?"

"I think it is." He dipped a finger through one of the holes in the cover, then pulled it out. "It's oil! Stand back, I'm going to try to light it, and with it being so old, it might erupt in flames." He backed away, nudging Murel so that he stood in front of her, and then extended the torch to the brazier.

The fuel wouldn't light at first. Then there was a great *whoosh* as it flared to life, shooting flames out of the punched holes in the lid. A moment later, the fire retreated, and the illumination steadied.

"Tomas, there are more!" She ran for one of the other branches and lit another torch while Tomas moved to the next sconce.

"The chains are brass," he said. "And they appear sturdy enough. Stand back when you light them. If something explodes, I don't want you doused in burning oil."

Together, they lit a total of six braziers, lending a beautiful glow to the entrance hall. The passageway was tiled in an intricate mosaic design. Still, there was not enough light to see more than a few paces into the main room of the temple. "This one is different," she said, noticing another brazier. "It's not hanging."

"Go ahead. But be careful."

Murel stretched out her torch to light the brazier, and like the others, it flared wildly before settling. But this time, a lick of fire erupted in a narrow trough running along the wall at the brazier's level. The tiny flame wasted no time chasing the fuel in the reservoir. A moment later, another, larger brazier erupted, again sending an offshoot to race to the next light. "Ingenious! There has to be one on your side, Tomas."

"There is!" he said, lighting the reservoir. "Wait here while I make sure our fire doesn't go out."

Murel nodded as she watched the flames light the evenly spaced braziers, mapping out the walls of the temple. It was much larger than she had anticipated, and when Tomas came to stand next to her, she slipped her arm around his waist. "It's extraordinary."

There was enough light now to illuminate the main space below them. A broad walkway girded a sunken floor, one reached by steps made of huge flat stones on all sides.

"Look," Murel pointed out. "Your flame caught up with mine. They're about to meet." No sooner had she said this, than the last of the braziers flamed, casting a warm, steady illumination to the underground temple. Hollowed out of the very stone that had been covered by centuries of drifting dunes, the space was supported by intricately carved columns, which soared three stories up from the smooth stone floor. They were evenly spaced, and from her vantage point, she could see no other rooms. The higher the ceiling rose, the darker the shadows grew, so that they were unable to make out the underside of the high dome.

Tomas took her hand. "Let's walk around. There must be a place to sleep. Or eat."

"Or prepare a sacrifice," Murel half-joked.

A continuous stone bench, interrupted by each column, girded the upper ring. Underneath, wood boxes—carved from one piece of tree trunk, for there were no joints or seams—were tucked into a small recess under the seat of each section. Tomas squatted down to pull one out. It slid smoothly on the polished stone floor, whispering in the quiet rather than scraping. Murel peeked over his shoulder.

He pulled out an earthen-made urn and, after removing the tightly fitted cap, smelled the contents. "Oil."

"That's convenient." She gazed about them. "I don't believe anyone has been in here for years, maybe decades, and yet, there's no dust."

"Just the mess from the storm when we entered."

"It's more like a tomb than a temple. Perfectly sealed against the ravages of time." She hated the idea of being trapped in the temple forever. "Let's try to find another way out. Sefrina said the oasis was protected, but I have a feeling it's taking a beating out there. Who knows what we'll find when we open the door?"

"If we can even open it from inside." He pushed the box back under the bench. "What do you suppose is over there?"

They continued, not seeing any hint of a recess or side room until they stood directly across from where they'd entered. Between the two columns and on the edge of the ringed tier, a giant wall rose to the curved ceiling. It was too thick for them to see around, so they continued their trek until they made it back to where they'd started.

The horses were huddled next to each other about halfway between the fire they had built and where they now stood. "The only way forward is forward," Tomas said, pointing to the shadowed area across the main floor.

The gloom made it impossible to discern what was on the wall. She reached for Tomas's hand, and thus linked, they took one step down the high, broad steps. "These could be seats, like stands at a tournament."

"But who was the audience?" Tomas asked, taking the next step and guiding her down. When they reached the floor, what they had deemed was polished stone was a thin layer of liquid. "Careful!" he hissed, then began to pull Murel away from where she had stooped to touch the liquid.

"Only water," she soothed after sniffing, then tasting it. "It's dry ahead." Together, they walked forward, leaving ripples in the shallow puddle, then footprints on the stone. "It's a spring!"

Before them was a deeper pool, its surface so calm it made a perfect mirror of the arching columns as they soared above them. And as they drew closer, their steps disturbed the settled water, causing the reflected flames to waver and warp.

"Another spring...right in the center of the temple," Tomas noted. "The water must've overflowed."

"Come on. Let's explore the area in front of that wall."

It was dark where they were walking, but she could make out some large shapes positioned here and there on the main floor. The puddles had dried up as well. The sconces, set back as they were, backlit the dark slab before them, making it difficult to make out its purpose.

"There's a large brazier," Murel noted. "More like a fire pit. What do you say we shed some light into this place? Together?"

"Yes. But be ready to jump away."

Murel waved her torch behind her to make sure there was nothing upon which to trip, then nodded. As one, they lowered their torches to the fuel. They staggered back at the loud *whumpf* that sounded. Flames shot up, temporarily blinding them. Then, like the sconces, the fire pit settled so that it cast a bright, steady glow.

Murel's eyes adjusted to take in what was before them, and she stumbled back. Tomas caught her before she fell into the pool.

"That's something to see," he finally said, like her, in awe.

Grander in dimensions than the perimeter flames, the central fire pit lit the entire cavern of the underground temple. But more than that, it finally lent illumination to the carved stone before them.

Murel and Tomas approached her. The Goddess. She had five arms and, seated as she was on her heels, was at least ten feet in height.

"She's made entirely of moonstone," Tomas noted. "I've never seen one this large and unbroken by crack or fissure. Look at what she's holding in her hands, Murel. Those gems are bigger than anything in the Known Realms." He stepped around the brazier set before the statue. "A pearl for Earth Caste. Sapphire for Kena."

"Emerald for Sylvain and amber for the Mother," Murel added. "And black opal for Umbren." The translucent stone, in the area of the statue's torso, was infused with crimson veins. "Blood Caste. She's both terrifying and beautiful."

"Those purple crystals in her eyes are likely amethysts," Tomas figured.

Murel jumped back and gasped—an even taller figure towered over the carved goddess. Tomas was at her side, hand poised to draw his sword. "No, it's all right." She pointed. "A trick of the light. Can you see the image etched into the wall behind the goddess?"

"Now that you point him out, yes. Handsome, isn't he?"

Murel smiled, drawing her first easy breath since she woke from her drug-induced sleep. "Trapped in a temple dedicated to a lost Sky Goddess. A sacred place, but one also used for her occasional tryst with her brother, the Wind God."

"Who is, at this very moment, outside this temple, trying to kill us."

"Not Wind, but the ancient spirit who enslaved him." She took a deep breath. "No, I only sense peace here, and love, even." She closed her eyes. "I don't know if you exist, or ever existed, but thank you for giving us sanctuary. When it's safe to depart, we'll leave everything as we found it so that when you meet again with your lover, it will be as if you never left your desert." When she was finished, she discovered Tomas staring at her. "What?"

"Nothing. You're wonderful, that's all." Then he smiled at her. "I'll see to the horses and our things."

"I'll find a place to make our camp for the night. If the spring rises, we don't want our gear to get soaked."

As Tomas headed back toward the horses, Murel spun in a slow circle. "Right," she said to the statue. "What are you hiding back there?"

The area behind the god and goddess had been hollowed out, creating a large, open storeroom that could be entered from either side of the statue. The back wall was lined with shelves. A convenient oil lamp hung from a hook just inside the room, and Murel used her torch to light it.

"The horses are wiped down and happily munching from their feedbags, and I extinguished the fire," Tomas informed her when he returned and found her exploring the storeroom. "We'll have a bit of clean-up to do when we leave. What did you find back here?"

"These lamps, for one thing. This seems to be a pantry." Baskets were neatly lined along the shelves of the wall closest to the main chamber. Each was filled with sealed, earthen jars. The carvings on the lids indicated the contents—different dried fruits and meats. "It's all perfectly preserved; well, maybe not the meat."

Tomas lifted the lid on a barrel that was pushed against the back wall. He dipped his hand in and scooped up some of the contents, letting the crystals sift through his fingers. "I would wager that whoever outfitted this place dried the meat and stored it in this salt. The lids are painted with an image of what's hopefully inside." He unsealed another barrel. "Grain, but this looks like it's for horses. Murel, how is it possible that it's fresh?"

"Maybe the dry climate in here… Sefrina acted as if no one has been able to access this place in hundreds of years. But someone had to have done so." She uncorked an earthen jug and smelled the contents. "Wine."

Tomas opened one of the jars holding dried meat, dug through the salt, and pulled out a strip, taking a small bite. "Tastes like venison…a little stale, but edible. Once you get past the salt, there are other spices that remind me of something I've had before."

"When?"

"I remember now. Madyan made this when she traveled with Princess Anwyl. Warin gave me some when I had to ride back to Ragallach. He said Madyan wouldn't give Anwyl the recipe—it was a family secret—but that the spices preserved the meat for years." He held out a piece to her.

"Tough," she said, trying to chew the small strip of meat. "But tasty. The spices are nice."

"There's also lamb, rabbit, and snake. And…" Tomas paused, and Murel made sense of the depiction on the lid.

They both turned at the same time and stared at where their steeds dozed. "There's a reason Fyrjians don't name their horses."

"I would rather eat dried snake." Tomas surveyed the stores. "Madyan's parents must have provisioned this place. It takes two people who are connected to open the portal. I wonder if she ever tried."

"When we find her," Murel stated, determined to maintain a positive attitude, "we'll ask. She certainly has been to this oasis, being the Malikáfyr. For now, let's make camp. Then we can explore whatever is behind that door."

"Agreed," he said, walking back toward the horses. He stopped. "What door?"

"Next to the bucket and brooms," she answered, following him as he went back into the storeroom. "At least it looked like a door to me, albeit one without a handle or latch. We're going to need more light."

While Tomas continued to search for a way to open the door, Murel moved to retrieve the lamp from where she'd set it upon one of the tables. "It'll probably take both of us to—" He was gone! She ran from the storeroom to see if he had gone into the main area, but he wasn't there either. "Tomas!" she cried.

• • •

Tomas lifted his lamp to inspect the back side of the stone door. It had slid so effortlessly open that when he stepped over the threshold, it hadn't occurred to him that it would immediately close again.

"Murel!" he shouted repeatedly, but his calls bounced back, echoing up the steep, curved set of stairs.

He pounded his fist against the stone. "That won't help either." Hopefully, Murel was on the other side trying to figure out how to open the door. "There has to be a release." He found a hook on the wall and hung his lamp from it, opening up the louvers and angling the light. Then, he let his fingers do the work as he glided them along the carved surround of the door.

"I should have paid more attention," he berated himself, trying to recall what he'd been doing when the door opened. He'd set his palm on the upper corner and leaned forward. He tried it again, to no avail. "Right. Now left." Again, nothing happened.

He refused to believe he might be trapped forever—without Murel. She was just on the other side, and dropping his chin, he rested his forehead against the door. And that's when he saw them, two paving stones shaped differently from the others...like footprints. Tomas carefully placed his feet in the exact spots. The portal had scarcely slid open when he stared into Murel's panicked eyes.

She threw her arms around his neck as he stepped forward and out of the vestibule. Behind him, the portal slid shut.

"I thought I had lost you! Don't do that again, Tomas!"

He squeezed her against his chest, so relieved and happy to be able to hold her. "I would never leave you, Murel." He took her face in his hands and crushed his lips to hers. She returned the embrace with equal passion. Slowly, he steered her backward until she bumped into the worktable with its baskets of linens and cloths. And there, trapped between his body and the table, he ravaged her with kisses and roaming hands. His heart hammered in his chest.

She was touching him everywhere, inciting him further. And then she began pulling his chemise from his waistband, tugging it up and growling until he lifted his arms to let her pull it free. Her gaze devoured him, roving over the expanse of his chest and the laddered muscles of his stomach. He couldn't help himself and contracted his pectoral muscles in response to her ravenous stare.

"Do that again!" she demanded, and he readily complied. "You are as beautiful outside as you are within." She lifted his arm. "Show me," she begged, cupping her hands over his bicep. He smiled and flexed his arm. "You're magnificent, you know that?"

She smoothed her hands over his shoulders and down to his chest. Once there, she circled his nipple with her fingertip, then traced down his sternum, following the dark blond trail of hair to where, just past his navel, it disappeared into his waistband.

That he was aroused by her exploration was evident, even in the dimly lit storeroom, and he held his breath. Her tongue flicked out and dampened her lower lip, and he almost lost it. She hovered for a moment, then the softest smile graced her mouth. With a pace that was excruciatingly slow, she ran her hands back up his chest, resting them on his pectoral muscles. She waited, and after a couple of seconds, he gave her what she wanted, and flexed, first one and then the other in turn, back and forth.

"Now it's you killing me," she said, her voice husky like he'd never heard before. "But I love it. You're rock hard and yet, so comfortable—a perfect fit for me." There was no mistaking her meaning, especially when she pressed her center against him. When he next flexed for her, it wasn't only his chest that tightened.

She pressed her lips to his nipple and sucked lightly. Nipped at him, even. Then swiped him with her tongue. "Sensitive," she observed.

"Now who's killing who?" he managed, tugging at her chemise. "Fair is fair." The offending garment was soon removed and tossed next to his. She arched back so that he could take all of her in. "Ah, Murel. You are exquisitely made."

Tomas didn't waste any time, and pushing aside one of the baskets, he lifted her by her waist to set her on the worktable. Then he dipped his head down and captured her nipple in his lips. There he played homage, massaging and kneading her voluptuous breasts whilst she moaned her pleasure, entwining her fingers in his curly blond locks and holding him to task.

"I've been imagining this for ages—wanting it," she moaned, and then gasped when he bit down.

"Again," she begged, sliding her hips forward to press against him.

He suckled her, gently at first, then harder, letting his teeth scrape her delicate flesh. When she flexed her hips, he slid one hand down her back and helped her to grind against him. The heat of her core burned through their clothing, making him harder than he believed possible. He wanted more than anything to bury himself inside her. She was panting now, her fingers flexing rhythmically in his hair. Her hips, too, rode up and down, again and again.

"Tomas! I need...I need..." She pulled his hand away from her breast and pushed it to the vee between her thighs.

Tomas wasted no time loosening the laces of her breeches so that his fingers could access her slick heat. "You are so wet, my love. Open your legs wider. Yes. Just like that."

And when he teased and delved, she began to shudder. "Come apart for me, Murel."

She arched, pulsing and shattering around his fingers. "Yes! Tomas!" She threw her arms around him and kissed him deeply. "That was...I don't have words."

"Good?"

She crushed her lips to his again. "So much better than good." She cocked an eyebrow. "But what about you..." She reached down to caress him.

He stayed her hand, not wanting her to be shocked by his prodigiousness.

For a brief second, emotion—hurt, perhaps—filled her eyes. She looked away. "Where is my—"

He touched her chin and gently turned her face to his. "I want you to, Murel. More than I can say. But that was for you. To show you that you no longer have to imagine us together. We *are* together. After we were marked, I didn't want to pressure you. Part of me worried that perhaps that flame that was kindled in Naca'an had been doused by the weight of being linked before we were ready."

"Definitely not doused," she said, a soft smile returning to her lips. "Just set out of the fire. But I know what you mean." She touched the marks on his arm. "We are more than these bands, Tomas. What we feel is not because of them."

"Good to know. Because, honestly, I've had feelings for you for years. For my entire life, in fact."

"Remind me to do bodily harm to my cousin when we return to Aurelia."

"So noted." He helped her back into her chemise, then off the worktable. While she tied her breeches, he shrugged into his shirt. "We should explore upstairs before making our camp for the night."

"Upstairs?"

"Mm-hmm." He pointed to the door.

"How did it open?" she asked, standing in front of the obstacle. "I tried pressing the designs and nothing."

"Slide your foot to the left...a little more. Good. Now look down."

"You're jesting," she said incredulously. "It can't be that easy."

"They're spaced a little too far apart to fit a natural stance. Go ahead, step on them."

Murel widened her feet, but nothing happened. Tomas pressed his hand against the stone portal. "Just a little pressure and—" The stone door slid effortlessly to the side.

"When you step through, your weight must trigger the door's mechanism, and it slides back into place." He grabbed Murel's lamp from the table. "It'll be a tight squeeze, but we'll enter together. Ready." She nodded, and they stepped through.

A mere moment passed, and the door slipped shut. Tomas handed her lamp to her, then took his from the hook on the wall. "I didn't go past this point," he disclosed. "I couldn't. I..."

She placed her hand on his chest. "I know. Me, too. When I couldn't find you, I may have panicked...just a tiny bit. But then I trusted that you would figure out a way to get back to me. You have always been able to find me."

"Let's explore," he said, holding out his hand.

She took it, and he couldn't help but think, even with the recent non-stop danger they'd been in for weeks, there was no one else in the world who he wanted by his side.

# CHAPTER TWELVE

# Mist and Missions

Tomas clasped Murel's hand and led the way up the narrow stairs. The walls were decorated with images of the Sky Goddess and Wind God personified. With each step up, the images became more and more amorous, until they were outright explicit. Behind him, Murel slowed, tugging his hand until she forced him to stop.

She was staring at an exceptionally creative rendering of the lovers, her head slowly cocking as if the different angle would give her an enlightened perspective. "How did he bend his leg like that?"

Tomas lifted his eyebrow at the image, then at her, and grinned. "That isn't his leg."

"Not his…? How…? Oh! I see."

He laughed, and she narrowed his eyes at him. When he nudged her up the stairs, she resisted.

"Hold on. She has a very happy expression; I think I would like to commit this one to memory." Then she regarded him with innocent eyes. "Are you blushing, Tomas?"

"Come on. We're here for at least a few days so you can copy them down if—" He stopped in his tracks, and she squeezed next to him to see what had arrested his words. In unison, they bent their necks farther and farther to the left to ascertain what was depicted on the wall.

"I'll have to come back to this one," Murel quipped. "Right now, I want to see what's up these stairs." She led the way this time, and after the steps curved around the dome, they finally saw an opening in the ceiling.

They came up through a hole in the floor, their two lamps illuminating a circular room, one that was centered at the top of the domed temple below. Tomas could make out the silhouettes of benches and low platforms. Around the room, the glow of their lamps was reflected back at them.

"We need more light," Murel said, and they split off to ignite the braziers and sconces placed around the perimeter. The walls, made up of highly polished stone, amplified the flames. A gigantic sleeping platform took up one entire quadrant of the room and was covered with stuffed cushions and plush blankets. "We're in a sleeping chamber."

At the same moment, their gazes fell on an awkwardly designed bench. "I don't think much sleeping happened up here," Tomas choked out.

Murel grinned. "Now we know how they managed that last position."

Tomas swallowed, suddenly imagining Murel—no, now was not the time. He walked over to the sleeping platform and pressed his hand down. Amazingly, the ticking was still fresh. There was a trunk at the foot of the bed, and he lifted the lid to find it filled with soft, fur-lined blankets. Here and there, cushions ranging from small to full-body sized were scattered about the space. The strange bench had relatives...banquettes and chairs—narrow, wide, and tapered. And one had an opening...

"Oh, hell," he swore, striding across the room to where Murel stood before a table, engrossed in the contemplation of some object.

"What do you suppose this is for?" she asked innocently, holding up a long, polished piece of wood. Then she giggled in the most engaging way, and Tomas had no doubt that she'd already divined the exact nature of its use.

"Let's get out of here," he said, not wanting her to feel uncomfortable.

But she stepped away from him before he could take her hand and sashayed to the platform. She turned toward him, threw her arms out wide, and fell back into the cushions. "This is absolute bliss." She propped herself up on her elbows to look at him when he didn't reply. "Come on over and test it out, Tomas. I promise not to bite." She patted the bed next to her. "Suit yourself," she said when he remained where he was, and then she laughed and plopped back down.

There was nothing else to do but join her, so he sat on the edge of the platform, and then eased back next to her. As he settled into the mattress, his weight caused the bedding to sink, and Murel rolled toward him. She repositioned his arm and rested her head upon it.

The tension in his shoulders, neck, and back loosened. "This *is* bliss."

"I told you. But then sleeping on the ground the last month may have something to do with it." She sighed and snuggled closer to him. "I don't know how to explain it, but I suddenly don't feel like I'm being hunted or even…"

"Responsible for the fate of the world."

"Yes! That's it exactly. This temple…*this room*…it feels like I should be nowhere else in the world but right here." She lifted her gaze to him. "With you, Tomas."

"I feel the same." He held her, and Murel closed her eyes, and soon her soft snore whispered in and out of his hearing. He held her in his arms as she slept, savoring the nearness of her.

• • •

Murel stretched, coming slowly awake and breathing in Tomas's scent. The first thing she noticed was that their belongings were piled neatly on one of the benches.

"You were napping, so I set up a perimeter for the horses in the entrance hall—they like to wander. I brought up our things on the way back."

"You smell good," Murel said, and nuzzled him. "Bath?"

He nodded. "In the spring. It was cold."

"Did you sleep at all?"

"A little."

An awkward silence stretched as they lay next to each other, staring up at the ceiling. Suddenly, a strangled gurgle interrupted the silence. Murel burst out laughing. "Hungry?"

"That wasn't *my* stomach!"

There was an amused glint in his eyes, and she placed her hand over her abdomen. "No!" Then her body betrayed her again by growling even louder.

"It's been two days since we've eaten anything substantial; we'll both feel better with some food in our stomachs." He sat up and retrieved the saddlebags.

"The good news is that we have enough to last us for at least a week," Murel said when he handed her the pouch from her tack.

"We'll be gone from here before that—I'm positive. We'll have to take some of what is stored down below. I'll find a way to repay whoever put it there once we find Madyan."

"Thank you, Tomas," Murel said. "I don't know what I would've done without you here with me."

"We're a team, Murel. Never forget it." He handed her some dates. "I've been saving this," he said, unwrapping a small, cloth-covered bundle to reveal a large chunk of hard Florestan cheese and several cured meats.

"Is that fideletto sausage?" she asked excitedly.

He grinned. "The best cured venison in all of the Known Realms. I thought you would like a taste of Pheldhain, and there is no better time than this very moment."

"I love you so much, Tomas," Murel blurted out.

He had been about to take a bite and paused. "You haven't said that to me before." His eyes searched hers. "I mean, not like that. That sounded like love-love. You meant love-love, right? I... Maybe you didn't. Oh, you said it because of the fideletto. Being trapped here with m—"

"I love-love you, Tomas."

"I love-love you, too." He paused, looking sweetly nervous. "When I told you before, maybe I said it too soon."

"You didn't." She pulled out a tin box, one that was about the span and length of his hand. She handed it to him. "You brought the sausage from Pheldhain, and I brought something for you. And do you know why? It's because I'm always thinking about you. I see something in a market or eat something new, and my brain wonders if you would like it. Always."

"It's the same for me."

Murel smiled. "And it started long before we came here. At court, I would watch how good you were with Jess and—"

"It was for you. All of it. Jess may be like a brother to me. But it was always for you."

"Open it," Murel said, pointing at the tin.

He pulled at the thread under the wax seal around the box. Then he opened the lid and stared down at the contents. His eyes shined with happiness. "Florestan millemiel. Where did you get this?"

"I wrote to your mother before we sailed. She was only too happy to send you a taste of home. She told me to save it for a time when you needed it most. Actually, she said *we*. And now feels like the perfect moment. The strangeness of this realm…this desert, it's changing us, but not in a bad way. More like a transition, another step away from what we were before sailing here."

"Like when the Fenrhi marked us." He gazed into her eyes. "But this pastry, and the sausage, they anchor us to who we are."

"Exactly." She smiled, but he frowned at her. "What's wrong?"

"I suppose that I'll have to share the millemiel."

Murel burst out laughing and smacked his shoulder. Tomas grinned, then used his knife to lift up one of the honey-soaked pastries. His mother's recipe used a combination of salted walnut meat and honey baked between parchment-thin layers. He handed the first piece to Murel, and she waited until he served himself. "To Floresta," Murel said, holding her square of pastry aloft.

"And Pheldhain," Tomas said.

They each took a bite at the same time. The flavors of honey, the salted nutmeat, and the crisp, thin layers of pastry exploded in her mouth. "S'good."

Tomas had closed his eyes, savoring the flavors of home. They finished their two-bite treats and stared down at the remaining ten pieces. Murel sighed as Tomas reluctantly closed the tin.

"I estimate that we're here for another day or so. And millemiel is a restorative. Besides, it's delicious for breakfast." He placed the tin in his satchel as she wrapped up the remaining sausage. "I brought up some wine from the storeroom."

Murel stretched, and Tomas got up from the bed. Grabbing their bags first to put with the rest of their gear, she walked over to where Tomas was standing by the rest of their belongings. "You found goblets?"

"Mm-hmm. Lots of useful things in that trunk over there." He cracked the wax seal holding the cork in place, then twisted it out of the bottle. After sniffing it, he raised his eyebrows. "I expected vinegar, but it smells mild enough." He poured them each a serving, recorked the bottle, then sniffed the golden liquid. "It smells like wine and something else I can't place."

"Pihaberries, I'm sure of it." She gazed about the chamber. "I have a feeling this place has missed being of use."

He cocked his head at her, and she wondered if he judged her words strange. But he nodded. "I was thinking the same. This will sound odd, but, like you, I sense that we were meant to be here." He took her hand and helped her to climb up on the high bed. Then he, too, climbed up, sitting across from her. "It's like this place needs us as much as we need it."

"So, we can simply relax for now."

"That's the plan." He held out his cup to her, and they tapped them together.

Murel repositioned herself so that she was leaning back against the cushions, and Tomas stretched out next to her. "What do you suppose Jess is doing?"

"Most likely, everything he can to get back here," Tomas guessed. "If the Fyrjians were smart, they would keep him dosed with that mala'eth. He would have seen the storm and known that coming back here would mean his life. But he would try."

They sipped their wine, then Tomas poured a little more. "Do you want to look at the scrolls? Try to unearth some clue as to what we're dealing with?"

"Not really," she replied, surprised by her lassitude. "There'll be time tomorrow morning. Or night. I have no concept of time right now. We slept at night, then slept during the day, then night in the oasis. And then we were drugged and woke up a full day later. I napped..."

"Only for a couple of hours," Tomas provided, yawning.

"It could be midnight out there," Murel went on. "Or midday." She echoed Tomas's yawn with one of her own.

"Then let's pretend it's night and get some real sleep." He took her cup and set it next to his on the table near the bed. "I'm exhausted, and you're exhausted. We can explore this place tomorrow. Open up some of those scrolls."

"Maybe there's a map of the Fyrost," Murel said, scooching down in the bed. Tomas followed suit, and she cuddled up to him and yawned again.

"Good night, Murel." He lifted her chin with his finger and placed a soft kiss on her lips.

She kissed him back and then settled herself closer to his warmth. Her eyelids were so heavy, and she struggled to keep them open. "Good night, my love."

She drifted in and out of near-sleep for a few moments, listening to Tomas's breathing even out and deepen, then finally succumbed.

Strangely, she was aware that she was sleeping. Tomas dozed next to her, softly snoring, and cushions were tucked behind her back. A blanket was pulled up over them, cocooning them together. Then she realized that she was viewing herself from above.

"'Tis an odd dream indeed," she observed, surprised that she was even speaking, for her face in repose remained still and peaceful.

"Because you drank the nectar."

If she'd been awake, Murel would've spun around at hearing the foreign woman's voice. Instead, she turned, as if slowly pirouetting in a dance. "Who's there?"

"Only a shadow," the woman spoke. "A shadow of what I once was."

In the dimly lit chamber, Murel searched for the disembodied voice. And then, slowly, a mist began to form, and a tall and terrifyingly beautiful woman emerged.

"You're naked," Murel said aloud, and a long, flowing gown developed around her. "Are you real or a figment of my dream?"

"I already explained."

"That you are a shadow."

The phantasm frowned.

"The nectar?" Murel asked.

"Now you see. The nectar gives you what you most need."

"More riddles. Are you the goddess?"

"No." She smiled wistfully at Tomas.

"You are part of her corporeal form." Murel finally understood. "Do you have a name?"

She nodded. "As I am of this place, I have been called Mitra. But I am naught but a wisp of that woman who spent time here."

"Please excuse us for disturbing your—"

"It is your very presence here that has permitted me to manifest." Mitra narrowed her eyes, sweeping them back and forth between Murel and

Tomas. She settled on Tomas's blond curls. "You and he are not Fyrjian. How came you to be here?"

"The storm forced us to take sanctuary in your temple. Even now, it is rampaging outside these walls."

The misty image suddenly retracted into itself, disappearing, then reappearing not a few inches from where Murel stood. "He's here?"

"If you mean the Wind God, then yes. That is what we've been told. But another is with him. He holds your bro—lover—the Wind God captive."

For a brief moment, something in Mitra's eyes hardened, and Murel felt her wrath. It was life and death and everything in between.

"You and this man..."

"Tomas. And I am Murel."

"You must love one another very much, for only hearts that are bound can enter this temple." She stepped back, then noticed the markings on Murel's arm—Murel hadn't even realized she was naked. "You bear the chalice, and your man is marked with the rod. Who did this to you?"

"The Fenrhi Artists. Would you like me to tell you about them?"

The apparition touched Murel's arm, then ran her cool fingers up her shoulder, across her collarbone, before settling her hand over Murel's heart. And Murel could sense her knowledge of the Fenrhi seeping into the ghost's awareness.

"I have waited thousands of years for this moment. What you showed me means that I have not been forgotten, nor am I gone. Like the one trapped in the storm, I, too, am another's captive. Do you know this Fanm...Larenne? She who holds my goddess form."

"You should not have taken my memories."

Mitra stepped nearer and regarded her with a frown. "You swore to keep the secret. Why? If I am here, even in this form, it may be possible for her to return."

Murel started backing away from her. "Her? You mean the goddess? That part of you who ripped this world asunder?"

"Do not be afraid, Murel. Without the destruction, you would not exist. You have shown me how far her children have come. You have also shown me their ugliness." She glided over to Tomas and trailed her fingers down his chest to linger over his heart. "But in him, I see your beauty and wonder.

That part of me, the Goddess, she *will* be full of rage, but I may be able to temper her. My success in this is in the hands of the Fyrjians. It is imperative that they separate my love from the betrayer."

"But how?" Murel asked.

"Two vessels are needed. Rottu and Malikáfyr."

"No, not Jess. He's been through so much already."

"Do not be distressed for your brother, Murel, for he will no longer be empty."

"But he will be held captive, like the goddess. Like the Wind God is being used now. You would damn him to be captive for the rest of his days?"

"Hush, child. The Rottu will always be the Rottu, and more. He is an empty cup begging to be filled. Can you deny it? Would you want him to live an unfulfilled life? Through you, I know what was done to him by the man who is filled entirely with bile and hatred for the world. But I also saw who your brother was before his ordeal, and he was never complete. If you were honest with yourself, you would admit that he has always been searching for more."

Murel recalled their childhood. The many adventures they went on—Jess always instigating, she always following. Watching and protecting him, even when they were young. "Say I believe you. How can I be sure he will not be hurt?"

Mitra laughed. "My, but you are strong. You bargain with a shadow, Murel. Nothing can change what is to come. But with your support, the Goddess may grant you a boon. It is your one chance to help the Rottu retain that part of him that makes him your brother."

"How?"

"You and your lover must be there to convince the Fyrjians to accept what is coming. For a millennium, they have prevented the change, and rightly so, for nothing was aligned as it is now. You and Tomas must guide the process. It is their best chance. For no matter your involvement, they will either be healed or consumed. The balance must be restored." Her fading apparition, somehow both shadow and light at the same time, directed her gaze upward to the dark center of the dome. "The light of day will shine down and show you the location of your brother. And the dark of night will illuminate your map and show you the path. Use the time you have here to rest and heal. And most importantly, to love. And when it is time for you to leave, I will find a way to travel with you."

The mist swirled and broke apart until nothing remained. And slowly, Murel felt herself sinking back into her body and the realm of strange dreams and forebodings.

. . .

"How is he still alive?" Danold whispered.

Diarmait kept his eyes closed, and not because he was feigning sleep. No, they remained shut for one reason and one reason only. At heart, he was a coward. He was afraid that the storm had blinded him, and he could not endure this life if he could not see.

"I don't know," Mirra replied. "I wish that I could claim that I healed him...that I have that power, but I do not." She lifted his arm and began unwrapping the bandage from his wrist. "Look at this, Danold. It's extraordinary. A week ago, this exact location was ulcerated. It oozed with pus and infection. I had slowed the progression of his illness but couldn't cure it. And now, it's as if the sickness was razed from his flesh by the very sand that came so close to killing him."

"What are you saying?" Danold demanded.

"I'm saying that whatever happened in his chamber that night healed him by flaying the rot from his body."

Diarmait's mind raced. He'd been healed precisely as the wind and sand had told him. He hadn't imagined the voice. Where his skin was exposed to the air, he felt the soft caress of a breeze as it swept through the chamber. With it came the unmistakable scent of the Fyrost.

"You haven't left his side once," Danold said. "You need to rest."

"I don't want to leave him alone...at least not yet."

"I'll take these trays to the scullery and then return to sit with him. Go on, Mirra. Go get some sleep."

"All right. But if he wakes, please send for me."

"Do you really care that much for him?"

Diarmait waited for her reply.

"Care? When he's shown us nothing but contempt?" she asked in return. "But I will concede that he's grown on me."

She touched Diarmait's head with gentle fingers, then pressed a soft kiss to the bandages. When they finally departed his chamber, locking the door from without, Diarmait exhaled. He tried opening his eyes, but his lids felt glued shut. He would have to wait. Not that he minded, for he had much to ponder. At the top of the list—how to harness the raw power that had swept through his room and scoured the disease from his body.

# CHAPTER THIRTEEN

# The Known Realms

A relentless current pulled at her, grasping fingers that coaxed and gently lured, trying to claim her as she drifted in the water. At the same time, the slithering sifting of sand weighed down upon her, forcing her to succumb to gravity. But Tomas was there, holding her anchored to his side with an arm banded about her waist, saving her from drowning.

· · ·

Murel woke as if floating up and out of her dream. Her first thought was to wonder why she was on her back, being a habitual stomach sleeper. Before she could forget, she pondered her vision-filled sleep. She was relieved to discover that she was clothed, for in her dreams, she and Tomas had been as naked as the day they'd been born. *"Mitra,"* she whispered to the chamber.

Silence.

Across the room, a lone lamp still burned, its horn panels turned to near closed. Murel gave a silent yawn, not really wanting to move or stretch from where she snuggled in the warm blankets. Beside her, Tomas still slumbered, and she took comfort in his smooth and even breathing.

She rubbed her eyes in the dim morning light and—

"Morning!" She shot to a sitting position and stared up at the curved ceiling. Next to her, Tomas grumbled in his sleep, rolling toward her and slinging a heavy arm over her lap. She shook his shoulder, eliciting a growl.

"The sun's barely risen, Murel. Go back to sleep."

"Exactly!"

Tomas blinked his eyes open and sat up, scanning the room.

Murel pointed skyward. In the center of the domed ceiling was a large circle made of thick glass. Only it wasn't mullioned, but one large piece about the span of a person's arms held straight out, like a giant crystal lens. Though it wasn't completely transparent, weak light was able to filter into the chamber. Now and then, a dark mass swept over its outer surface, throwing the chamber into darkness. The storm still raged, blowing sand and dust and blotting out the sun.

"'*The light of day will shine down and show you the location of your brother. And the dark of night will illuminate your map and show you the path*'," Murel repeated aloud.

"Is that some prophecy?" Tomas asked.

"No, Mitra said those words last night."

"Mitra?"

Murel quickly related the details of her dream. The room grew brighter again as the portal to the sky was swept free of the strafing currents of sand. On the floor, the rug was washed with a large circle of light, one that was centered perfectly under the dome.

"Come on," Tomas said, rising and striding across the room. "Let's take a look at what's under this carpet." He lifted the corner. "There's something carved on the floor...a sun and moon." He rolled up the rug and dragged it to the side.

"Is that a trapdoor?" she wondered, pointing to the planking that had been laid out in a circular shape. A single ring was set flush with the thick boards. One side had been carved to represent the sun while the other half, the moon.

"Let's find out. I don't see any hinges, but if those grooves in the floor had been on this side, I would have said they were guide tracks."

"Be careful, please."

He smiled at her warning and then pulled the ring, arm and shoulder muscles bunching. The planking didn't budge. He tried again with more force. Nothing.

Murel studied the faces of the sun and moon, depicted as a man and a woman. An emanating glow had been etched into the stone floor surrounding the sun's half, while rays beamed from the moon's side. "Try moving it to the side. Hold on, I saw something that could help in one of the trunks."

She lifted the lid of the chest near the table with the scrolls and selected one of the thick robes. It had been folded into a bundle with an ornate sash wrapped around it. She next threaded the sash through the metal loop and tugged sideways. The wood circle grated against the stone as it shifted. "The pattern is wrong—the rays from the moon belong to the sun and vice versa."

"You're onto something! Here, let me." Tomas took the sash from her hands and used it to turn the circle. Once realigned, there was an audible click, and the wood popped up. "Stand back. I don't want you to fall." He pulled again, and the circular panel slid up and over the rim, sliding easily along the parallel tracks.

Murel grabbed two large cushions and slid them to the edge of the aperture. She got down on her stomach and inched forward, propping herself up on her elbows to lean over the lip of the hole. Tomas followed her lead. They glanced at the skylight above—it had darkened again.

The sconces below still lit the vast space, as did the large brazier before the statue of the goddess. It was strange looking down at the top of her head. Nothing they saw revealed anything that would give them a clue as to how to find her brother.

"The floor is covered with water," Tomas pointed out.

"All right, Mitra. Help us to see."

"Maybe we should be asking Kardia," Tomas suggested.

"Kardia?"

"If your dream ghost is Mitra and this is her temple, then it stands to reason that we can call her counterpart Kardia, especially as he's the one in the storm."

"Right. Kardia, could you maybe shed some more light for us? Please." The mineral scent of the spring-flooded cavern below wafted up through the opening. With it came the unmistakable spicy scent of the desert. Above them, the crystal eye brightened, and a column of light shone down, bathing them and the hole in the floor with warmth and sunlight. She glanced at Tomas, who smiled and shrugged. "Thanks," she threw out to the entity in the storm, then stared down into the heart of the temple.

"It's a map, Murel! It's…it's…"

"The Known Realms!"

They were directly above the spring. "Remember how the floor was uneven? Look! The places not submerged are land masses—Aurelia, and the Southron Isles over there. And all of Nifolhad below us."

"The spring in the center is this oasis." The stone floors had been stained, and in a rusty hue, the outline of the Fyrost desert was spread below them. "There," she called. "The brazier must be Kardia!"

"If that is where Sophiana lies," Tomas said and pointed, "and that is Naca'an, then we can determine the distance."

"Oh, no. It's so far away. And over there, that must be Palamia. It's half the distance than it is to Kardia. We could make it to Sophiana and secure reinforcements." She paused. "But Jesper."

"I would be lying, if I didn't admit my fear that the two of us alone can't make it to Kardia's temple. But he's your brother, Murel, so you should decide. You already know I would follow you all the way to Mount Kanta and Diarmait's stronghold if you asked." The light streaming through the skylight above them started to dim, and they both turned their attention back to the space below, watching as the outlines and borders of the realms faded away.

Easing away from the hole, Murel sat back on her heels. "I don't think we'll be alone. Mitra said she would find a way to join us."

"A ghost?"

"More of a shadow. I know," Murel said, "it is difficult to believe. But we would not have found this without the vision I had. And then we asked them to share their light. It's probably a coincidence, but…"

"We've seen too many strange events to not take a simple dream seriously." Tomas pushed the wood disc over the opening, twisting it a bit to the side to lock it in place. "No sense closing it completely, as we'll need to open it again this evening."

"Tonight?"

"You said it already, '*the dark of night will illuminate your map…*' Knowing the distance and direction is all well and good, but we could travel northeast in the proper direction, and with no sun to orient us, the dunes will put us off course—we might end up riding in circles."

"And forever lost in the Fyrost. It's important to find Jesper. And Madyan." She frowned, knowing that she was missing something. And then it came to her. "Mitra told me that we must guide the Rottu and the Malikáfyr. It stands to reason that the Fyrjians took Jess to save Madyan. Only, they plan on sacrificing him. They don't know that it's time to finally heal Mitra and Kardia."

Tomas nodded but looked worried. "Let's see what happens tonight first. Then we can make a decision about finding Jesper or seeking more help. In the meantime, you can tell me everything about our nighttime visitor."

Murel nodded, then pressed a quick kiss to his lips.

"What was that for?"

"For making me feel better. For always being positive. Especially as this journey that we're on is the last thing you ever wanted to happen."

"What do you mean? Because the way I remember things, we *both* hoped we weren't going to be pulled into this mysterious prophecy." He took her hands. "Somewhere along the way, I changed my mind, Murel. I welcome any adventure that comes my way, so long as you are by my side." He pulled her into his arms and rubbed her back. "We don't have to decide our course today. Let's see what visions reveal themselves tonight."

"All right."

"I'll go tend to the horses," he added. "Can you copy the map below? You're the better artist."

"I was thinking the same," she said. When Tomas laughed, she swatted his chest. "About drawing a map while it's fresh in our minds."

While Tomas watered and fed the horses, Murel pulled out her notebook and began sketching the borders of the Fyrost, lightly tracing in the three oases. She pictured the way the stone floor had been stained with different colors—the high desert was slightly lighter than the area to the south. The darkest region was along the coast of the Virin Sea to the west. If the stains indicated elevation, then the terrain around Kardia could very well be arid highlands, for its shading was the lightest.

She turned a page and quickly drew what she'd seen of the Southron Isles. It was the one area on the floor that was stained darker than where the water from the spring pooled. It wasn't much, but it might be helpful in the months to come. She heard Tomas's boots coming up the steps and flipped back to the drawing of the desert.

"How are the horses?"

"Content," he said. "Maybe the peace of this place has affected them as well. How is the cartography going?"

"I'm almost done, but I wanted you to take a look before I add ink to the charcoal."

He sat next to her and pointed at her map. "You've added shading for elevation. We have a climb ahead of us if we travel to Kardia."

"Yes." She repositioned the notebook so they could study it anew. "Something is off. I haven't accurately noted the distance between here and Kardia."

"It's pretty close. Why don't we eat something? Then by the time we're finished, the water below will have receded, and we can go down and pace off the distances. And if we use the wall sconces as reference points, we can confirm that the angles are true as well."

They ate a few dates and a bit of dried meat, then drank some water. Tomas grabbed their waterskins to refill, and together, they went back down the stairs. Most of the overflow from the spring had evaporated, and they paced off the distance between Mitra Oasis and Kardia. "What you've drawn is accurate, except where the Fyrost fades into Sophiana."

"Kardia is slightly more south than I drew."

"It's close," Tomas added. "But you're correct. Being even a fingernail's width off could mean we miss the oasis by several leagues." He took her hand, steadying her. "We can do this, Murel. We will find our way."

She leaned into him, taking what strength he offered. "I should draw the Southron Isles—it's the most detailed depiction of the region that I've ever seen. It's even better than what Warin has shared with the king and queen. He'll want to see it when we return to Aurelia."

"You take care of that, and I'll see to refilling the oil reserves down here. We want to be good guests and leave the temple ready for its next visitors."

• • •

As Murel lay on the cushions they'd placed on the floor, she stared up at the domed ceiling, waiting for the light of the moon to reveal the secret to navigating the Fyrost Desert. Tomas had opened the trapdoor so they would be ready to peer into its depths. He sat beside her, poring over the map of the Southron Isles she had copied from the floor below.

"So many islands," he wondered aloud. "I don't think anyone realizes how large that realm really is. I wonder if Captain Grieg ever said anything to Warin."

The orifice at the top of the dome remained dark, and Murel willed the sands above to move and let in the light of the heavens. "I doubt it," Murel finally replied. "Even now that he is banished forever from his home, his honor will not allow him to reveal the truth about its geography."

Tomas set her maps to the side and then reclined next to her. "No change?"

"Not yet. Did you dim the lanterns below?"

"I did. To the minimum level. Did you try asking Kardia again?"

"Asked, prayed, begged."

"Come here," he coaxed, holding out his arm. "Rest your eyes for a bit while I keep watch."

Murel scooted closer to him, resting her head on the crook of his shoulder. She drew lazy circles on his chest, then eventually closed her eyes.

"Murel," Tomas whispered. "Murel."

"*Mmmph.*"

"It's happening. Murel, wake up."

She rubbed her eyes. "What's happening? Oh, the moon." She immediately rolled onto her back and stared up at the black skylight directly above them. "Are you sure?"

"It's possible that I've been looking at the dome for so long that I might've imagined it. But I thought I saw—there!"

Above them, the dark circle brightened. A dusty glow from the moon's beams penetrated the blowing sand above. Murel gasped as the sand disappeared and a beautiful, nearly full moon shone down through the aperture.

Tomas flipped over onto his elbows. "Let's see what the light reveals."

The spring's surface was completely still and reflected the incomplete orb back up at them. "Do you see anything that might guide us?"

"No, only the reflection of the moon. You?" he asked.

"No. Hold on to me." She inched forward, her head and shoulders hanging over the edge as she peered into the dark recesses below. "Nothing," she said flatly, not bothering to hide her disappointment.

"Let's give it some time," Tomas suggested. "I'll keep watch below, and you keep watch above."

Murel scooched back and flipped over to track the hazy shape of the moon. Its brightness would dim and intensify with the shifting of the windblown sands. Slowly, the orb continued on its course, its bright shape disappearing past the rim of the glass above until all that remained was a soft glow. And then the wind must have picked up, for the light vanished altogether when sand once more blotted it out.

She sighed. "That was disappointing."

Tomas stood up to secure the aperture's cover. "We'll think of something."

Murel had a sudden urge to kiss him. "Do we have any wine?" she asked nervously.

"I brought some up to celebrate our eventual escape." He held out his hand to her and pulled her up.

She followed him across the chamber, and then took the wine he'd poured for her and sipped, before offering him a drink from the same cup. His gaze was steady on hers as he swallowed. When he passed the cup back to her, she guided it to the table, her fingers lingering over his. They continued staring into one another's eyes as she traced her fingertips over the back of his hand and up his wrist. She smoothed her hand up his forearm, squeezing and waiting. A tiny lift at the corner of his mouth was her only hint, and then his bicep bulged, turning as hard as a rock. Murel drew a deep breath through her nostrils. "It's not like I haven't seen a man's muscles before, and I don't know why," she drawled, running her hand to his chest, "but when you flex like that, I want to swoon."

"Maybe because when I do it, it's for you alone," he replied. "That day I almost lost you to the tide, I vowed that I would never be weak again. I started training with Warin, and every free moment thereafter, I practiced with my sword and staff."

"No wonder you are so good at it," she mused. "You changed the course of your life...for me. I...I'm humbled."

"I would do it again and more, Murel." He took her hand and set it on his chest, then flexed. "Only for you."

Murel gave him what she hoped was a sultry look. "Take it off," she demanded. "Take it off and do it again."

Tomas stepped back, took a sip of the wine, then propped his hip against the table. He reached down and leisurely pulled up his shirt, revealing one glorious abdominal ridge after another, until finally, he lifted the garment away. He tossed it aside, then crossed his arms over his chest, defining his biceps even more.

Something like a mewl escaped Murel's lips, and he opened his arms to her. "I'm not sure if I should like being objectified like this," he teased, clearly not put out in the least as he flexed his chest muscles in tandem, then one after the other, putting on a show for her. "Perhaps if you were to show me yours, I wouldn't feel so used."

"I don't have any."

"*Mmm.* But you do."

She let him draw off her chemise. Then he ran his hands over her shoulders and arms. "Come on. Your turn. Show me."

Murel could feel a blush flushing over her cheeks, neck, and chest, but she obliged and raised her arm, bending it at the elbow to show him her tiny bicep. He smoothed his fingers over it, cupping the muscle. "See," he said. "You have long, sinuous muscles... They're beautiful." His hands came around and lifted her breasts.

"I'm too curvy," Murel stated. She'd always been slightly embarrassed by her bountiful bosom, especially compared to the other ladies at court.

"Look down, Murel. See how perfectly you fit in my hands, like you were made for me to hold." He kneaded her flesh. "To play with." His thumbs turned up and moved in circles over her nipples. "And to stroke."

Her breasts rose and fell, and for the first time, she was proud of them. She arched her back, watching how his fingers teased her nipples into hard buds. Tomas made her feel beautiful.

"So perfect. I need to taste them," he purred, then dipped down to kiss her nipples while his hands continued to massage.

She watched as his tongue swirled around her areola, and then flicked at her bud, before shifting to her other breast. He brought it higher, then pulled the nipple between his lips and sucked. When Murel's knees buckled, he lifted her by the waist and spun them around to set her on the table. Then he attacked her breasts with his tongue and lips, drawing her into his mouth while his thumb and fingers pinched and squeezed her other nipple.

"You might admire my chest muscles, Murel," Tomas murmured, kissing a trail up her neck until his mouth hovered over hers, "but your breasts made me want to strip you naked every time I saw you at court."

"I always assumed you were the one nobleman immune to them," Murel confessed.

"What do you mean?"

"Most of the men at court are unable to look any higher than my bosom."

"Then I feel sorry for them," he said, and elaborated. "It's not these beauties that I dream about at night, but your smile."

Murel felt her eyes glistening.

"Hey, I'm sorry that we—men, I mean—can be such idiots."

"Thank you. Now be quiet and kiss me."

"As you command." He crushed his mouth to hers.

Slowly, as if on purpose, he pressed his naked abdomen to her stomach. He looped his arm around her waist, drawing her in, until her sensitive breasts met the planes of his rock-hard chest. She managed a gasp in the onslaught of his mouth and tongue, and twined her fingers in his blond curls, angling her head to deepen their kiss.

Tomas growled in a way that vibrated through his chest and went straight to her core. And when he picked her up to carry her to the bed, she wrapped her legs around his waist. He eased her down, following her onto the blankets, and thoroughly ravished her lips and mouth. His arms strained as he held himself above her, and Murel took a moment to run her hands over his triceps. She couldn't help herself. She needed to touch him, to feel him. He lifted and smiled at her. "You're objectifying me again."

"Do you mind? Because I can't seem to stop."

"As long as it's you. And I get to do the same," he replied. "Damn, but you are one curvaceous woman, Murel. Absolutely, perfectly, lushly...mine." He kissed her again. "Before you start worrying, it's not the wine, or the markings, or this place. It's you and it's me. And we can go at whatever pace you want to set. I'm in this with you for life, Murel. So, you can tell me if you would rather wait until we're free of the temple, the desert...hell, even Nifolhad. I will simply content myself with kissing your luscious—"

She pressed her fingers to his lips. "It's not the wine," she repeated. "Nor the markings or even this place. It's you and it's me. And I want you, Tomas. I want all of you. Tonight. Now."

"Then I'm yours." He lowered himself to her side, then kissed her. Deep and penetrating, pulling her passion to him. He nipped along her jaw, then down the column of her neck before burying his face in her ample bosom, turning his head from side to side. He leaned back, propped up on one elbow beside her. His strong hand cupped one of her breasts, and he squeezed and teased and kneaded. His thumb brushed over her nipple, and he stared down at it, as if contemplating how his ministrations were affecting her. His fingers tightened on her flesh, and he leaned forward as he pulled at her, serving her up to his mouth.

Murel hummed as he sucked her, and impossibly, her hardened nipple grew even larger. She gasped when, as he fondled her other breast, he tweaked her a little more forcefully, at the same time drawing her deep in his mouth and nipping. The intoxicating sensation was just shy of pain and so exquisite, it left Murel aching for more. Her hips shifted.

"Please do that again," Tomas begged. "Your body was made to move that way." He skimmed his hand down her side, where he traced lazy circles while his lips and teeth suckled and nipped her breast, slowly moving lower and leaving a trail of kisses down her stomach. He finally stopped at her navel, taking time to pay homage to the indentation, and Murel felt the heat of it shoot straight to that juncture between her legs. She undulated again, and Tomas groaned.

"I need to see all of you."

The way Tomas was worshipping her curves gave Murel courage. Though she was fit, she wasn't lithe and toned like her friends. She smiled at him. "Only if you show me yours first," she teased.

With a cocky grin, Tomas climbed off the end of the bed, and Murel propped herself up on her elbows to watch. He started by undoing the laces of his breeches, letting them ride low on his hips, but not taking them off. With amazing grace and balance, he removed first one boot and then the other. Murel sat up, hugging a cushion to her middle, when he hooked his thumbs in his waistband to tug them a little lower.

She was helpless to do naught but stare at his torso and the deep vee-cut that disappeared into his breeches. She hadn't had a chance to really gauge his size before, but from the way he was straining inside his trousers, he was a large man. More. She needed to see more.

"Do you now?" Tomas asked.

"Oh, dear. I said that out loud, didn't I?"

He twisted around, slowly—shoulders first, then torso, followed by hips—letting her see the interplay of his muscled form until finally, he faced the opposite direction. And, oh heaven above, his posterior was a work of the divine. Murel bit her lip in anticipation as he tugged his garment lower, revealing two identical dimples where his waist met his buttocks. And his back...how had she ignored his back? "Just lovely," she gushed, and he grinned at her over his shoulder as he slowly came around again.

"Remember how I said that I love the way you move?" he asked.

She nodded and swallowed. The cushion she'd been holding fell away, forgotten.

"It looks a little like this." He tensed his abdominal muscles, rolling his torso and hips, undulating all the way up to his shoulders, then releasing the wave back down and up again.

Murel knew her mouth was hanging open when she rose to her knees. Her hand dropped away from her lips and drifted to her breast where she touched herself, half-conscious of what she was doing. She pressed her other hand lower, desperately in need of connecting with the inferno between her legs.

Tomas watched where she touched herself, and a sudden feralness lit his eyes. He brought his dance to a smooth close and stepped forward. Hooking his thumbs into his waistband, he leisurely drew the garment down, revealing the dark blond hair that trailed lower. Then he smoothed his hand up over his still-covered erection, and turning, continued to push his garment lower, over his hips.

"You're teasing me," Murel said in what sounded like a plea.

With his back to her, his breeches came down over the glorious globes of his buttocks, and he bent slightly at the waist as he pushed the snug pants down his muscular thighs, until finally, gravity came to the rescue, and the garment fell about his ankles. He stepped out of his breeches, first one leg and then the other, as Murel ogled him. This man, he loved her. He had the visage of a carved angel, but his body was made for all sorts of deliciously wicked things.

. . .

Tomas wasn't sure what Murel would make of his size. He had allowed rumors of his prowess with the ladies at court to grow to the level of a rake. But they were only that—rumors. Other than one or two dalliances, and not with anyone Murel would consider a friend—or possibly even know—he mostly kept to himself.

Truth be told, the few women he'd been with had found him too large, so he'd spent those few evenings pleasuring them so sufficiently that the lack of consummation was the last thing they would miss. There were what he preferred to call one-offs, consisting mainly of women who ran taverns or inns and had no expectation of forming a lasting relationship. He'd stopped those activities years ago though when word got out at his resting places amongst the female staff about his prodigiousness, and he found himself the object of wagers. He was a challenge for them, and it left him feeling...well, dirty and used.

But Murel, with her soft curves and welcoming body...for her, he would risk trying.

He slowly pivoted on the ball of his foot, his arm down and covering his length and girth. She'd felt him before so had already ascertained that he was large. He didn't know what her past experiences with other men had been, and frankly, he didn't care. But the last thing he wanted to do was to shock her. No, better to conceal himself. Let her discover him by touch and feel. Besides, seeing him up close might make him seem smaller than if he exposed himself from this distance. Less perspective that way.

He approached her on the bed, her one hand clenching and unclenching her breast and the other slowly rubbing herself between her legs. He wasn't even sure if she realized what she was doing, and it was so arousing that his cock twitched like a divining rod in her direction. She bit her lip, and her eyes looked a little glazed, and Tomas wanted to ravish her right then and there. His thighs hit the edge of the bed, and he lifted a knee to climb toward her.

"No," she panted. "I want to see all of you." She stared at where his arm and hand obscured his arousal.

"That's not very fair," he reasoned, admiring her still clad legs. And before he could explain, she hurried to undo her breeches, falling back to peel them off and fling them to the floor.

She scrambled back up to her knees, baring her gloriously naked body. "Can you do that thing again, where you writhe like a serpent? Please."

Tomas thought for a moment that she might be poking fun, but her features were serious, and she was biting her lip again. He undulated his body for her, once more slowly turning in a circle. When he came back around, she was touching herself as she had before. Her chest rose and fell with her heavy breathing.

"Let me see. Please. I need to," she begged.

With infinite patience, he pulled his hand up and away, and his erect member bobbed in her direction. Her eyes widened, and heaven preserve him, she licked her lips.

"You are...magnificent. Come closer. I want to see more."

He stepped back to the bed, watching her eyes for that telltale flicker of hesitancy. But she kept staring in rapt fascination and continued to stroke herself. He reached back down and took himself in his hand, moving it up and down, keeping time with her increasingly deeper delving finger. She grabbed his other hand and placed it on her breast. He squeezed her soft globe, and she moaned. She left him to his own devices and ran her free hand over his shoulder, down his arm to his wrist and hand. He nearly lost it when she placed her delicate fingers over his as he stroked himself up and down.

He massaged her breasts, tweaking her nipples and rolling them between his thumb and forefinger.

"Tomas!" she gasped, while her hand remained in place on his cock. And then she arched her back and screamed his name again as her body bowed and broke into convulsions when her climax took her. She fell backward on the cushions, her eyes squeezed shut, and she struggled to catch her breath. And then she propped herself up on her elbows and smiled at him. "Why are you still standing so far away?"

He climbed up onto the bed and reclined next to her. She rolled into him, then put her hand on his erection. She stroked him, lightly at first. "You're so hard, and yet soft at the same time. And so very beautiful."

Tomas would spend in her hand if he didn't take control, so he rolled forward, pushing her to her back. "My turn to examine you," he insisted. Supported by one arm, he ran his hand over and around her breasts. Everywhere her skin was like silk, everywhere except on the third rib on her left side. He felt the small pucker, the place where, when they were younger, she'd fallen from a tree they'd been climbing and was punctured by a broken branch on the way down. He remembered that day in great detail, how he'd knocked Jesper to the ground for laughing at his sister's clumsiness.

He kissed the scar, and Murel sighed and shifted on the bed. He kissed her again, this time a bit lower. He wanted so badly to taste her, and he gave in to his desire. Murel gasped as his tongue made contact with her still sensitive nub, so he placed his forearm over her stomach and proceeded to lick lower, taking long swipes of her seam. With each stroke, he lapped a little deeper, until he tasted all of her delicious essence. He dedicated his mouth to her center, stroking and sucking, bringing his tongue ever closer to where he knew she was aching for him, but giving her the time she needed to endure what was to come.

When her hips began to move, he knew her to be ready again for his touch, and so he licked, gently at first, then suckling her and drawing her between his lips.

He moved between her spread thighs and pushed them wider with his broad shoulders. And as he feasted, she thrashed her head from side to side. That's when he touched her with his finger, slowly inserting the digit deeper and deeper into her. When she lifted her hips in a matching rhythm, he introduced another finger, thrusting in time with her motions, all the while licking, and stroking, and drawing her deep. She moaned his name and something unintelligible, and he inserted a third finger, thrusting gently and twisting his hand in and out of her body, trying to prepare her for him. It wouldn't be enough, but it would help.

"More," she begged. "Tomas, more. Please. I want you inside me. I want us to be together in every way."

He withdrew his fingers from her tight sheath and gentled his mouth. Slowly, he crawled up the bed, holding himself suspended above her. "I don't want it to, but this will hurt."

She smoothed his brow with her hand and stared up at him, her eyes heavy with desire. "I've heard that about a woman's first time. But I'm stronger than I look. Please, Tomas."

He kissed her, lowering his hips and letting his cock rest in that crease where her hip met her leg. To his amazement, she reached down and touched herself, taking the slick heat from between her legs and transferring it to him. Tomas lowered his body to hers, resting his elbows on either side of her, then positioned himself at her entrance. She stroked him against her cleft and lifted her hips, but Tomas slowed. "Not yet, my love. I need more of you on me. It'll make it easier." He shifted to reach down.

"Let me," she said, and she held him, rubbing him everywhere.

Tomas squeezed his eyes shut.

"Am I hurting you?" she asked.

"No. You're perfect." He kissed her while she continued to make him slick with her juices. "Are you ready? Because much more of this, and I won't last."

Her answer came in the subtle shift of her hips. Slowly, Tomas entered her. An inch, two, more. When she held her breath, he waited until she was ready, kissing her neck and breasts, then pressed forward. More. And then more, until he reached that thin barrier.

"Why did you stop?" she panted. "Oh. This is the part they told me about."

He nodded and pulled out, but not all the way. Then slowly, he slid back to that point, and withdrew again, letting her get accustomed to the rhythm of his thrusts, short though they were. Soon, her hips began to match his movements, and she moaned his name.

She felt exquisite around him, even though he was nowhere near close to being seated within her. "My Murel." She flushed, and her moans grew more ardent. He was on the verge of moving deeper, when she took matters into her own hands, and thrust up her hips.

She didn't exactly yelp in pain, but she chirped and froze with her pelvis lifted off the bed. Her eyes went wide. "Oh. That burns a bit. What do we do now?"

He couldn't help chuckling, and he kissed her forehead, her nose, her lips. "I'll follow you back down…when you're ready."

She bit her lip and slowly, vertebra by vertebra, eased her hips to the bed. Tomas focused on matching her, neither pushing forward nor pulling back.

"You're so tight, Murel."

"Is that bad?" she asked, worry filling her eyes.

"No…no…it's not bad."

"But you look like you're in more pain than I felt."

"Definitely not pain," he said.

"What next? Because that can't be it. Oh no, it is, isn't it? I'm sorry. It was very nice and—"

Tomas stopped her from saying more with a deep kiss, one that had her tongue entwined with his. Carefully, he shifted the weight of his upper body to one arm and reached for her breast with the other. He continued kissing her and massaging her breast, rolling her nipple. He ran his mouth to her neck and up to nibble on her ear. Beneath him, her muscles loosened, and he thrust a little deeper, then withdrew, but not completely. He rocked her forward again, and she moaned into his mouth as he kissed her.

"Oh, I see. Yes. This is much better. Ooh," she moaned, and her hips began moving in time with his again.

Still balanced on his elbow, Tomas continued to fondle her breast as he thrust forward. He skimmed his hand down her waist, reaching between them where he could touch her, finding her wetter than before. She was panting, and when he connected with where their bodies were joined, she groaned in pleasure. He plucked, gently strumming her most sensitive nub, watching her as she grew closer and closer to coming apart. When her orgasm broke, she arched her back, thrusting her hips toward him and crying out into the domed bedchamber. It was the sweetest sound Tomas had ever heard. She drifted back down, and he once again followed her.

After a few minutes, she opened her eyes and stared up at him. "That was...amazing." She ran her hands over his shoulders and down his arms, where he still held himself above her. "You can let go. You won't crush me." She put her hand on his cheek and then kissed him, long and slow. Still buried in her, his cock twitched. She pulled back, her eyes wide.

"Uh, Murel..."

Before he could finish, she reached down and touched him where he was seated within her. Her hand glided up his length to his body, and her eyes widened even more. "That's not fair," she stammered. "I mean for you."

"There's no fair or unfair in this, Murel. I love you and—"

"Stop," she put fingers to his lips. "I love you, too. And I meant what I said when I told you that I want all of you."

She caressed him up and down his exposed length, and Tomas groaned. "Please, Tomas. I want you to lose yourself in me like I lost myself in you. Please." She kissed him again. Her tongue dallied with his, and then her mouth was on his neck and collar, licking and sucking and scraping her teeth on his skin. Her hands weren't idle, running all over his back and sides, until she reached for his buttocks and tried pulling him closer. She adjusted her hips, angling them to take him deeper.

"Use your heels," he managed, as his control began to fray.

"Ohhh," she said, on a sigh filled with pleasure, then dug her heel next to his thigh. Her hands reached as far as she could, grabbing his buttocks and urging him to rock forward.

Tomas moved, a tiny bit, then withdrew. She pulled him up again, and he plunged a bit deeper than before. Below him, Murel's hands were wild, touching him and fondling herself. He lowered his head to take her breast in his mouth again, and she gasped.

"Harder," she demanded. "Suck harder."

He obliged, stoking her fire again, heightening her pleasure once more. He drew her nipple into his mouth, sucking hard, and then he bit down, just a little.

"Yes. Again." He moved to her other breast, drawing her abundant flesh into his mouth and pressing and lashing her with his tongue, all the while moving in and out of her warm sheath, a little deeper with each thrust. Murel was panting and gasping below him, her hands touching them where they were connected, and her heels now urging him deeper and deeper. Her hips thrummed, and she lifted herself more with each plunge. "Harder, Tomas. Oh, it's happening again! Harder, please. I need...I need..."

"Tell me!"

"I need..."

"What? What do you need?" He felt her fingers on his cock, still not completely sheathed within her. "Tell me!"

"All of you. Oh, all of you." She planted her feet on either side of his hips and pushed up. "Now. Deeper! Take me all the way!"

Tomas thrusted then, filling her all the way to the hilt. And she took him, all of him. And he rocked harder and harder against her. He reached down and hooked his arm under her knee, opening her even more. And plunged. Again. Again.

She thrashed and writhed below him. "Harder! Yes! Oh! Tomas!" She flung her arms wide, arching her back again.

Driving into her, his hips pumped faster and deeper than he had ever done before with a woman. He pushed her over the edge, and she screamed his name as her muscles quivered and spasmed around him. And with another thrust, he followed her, shouting, "Murel!"

He collapsed on top of her, his hips still bucking as he rode out the most intense climax of his life. She wrapped her arms around him, her fingers clenching and grasping his back. He set his lips gently to hers, then slid to the side, his leg and arm draped over her. Their bodies were slick with sweat, so he reached down to pull a blanket over them.

"That was...I have no words."

"Did I hurt you?"

"No. I mean a little at first, but later, no. It was perfect. Never hold back with me again," she ordered. She shifted to her side so that she could smooth back some of the hair that fell onto his forehead. "It was so much better than I ever fantasized it would be with you."

"You've been fantasizing about me?"

She bit her bottom lip. "You haven't?"

"You have no idea. And that night at the inn?"

She blushed.

"Tell me."

"I called your name and kept silent, merely to hear you say mine," she confessed. "And you said it...twice. I love your voice. It seems to vibrate...deep within me."

He kissed her. "I like watching you touch yourself," he professed, running his fingers lightly over her. "Stay here; I'll be right back." He rolled over and swung his legs off the bed. After grabbing a soft cloth, their wine, and one of the waterskins, he made his way back to her. She stretched and yawned. He dampened the cloth, then looked into her eyes for permission. She pulled back the blanket, and he wiped away the scant smudge of blood from her thigh. As gently as possible, he cleaned between her legs, noticing her slight wince. When he finished, he handed her a glass of wine, and she sipped. She yawned again, and Tomas took her cup and set it aside, then reclined back, drawing her to his body. He pulled up the blankets, and she snuggled next to him, finding a comfortable position. Within minutes, she fell into a thrice-sated sleep. Tomas stared up at the darkened dome, thanking whatever gods and goddesses who were listening for the gift in his arms. And then he, too, drifted asleep.

# CHAPTER FOURTEEN

# The Storm's Eye

The colors and sounds were simply too fantastic to be real. It was a strange sensation, not unlike the evening before when Murel had conversed with Mitra. Above her, though, the light from the full moon cast its beams down upon the bed, washing her in its milky glow. Another aspect of her dream state, for the dome above was so clear that she could pick out the individual stars.

Mitra was nowhere to be seen. Tomas lay next to her, and Murel took her time studying the man in his repose. She reached over, running her hand over his muscled arm—she could never seem to get enough of touching his beautiful physique. When separated, she found herself longing for the low rumble of his voice.

He stirred, then reached for her hand, tugging it lower to where his arousal had grown—and again, Murel wondered how much of this was a dream. She got up on her knees and stroked him, and he in turn applied feathery touches to her body.

"Murel," he whispered into the night. With infinite care, he lifted her by her hips and settled her over him. She straddled him and leaned forward, resting her palms on his chest. Tomas's eyes had yet to open, but he guided her hips down and forward, helping her to grind against him. The sweet pressure grew and grew in intensity, until she could no longer wait, and took his arousal in her hand to guide him to her entrance. She lifted away and settled down around his shaft, again and again.

She rode Tomas. For how long, she didn't know, for there was no passage of time in her dream, only the relentless slipping in and out, and the stoking of her passion. He encouraged her to take him deeper, and she experienced a new level of sensation. She continued their dance, her hands still braced on his chest. He was staring up at her in wonder, and a strange glow surrounded their bodies, one emanating from their hearts. As their combined passion grew, their auras pulsed, as if one with their heartbeats, and those pulses lifted her hair—and his—so that their locks twisted and waved in a miniature cyclone created by their lovemaking. Tomas's fingers tightened on her as her pleasure burgeoned, intensifying her motions and rushing her, pushing her, until they were both barreling headlong to their combined release.

"Murel!" he shouted.

"Tomas!" she cried out at the same time, climaxing and flinging her arms wide. She was aware of every pore on their joined bodies, every strand of hair. And as her chest rose and fell, sparkling motes of light popped on and off as if moonbeams became physical matter around them. Tomas gazed wonderingly up at her with rich brown eyes full of love. He reached up to caress her face, then settled his hand on her heart—they were sharing this dream.

She rested her hand on his chest, and he smiled, then closed his eyes and drifted back to sleep. Around her, their auras had ceased pulsing and now eddied slowly about them, settling and lifting again, as if she were being caressed. Her hair finally wafted down, but the sense that time was suspended continued.

She was still joined with Tomas, when she realized they were no longer alone in the chamber. "This isn't a dream, is it?" she asked. "Did you do this? Did we make love because of you?" she asked when a shadow in the corner stirred.

"No," Mitra answered, slowly coalescing, and Murel wasn't sure if the answer was to one or all of her questions. "But your union with Tomas allowed us to be together, for a short while at least."

A hand rested on Mitra's shoulder, and briefly, the outline of a man stood behind her. "Kardia," Murel breathed, and his wavering form strengthened at the pronouncement.

"He is already fading," Mitra said, covering his hand with hers. "We felt your love and remembered our own. And it made us stronger."

"The glow, was that your doing?"

"It was a gift that we gave in exchange for the one you gave us. You are unhappy. Why?"

The outline of Kardia was all but gone, and Mitra turned to kiss the hand on her shoulder. When he disappeared altogether, a great sadness filled Mitra's eyes.

Murel tempered her anger before replying, "A gift is not a gift when it is not freely given, Mitra."

"This has no meaning. Would you not have wanted to help us?"

"No. Yes. But not that way. What is between Tomas and I cannot be shared. *Should* not be shared."

"We only wanted to increase your pleasure and to heal you from your earlier lovemaking. He is quite endowed, for a man."

Murel wondered again about this dream that wasn't a dream. She had felt no burning, no ache or soreness. "Still, it is not a gift when a thing is given for something taken in exchange."

"This I understand. A trade was made."

"And an agreement must be made before a trade is realized," Murel added.

Mitra seemed to weigh this and then nodded. "Did you find the map and route?"

"The map, yes. But the moon revealed nothing of the path below."

Mitra shook her head. "To understand your path, you must look up, not down." She stood and reached out to smooth down Murel's tresses. "There. That is better. You are now prepared to receive the gift that I will give you tomorrow."

"But I do not—"

"I understand your concern," Mitra reassured. "This is a true gift. A part of the Fyrost. Not a trade. Don't forget, seek the moon and the stars to find the path." And then Mitra faded away.

Murel looked down, for she was still astride Tomas. She could still feel him inside her, heavy and large against her womb. Her aura flared, and then a moment later, it faded.

"Go to sleep, Murel."

She drifted forward, settling on Tomas's chest, then sliding off him to his side. Her eyelids drooped, and she was suddenly cocooned under the blankets next to him. Sleep pressed her mind, and she wondered if they would remember what had taken place.

• • •

Murel woke to a gray, anemic light coming through the dome's eye—for that's how she now thought of it, as if it kept a constant watch. She was naked and curled up next to Tomas. Rubbing the sleep from her eyes, she tried to process what had happened during the night, more assured than ever that their lovemaking had not been a dream.

Beside her, Tomas stirred. She sat, pulling the blankets with her, and leaned back against the wall. She ran her fingers through her hair, pushing it back and behind her shoulders as she pondered the conversation with Mitra.

"Good morning," Tomas murmured.

"Morning," she replied after a moment.

He sat up next to her, taking her hand in his. "That took some time. How are you feeling?" he asked. "Are you...hurting?"

She lifted his hand to kiss his knuckles. "I'm not sore in the least. Another unasked-for gift from Mitra."

"Mitra? Last night..." Tomas closed his eyes and frowned. When he opened them, he stared at the bed. "These extra blankets...they weren't here last night. Did we? You? We made love again," he finished. "It wasn't a dream."

"No, it wasn't a dream," she confirmed.

"And this upsets you..."

She turned to him then. "I could never be upset about that. Never," she repeated. "Mitra was here. And Kardia, though he was as weak as this morning's light. They gave us some encouragement. She called it a gift. Something in exchange for what they took from us."

"That's not a gift, then," Tomas pointed out, saying it aloud to the chamber as if Mitra was still there.

"I already told her," Murel said with a soft chuckle.

"Er, what sort of encouragement? And what did they take?"

"She healed me, for one. And when we made love…I don't know how to describe it…"

"We glowed," he said, remembering. "That seems harmless enough, considering our friends. But it's not, is it?"

"I'm afraid not. You fell back asleep, and Mitra and I talked. About the difference between a gift and a transaction. About how Kardia was able to make a brief appearance… Our love made it possible for them to be together. She told me how to find our route, that we had to try again tonight. We got it wrong, Tomas. We needed to look up to find the way. And that means being in the main chamber below, not up here. She said to seek the moon and the stars to discover our path."

At her comment, the dark, swirling dust above them lessened, and the room brightened. Tomas gasped. "Murel, your hair!"

"My hair?" She grabbed a lock of it. "What's wrong with my—" Her near black Pheldhainian mane was frosted white. She pulled more forward, and everywhere, the same. Wrapping a blanket around her, she went to stare at herself before one of the many reflective surfaces in the bedchamber. It was as if someone had threaded her hair with strands of fine silver. Underneath, her dark tresses peeked out. "What kind of hell-cursed gift is this?" she demanded. "I look like—"

"Madyan," Tomas finished for her.

She spun around. "I was going to say a skunk. But you're right." Her eyes flew to Tomas's. "She touched my hair. She said she gave me a piece of the Fyrost and that I was now prepared for another gift. I thought she meant showing us the route." Murel shouted to the chamber, "No more gifts! I don't want them!"

Tomas drew her into her arms, and Murel was helpless to stop herself from doing the one thing she absolutely hated. She cried. Great heaving sobs. Tomas simply held her. "This realm," she gulped. "It takes and takes and takes. Our friends, my brother. It's changed us too much already." His arms tightened around her until her tears dried and she only gave the occasional sniffle.

"It's also given us one other gift."

She looked up at him.

"Each other." He kissed the top of her head. "And your hair is beautiful, no matter the color. Besides, the contrast always lent an air of mystery to Madyan." He rubbed her back. "Come on. Let's dress and then pack. From the way the sunlight is streaming through, I would hazard that the storm is finally giving up on us. We'll want to be ready to leave tomorrow."

"Oh, heavens," Murel swore. "Your hair...it's touched with silver, like mine. I couldn't see it until the chamber brightened because the color is already so pale."

He sighed. "There's nothing to be done about it now. I suggest we dress and then provision our packs—we'll need to carry as much water as possible. Then we can wait for the night to reveal our path, rest, and pray that we can break out of this temple in the morning."

They spent the day seeing to their gear and the horses, cleaning the entrance hall by sweeping and moving the storm debris to the portal so that it would be easier to carry outside when they opened it. While Tomas replenished the sconces' fuel reserves and straightened the storeroom, Murel unrolled a few scrolls. She couldn't decipher what was written, so she copied a few, then made a drawing of Mitra's statue with Kardia behind it. She slipped to the stairs that led to the bedchamber and sketched some of the diagrams that were of a more private nature, blushing as she went along.

When the light from the dome began to wane, Tomas joined her in the bedchamber. Together, they opened the trapdoor, and then made their way to the lower level. They'd already doused most of the sconces. The spring had ebbed, so they set out their sleeping rolls on the floor to rest side by side, staring at the ceiling.

After some time, they stopped talking. Tomas squeezed her hand.

"Did I fall asleep?" she asked.

"Only for a short while. It's starting." He pointed to the aperture above them.

First, there was a soft glow, then an increasingly larger piece of the full moon as it filled the skylight. She grabbed her notebook and charcoal and waited.

"It's so bright," Tomas said. "The storm must surely be gone."

When the aperture was completely filled, an amazing thing began to happen. The opening in the floor above acted as a lens and focused the beam directly onto the pool made by the spring. The light hit the still surface and bounced back to the ceiling.

"It's the heavens, Tomas," Murel whispered. "The builders of this place must have set crystals in the ceiling to catch the moonlight." She pointed. "Do you see those five stars? They make up the weeping sisters that Claire told me about. And that's the Boar's Eye!" She began to quickly sketch the constellations, marking the ordinal positions for east, north, west, and south.

"If we align ourselves with those two stars," Tomas noted, "we can navigate the desert at night and find Kardia."

"And my brother and Madyan."

Above, the moon was already passing over the temple's lens, and the crystals dimmed. Murel looked south, studying the ceiling above the Southron Isles, and furiously sketched the other constellations.

"Did you get it all?" Tomas asked.

"I hope so. I don't know why, but I thought it important to capture the night sky over the Isles."

She tucked her things back into her bag, and they rolled up their bedding to set with the rest of their gear. Then, they headed back up the stairs that led to the chamber above to sleep for what would hopefully be their last night in the temple.

"Mitra?" Tomas called to the dark recesses of the chamber.

"She's not here. Maybe because Kardia has departed with the storm. I think she's giving us our privacy."

"That's good because, seeing as this may be the last time for a long while that we sleep in a real bed, I plan on making love to you."

"I was hoping you would say that," Murel said, drifting into the embrace of his arms. They stayed up as long as possible, knowing they would sleep in late so as to be ready to once again travel by night. Eventually, they fell asleep, sated and holding one another.

• • •

Tomas woke first to a chamber brightened by sunlight. Murel in repose was as beautiful as ever, and he gently brushed back a lank of her silver-kissed hair. He hadn't been bothered by dreams during the night, and Murel's features were the epitome of a peaceful slumber. She shifted, slowly coming awake, and he kissed her forehead, the tip of her nose, then her lips, and she hummed her appreciation.

He drew back. "Blue skies above."

Murel opened her eyes, and she smiled before facing him.

Tomas reared back, jumping from the bed. She followed him, leaping toward him and turning to stare at the blankets. "What is it?" she cried.

To his ears, it was Murel's voice. He managed to hold his ground when she took a step toward him. Not wishing to cause her more alarm, he resisted flinching when she set her hand on his arm.

"You're scaring me," she said regardless.

"I'm sorry, it's just that..." He took her hand and drew her to the center of the room where the light was best. "Your eyes were glowing purple, like amethysts. They're blue again, but different. It's like I can see the color of the goddess's eyes in yours."

Murel stumbled back to the bed. She sat heavily. "Her parting gift, except it's anything but." She looked so helpless.

"Was she here again last night?" he asked.

Murel set her hand over her chest. "No, she's here with us now."

"With us?" Tomas demanded, though he already knew the answer.

"Mitra said she would find a way to journey with us. Two nights ago, she said she would prepare me, and then this happened." Murel raked her hands through her hair.

"Who am I talking to right now?"

"It's me. Murel. I can't explain it, except to say that she is here, too. In the recesses of my mind. Like a shadow, hovering out of reach."

"Can you communicate with her? Does she know your thoughts? Can you—"

"Stop!" Murel cried. "I don't know. It's not like this has ever happened to me."

He checked his anger and sat next to her, wrapping his arm around her shoulders. "I know, I'm sorry. This all sounds suspiciously like something that the Kena of the Fenrhi could do, manipulating a person to control their actions.”

“It’s not like that. Mitra isn’t controlling anything. These are *my* words and *my* actions. I promise. It’s like she’s a…a passenger.”

“You’re sure?” he asked. “Because—and I’m talking to Mitra now—if you harm one hair on Murel, I will personally see to it that you are trapped in this temple for another thousand years.”

“Maybe not my hair, since that ship has sailed,” Murel joked.

“Everything else, then,” he said, taking her hand in his.

“I believe she wants to help us. You know how I feel protected when I’m with you? I get that same sense from Mitra.”

“Just promise to tell me if that feeling changes.”

“I promise.” She leaned forward and kissed him. He deepened the kiss, his tongue playing court with hers.

Murel shifted around, swinging her leg over so that she straddled his thighs. They continued kissing, and when she reached down to stroke him, he fell back against the cushions and touched her in turn.

“Tomas,” she moaned, and then gazed down at him.

“Absolutely not!” He lifted her and tossed her unceremoniously onto the bed.

“What’s wrong?” she demanded.

“Your eyes glowed purple. You may be in complete control, but Mitra is definitely aware of what is happening to you. Until she’s gone, I…we…”

Murel flopped back and threw her arm over her eyes. “I understand.”

He took her wrist and pulled her arm away. Her eyes when she gazed back at him were their usual blue. “What is between us…it’s ours. Not Mitra’s. Not Kardia’s. Ours.”

She heaved a sigh and pouted. “Thanks, Mitra,” she said to the room. “Come on, then. Let’s get dressed and out of here.”


...


Murel stood by the main pool and spun in a slow circle to inspect the damage. “So much for collecting any dates for our trek,” she complained.

It was already late afternoon, and she and Tomas had spent hours clearing away enough of the detritus piled against the portal to lead the horses through. Once outside, they spent a few minutes simply staring up at the azure skies and breathing in their newfound freedom. Then they got to work again, moving dead branches and splintered tree trunks, piling everything behind the small olive grove. Amazingly, except for one or two casualties, the wizened fruit trees had mainly survived intact.

Tomas was using a branch to drag palm fronds floating in the pool toward the edge where he could haul them out. "Look what I found!" He walked over and presented her with a palm frond. Tangled up in the spiked leaves was a cluster of dates. "Not a total loss, after all. Dates from the Fyrost…fruit fit for royalty." He paused. "Ah, sweetheart, what's wrong? Why are you crying?"

"Am I?" She touched her cheek. "This destruction… It's so very sad."

"Maybe that's a little bit of Mitra's feelings that you're sensing." He set the dates aside and pulled her into his arms. "This place has seen more storms than we can ever conceive; it will survive this."

Murel nodded, and at his assurances, the melancholy she'd been feeling melted away.

"Good. I think we've done enough. The temple is tidied and sealed up, and the horses are settled. Let's eat a couple of these dates, drink some wine, and rest. We have a long night ahead of us."

"That sounds like as good of a plan as any," Murel agreed.

. . .


## Kantapan Castle, Mount Kanta

"Danold," Mirra whispered somewhere to the left of his bed. "Danold. It's my turn to sit watch. Go find your chamber and get some sleep."

Diarmait, eyes sealed closed, heard Danold walking over to him, sensed him staring down at him as he feigned unconsciousness.

"I'll help you change the bandages."

"There's no need. I can handle it."

His son groaned, and Diarmait heard joints popping as Danold stretched.

"I'll see you later this evening. Do you need anything from the servants before I hit my bed?"

"Just the usual fresh linens. These will need changing. And can you have them send up some broth?"

"Sure...if he wakes..." Danold said, yawning.

His son's footsteps retreated across the room, and he heard the door's latch being secured. Mirra came to stand by his bed.

"Let's see if we can't clean you up a bit. Starting with your eyes. You'll never get them open if I don't clean away the dried honey. I imagine that it's painful."

Did she realize that he was awake? He didn't acknowledge her.

"Come now. I can tell that you are listening. What did you expect to hear, old man? That we spent days keeping you alive, cleaning you and changing your soiled bandages and linens, only to plot some nefarious act against you?"

He remained unresponsive.

"We could easily smother you with a cushion or simply let you starve. Heaven knows you've never given us cause to do otherwise."

Diarmait grunted at her comment.

"Was that an attempt at laughter? So, I found you out. Now we can work on getting you strong. Your linens need changing, but first, your eyes. You're most likely frustrated that you can't keep watch on us."

"Piss," he managed in a gravelly voice.

Mirra pulled back the sheets. "Well, look who hasn't made a mess of the bed. Still, this was easier when you were unconscious," she warned, and then began adjusting the bandages that covered his genitals. She eased a chamber pot in place and held him. "Go ahead."

Diarmait would've cried with relief at the sensation of emptying his bladder, but he couldn't open his damn eyes. When he was finished, Mirra adjusted his bandages and dumped the urine into a privy pail. "No blood in it this time, but still too dark. We need to give you something more than water today. It's why I ordered the kitchen to make a hearty marrow broth."

He heard her step away. "Just warm water and soft cloths," she explained. "The honey and balm I used to treat your burns dried and glued your eyelids shut." She sat on the edge of the bed. "I'm going to apply warm compresses to soften the crust, then we'll see to cleaning it away."

She repeated the process several times. "Just a little longer. Let me wipe this gumminess away from your lashes. Your flesh was burned, and I'm not sure if your eyes were damaged. Can you sense light?"

"Yes." His answer came out in a hoarse grumble.

"That's good. I have to caution you, if the sand abraded your eyes, then it might be some time before you can see clearly." She paused in her ministrations and set her hand on his shoulder. "I don't want you to worry that it might be permanent. Now, your eyelids are a bit chafed, so I'm going to put some liniment oil on them to soothe away the redness. All right, I'm finished—you can open your eyes when you feel ready."

He furrowed his brow, scrunching his eyes tight, then slowly, bit by bit, opened them.

Mirra hovered over him. "Bloodshot," she said. "But your irises are clear and blue." She peered at him. "There doesn't seem to be any damage. Can you see?"

He gave a slight nod.

"Good." She sat next to him and carefully unwound the bandages from his fingers and forearm. She lifted his arm, holding his wrist and hand aloft. "Fresh as a newborn, Father. Even your sores are gone." She gently rotated his wrist, showing him his newly grown skin.

Diarmait tried to recall what the storm had whispered to him. "I had to die first," he rasped to himself.

"Yes, Father. You died," Mirra soothed, patting his shoulder. "Now rest, like a good patient."

Diarmait focused his cold blue stare on his daughter. Before she could react, his hand whipped out to slap her. She yelped in surprise at the stinging blow and scrambled backward off the bed. "You will address me as your king, for I am reborn."

His cackles chased on her heels as she fled from his chamber.

# Race and Ruin

Even at night, the heat of the sunbaked earth pulsed, as if the Fyrost were one massive heart. Tomas pulled up beside Murel where she sat atop her Fyrjian horse, and together they stared out over the rim of the dune. As he cracked his neck from side to side, stretching in his saddle, Murel took stock of her own physical state—stiff, but no longer aching, and her sit bones had gone numb several days past.

Under the light of the waning moon, she consulted her notebook, comparing what she'd drawn to the stars. "We should ride to that ridge," she said to Tomas, "the second highest one, then recalibrate."

"We didn't need your notes to tell us that," he said. "Take a look."

Spread below them, spearing out from the oasis in a straight line, was the aftermath of the sandstorm. "No wonder the clean-up was so easy," Murel said in awe. "Now we know where the missing palm fronds and branches are. Is that a tree?"

"It is. And transplanted upside down."

He nudged his horse forward, and Murel followed. The going was slow at first, the sand being recently redistributed and loose. They eventually made it to the top of the ridge and reset their course, veering slightly south from the path of ruin. Tomas sat up in his stirrups, narrowing his eyes to better see into the distance. They were not traveling a direct route to the Kardia oasis, as they needed to replenish their water along the way.

"Good thing you were able to link some of the lower areas on the temple's floor to signs of desert springs," Murel said. "I prefer our puddle jumping to following the storm."

"Agreed. And as long as the springs are not buried, we should just be able to make it to Kardia without running out of water."

They rode through the night and into the morning, then pitched a canvas canopy in the lee of a dune and waited out the day, sharing the shaded space with the two horses.

"We're not being pursued anymore. Can you feel it?" Tomas asked when he roused her so that he could take his turn at rest.

"No, but...there's this strange draw in my chest, like a rope that's being stretched too far."

"Where's the other end?"

"Back at the Mitra Oasis."

"I imagine every step we take farther from her temple is difficult for her," he said, gazing deep into her eyes, as if he were speaking to both Murel and Mitra. "Uncomfortable."

Murel nodded. "Try to get some sleep. I'm going to stretch my legs."

As she climbed the dune, moving farther away from the temple, she felt the weight of Tomas's observation. The sun was behind her now, and she was grateful for the light desert garb given to them by Sefrina. Though it was late afternoon, the heat was intense enough still that she pulled her hood up to protect her head.

*He is remarkably astute, your man.*

"Mitra," Murel greeted, sitting on the rim of the dune. "I wondered when you would talk to me."

*I waited until your anger subsided. I did not understand it at first. Did you not seek my aid?*

"Your help, yes," Murel said. "But you could have asked before possessing me."

*Possessing? Is that what you think? The entity residing in her laughed. This is not possessing, Murel. I promise you, you would know if I was doing more than simply riding along. Sharing is a better word.*

"Sharing, then. Still, you should warned me." Murel stared ahead at the rolling sea of dunes, the sun burnishing them in bronze and gold.

*Is my desert still beautiful?*

"You cannot see it?"

*That is the difference between possessing and sharing. I can sense your feelings and thus converse with you this way. I sense Tomas's as well—it must be through your bond. But I cannot see the beauty of the desertscape or appreciate the texture of the sand under your fingers. Nor can I hear the voice of the wind or smell the heat of the sun at your back. It stirs your emotions, and that in itself is exhilarating.*

Murel sighed. "Would you like to see?"

*You would do that for me? You would trust me enough to let go?*

"Yes."

*I should not, Murel. I may not be able to give up what you will allow.*

"Then I trust Tomas to help me find my way back. It would give me peace to gift this to you." Murel closed her eyes. She didn't need to speak the words to let Mitra know that she was ready.

A moment later, Mitra soaked in her desert. Murel's human eyes beheld the expansive vistas in an entirely different way than Mitra could have ever imagined, adding to the majesty and wonder of the landscape. She scooped up a handful of sand, watching the tiny grains wink and sparkle as they sifted from between her fingers, catching on the light breeze. Dust and heat had never smelled so lovely as they did now.

Her sun was glorious in its setting, picking out layer upon layer of dunes in an ever-changing palette of hues as the day transformed into dusk, and the stars winked on one by one until the heavenly sparks shone down upon them.

"Thank you for this gift," Mitra said.

*You are welcome.*

Mitra closed her eyes to the splendor for which she longed for centuries. Though she wanted the opposite, she tucked herself back in Murel's mind. *You should ready the horses. Your man will wake soon, and you must make better time this evening. You must push your steeds if you are to survive. Once they sense the spring toward which you ride, you will not be able to curb their desire for water.*

"But they were not born in the desert; they do not know the way."

*Perhaps not, but they possess the instincts of a fyrjór. It is time to stop chasing the storm; we must arrive at Kardia before it.*

"How does one travel faster than the wind?"

*By distracting what drives it forward.*

"Kardia?"

*Thanks to you and Tomas, he is aware again, and he will do what he can.*

• • •

The Fyrjians weren't taking any chances, and Jesper was helpless to do anything but swallow the soporific draught they poured down his gullet. Swallow or drown, Sefrina had said. In his stupor, his instincts had kicked in, and he reflexively gulped down the drugged mead.

After his second—no third—escape attempt, they had kept him contained in his own brain. He supposed his plan to ride back and find Murel and Tomas was a futile one; he would never have survived the Fyrost on his own, let alone the storm that'd been heading toward them until it suddenly veered north. Sefrina had chastised him for wanting to throw away his life. What did she know? The dosed quaff made him a walking corpse. Awake, able to sit in a saddle if tied to it, but unable to otherwise move. They fed him; his body swallowed. They led him behind some stone outcropping; his bowels and bladder emptied. He couldn't string more than two slurred words together. But he could think. And plan. At least when he wasn't dozing, which seemed to be most of the time.

That's when he figured out how to beat them. For as they watched his every move, so, too, did he watch theirs. They only dosed him when they sensed that he was too aware, being able to curse them being one major predictor. When next he came to, he feigned stupor, even letting someone clean his arse—it had almost proved his undoing. But it had been worth it, for he now had nearly two hours of clear-headedness between the draughts they gave him. And when he caught Sefrina studying him, he added acting up to his repertoire to allay suspicions.

Jesper struggled to keep from smirking. His plan had been successful; for even Sefrina—as they'd climbed the hill to the massive fortress ahead— had taken to ignoring him.

Even if the frequency of the dosing hadn't lessened, Jesper had a hunch that he was slowly becoming immune to its effectiveness. His ability to remain aware of his surroundings lasted longer and longer, and so did his control over his muscles. When, once inside the fortress, they had secured him into a large wood trough, he hadn't resisted. It was the one time he'd lost control of his carefully constructed façade. They pushed him over the edge of what he feared was a bottomless pit. His heart dropped as gravity took hold of the trough. Those two or three seconds of freefall had lasted a lifetime, and then the ropes caught and the contraption jerked to a stop. Only their inattentiveness had prevented them from seeing his abject horror and his white-knuckled grip on the trough as he was plunged into the dark for those brief moments.

Quick to recover, he had stared dully at the Fyrjians standing so casually along the rim of the hole. And then, chains clinked, and ropes creaked as his sled was sedately lowered. When he was sure they could not see, he peered over the edge into the pit. It was a long while before a faint light grew, and he discerned that the glow came from strange plants sprouting from the walls, lending enough illumination to reveal that steps had been carved into the natural, near-perfect vertical corkscrew within the tube. That was when he began formulating his escape from the depths of the mountain and its vast subterranean city.

But that had been weeks ago, and now, he glared at the Fyrjian guard from where he sat on the flimsy pallet they'd allotted him in the spacious and richly appointed underground chamber. A shackle encircled his ankle, making him no better off than a dog lying in the corner. At least he was clean. They'd made sure of that.

He supposed he hadn't given them much choice, having believed he was docile, only to later find him lost and wandering in one of the many tunnels in the maze-like structure within the mountain. The elders had been none too happy, but Sefrina had intervened, saying that it was the nature of the Rottu to always seek more.

He glowered at them now as they filed into the chamber. As they did every day, they ignored him, disappearing behind a set of ornate screens that blocked the opening to a recessed area. One of them—an elder he'd come to learn—entered with another guard carrying a tray of food. She took a plate off the tray and walked over to him.

"Who's the other prisoner?" he muttered.

"What makes you think—"

"There wasn't enough food on that tray to feed everyone back there. I hope their sleeping arrangements are better than mine."

The elder noticed for the first time the tattered mat they'd given him. She frowned, then held out his plate to him. He refused to take it from her. "It's simple bread and fruit. Water, too," she said, pointing at the ewer and cup that he'd left untouched. "We should've known our sleeping draught would lose its effectiveness."

"Where's Sefrina?"

The elder ignored him and set the plate on the floor.

He pushed it out of reach, and then turned away from her to lie down, facing the stone wall, using his arm as a cushion.

"Rottu," she called, touching his shoulder.

He was surprised by the concern in her voice, but he was in no mood for conversation. He'd made a mistake once in assuming that Sefrina was a friend. She wasn't. No one here was. He shrugged away from the elder's touch. If he'd had a blanket, he would've pulled it up over his head. She made an exasperated noise and eventually left him to join the group arguing in hushed tones on the other side of the screen. Moments later, they shuffled from the room, and if any of them spared him a glance, he didn't see it, set as he was to ignore them all. After staring at the stone wall for what seemed like a lifetime, he finally fell into a troubled sleep. One where he dreamed of a beautiful woman with brown hair that was frosted white. She called to him, *"Rottu. You must free me. They are terribly wrong, but they shouldn't die for their bad judgment."*

. . .

"Kardia," Murel stated, staring up at the fortress carved from the very mountain top. "It's not quite the oasis we expected."

After dismounting and crawling the ridge, he and Murel surveyed the cracked basin spread below them, and Tomas whistled at the massive fortress. "We'll need to traverse that barren expanse before climbing the mountain. I'm betting that it's riddled with traps and pitfalls. We may be the first non-Fyrjians to lay eyes upon this place."

"If any outsiders preceded us, we would never know. The Fyrjians no doubt killed any who happened upon it. Neither the temple at Mitra nor this fortress appear on any map that I've ever seen in Aurelia or in Sophiana. We've only ever seen this desert's borders, and even those are as fluid as the shifting dunes."

"Let's hope Mitra is our key to access." Tomas looked back at the desert through which they had ridden. The rise they had climbed and the setting sun at their backs would hide them from anyone on watch. "We'll backtrack and make camp."

Murel had told him of her conversations with Mitra...conversations that happened less and less the farther they rode from the goddess's oasis. But like a constant humming in their ears, they felt Mitra's silent urging to ride faster, to rest in the brief time when the sun was near its zenith and start again shortly after its passing. For Tomas, she was a shadow of some hovering being.

Over the past week, the desert's terrain had shifted from an ocean of sandy dunes to hard-packed earth and rock, always climbing higher and higher. A gust of wind tugged at his cape, and it billowed out behind him. Murel's hood flew back, and her ebony locks appeared even more bleached than before. Like Madyan's hair, the light and dark combination seemed an impossibility. Yet it existed. He watched as her hair settled around her shoulders, and she drew her hood back up. From their elevation, they could see for leagues. The horizon from whence they traveled revealed nothing but sky and earth. But he was aware, as was Murel, that somewhere out there, a sentient storm raged.

"We shouldn't tarry here," Murel cautioned, echoing his earlier thoughts. "It feels too exposed."

"The outcropping we passed will hide us from anyone watching these lands."

They had pushed the horses beyond what Tomas judged they could endure, but the creatures continued to surprise him. After an hour or two of rest, taken when the sun was at its highest, they had ridden both day and night. Each step had brought them higher and higher and past scree-covered slopes that dropped into hidden ravines. They would make up for their exhausting pace this evening, for the slope that dipped into the basin and the steep switchback trail to the fortress was too treacherous to attempt in the dark.

He led the way to the outcropping, once again trusting his mount to pick out a secure path. "No one ahead that I saw, but I'll take first watch. You get some rest."

"I'll help you settle the horses," Murel stated.

The brittleness in her voice was growing with each step away from the Mitra Oasis, as if she were fissuring inside. He opened his arms to her. "They can wait for a few minutes. Come here." She stepped into his embrace and rested her cheek on his chest. He hugged her until he felt some of the tension slip from her muscles.

She inhaled, then let go of her breath. "Thank you. I needed that."

He held her at arm's length and examined her. No doubt about it. The communion with Mitra was taking a toll.

"I'm fine. Mitra is..." She seemed to look inward. "Mitra is fine. And I can help with the horses."

"I know you can," Tomas said, "but why not see to our bedrolls instead? Maybe check what we have left to eat."

She nodded and turned away.

Their stores were nearly depleted. They hadn't set snares to try for a stray hare—there wasn't much use. Nothing moved under the scorching sun of the Fyrost during midday hours. "Nothing but us," Tomas said to the horses. He pulled off their tack and wiped them down. Then gave them their ration of water and the last of the grain, about a handful or two for each of them. "Fresh feed and water for you both tomorrow morning."

His horse nickered low, then dipped his head to the ground to pull at a twig that poked up through the dust and scree. His companion joined him, pawing at the earth with her hoof until a bulbous root popped out of the ground. The horses took turns biting chunks out of it, revealing the white, pulpy meat inside.

The Fyrost gave sustenance only to those who knew where to find it. He left the fleshy tuber to the horses. Murel was sitting on her blanket, and she smiled sadly at him, indicating with her hand their paltry meal. She looked tired to her bones.

"Our feast awaits." She laughed, but the sound rang hollow.

He sat close to her and helped her divide the food.

"Take it back, Tomas."

"What?" he asked, feigning innocence.

"Your portion of meat. You need it as much as I do. More perhaps."

"Murel..."

"I'm fine, I swear it. I'm just tired. Nothing that sleeping for a few years won't cure." Smiling, she held out his piece of venison, and he reluctantly took it. "They'll see us coming tomorrow," she said.

"From the moment we ride over the ridge and into the basin," he agreed. "What else do we have?"

"Some water and the last of our dates."

Tomas scanned the ground around them. He espied a lone twig near the foot of his bedroll. Using the butt of his dagger, he scraped at the loose soil, then pulled. The tuber came free with a pop, and he held out his ugly prize to Murel. "If it's good enough for the horses…"

Murel laughed, and this time, it sounded as if there was some weight to it. "Give it over. I'll see if I can cut it into manageable pieces. If it's edible, I say we save the dates for breakfast."

"Good plan. It would be rude to meet our welcoming party with grumbling stomachs." While she worked on cutting through the bulb and carefully paring away the dirt-crusted rind, he tucked his venison into his bag to share with her in the morning.

"You first," she said, holding out a wedge of the white root.

He took it from her and smelled it. "A cross between stale beer and smelly feet," he decided, then took a bite. It was like eating a raw, sour turnip, and he nodded to Murel to try hers.

"Crunchy," she said, then turned to the side and made a dainty spitting sound. "I got a little grit on mine." She drank some water. "Our loyal mounts are still standing, so they're not poisonous."

They ate their meal in silence. Murel picked up her venison strip and tore a chunk off. "Since you're saving yours for tomorrow, it's only fair that I share mine this evening. Besides, we need something to take away that delicious taste of dirt."

"And here I was, trying to be sneaky. Maybe we should split one of the dates as well. To help with the aroma."

"Good idea." She pulled one from the bag and cut it in half. "I wonder if the Fyrjians will send someone to escort us to the fortress."

"That, or simply try to kill us first. Has Mitra offered any advice?"

"No. She's like a bear, hibernating. But one thing that she did warn me about before she began her slumber is that we must not be separated."

"Sound advice," he said, moving behind her so she could lean back against him. Together, they watched the last rays of the sun disappear, leaving a copper glow on the horizon that faded into the deep indigo of a starlit night.

"Always being on the run this entire journey, I've been blind to the beauty of the Fyrost. Bathed the way it is now in the moonlight, with the stars holding vigil, it could be an ocean before us and not the sere dunes of the desert. It lives and breathes," Tomas added, and Murel nodded her head where it rested upon his chest. "Murel..."

"Yes."

"While the bear is still asleep, I would dearly like to kiss you."

"I thought you would never ask." She tilted up her chin, and he set his lips to hers. They kissed, softly, gently, taking their time, careful to not over-stoke their passion, lest their ursine companion wake. As he did for Murel, so, too, did she give him what he needed...love and caring, enough to sustain them through the night and what would come for them in the morning.

One of the horses strayed near, sniffing out the sour-smelling parings from the root they had shared, and munching noisily on them. Murel pulled back from the kiss and smiled up at Tomas, caressing the scruff whiskers on his cheeks. "Your beard has grown thick again; I like it."

"Will you care when I shave?" He had done so while they rested in the temple.

"I won't mind. With or without it, you're still my Tomas."

"Good. Because I'm well past the point when I can't stand the itch. How Trian manages to sport a full beard, I'll never fathom."

"He conditions it," Murel stated matter-of-factly.

"He—"

"Conditions his beard. Claire makes a special cream for his skin. Warin and Lark use something as well."

Tomas laughed. "Of course they do." He kissed her again. "Try to get some sleep." She curled up on the blanket, and Tomas leaned back. At this elevation, the desert temperature dropped at night, but they had decided against making a fire. No sense drawing attention to their location if they had not yet been detected. He pulled a blanket over Murel's shoulder, and she took his hand and held it. It wasn't long before her grasp loosened, and her fingers slipped from his.

Quietly, Tomas stood. He hobbled the horse that had encroached close to their blankets and then went to the other to bring it nearer. He scratched them both behind the ears, wondering why, like the Fyrjians, he had not made a bond with this horse as he did with his Chevlain steed in Aurelia. Perhaps it was a trait of the breed itself, as if the desert horses were cognizant that they served their masters and could be ridden one day and put into a stew pot the next.

"I'll see to it that you're not eaten, at least not while I still breathe," Tomas promised. His horse simply stared, unblinking, with its shiny black eyes. He scratched its ear again, and the gelding pressed its muzzle into his chest. One last pat on its neck, a quick check on the mare, and then Tomas silently climbed the ridge. He stayed low and surveyed the basin that was lost in shadows. The fortress was alight with many fires—a lone beacon in the night. "Give me the strength to keep Murel safe tomorrow," he begged of any benevolent gods or goddesses that might be listening.

Then, as he made his way back to Murel, a slip of a breeze caressed his neck. Tomas shivered at the sensation of something sniffing his flesh, and he instinctively sought whatever it was to the northwest. On the blankets, Murel was still sleeping, and he sat down, vigilant to any disruptions. But the only noise came from the horses when they shifted in their sleep. Even Murel slumbered in silence.

"Go back to sleep," he whispered, when hours later she roused.

"No, it's your turn," she insisted. She sat up, then scooched back, patting her thigh and drawing Tomas down so that he could rest his head there. Her fingers twined in his hair.

"The bear is awake, isn't she?" he asked, closing his eyes and enjoying the sensation.

"Mm-hmm." Her fingers continued to twirl and swirl, lulling him to sleep. "There will be time to talk about it in the morning. Get some rest while I watch over you."

# CHAPTER SIXTEEN

# Mother Bear

Even into the pre-dawn hours of night, the worn rock behind her radiated a gentle warmth. Unlike during the day, the nighttime desert was alive with sound. Always, the sibilant whine of air as it sloughed over the sharp edges of the rocks and crags sang out a melancholy tune. Below their outcropping, Murel caught a glimpse of some furtive, doglike creature. A desert fox, perhaps, but lean and rangy, with large ears that perked in her direction when it stopped to regard her before determining she was not a threat and continued on its hunt.

One of the horses shifted, its hoof making a muted scrape through the dirt. Unlike the terrain of the seemingly endless dunes with its cloying heat and choking dust, the air at their current elevation was lighter, purer. Murel could see for leagues. She stared up at the stars, envisioning the reverse of their route, trying to pinpoint on the horizon the location of Mitra's oasis. And with the thought came the realization that her companion was fully awake.

*What is a bear?*

Murel smiled. "A great and honored beast in the mountains of Aurelia. The bear is strong and fierce. It is said that the mother bear, when protecting her young, is the most formidable creature in the Known Realms."

*I sense humor when you and your man call me a bear.*

"Because a bear is also unpredictable and dangerous."

Mitra had no reply.

"You miss your temple. Your longing is like a cord stretched too far. If it snaps, will you be able to return?"

*Perhaps. Perhaps not. It is different this time. I do not have Kardia drawing me forward. In our corporeal forms, we were anchors in the desert and could travel where we wished. But when my goddess part was cast to the Virin Sea and her brother disappeared, the ties were severed.*

"Is any part of Kardia in his temple?"

Mitra was silent for a long while, and Murel felt her heartache. *His presence, however brief, graced my oasis. But he was less than a shadow…less than me. I do not know if he will ever be again. If we can separate Wind—as you call him—from the storm, Kardia could be lost forever. This does not change the fact that Wind must be freed.*

"And what will he do when he is free?"

*Heal. Seek. Find peace.*

"He is seeking now. And I believe he has found us," Murel stated. All along the horizon, Murel could see stars. Everywhere except to the northwest. A vast, unnatural darkness billowed there.

*You should wake your mate now. Explain what needs to be done.*

Beside her, Tomas stirred of his own accord. He ran his hand over his face, then pushed himself up. "Good morning."

"I was about to wake you," Murel said. "We need to leave."

Tomas followed her gaze. "It's far, but so much larger than before."

"And moving fast. Toward us. It senses Mitra."

Tomas stood, then pulled up Murel. "Let's go then."

She set her hand on his arm. "Tomas, Mitra is very much here. And she may need to—"

"I already know. If you trust her…"

"I trust *you*…to keep me safe when she is present. She has thus far waited for my approval to become dominant. But I suspect, with what is coming, she might simply take over."

"She can do that?"

Murel nodded.

"What is it like for you?"

"I can't see or feel but, from her viewpoint, I know everything that is happening. It's so very lonely. I think that is why she has been sleeping. When we started this trek, I allowed her to see her desert. She was so happy, and yet so sad. Even now, I can sense that she understands, and that talking about her this way adds to her grief.”

“Then we’ll focus on reuniting her with Kardia and on finding your brother and Madyan. And when we do, she’ll be free again.”

Murel smiled at him, and then looked inward, testing her ability to let a tiny portion of Mitra through. “Thank you, Tomas. I will protect Murel as I will protect you. Your lives are more important to me than restoring who I once was. Kardia would understand this as well.”

*Mitra, you should have let me warn him.*

“Oh, my dear, your man already knows. He is beautiful, and loyal, and brave, and so in love with you it makes my heart sing.”

Murel felt Mitra’s awareness swing back to Tomas, and she felt her admiration and perhaps even a touch of lust.

“It is time for you to hie from this place. Be on guard...the danger is not only coming from behind you. Trust your mounts and ride.”

With the pronouncement, Murel was once again gazing into Tomas’s eyes. He grabbed her shoulders and pulled her to him to hold her to his chest.

“I’m sorry. I should have warned you.”

“No need to apologize. She’s on our side for the time being.” He let her go, and together they saddled the horses and packed their gear.

He helped her up, then mounted his gelding. It was still dark as they rode over the ridgeline, and they gave the horses their head, letting them pick their way down the steep slope and into the pitch-dark basin. Murel divided her attention between the looming darkness chasing them and the fortress city of Kardia ahead.

It wasn’t until they reached the level floor of the basin were they able to discern the make-up of the terrain. Tomas pulled up next to her, and they rode forward. “They’ve spotted our arrival by now.”

Murel nodded.

“I don’t like that we are so exposed. And this pace is too slow.”

“I agree.” They nudged their horses’ flanks, kicking them forward into a gallop. As if they’d been born in the desert and not the lush valleys of Chevlain, the Fyrjian horses nimbly veered left and right to avoid brush and boulder alike, but always side by side. It was as if some divine hand guided them. They flew over the hard-packed ground, wide hooves clopping out a staccato rhythm.

Faster than she could imagine, they were halfway across the basin, and the sun had yet to rise. But in the pre-dawn light, three riders appeared, racing to intercept them.

"They mean to flank us," Tomas shouted, and Murel saw even more riders coming at them from the north and south. "Keep going. If we have to, we'll punch a hole straight through them." He drew his sword.

"I see the road to the fortress," she shouted. "To the left." They tucked in, and their mounts kicked up their speed.

Arrows whistled their deadly songs as they cut through the air to their right, and she and Tomas veered away. Their riders on their southern flank were much closer. But the three ahead moved to intercept them, and Murel could now see them—dark-cloaked Fyrjians, aiming their bows directly in their path. Again, they were forced to adjust their course.

"They're herding us," Tomas shouted.

It was a well-coordinated strike—the Fyrjians adjusted their speed and direction, even the shooting of the arrows, always near hits, but never striking. And suddenly, a gaping pit opened before them. Murel wanted to pull back on her reins, but Mitra's voice urged her on.

*Trust in your steeds.*

It was too late to stop, so she urged her mount forward. Beside her, Tomas did the same. Their horses leapt into the air, and Murel focused on the opposite edge of the trap instead of the horror of jagged rocks below that would rend their flesh and break their bones should they fail to reach the other side. Time slowed, as it had in the Fenrhi temple when she and Tomas had occupied what seemed to be their own space. Their horses carried them forward, ten, then twenty, then impossibly more feet over the deadly chasm.

She turned to Tomas, and he stared at her, exhilaration lighting his features. She reached out, and he took her hand as wind and sound flowed around them, not letting go until four hooves slammed into the heat-cracked dirt, sending shards of hardened mud in all directions. Murel shifted in her saddle to counteract the momentum of her body lurching forward. Her mare's haunches bunched as it tucked its rear legs, extending them so its hooves hit solid earth, and she and Tomas were once again away. Their horses never broke stride as time sped up to catch them.

They were now ahead of the forward riders, and they charged across the basin and up the opposite slope until they crested its rim. Fyrjian arrows rained down around them. Tomas's gelding screamed when one grazed its haunch, but it didn't falter. They hurdled toward the crevasse in the rocks where they could climb the road that would take them up to the fortress. Suddenly, a score of archers rose from either side of the path. But behind them, a lone rider careened down the mountain, shouting, "Hold! Hold!"

It was too late. Arrows shot forward, arcing above them, deadly missiles intent on spearing everything below. Murel ducked her body along her mount's neck, giving as small a target as possible, watching in dread as another volley was nocked in case the first launch failed. Tomas held up his sword, perhaps hoping he could shield them. The first wave was upon them, and time hung suspended as Murel pinpointed each lethal tip. If she and Tomas managed to somehow survive the onslaught, their horses wouldn't. And at this speed, a downed horse would kill as easily as an arrow.

Her hood had long since been blown back, and her hair streamed wildly behind her. A sudden welling of light flashed inside her as Mitra took over. She could feel her anger, and something more. A deadly eagerness. *Mitra, no!*

• • •

Tomas sensed the very moment when Mitra possessed Murel. No longer crouched over the neck of her mount, the woman he loved dropped her reins and swiped her arm across the sky as if wiping away condensation from glass. The arrows glowed brightly, bursting into flames and disintegrating into ash.

Murel's—no—Mitra's eyes were an incandescent shade of amethyst. Sensing his scrutiny, she turned to him, and he suddenly could hear Murel's plea in his mind. Before he could stop her, Mitra made a circular motion with her hands and wrists, and then pushed them out toward their flank where the Fyrjians were readying to release another barrage. Their nocked arrows exploded, then their bows, driving shrapnel into the necks and faces of at least half the warriors. At the same time, the marking on Tomas's arm burned with a cold heat—Mitra was drawing her strength from him and using Murel as the conduit.

She drew back her arms and began the intricate circling to send another push, this time to their left flank. Half of the remaining archers, their expressions registering the sheer horror of the invisible attack, scrambled across the road to try to aid their brethren. And Mitra, in her lust for vengeance, for that was the only emotion Tomas could sense from her, focused her hatred upon them.

Tomas veered on his mount, sending his horse's shoulder into Mitra's mare, knocking her sideways and breaking her focus. Her wild tresses settled, and whatever power she'd taken from him abated.

She snarled.

"Murel would not want this!" Tomas yelled, grabbing the reins of her horse and muscling them to a wrenching halt. "Enough, Mitra. You could have stopped the arrows. There was no need to attack."

"They tried to kill me! I will not suffer again a man's spears."

"The Fyrjians do not know that it is you. They only see two outsiders. I understand your need for vengeance, but these are your people." He recognized the lone rider cantering toward them. "Sefrina, stay back!" Her horse skidded to a stop, sending loose rock and gravel spitting down the slope. He held tight to the reins of Murel's horse as Sefrina yelled to her people to stand down.

Mitra narrowed her eyes at Sefrina, and the formidable woman paled and lowered her head.

Tomas eased forward, positioning his gelding between the raging entity and the Fyrjians. Several of them had come forward and were standing on either side of Sefrina. Their arrows were still nocked, but the tips pointed to the dirt. "Do you trust Murel?" he asked Mitra.

Her glowing gaze fell upon him. The anger rolled off her in waves, and he felt it soaking into his pores. But she gave him a curt nod.

"Then you trust me."

She didn't reply, but there was a palpable ebbing of rage. And as if they resided in a space wholly separate from everything and everyone around them, Tomas sensed a lessening in the closed, tight air.

"Murel would not want to hurt these people," she repeated, still glaring at the archers.

Sefrina kicked her horse forward, keeping. "Welcome back to Kardia. We have waited centuries for your return; I am honored to bear witness on this auspicious day."

"And you are?"

"Sefrina, high captain of the Fyrjian army, Umbren Master of the Fenrhi, Protector of the Malikáfyr, Finder of the Rottu, Keeper of the Temples, and Reader of the Signs."

Mitra settled back into her seat and smirked. "All that."

Tomas let go the reins, hiding his grin at the sarcasm that dripped with Murel's dry wit.

"Allow me to escort you to the temple," Sefrina offered, and then pointed to the northwest. "The storm will be here on the morrow, and there is much to discuss and prepare." Sefrina steered her mount back toward the road. Those assembled bowed or knelt as they passed.

But Mitra pulled her horse to a stop and dismounted. And when she faced Tomas, her eyes were the beautiful indigo of the woman he loved. He slipped off his horse and drew her into his arms. Ignoring the curious scrutiny of the Fyrjians, he gave her a brief kiss.

"I need to help the injured."

Sefrina jumped from her horse. "Murel. It would have been better if Mitra remained present." The other warriors were inching forward, slowly crowding them.

"Mitra cannot help your people like I can—" She reached out to take Tomas's hand off the hilt of his sword. "Like we can." They walked over to those who'd been hurt. One after another, she checked their wounds, tended to them, touched them and drew upon her healing strength, all the while fortifying her energy with Tomas's.

The Fyrjians watched, edging forward, some touching her hair in wonder as Sefrina tapped her foot impatiently, waiting for Murel to finish. And when she finally did, instead of remounting her mare, Murel tended to Tomas's horse, treating the gash on its haunch.

"They are still in a state of awe that Mitra was among them," Sefrina whispered. "But I do not know if that will prevent them from attacking you and Murel. We must get you both inside the temple."

"I don't think you have anything to worry about," Tomas observed, then nodded toward Murel. One of the archers had brought her water to drink. Tomas took the reins of their horses and joined her. He, too, took an offered waterskin, drinking only enough to quench his thirst. Two more Fyrjians stepped forward with water bags for the horses.

Tomas turned to speak to them. "The storm is coming, and it will destroy anyone in its path. You mustn't remain here." He took Murel's hand, and he sensed Mitra's impatience to be off. "Kardia's fortress and temple...can it hold all of your people?"

"Yes, and more, if necessary. But our outer settlements have withstood the storms of the past."

"What is coming is every storm you've ever weathered, all rolled into one," Murel stated. "It... He will tear apart your shelters if he senses life within." Her eyes flashed amethyst for a moment, and the others stepped back. "Mitra agrees. Everything alive must be protected, including your horses and cattle. Who leads your archers?"

"I do," a man croaked out, getting up from the ground where she had tended to him. As he moved, one of the bandages fell away—the laceration had not only stopped bleeding but had scabbed over completely. Those closest to him stared, amazed, and they placed their palms over his heart before touching their own breastbones.

"Send someone to bring drays for your wounded," Tomas ordered, breaking the spell. "Then hie to the fortress and send signal flares to alert your people."

The archer sought confirmation from Sefrina. "Do as he says. The rest of you take the fastest horses and ride to the outposts. Bring everyone back. If you are able, go to the periphery lookouts and give them the order to seek refuge within the fortress." She wheeled around as three more riders pulled up.

"Sefrina, the Malikáfyr needs you."

"We're coming now. Ride back ahead of us. Everyone is to assemble in the fortress. Now," she ordered, before looking back at Murel and Tomas.

"Do your horses require rest, or are their spirits strong enough to carry you up the mountain?"

"They've traveled the sea and your desert and are eager to see their home for the first time," Murel said, lifting her foot to her stirrup and swinging up into her saddle. She patted her mare's neck. "Right, girl?" Her horse pawed at the ground, impatient to be off.

When Tomas settled into his saddle, they set off at a trot. The archers moved from the path, lowering their heads and touching their hands to their hearts again, just like the gestures made by the Southron Islers. "Respect for Mitra, even after she nearly slaughtered them?"

"Not for Mitra," Sefrina corrected. "For you. And for Murel."

# CHAPTER SEVENTEEN

# Vessels

She and Tomas followed Sefrina into the fortress. Unlike the Fenrhi Temple, Kardia's layout was simple. There were no confusing halls or twists and turns, only blocks carved from the thick, gray stone of the mountaintop. Flourishes and filigrees were non-existent. Like the Fyrjians themselves, the place where they lived was utilitarian. They followed Sefrina across an open square.

The screaming sound of javelins, released in succession and spaced apart by a few seconds, split the quiet of the moment. "Efficient and ordered," Tomas noted.

To their left, several warriors stood, looking up into the sky. Murel tracked two of the javelins as they were launched. First, one flashed bright against the backdrop of the darkening sky. Before the second ordinance exploded, the air was rent with an enormous crack, booming and sending concussive echoes across the desert. Then the next burst, and another, and another, until Murel could no longer count them, as the explosions were lost in the repeating cacophony.

"So many," Tomas noted. "They'll hear your alarm in Aurelia."

"Eight to signify the last storm," Sefrina supplied as the echoing rolled farther and farther away. "If you can hear the signal, you are in its path."

Out in the desert, another volley was released, and Murel held her breath, waiting for the retort—a flash, then a darkening blot of smoke in the dusty blue. It took longer for the explosion to proclaim its presence, and its rolling echoes passed back over them.

"What if they can't make it to the fortress in time?" Tomas asked.

"They'll go to ground. The desert is riddled with caves—if you know where to find them."

Spread below was the road they had climbed, one that was lost in the jumble of structures the higher it rose to the top. Already, she could see a line of people, horses, and carts making steady progress up the incline. The efficiency of the Fyrjians was a wonder to behold. "How many roads?"

"Eight at the base, merging to four, and then finally to two. There is another square like this to the east."

"And to the north and south?" Tomas asked.

"The upper fortress spans the diameter."

"And where is the temple?" Murel asked. "Where is my brother?"

"In the center, but down, into the heart of the mountain."

"It *would* be underground," Tomas noted, not sounding too pleased.

"Where else should it be but near the spring that nourishes our people?"

"She has a point," Murel said in an aside to Tomas as they followed their guide through a deep-set archway and into an enormous structure.

"We've gained an escort," Tomas pointed out, nodding toward the four heavily armed Fyrjians dogging their footsteps. Cloaked, hooded, and with scarves covering their lower faces, their genders weren't discernable. "At least we haven't been disarmed."

Sefrina drew to a halt. "I must go to the temple to see the Malikáfyr. You and your man will be taken to the bathing house; afterward, you can eat and rest." She signaled their escorts, who stepped forward, trying to separate Murel from Tomas. But Tomas would not be diverted, especially as Mitra had warned them to never split apart. There was a tense moment when the warriors appeared to be reaching for their weapons. "The palms chamber...for them both."

"I will be taken to my brother immediately," Murel demanded, not moving to follow the escort.

"He'll be brought to you...after you've bathed and eaten."

"Not acceptable."

Sefrina looked as if she'd lost all patience. She opened her mouth to shout, then stopped, ending on a weary sigh. "Come with me."

She turned and strode away. One of the escorts had a wry glint in their eye and took Murel's measure. Pulling down her scarf to reveal that she was a young woman, she nodded. "That's a first."

"What is?" Tomas asked.

"Sefrina backing down," the escort replied. "We'd better catch up. She does not suffer laggards."

"We're well aware," Murel noted.

"I'm called Dina, by the way." She pulled a pouch from a hidden pocket in her cape. "Here, you must be hungry after your journey. Few survive the trek from Mitra to Kardia without a guide. And never one not Fyrjian born. How did you manage it?"

"Who said we didn't have a guide?" Tomas provided cryptically, opening the small sack and holding it out to Murel.

She reached in and pulled out a handful of dried fruit and nuts. "Careful, my love," Murel mock-warned in between bites of the sugary-salty mix. "You're beginning to sound like a Nifolhadajan."

Dina hooted with laughter. "Truer words." She peered ahead. "We've lost Sefrina. No matter. I know the way." She reached back into her cape, extracted a waterskin, and handed it to Murel.

"It's mala'eth! How came you by the Fenrhi mead?" Murel demanded before passing the skin to Tomas.

Dina shrugged and pulled up her sleeve, revealing the markings of the Fenrhi Earth Caste. "One of the benefits of being a master brewer."

"Thank you," Tomas said, handing back a much-depleted sack. "You are obviously trained for combat. Are you also marked for Umbren?"

Dina snorted. "Oh, your question was in earnest. You've traveled the desert, your garb is Fyrjian, and Sefrina even put you in the quarters reserved for visiting leaders of the other Fyrjian sects. I forgot that you were outsiders and do not know our ways." She pulled her sleeve back in place. "All Fyrjians are trained as warriors. How do you suppose the Umbren Caste came to be so good at what they do?"

It was Murel's turn to laugh. "That explains quite a bit about the Umbren."

Dina stopped, suddenly serious. "Can you help the Malikáfyr? News of your skill as a healer reached the fortress ahead of you."

*Show her. The runes will smooth your way forward.*

Murel tossed pulled up her sleeve, revealing her markings. It was a risk showing her the runes, but she did not trust that the Fyrjians had her brother's best interests at heart, nor even hers or Tomas's. Better to give them something greater to consider than just her skill as a healer.

"Sylvan," Dina admired, then noted the darker markings. "And Umbren?" She looked in Tomas's direction when he revealed his upper arm as well. "I see. You are bonded in the old ways." Her gasp informed them of the exact moment that she noticed the Fyrjian symbols, and she took hold of Murel's arm to inspect the design again. When she lifted her head, a mixture of fear and awe and hope filled her expression. "No wonder Sefrina spared your lives. The elders will be hard put to atone for the punishment they doled out to her for her disobedience."

"She was punished for allowing us to live?"

"She was given a choice. Lose her rank or endure a week of banishment in the high desert with neither food nor water nor weapon. She chose the desert." Dina lowered her voice. "She survived, obviously, but our healers weren't sure if they could restore her sight."

"She went blind?" Murel asked, horrified.

"No. She was blinded. When she was asked why she had spared you, she would only say that she had seen a sign. Because she refused to share that which she saw, they administered a tincture to take her sight as further punishment."

Murel pulled down her sleeve. "Blinded and alone. I had my sight and was with Tomas." —He took her hand.— "We almost didn't make it."

"That was the deciding factor for the elders…in sparing you, she risked giving you an inhumane death. Such an act is forbidden. How did you survive the storm?"

Murel and Tomas shared a look. "It wasn't easy," Tomas offered, not revealing that they were inside the temple. Murel felt Mitra stir inside her, sensing her agreement with his decision.

Dina narrowed her eyes. "Right. Perhaps I do not need to know. But the elders will want answers about how you and your horses survived."

"They can ask any questions they want," Murel replied.

Dina smiled. "But you need not answer, is that it? I like you, Murel." They continued down the corridor. "'Tis strange, though."

"You find something strange in all of this?" Murel remarked, letting a little sarcasm lace her words.

Dina laughed. "The desert can be fickle. But what is happening here is more than its usual oddness. First the Rottu, and now you," Dina continued. "We thought we only needed the one, but now there is a third and fourth vessel to help save the first."

Murel touched Tomas's arm, and they let Dina pull ahead of them. "That sounded eerily similar to the prophecy."

"I know. But isn't your brother a vessel?"

"I carry Mitra," Murel whispered back. "And the storm carries Kardia and something else. That's but three."

"Any ideas coming from Mitra?" he asked.

"She's here, but except when she urged me to show my marks, she's been oddly quiet since we left the archers. I think she regrets her actions."

"Dina already knew that you healed the wounded, but she has no news of Mitra. I wonder...did Sefrina have something to do with suppressing the knowledge? She made some hand signals to the archers earlier."

"We'll have to ask when we catch up to her." They were trailing farther behind Dina and sped up their pace.

Ahead, two enormous wood doors soared at least twenty feet high. Upon recognizing Dina, the sentries admitted the trio entrance. If the doors were impressive, the massive hall that they entered was even more so. Supported by soaring columns, Murel could see no end to either side of the hall. But the Fyrjians were busily preparing. Row after row of sleeping mats had been laid out to the left; opposite them, hundreds of long benches had been set, and sustenance was arriving by the cartload. Murel had admired the efficiency of the exploding alarms, but this was organization at a whole new level. Beside her, Tomas whistled.

Without breaking stride, Dina threw back, "This isn't the first storm we've had to ride out, but with luck, it'll be our last." She came to an abrupt halt and got down on one knee, holding out her arms. A little boy, perhaps five or six years old, ran to her.

"It's my first storm! We saw the signals! Gama covered my ears, but I can still hear the *boom boom!*" Dina hugged her child as an older woman approached, and Murel realized, perhaps for the first time, the true import of what was coming.

Inside her mind, Mitra suddenly stirred, and Murel grabbed Tomas's hand for strength. She allowed her to emerge, feeling only joyful love and warmth residing in Mitra's heart.

"Mama," the little boy said. "She has such pretty eyes. Like the Mitra."

Murel could feel Tomas anchoring her, and somehow, she was able to see what was happening. The older woman knelt. Dina notice last, preoccupied as she was with trying to control her son's cowlick. She gasped and maneuvered her child behind her. Still, she bowed her head.

"I would not have been so… I did not know who—"

"You have welcomed us. But I must attend to my Malikáfyr."

"Yes, of course."

"Kiss your child and say your goodbyes. We have much work to do before the coming day." The boy snuck around his mother and hesitantly stepped before her. Murel could feel Mitra's smile as she reached down to touch the boy's head and then chest.

"Thank you for your blessing," his grandmother said.

"Good night, Mama. Come on," he said, pulling his grandmother's hand. "If we help the bakers, maybe they'll give us a treat."

Mitra receded—Murel's transformation had not gone unnoticed by the others in the hall.

"A guide across the desert, indeed," Dina surmised. "Come. We must get to the elders before word of this reaches them. They'll not be happy to be the last to know of our good fortune."

"Good fortune?"

"It seems that the chalice is already full," she replied. "There may be hope after all."

"Hope is a thin cloth upon which to pin one's strategy," Tomas stated.

"But it is a good place to start." Ahead, Sefrina waited impatiently for them, then disappeared around a corner. "We have to hurry now," Dina urged, pirouetting to run to the opposite side of the hall. Murel and Tomas sprinted after her.

# Kardia's Temple

Dina skidded to a stop at the lip of a giant opening in the floor, revealing broad circular steps that had been carved into the wall. Sefrina was already moving down the tube. Fortunately, the stairs were wide enough that Tomas and Murel could walk side by side, and they followed Dina into the unknown depths.

The stairs were alight with sconces similar to those in Mitra's Temple. Despite the half wall that spiraled down with the steps and protected people from tumbling into the abyss, she hugged the opposite side. They descended forever, at least it seemed that way.

She became disorientated as the unending spiral played tricks on her mind, and she took a deep breath to clear it. Loop after loop after loop, deeper and deeper into the mountain.

"Not much farther," Dina announced, noticing her discomfort.

"Just a moment, Dina," Tomas said, pulling Murel to a stop and taking her face in his hands.

Murel's brain continued curling endlessly downward, as if her feet were still descending the spiral.

"Look at me," Tomas urged.

She did, and he smiled, then pressed his lips to hers.

"What was that for?" she asked when he pulled back.

"I could feel you becoming too entrenched. And because I'm not sure what we'll find down there, I wanted to kiss you. And tell you again that I love you."

Murel could feel the pleased blush steal up her neck and cheeks. "I love you, too."

"Better, then?"

She nodded, then stepped to the edge to peer over the half wall. That was when she noticed a complicated series of ropes and chains. She turned to Dina and pointed to the cables.

"Pulleys," she said. "For supplies. And if someone is infirm, we lower them down."

"Do you bring up water from the spring?"

"We have pipes and screws that do the work for us." She pointed to the opposite wall a bit lower down. "You can see how the column's walls are widening. That's how I know we're almost there."

Indeed, Murel could detect a bowing out of the stairs, like an inverted funnel, and when she looked straight down, she could see a soft glow emanating up from the bottom of the conduit. "It must be another thousand feet."

"That's about right," Dina agreed. "Let's go. It won't be so monotonous after the next few screws. There are storage areas and even living accommodations."

"You have people who live down here all the time?" Murel asked. "I could never survive it, not seeing the sun or the sky."

"We rotate with each new moon," Dina explained.

"I guess that would save you from having to climb these stairs every day," Tomas added.

Dina grinned. "Exactly!"

After a few more screws, as Dina had called them, Murel did indeed start to feel better. They passed cubbies, and then larger, hollowed-out spaces. Places with sleeping pallets and low tables and pillows for dining.

"The light is moving down there," Tomas pointed out.

"It's the limchens reflecting off the water."

"What are limchens?"

"Growths, much like lichen, except, down here, something makes them glow. Come, you can see them for yourselves."

They made their way down, earning more than the curious stare. Soon, Fyrjians were coming out of their rooms and following them. Dina looked back over her shoulder. "We've never permitted outsiders here. And I've read the annals; such a moment would have been recorded."

"Until Jesper, that is," Tomas reminded.

"Jesper?" She stopped, pausing on the steps, and Tomas and Murel drew to a halt. Those behind them also stilled. "Oh, you are referring to the Rottu. He is not considered an outsider, nor a Fyrjian. As he is empty, he counts as neither." She took a step closer and lowered her voice. "There is an old Fyrjian saying about the day of healing and the night of death."

"And…" Murel prodded when Dina seemed unwilling to share more.

"That healing or death will be decided by one who is both stranger and Fyrjian," she finally said. "Is that you, Murel? Will you be strong enough?" She next took Tomas's measure. "You chose well in your bondmate. But, in truth, there was no choice, was there?" And with that, and the flash of a smile, Dina turned and continued down the ever-widening column, until the steps themselves broadened, creating tiered seating, much like in Mitra's Temple. Only, it was not a temple under a dune, but an enormous cavern, one large enough to hold not a spring, but a small lake. It was at least a hundred full paces across and oblong-shaped.

"Pijala trees!" Tomas exclaimed. "How is it possible without sunlight?"

"The limchens provide the illumination, and the trees thrive. During the day, their light is soft, but as night descends, the hue will deepen and barely cast any glow."

"Are they plants?" Murel asked.

"More like moss. They would take over completely if the light tenders did not keep them contained. If you see one on the ground, don't step on it."

"Are they sacred to Fyrjians?" Murel touched one of the strange growths on the wall next to her.

Dina laughed. "Oh no! They stink worse than a striper!"

"That's a skunk," Tomas provided.

"How did you know that?" Murel asked.

"Princess Anwyl told me once. She's had experience with them."

"I've met the princess," Dina added. "She's a force to be reckoned with, and I would not want to be in the striper's shoes."

Tomas chuckled.

"This is the largest cavern, but there are tunnels to other, smaller spaces. The atmosphere is always fresh because there are natural air conduits.

We'll close off the larger openings to prevent the storm from entering the mountain."

Murel appreciated the information, but she was impatient to see her brother.

"Come. I'll take you to Sefrina. She's gone ahead to speak with the elders." Dina once again led the way, walking along the edge of the subterranean lake.

Murel followed close behind with Tomas striding beside her. Their path took them close to the water's edge, and she peered into its depths. Near the shore, some of the limchens glowed from under the water. The surface was perfectly still and reflected the growths growing on the cavern's ceiling, creating an echoing sky full of strange constellations.

Farther out, the water darkened to a midnight blue. "It looks deep," Murel noted.

"It is The Source," Dina provided.

"The source?" Tomas asked. "The source of your water."

Dina threw an amused smile over her shoulder. "It is The Source of everything. Of the goddesses and gods. And of flora and fauna alike. And it is the source of Life. And Death." She continued without breaking stride. "We've dropped weighted lines and have not yet hit bottom. The elders finally stopped trying, stating that there was no benefit to knowing the exact depth and that there is more beauty in the mystery of the unknown. The water is extremely pure."

"It's the same color as your eyes, Murel," Tomas noted.

"Indeed, it is," Dina agreed. "And it's not an illusion created by the limchens' glow—the water is actually blue." She continued leading them around the lake, and the broad band of earth narrowed with each step, taking them to the far wall of the cavern.

Dina kept walking toward a massive rock promontory that jutted into the lake, and Murel wondered if they would have to wade through the water's edge. A trick of the light, it seemed, for their trio passed under a natural arch in the stone, one that led to another cavern. Though nowhere as large as the main space, it was still expansive.

"About the size of Mitra's Temple," Tomas noted with a whisper.

Upon their arrival, the group of gathered people stopped talking. They stood in an arc facing Sefrina, glaring daggers back and forth between her and Tomas and Murel.

"If looks could kill," Tomas commented, loud enough so that everyone heard.

"Well, good luck!" Dina stated, before beating a hasty retreat.

"Coward," Tomas threw back with a grin. He took Murel's hand and headed toward the group, positioning himself slightly in front of her as if he would shield her from any thrown daggers, real or imaginary.

Sefrina approached them first.

"What do they know?" Murel asked.

"That you survived the storm. I haven't revealed anything else. And I reached them before word of your actions could. No one else has been here."

"Dina knows, and her son, and I'm guessing, her mother."

Sefrina smirked. "Good. Then word will spread quickly, and there'll be nothing the elders can do to stop you from being here."

"I don't see Jesper anywhere, nor Madyan," Tomas noted.

"Like Mitra's Temple, there is a private area for Kardia and Mitra to meet. The Malikáfyr and your brother await you there. But we need to get past the elders and—"

. . .

The flashover as Mitra took control of Murel was so quick and without warning that Tomas grabbed her wrist to get a sense if Murel was all right. All that he could sense was her impatience.

"It wasn't me," Mitra said defensively, staring at Tomas's hand gripping her wrist. She kept her eyes down, avoiding drawing unnecessary attention to the ethereal quality of their peculiar hue. "Murel feels the best way forward is for me to confront the elders. I don't think she cares if I change them into horned toads, if it means she gets to see her brother that much quicker."

Tomas let go of her wrist. "You can do that?"

Mitra laughed, drawing the elders over. "I've never tried. Besides, who would do such a thing?"

"You are strangers here and must leave immediately!"

Mitra trained her gaze on the frail-but-brave woman standing before her, slowly drawing up her chin to peer into the rheumy eyes that were glaring at her. "I am surprised to find you still alive, Palinah."

"Not strangers, after all," Sefrina murmured.

"How do you... You've been gone for... I don't understand, Beloved Mitra," Palinah strung together.

"I was always in my temple. Trapped. Unable to manifest until Murel and Tomas healed that part of me, that part of the Sky Goddess. They gave me a place to exist again. But tell me, Palinah, Custodian of the Temples, why was the Malikáfyr never brought to me?"

Tomas stepped closer to Murel, sensing Mitra's growing ire.

"The Malikáfyr was not here. She had to fulfill her promise to her parents, a promise that took her from the desert for many years. She has only recently returned. And the storm is always lurking. We could not risk the crossing. If she were taken...it would be as if the Sky Goddess lived again to rain down her wrath upon the Fyrost."

Mitra looked to Tomas for confirmation.

"It is true. She has journeyed across this realm and mine, but she has been missing for over a year with no word as to her state." Tomas sensed her consulting with Murel, and her anger cooled. Others came forward to meet the person who contained the embodiment of their long-lost goddess. Murel blinked, and her eyes were once again the beautiful blue of deep waters.

"Now that we've established that we are not exactly strangers, I demand that you take us to my brother," Murel intoned.

"*You* may not be a stranger, but your—"

"Tomas is her bondmate," Sefrina interrupted Palinah. "As such, he is considered to be one of Mitra's consorts, is he not?"

Palinah pursed her lips together but conceded her loss with a respectful tilt of her head.

"And Sefrina joins us," Tomas added, when he noticed some of the elders pulling her to the side. Murel nodded gratefully in his direction.

Palinah narrowed her eyes, but spun on her heel, dropping her old woman persona and walking spryly toward an arched opening in the wall. Two guards on either side pulled back the double doors, and she marched through.

Tomas took Murel's hand, and they followed. Sefrina came next, leading the queue of the elders.

Murel stopped abruptly and addressed them. "Just us, thank you."

Through the doors they went, and like the chamber in the Mitra Oasis, the one in Kardia was reached via a steep, narrow staircase. Murel tightened her grip on his hand. "I know," he said, "but I'm sure it's not much farther."

"I'm all right, as long as I'm connected to you."

"Always."

Above them, Palinah rounded a corner and disappeared from view. They reached the spot, a small landing, and then passed under a low arch. Despite being located in the heart of a mountain, the space somehow felt light and airy. Beside him, Murel let out a sigh of relief. To one side, a low wall spanned the length of the chamber and overlooked the lake. Limchens grew everywhere, tucked into nooks and crannies in the stone walls, overflowing like waterfalls from baskets suspended from the craggy ceiling, and artfully arranged in pots and urns and placed about the room.

That's when they laid eyes on the giant sleeping platform across from the opening. Tied by her ankles and wrists, an unconscious Madyan was secured. The sound of a chain being dragged on the stone floor had them turning toward the third wall. "Come to force-feed me again?" a rough voice croaked out. A thin man with a scraggly beard shuffled from behind a partition. He was in leg irons, and so had to take small steps to move. "Murel?"

Tomas let go of her hand as she flew across the room to reunite with her brother. "Jesper! What've they done to you? You're so thin!" She hugged him, then took his face in her hands to peer into his eyes.

"Except for the leg irons, they've been reasonably hospitable, at least of late."

"But why?"

"I took to exploring the caverns one too many times, so they tried putting things in my food. A benefit of being the Rottu, I'm immune to their concoctions. One night while I slept, the guards got the jump on me; I woke with these chains connecting my ankles. The length is too short to navigate the steps. I have the bruises to prove it. After finding me the last time, they attached me to the wall."

"The Rottu is extremely stubborn, and not a very polite guest," Palinah intoned.

"Palinah!" Sefrina gasped in outrage, gesturing to one of the guards, who produced a key and moved at once to free Jesper from the leg irons. "I am sorry, Jesper. The elders have become lazy. They should have assigned you an escort. There are places under this mountain into which you could fall and never be found."

Murel threw her arms around her brother again and held him. "I've been so worried about you."

"I knew you would survive. Never doubted it, in fact." He grinned at her, then touched her hair. "I like the new look, Sis."

"I'm glad to find you alive," Tomas said. "But right now, we have bigger problems."

"I'm guessing it has something to do with why they keep Madyan sedated and tied up, and why you both have the same hair."

A guard stepped into the room and conversed with Sefrina and Palinah. Sefrina gave him some curt instructions, and he hied away. The two women approached them.

"The storm?" Tomas asked.

"Yes," Sefrina replied. "It will be here tomorrow afternoon."

More people came into the room, some carrying baskets of food, others, pails of hot water. "But there is still time for you to bathe. We have fresh garments befitting your stature. And then we can determine our course of action."

"You are overstepping, Sefrina!" Palinah shouted. "The elders will decide what—"

Mitra came forth again and squared off with the old woman. "You will decide nothing. It is a courtesy that I allow you to remain in our chamber.

Make yourself useful and see that my Malikáfyr is roused. For now, Murel wishes to bathe." She crossed the room to the partition.

"What in all the heavens?" Jesper cried out when he caught sight of Mitra's glowing eyes. He shot forward toward Sefrina. "You promised me she would be safe from this!" He hooked his foot around her ankle and twisted his weight, slamming her down to the floor.

"Jess!" Murel yelled, hastening back. "It's not what you think! I'm all right. I swear it."

"Tomas?" he asked, not letting Sefrina up from the floor.

He nodded to his friend, then added, "She's starting to turn blue."

Jesper released the pressure of his forearm off Sefrina's neck.

"I was not turning blue!" she sputtered, and then held out her hand to Jesper, who reached down and hauled her up. "And you! I would have never taught you that move if I imagined you would use it against me. But well done!" She slapped his shoulder.

While Murel bathed, Tomas filled Jesper in on everything that had transpired. "Your sister and I...we're..."

"They're bondmates," Sefrina threw in. "Ever since the Fenrhi Temple." For once, Palinah held her tongue, clearly intrigued by the accounting. "I gather you managed to enter Mitra's Temple and—"

"You entered the temple! But how—"

"Show her, Tomas. Then maybe she will stop interrupting."

Tomas rolled up his sleeve, revealing the markings on his arm.

Palinah's eyes widened. "The mark of the rod. Then Murel must bear the chalice. Sefrina, forgive me. We should have trusted you when you said you saw a sign. Instead, we—"

In true Fyrjian fashion, Sefrina scoffed. "The journey—"

"Banishment," Jesper corrected.

"Only made me stronger," Sefrina finished.

"They blinded you," he persisted in true Jesper fashion.

"And now I see so much better."

Jesper glared, then turned his sharp words in Tomas's direction. "I want to hear more about this 'bondmate' thing," he demanded.

"Only true bondmates are able to enter Mitra's temple," Palinah explained, before Tomas could answer. "Bondmates are linked by more than their love. They are linked by their faith in one another, by their willingness to sacrifice everything if it means the other will be safe. It is stronger than handfasting and more binding than what you call marriage."

"That doesn't sound too horrible," Jesper grudgingly allowed.

"We wanted to tell you, Jess," Tomas began. "But Ni—"

"Ni'mala knows little," Palinah scoffed, interrupting Tomas at the mention of the Fenrhi Mother. She then raised an eyebrow and appeared to be measuring Tomas's worth. She prodded his arm, then chest, and made no attempt at hiding her examination of the fit of his breeches. An appreciative hum emanated from her throat before she added, "Bondmates must also consummate their union. And Mitra's Temple would've been an excellent place to do so. Did you find the passage to the bedchamber?" she asked, waggling her eyebrows. "The artwork is—"

"Palinah," Tomas warned.

Sefrina put her hand on Jesper's arm. "No place is more sacred than Mitra's Temple, the place where she and Kardia met in corporeal form to love, for bondmates to join."

"You're not helping," Tomas growled.

"I don't want to know about any joining!" Jesper croaked. "You're talking about my little sister!"

"Relax, Jess," Murel said, coming up behind him.

Tomas drew her next to him and kissed her hand. "And don't forget, you've gained a brother."

"Go clean up—they changed out the water—and I'll fill them in on the rest. Then it's your turn, Jess. You need a bath and a shave."

• • •

"Does Madyan need to be restrained like that?" Murel asked, not bothering to hide the accusatory glare leveled at Palinah. They had been slowly dripping a tincture of some herbal remedy on her lips, and though she was beginning to stir, it was as if she were still locked in a dream state.

"The Malikáfyr ordered us to do so herself," Palinah was quick to defend. "She'd only just stepped foot into her desert when she was nearly taken from us. Many of our people were injured trying to protect her, and not only by the storm."

Murel took Madyan's hand in hers, stroking the smooth skin, and then looked up when Tomas returned. "There's something I don't understand. It was over a thousand years ago when the Sky Goddess was lost, and her brother and Kardia were taken. Yet Mitra was aware that Madyan had not visited the temple. The timeline is wrong."

"It's a long story, and—"

"We seem to have an abundance of time," Tomas put forth.

"I was going to suggest that you eat while we recite the history," Palinah said, finally accepting their presence in the Kardia Temple. "The food is not dosed," she added, throwing an arched eyebrow at Jesper.

They filled their plates and sat in a ringed area with thick cushions and low tables. "After the Wind God cast his sister into the depths of the Virin Sea, he regretted his actions—he searched for her for decades. He continued to travel to the Mitra Temple so that Kardia and Mitra could be together. What he did not know was that the man, the one called Be'alu, who he had saved from his sister, had taken part of his power.

"Be'alu hid in the Fyrost, gathering his strength and feeding his own rage until he became a storm that scoured the desert, destroying any living thing in his path. The Wind God would intervene, averting the storm from its targets, but each time losing a little more of himself until the storm consumed him."

"And Kardia?" Murel asked, sensing that Mitra needed to know.

"Kardia was lost. I am sorry," Palinah stated, and Murel wasn't sure to whom she spoke—herself or Mitra. "Over the centuries, our leaders continued to honor Mitra. To stay in her temple and invoke the old rites of union. Every new generation until..." She paused and stared down at Madyan.

"Until Madyan's parents were murdered by the Steward King Diarmait."

At the mention of the name, Palinah and Sefrina turned to the side and spit in unison. "Death to the Usurper," Sefrina stated. "We have sworn it. It is why we infiltrated the Fenrhi, to gain access to the spawn of the storm."

"Wait a moment," Tomas said, standing and then pacing. "You're saying that Diarmait is a descendent of the man, this Be'alu, who ultimately destroyed your god and goddess?"

"Yes," Palinah stated coldly. "When Diarmait's mother, sister to King Jarold, Queen Aghna's grandfather, married Lord Farnad, the bloodline—long ago purged from the royal line—was reintroduced. He wears the same facial mark as his father. And probably his heir."

"Lord Roger did not have a mark, but I'm not sure about Prince Bowen. He wore a beard," Tomas said.

"The strength of the storm coincides with the rise of Diarmait," Palinah intoned. "They are connected. But we have a chance now. We thought Mitra was gone, extinguished when both the Sky Goddess and her brother were lost to us. But she was aware that I had been in her temple with Madyan's parents. And if she is here, with you, she is not lost forever."

"You keep saying that Kardia is lost to you...to Mitra. But we saw him, or at least his shadow."

"When?" Palinah demanded, jumping from her chair so forcefully, it toppled backward, nearly taking the old woman with it. Sefrina set it aright and helped her to sit. "I'm sorry. You saw Kardia. When?"

"The storm almost killed us before we were able to enter the temple. And while it raged outside, Mitra visited us one evening... He was a mere wisp, but Mitra embraced him. If it's possible, he rides with the storm. We don't believe the storm realizes he's there. Somehow, he slipped into the chamber."

Palinah began wringing her hands. "All these centuries, Mitra's existence gave us hope—for she is a small part of our lost Sky Goddess. When Kardia disappeared, we assumed only the storm remained. But if what you say is true, then there is a chance we can vanquish the storm that killed the Wind God, and free Kardia!"

Murel shot a look at Tomas. He gave her a tiny shake of his head. Now was not the time to reveal that perhaps their Sky Goddess was not gone but held captive. And if she still existed, then there was a chance that her brother could also return. Deep inside her, Mitra rumbled her agreement to remain quiet about her other incarnation.

"...and one Rottu," Jesper was saying. "They want to use me to contain the entity in the storm. And then, I assume, to kill me."

"Once, that may have been our intent. But no longer," Palinah interjected.

"Explain," Murel demanded.

"The discovery of your brother is the miracle for which we have always searched. The Rottu exists so that he or she can be filled with either Mitra or Kardia. Without Kardia to fill him, we planned on using your brother to trap the storm. Held within the Rottu, we could defeat him once and for all."

"By killing me," Jesper repeated.

"True, but so much has changed," Palinah went on. "If Kardia rides the storm, then he may be able to fill you and protect your life. This happens simultaneously to the Malikáfyr with Mitra. Two people, bonded by the love between them can—"

"But I don't want to be bonded!" Jess shouted, and Murel smiled at her brother's abject fear of the idea.

"I don't much like it either," came a gravelly voice from the other side of the room. Jesper rushed to Madyan's side, taking her hand.

"Your brother's actions belie his protestations," Tomas whispered.

# CHAPTER NINETEEN

# The Prophecy Revealed

"We discovered that the Rottu has been communicating with the Malikáfyr while she's been in and out of her sleep," Palina explained, nodding toward Madyan who seemed not at all nonplussed that Jess had left off holding her hand and was smoothing back her hair. "Whether he wishes it or not, a bond has grown between them."

"Murel," Tomas said, keeping his voice low. "If you *and* I are the fourth couple in the prophecy, then it stands to reason that Madyan *and* Jesper could be the fifth. We are meant to—"

"Did you say prophecy?" Sefrina interrupted.

"Er, yes."

"Does it concern five women?"

"Yes," Murel answered. "Six. But not only women—their partners as well. It comes from an old Fenrhi translation. Why?"

"I'll explain in a moment. But first—and as much as I hate to say this— we need to convene the elders." Sefrina marched away to confer with Palinah, leaving Murel and Tomas to approach Madyan and Jess.

"It's good to see you, Madyan," Murel greeted. "You have many friends who are worried for you."

In an uncharacteristic show of emotion, Madyan gave a soft smile. "I've missed you. How is Claire? And the princess? Is she keeping Warin in line?"

Tomas snorted. "They are keeping each other in line, more like."

"Good. Any fool could see they were meant for one another."

Murel grinned upon hearing her usually pragmatic friend sound a bit more like herself. "Do I need to introduce you to Jesper or…"

"She knows all about me," Jess replied. "Except for the times when they would tend to Madyan's needs, I was pretty much left to my own devices here. So, I talked and, I don't know, I felt like Madyan could hear me." He turned to her. "Even when you were sleeping, it was as if you were listening."

Madyan smiled again, in that special way that one does when they're falling for someone. "I *was* listening. And I could sense that you were by my side."

"The chains were just long enough to reach her," he explained.

Madyan sighed. "When the echoes of the storm would resonate through my skull, caroming around, trying to find me, I would focus on you. On how calm you were, and it centered me."

"Happy to oblige. I am the Rottu, after all."

This time, it was Madyan who took Jess's hand. Only...she reached for the stump at the end of his arm. Jess didn't even flinch when she held him there. "You're more than an empty shell, Jesper. Don't let anyone tell you otherwise."

Murel blinked back her happy tears. When Tomas slipped his arm around her shoulder, she felt complete.

Madyan, sensing an audience, adopted her signature scowl, but eventually relented. "I guess I'm in good company. Your sister was always the most sensible of you Aurelians when it came to matters of the heart. But it seems she, too, has finally fallen victim to"—Madyan grimaced—"love."

When Jesper audibly swallowed, Murel and Tomas laughed. Madyan took pity on him. "I'm not saying that we're in love, Jesper. But something connects us."

"I spent my life wondering if there was another person out there for me," he divulged. "And then this happened." He held up his arm. "I had pretty much given up on everything, including finding a...a...soulmate. Then I saw you, and something clicked. This Rottu thing... Imagine existing solely to be filled to save another. I thought it nonsense."

"And now?" Murel asked.

"Bring on the storm, I say." He turned back to Madyan. "Anything to protect you."

There was a flurry of activity behind them as the elders came up the stairs and entered the chamber. Upon seeing their Malikáfyr aware and sitting upright, they immediately bowed and then began muttering amongst themselves. Sefrina and Palinah quickly put a stop to their quibbling about what to do and herded them over to a place where they could convene.

Despite his reduced weight, Jesper scooped up Madyan with ease and carried her to the screened-off area in the far corner of the large chamber. Murel followed and helped Madyan complete her necessaries while her brother waited.

"How much do you hate this?" Murel asked, knowing Madyan at full strength was a warrior who could rival even Lady Anna of Chevlain, a woman who could best even the strongest of soldiers.

"I'm not as weak as they believe," she whispered. "Jesper knows. He would swap out the dosed food they gave me with his own when they were not paying attention. His carrying me was a ruse so that they would not suspect that I've been awake, at least for short periods, each day for the past week. Murel, I've never met someone as resilient as your brother. What he endured changed him, hardened him. Yet, he remains kind."

"He lost himself for a while," Murel said, worried. "The part of him that was stolen...he'll never get it back."

Madyan slowly stood. "But now there's room for something more in that hollow space, isn't there?" She called out, "Jesper."

He was by her side in seconds, once again lifting her with ease, and then carrying her to where the others had arranged themselves in a circle. While Murel and Tomas stood apart, Jesper lowered Madyan to the pile of arranged cushions and then sat next to her.

"Remember our oath to the others," Tomas whispered. "Until we know more about what they are planning with the storm and your brother, I think we should not reveal all that we know."

"Just the prophecy, then," Murel agreed, and they joined the group of Fyrjians. She was surprised to find that many of the elders were not actually old. Sefrina was numbered among them. And she indicated a spot next to her where she and Tomas could sit.

"We wish to hear this Aurelian prophecy," Palinah requested, and the murmuring in the chamber was silenced as all eyes settled on Murel and Tomas.

"It is not an Aurelian prophecy by origin, but one from Nifolhad. With the aid of Princess Anwyl, Queen Juliana was able to decipher some ancient texts in the royal library." Murel took a calming breath, feeling Mitra stir restlessly within her, then slowly recited the lines.

> *"Duty and shield to cast out blind obeisance*
> *Truth and healing be a warrior's protection*
> *One saved by four*
> *Five control the sixth*
> *But first and last, there will be blood."*

"That's it?" a wizened man wheezed. "That's all that your queen has? And the great Sophianan Scholar, Princess Anwyl?" He started coughing, and his entire body was racked with spasms.

Murel suddenly realized that the man was laughing.

"Forgive him," Sefrina begged. "He's old and feeble and—"

"You're feeble!" the man shouted at her.

"You should not even be here," Sefrina countered. "Your days as an elder are over. You agreed."

"Yes, I agreed, Granddaughter. I agreed to step back so that you could take your place. Younger minds are needed if we are to survive the storms. But that does not mean that I can't make a contribution."

"We pray that this will be the last storm that we must weather," Palinah added, trying to soothe the tension.

The man began laughing again, and this time, his cackles morphed into real choking, contorting his bony frame. Sefrina pressed a cup of water to him, holding it steady while her grandfather sipped from the vessel. He held her hand while she rubbed his back. "You always were my favorite granddaughter."

"She's your only granddaughter," several elders spoke in unison, revealing that it was an old and probably oft-repeated joke.

"I did not say that your mind was feeble, Grandfather. Merely that you are old and—"

"And feeble," he finished. "I am at that." He next addressed Murel. "How did your queen come by this prophecy?"

"From a piece of Fenrhi exiflos," she provided.

He grumbled. "Those Fenrhi women, always with the sixes. The honeycomb, the castes, the exiflos. Five lines of prophecy pointing to six to save the world. Except the Sky Goddess holds dominion over five realms, not six."

"Five realms?" Tomas asked.

"Not like you are envisioning, young man. These realms have no borders, no armies, no castles or fortresses. They are the realms around us." He held up one finger. "First, the sky, of course, and all that is contained within it. Then there is both the earth and the water in all their forms. And the creatures"—he turned, holding up three more gnarled digits, and winked at Sefrina—"that would be you and me and all the living beasts that roam. And finally, those things that grow: forests, plants, and even these limchens that light our caves. All connected to the heart of the Goddess."

"But from what I understand of the Fenrhi is that there are six castes," Jesper noted.

"Blood Caste and the Mother are the same," Murel guessed. "What is our prophecy missing?"

"I wish I could tell you," he replied. "The Fenrhi have applied their logic to an illogical being. Wrapped it up tight with their adherence to symmetry. Our Goddess is perfectly imperfect. She is subject to the same whims as her children, and the same weaknesses."

"Love and jealousy," Murel said, and he nodded. "And if blood and the mother are the same, then it would explain why she has five arms and not six."

At that, every person in the room snapped to attention. "When did you see the Goddess?"

Murel had almost let slip something vital about Warin's drawing from the Southron Isles, but Tomas was quick with an answer.

"In Mitra's temple," he explained. "Her statue is hard to miss."

The elders relaxed, but Sefrina's grandfather continued to regard Murel with knitted brows. Before he could ask more, a woman burst into the space. "The storm nearly is here!"

"So early?" Palinah cried. "The Rottu is not prepared."

"Go," Sefrina said calmly. "I will explain what to expect. We still have at least an hour before it finds the mountain's heart and this chamber. Take care of the elders and my grandfather."

"I need a few moments to recover from that last coughing fit," he claimed, suddenly acting much frailer than he had before. Most of the others had already filed from the chamber, making their way down the steps to find safe sanctuary in the many chambers carved from the solid rock.

Sefrina stood and, hands on hips, stared down at her grandfather. "I can handle this."

"That you can, I have no doubt," he said. "But these two know more than they are letting on. And our Malikáfyr and Rottu are in on it."

Sefrina turned to where Murel, Tomas, Jesper, and Madyan all waited in silence. "We haven't much time…"

"How much do you know about the Southron Isles?" Murel asked.

"Very little. Fyrjians rarely travel farther than the desert, with a few exceptions… You, of course," she added, nodding to Madyan. "From what I do know, they may be the only people in the Known Realms who are more secretive than we. One people, surrounded by a sea of sand; the other by water. Dunes and waves."

"And the legend," Murel prompted. "The Sky Goddess thrown from the desert sky into the Virin Sea…"

"What about it?" Sefrina asked.

"You've seen the image of our goddess elsewhere," the old man guessed.

"Not Murel, but her cousin, Warin," Tomas stated. "When he visited the Southron Isles. He saw a shrine to a five-armed goddess…in the home of an Isler named Marlita."

"They found her, you see," Murel added. "They found Sky and drew her from the sea. They saved her, and she blessed them with prosperity. Warin and Princess Anwyl were saved by Marlita when she asked a boon of their goddess. But Marlita and her brethren are controlled by one who is corrupted. This woman, the Fanm, she uses the goddess to not only destroy her enemies, but any person who does not agree with her."

Sefrina's grandfather slumped in his chair. "An angry goddess does not bode well for the world. No wonder Mitra and Kardia have survived. And if the Sky Goddess yet exists…"

"Do you have a sense from Mitra that she is connected to her goddess form?" Madyan asked. "Can the two be aware of one another?"

"She knows because I know," Murel replied. "But distance and time have severed the connection between them."

Madyan looked thoughtful for a moment.

"How exactly does that work?" Jesper asked. "Brother and sister, but husband and wife in another form? And how was it that the Sky Goddess fell in love with a man? That's one hell of a triangle."

"Exactly," Sefrina's grandfather said. "Be'alu loved the goddess of the trees, for he made beautiful things from her bounty. And terrible weapons. Her largesse inflamed his hunger for more power. But she could not give him more. The Sky Goddess always ruled equally over the five realms. In giving the Forest Goddess more rain, she would be stealing from the sky and the earth and the creatures. It would upset the balance of the world. It is the reason Be'alu pretended to love her—the grief caused by his betrayal would strengthen his Forest Goddess. And it did, but not enough."

"What made him that way, I wonder?" Jesper asked, staring at the space where his hand should've been. "So evil that he scours the desert with the sole purpose of destroying life. Even his progeny…they live to inflict pain. They take pleasure in it."

Madyan placed her hand on his forearm. "The world will always need balance, but I believe Diarmait and his sons, Roger and Bowen, are evidence of Be'alu's growing strength."

"There has always been a balance between good and bad," the old man stated. "What we conquer today will only manifest another day—perhaps in a decade or a millennium. There is no way to tell."

Everyone fell silent, and that was when Murel heard it…the soft wail of wind, low pitched as if blowing through hollowed-out logs. "How do we help Jess?" But Murel didn't hear the reply, and she swayed on her feet. Tomas caught her before she hit the floor. A gust of wind that had nothing to do with the storm swept through the chamber, one that had emanated from her chest, only to direct its flow toward Madyan.

Murel blinked, then focused on Tomas. "Mitra left me." Madyan's eyes flashed amethyst for a brief moment. The storm wailed louder.

Sefrina helped her grandfather to rise. "You must get to safety, Papi."

"It is too late for that, my dear. If my time is finished here, then I will end it fighting."

"You will not! You will stay hidden. With me, Grandfather, when the time comes." Sefrina took his hand and held it to her heart. He nodded, and she turned to Madyan. "He'll come for you first. I don't know if he realizes yet that Mitra is here, but once he is in this chamber, he'll sense her. It will incite him."

"And what happens to Kardia? Does he fill Jesper?" Murel asked.

"It is not Kardia—if he is even able to manifest—who will fill your brother," Sefrina rushed to say as the wailing of the wind grew to a crescendo. "As I said, Be'alu will sense Mitra, and he'll attack Madyan first. He'll try to consume her for her power. That is where Jesper comes in."

"What do I need to do?" he asked, taking Madyan's hand.

"Block his path. Force him to fill you instead. You are the Rottu. An open vessel with nothing for Be'alu to latch onto. Nothing for him to use to grow stronger. Kardia will also sense Mitra, and I believe he'll be able to shear himself away from Be'alu. You must welcome him into your mind."

Murel wondered not for the first time where Kardia would go, but she would worry about that after making sure her brother would be safe. "How do we protect Jesper? He can't be expected to carry this storm around inside him for the rest of his days."

Though it was not the time to laugh, Sefrina's grandfather chuckled. "I like an optimist."

"Papi!"

Murel narrowed her eyes. "Tell us, Sefrina."

"The Rottu is not meant to live"—she held up her hands to stop the ensuing argument—"but your presence changes that. Yours and Tomas's. You are more than bondmates; you are the fourth and marked by runes that were used during the creation of the world. You and Tomas can fight to save Jesper! Your combined strength can control Be'alu until he is weakened. And Jesper will keep him trapped until nothing remains of him."

"Jesper, I don't like this."

"The cycle of hate in Nifolhad, it is fed by Be'alu," Sefrina continued. "Diarmait will never be defeated until the storm is eradicated. Where do you think the steward king got his power? He will continue to plot and kill and maim and torture…for no other reason than it feeds his lust for more. He will not stop. Even if you survive today and return to Aurelia, he will come for you, again and again. And when he dies, one of his spawn will take his place. Princes Roger and Bowen might be dead and buried, but Diarmait has countless legitimate daughters and bastard sons."

To punctuate her statement, the wailing grew and the air pressure dropped. The limchens flushed, beating as if the center of the mountain was a giant heart, pumping blood in and out of the chamber.

"Grandfather, we must hide!" Sefrina pulled him to the wall that partitioned off the bathing area.

"I'm ready," Madyan announced, her eyes flashing over and proclaiming that Mitra was present once more. "Rottu, will you stand by me?"

The very air in the chamber seemed to be sucked from the room in a great *whoosh*. Mitra's eyes glowed, and her hair lifted as wild gusts swept through the chamber. Tomas pulled Murel to his side, his arm banded around her waist, as if afraid she might be sucked out of the room.

No sooner had she pictured herself flying over the open edge of the chamber's overlook than she felt the malevolence behind her. A dark, twisting entity oozed and pulsed over the half-wall. It was as if the entire storm that had scoured the desert had shrunk down into a gaseous concentration of evil. Its tendrils flicked out like long tongues, tasting the air for the occupants of the chamber.

It homed in on Madyan, withdrew slightly, as if gathering its strength, then lunged forward with hundreds of dark, spear-like tendrils, each aimed at her heart. Jesper jumped forward and in front of Madyan before the mass had a chance to reach her.

It was too late for Be'alu to veer away, and sooty daggers of smoke and dust stabbed into her brother, one after the other. His body jolted with each puncture. About half of the dark mass remained, and Jesper—eyes closed and teeth gritted in pain—leaned into the onslaught. He took a step forward, his arms down and his one fist clenched, and then another step, shortening the distance and not allowing what remained of Be'alu to circumvent the trap.

The wailing of the storm morphed into a roar of hatred, its last notes dwindling into something that sounded like an anguished cry. And when the last of it entered Jesper, he closed his eyes and swayed. When he opened them again, they were black with animosity. He sneered, then fixated on Madyan...only it was Mitra he confronted. He raised his arms as if to strangle her and then noticed he had but one hand. The roar that came from Jesper's mouth was inhuman. Mitra matched his ire, her eyes blazing brightly to cancel the blackness that had entered Jesper's soul.

"Now!" Sefrina shouted. "Murel, give your brother your strength!"

Together with Tomas, Murel stepped forward. Tomas grappled with Jesper from behind, using one arm to loop around him and pin his good arm to his side. He held fast to Murel's hand. The full import of their connection was made clear—her strength fed Tomas as much as his fed her. Mitra placed her hand on Jesper's cheek. He twisted his head, gnashing out with his teeth but stopping shy of ripping at Mitra's fingers. He howled in rage and confusion.

Then, in the dead black of his gaze, Murel saw it—a spark of light.

She reached across her brother's chest and placed her hand over his heart. Mitra took his face in both hands, tenderly and with love. She too had seen the spark, and she stared into Jesper's eyes, forcing him to see her.

Murel squeezed Tomas's hand, felt the welling of his concern and love for her, felt it move physically through her arm and into her chest, where it joined the care and love she felt for her brother. She imagined it was a sphere and rolled it down her other arm and into her hand. From there, she pressed it against—no, into—Jesper's heart.

Be'alu roared again, but the spark that was Kardia grew, and his light burned through the ruin of Jesper's eyes in a violent coup. The strange circle in which they stood shrunk, then exploded outward again with such force that their connection was blown apart, forcing them to stagger back from Jesper. The mountain trembled, and the bedrock fissured below their feet. Shards of light shot up, hitting the ceiling and rebounding in brilliant, frenzied patterns throughout the chamber.

# CHAPTER TWENTY

# No Longer

Murel hit the floor hard, as did Tomas. Mitra managed to keep her feet but appeared stunned.

Murel felt…singed. The air reeked with the acrid odor of lightning and the coppery scent of blood. The blinding rays emanating from her brother had zigzagged across the room. Several larger bolts had struck Tomas, and he lay unmoving on the floor. Only the steady rise and fall of his chest stopped Murel from running to him. A thick, sooty mist had settled around her brother's feet, not so much dissipating as it touched the floor, but rather seeping into the crevices in the stone.

First to recover, she sprang up and rushed to her brother. He hung his head, eyes downcast. "Jesper?" Murel whispered as he slowly lifted his chin.

The same golden light that had pulsed and sent them all flying blazed from his eyes, burning with such intensity that Murel was forced to look down, where she saw that even the floor had cracked. Fissures radiated outward from Jesper's feet to where she had been flung. She slid her foot to the side, revealing a finger's width crevice below her boot. The strange glow from her brother played tricks with her vision, causing the shadows in the crack to pulse and writhe.

Across the room, Tomas rose to his feet and stared spellbound at Jesper. When Murel looked again upon her brother, his blinding gaze had been replaced with the cool amethyst glow of the Wind God's earthly entity. "Kardia?" she wondered aloud, and he nodded. "And Jesper?"

Kardia frowned. "H-he," he stuttered. "I…I am…unused to words."

Behind him, Madyan stirred, but her eyes were those of Mitra. She eased her way to Kardia, placing a gentle hand on his arm. "You survived all these years, my love. I've missed you."

Kardia caressed Mitra's cheek. "I have screamed for so long, I feared not remembering how to speak." He turned back to Murel. "The Rottu is no more."

Murel gasped, and Tomas hurried to her side.

"No, Murel," Mitra explained. "He means that now that the Rottu is full, he is no longer empty, and therefore, no longer the Rottu. Your brother is now your brother."

"Yes. He is only Jesper," Kardia added. "How came you to care for these strangers to the desert?"

"They freed me, my love," Mitra replied.

"Then I will love them as well."

"Will you let Jesper come forward?" Murel asked.

"In time," Kardia answered, slipping his arm around Mitra and pulling her to him.

"Patience," Mitra soothed. "There are ceremonies and rites."

"I care not. I have been apart from you for too long."

"But the Rottu and the Vessel, they are not prepared." She nodded toward Murel and Tomas. "Many centuries have passed, and these young people have been teaching me about their world. The gods and goddesses of old no longer rule. Look inside yourself. Listen to Jesper's voice. Our love will be tainted without their consent."

Kardia closed his eyes for a few seconds. "We shall wait. Your brother tells me that we are not finished here," Kardia intoned, settling his palm over Murel's heart. "*Your* trials have yet to conclude."

An overwhelming sense of dread filled Murel's chest, and she staggered backward. Tomas started for her, but she held out her hand to stop him as a black haze crept up the inside of her body, suffocating her and clawing its way up her shoulders and throat. The last thing she saw was Tomas's frantic eyes and his glowing blond hair. The smell of rank, rotting earth clogged her nostrils.

"Do not touch her!" Mitra cried out, and Murel heard no more.

But she could feel Be'alu's vitriol and taste his never-ending desire to destroy. She struggled to find something more, something of herself, of her love for Tomas, but could sense naught but immense anguish under the hatred. And something else...an all-encompassing appetite for power.

Be'alu searched for her; she felt its desire to root her out, to rip her painfully from existence. And she, though she no longer knew who or what she had been, made herself small and hid.



A rage like he'd never experienced before consumed Tomas as the woman he loved disappeared, morphing into something hideous. Her eyes were black and bottomless. It, or Be'alu, swiveled its head as if considering its new form. It twisted its wrist in elegant circles, the movements going from hand to elbow and arm, and then to its shoulders. It breathed in, deep, moving its body seductively, and when it exhaled, a dark fog swirled from its nose and mouth. It smiled then, beautiful and deadly, making a mockery of what had been Murel.

Tomas was helpless to stop Be'alu as it ran its hands down Murel's body. Touching her, pinching her breasts and taking pleasure in the self-afflicted pain. It reached lower, between Murel's legs, cupping her, and moaning in pleasure. Be'alu's grin widened, and it dipped its fingers into Murel's Fyrjian leggings.

"Don't you dare," Tomas commanded, drawing his sword and raising it to knock the thing unconscious. They could trap Be'alu in a deep sleep until they could figure out how to bring back Murel.

"No," Sefrina's grandfather shouted, stepping between them. "Be'alu is too strong. He will use the very power that now resides—"

A hand—Murel's hand—gripped the old man's shoulder, digging its blackened fingernails through the cloth of his tunic and into his skin, twisting and breaking the bones as if they were made of brittle ice. Sefrina's grandfather screamed, and the thing wrenched its body sideways, flinging the man into the partition, where he crumpled into an unmoving heap.

Be'alu next faced Tomas and took his measure. It undulated its body, and a black tongue slicked slowly over its lips.

Tomas dared not glance at the old man cradled in Sefrina's lap.

"No, Papi," she cried over and over.

Attracted by the anguish in Sefrina's pleas, it stalked its new prey. Kardia and Mitra moved to block its path. "You won't touch her, Be'alu," Mitra seethed.

It pulled back in surprise. "Be'alu," it drawled. "Thank you for reminding me. You won't be able to stop me, Mitra. Not even with Kardia's help. You are too weak. You should not have gifted any of your power to the chalice. It is mine now. Mine to use. And with this new body, I will torture and kill every tiny ant in this hill." It shuddered in pleasure at the image it invoked, and a wall of black dust cut off half of the chamber, trapping Mitra and Kardia where they stood. Kardia pounded against the barrier, but to no avail. He paced like an angry mountain cat whilst Mitra went to Sefrina to console her.

Be'alu laughed at them. "There is so much to do here. I promise to return to settle our score. But first, I must slake my needs." He slowly stalked toward Tomas. "This body knows you. Covets you. I should like to feel what it felt."

"I do not want to hurt you," Tomas stated, raising his sword.

"That is why you are weak." Be'alu laughed. "Besides, you are a fool if you imagine you can."

Tomas advanced, lifting his sword with both arms. His mind cried out for Murel, trying to reach her, but all he could feel was her absence. He prayed, begging her to let him somehow get close enough to knock Be'alu out. His heart held that small hope as he reached striking distance of his goal, and he brought the flat of his blade down. Be'alu's black eyes stared, and he cowered. Tomas faltered. Then it laughed—the monster was simply toying with Tomas. With one hand, it wrenched his weapon from his hands. Pain wracked through Tomas's wrists, and his sword went flying across the room.

"I've forgotten this feeling." It grabbed Tomas by the throat, its blackened fingers squeezing. "Enjoyment. Yes, I like this very much."

Tomas uselessly groped at the fingers choking him, and the pain in his broken wrists intensified. Be'alu was impossibly strong, and black spots dotted his vision.

"And"—it drew in a deep breath through its nose, sniffing back and forth in the air—"arousal." It forced Tomas onto the bed.

Tomas gulped air into his lungs as Be'alu climbed atop. In seconds, it ripped open Tomas's tunic and chemise.

"You might be stronger than me, Be'alu. But you can't force this."

"Can't I?" it said, in the softest of voices, sounding like Murel. "You must, Tomas," she begged, "or he will kill you. Please, Tomas." Delicate fingers caressed him. She straddled him, pressing down and rubbing against him like a cat in heat. "Please, I beg you, Tomas. Please." A black cloud of dust and mist swirled around them, closing in on all sides, and obliterating all light save that which came from the limchens that had fallen from the ceiling onto the bed.

"Murel, no," Tomas pleaded. "If you are in there, don't do this."

"We must, Tomas. It is the only way to save you. I am already lost. Do this last act for me, before I am gone forever."

The limchens cast an eerie glow upon her visage. Murel. The woman he loved. She ground herself against him. A strange heat filled Tomas's heart, traveling outward and up to his shoulders, down his arms, and to his wrists. There it pooled, and he gasped in relief as his snapped bones reset and mended themselves. She was healing him.

*It is not the woman you call Murel who heals you.*

The voice had come from within him.

*And you know the thing above you is not Murel.*

"Please, Tomas," she urged, and without the fog of pain, he could see the wisps of black seep forth with each word. Inky eyes looked down at him and frowned. "These plants must go."

"Why, my love?" Tomas asked, stalling for time. "I cannot see your beauty without the light."

"I am shy, Tomas," she murmured, oblivious to the dark, oozing mist from her mouth that spilled down her chin and chest. She swept the limchens away, extinguishing all light from the enclosed sphere.

His Murel abhorred tight, dark places.

*Close your eyes.*

*Who are you?* Tomas silently wondered.

*You know already. You wear my mark.*

Not Kardia, the Wind God himself. Then Tomas remembered how he'd been struck in the chest by its golden light.

*Now you understand. You must close your eyes, or Be'alu will know. I will try to save you.*

*Save Murel instead,* Tomas impressed to the power inside him. A solution fomented in his mind, and he silently swore. *She wears the mark of your sister, the Sky Goddess.*

The thing that had taken Murel writhed sinuously over him. "Please, Tomas." Nails raked down his chest, leaving a searing trail of pain. "I desire to feel you inside me."

*I will try. But you need to be connected to each other.*

Hope surged in Tomas's heart, and before Be'alu could reach down to touch him, he pretended to be incapable of lifting his arms and faked a painful groan. "I need to touch you, my love, but my wrists…"

"Yes, touch me," it said in the dark. He felt Murel's body shift forward, then her cold hands on his shoulders, slicking their way over his biceps and elbows, down to his wrists. Be'alu squeezed, and Tomas feigned a cry. "I'm sorry, my love," it falsely expressed, lifting Tomas's marked arm, heedless of his pretended hisses of pain. "Am I hurting you?" it asked with an eagerness that belied its concern.

"I can bear anything if it means giving you pleasure one last time. Help me to touch you where you like it best," he pleaded, his words tight with the disgust he felt at the idea that Be'alu was taking pleasure in using Murel's body.

"Yes, my love." Be'alu reached forward in the dark, scratching its nails up Tomas's arm and lifting the dead weight. With Murel's other hand, Be'alu gripped Tomas's wrist and moved it so that his hand skimmed over Murel's chest and up her shoulder. "Caress me."

"I will try," he said, ungracefully circling his fingertips.

Be'alu reached for Tomas's other hand, pulling it up, heedless of any broken bones. Before it released his upper arm, Tomas let his hand slip from Murel's shoulder.

*Try to reach her. Be ready to open your eyes.*

Tomas tightened his grip, encircling the banded marking on Murel's skin. "Murel," he called. "Murel, if you can hear me, you must come forward." The hand on his bicep tightened.

"But I am here, Tomas," Be'alu crooned unconvincingly.

"Murel, I love you," Tomas tried again. "Hear me, Murel. Fight."

Be'alu suddenly realized that the connection between the bond marks had been made. It tried to pull its hand away, but Murel's fingers would not obey.

*Now!*

Tomas opened his eyes, and a golden light pushed at the dark mist. Black tendrils of malice streaked out like worms from her mouth and eyes, staining her face. Tomas twisted his other hand around, capturing her hand and wrist. Without breaking the contact between them, he pulled Murel forward, trapping her palm to his heart and his to hers.

She twisted and bucked as Be'alu tried to break free, but the golden glow from Tomas took on a physical force, shredding the dark mist.

Then he felt her. Tiny. Lost. Hiding. He urged her to come forward. "I'll protect you."

He felt her reluctance. *Not yet, Tomas,* she whispered in his mind. *Give me time.*

"You have it. Hand and heart. Heart in hand."

Be'alu screamed and threw Murel's body back. But the connection to their markings and where their hands touched their chests could not be broken. The room around them coalesced, and Be'alu continued to rant, thrashing Murel's head from side to side.

Tomas couldn't risk looking away, but sensed that the veil separating Mitra, Kardia, and Sefrina was breaking. He could hear them shouting.

"Murel, see me. I am here," he encouraged, trying to break Be'alu's hold over her.

*Your eyes burn me.*

"No, they will heal you. They are burning Be'alu. The pain you feel is his."

*Of course. The pain is his.*

. . .

The waves crashed and pounded on the shell she had erected around herself. Relentless. Cold. Black. Deafening. Murel screamed as Be'alu came for her. Dark whispers seeped through the fissures, and she fought them.

Steeling herself against the onslaught, she tried forcing the inky fingers back. The pain was too much to bear.

And always the roar and the blackness. Whatever it was that was clawing its way toward her was trying a new tactic. A blade of light was spearing its way through her dome. If she had thought she was in pain before, this was a new level of hell. She screamed again, and this time, she wasn't screaming alone. Bright gold pierced her flimsy canopy, and a thousand veins of light cracked her protection. The walls exploded outward, taking the dark along with it.

Almost. She sensed something near her. Someone. An ill-formed figure trembled in pain and rage—the malevolence that had taken her.

But who attacked her now? She tried facing the light, but it was too radiant to behold. The figure that emerged was divine. And terrible. It was the greater of the two raging entities.

Waves of light from the being continued to throb and pulse. And the evil thing rose from where it had lain. A war was about to be waged, and she was all that stood between the two enemies.

"Stop!" she ordered, holding her hands against the opposing forces. Pain seared a path through her fingertips, up her arms, and across her chest, where it clashed in an explosion that left her heart in fragments. "Stop," she cried out again, but with less conviction, bracing herself as the second onslaught of the dueling waves of light and dark crested through her. "Neither of you can win. I'll be the lone casualty in this war."

She sensed that neither being cared. She focused on what she believed was the Wind God. "This is what you want? To continue in this trap? Don't you see? It's the same as being caught in the storm."

The pain ebbed, but Murel held onto it, grabbing it with her outstretched hand and squeezing it in her fist. She shifted her focus to Be'alu. "You've raged for centuries. Aren't you tired? Don't you want to rest? You deserve peace after all this time." Again, not a cessation in the assault, but a slight retreat. Murel latched onto it and held it fast in her hand.

On either side of her, the light and dark coalesced into indistinct figures, tethered to her in ropes of shimmering golden waves and oozing tendrils of ink. She stepped back so that she could see them both, holding their leashes. It was a tenuous control at best. Then she felt it. A stirring in her heart. Somewhere, Tomas was feeding her his strength. Colors whirled in her mind, but always the subtle glow of green—emerald and moss and pine and mint. Shades of nature and earth and health. She could smell them, and she allowed the scents to radiate from her core, outward toward the two diametrically opposed wills.

"How is this possible?" Be'alu gasped. "You smell of the forest. She is gone forever, yet you evoke her essence."

"She's not gone," Murel explained.

"Liar! I witnessed her death. He ripped her asunder, flinging her to the sky to be consumed by his sister."

"At first," she said. "But then he carried her children to safety. She is alive, right now, in the forests that thrive in the valleys and mountains and plains of our realms. You've hated the world for so long that you forgot that other climes exist."

"It is still too late," he said. "If I leave here, she will destroy me. He will help her."

"He saved you," Murel revealed. "He sacrificed the Sky Goddess to save you." Be'alu's rage was slowly being assuaged, but the hatred radiating from the Wind God expanded.

It was time to reveal the secret that she and Tomas had kept hidden. "Just because you never found your sister does not mean she perished. Let go of your animus, and Tomas and I will help you find her." Then, she released the two vines of light and dark, and with them, the pain.

• • •

In his arms, Murel screamed. But he held her, willing his strength into her, taking what pain he could into himself. Then he screamed as well when the Wind God flooded back into his mind, scouring it for information, and upon confirming what Tomas suspected Murel had imparted, settled. Outside their circle, he felt the eyes of the others upon them.

"*Ma Lah*," he heard Sefrina swear, and he realized that his eyes must be glowing golden again.

When she opened them, Murel's were dark against his light. And as she grew stronger and more aware, the black poison inking her skin withdrew, and the whites of her eyes were once more visible. Streaks of dark winked on and off in the brilliant ocean blue of her irises, mere shards that told him that Be'alu was still with her.

Tomas could feel the golden light in his own eyes dissipate. He blinked.

*Neither of us will be healed until we are whole again and reunited with what we lost.*

"They must remain with us, Tomas," she said, as if she could hear the voice speaking in his head. "But they understand now. And it will take some time before all their anger is gone."

"I can see him in your eyes," Tomas said. "Tiny dark tendrils."

"The same is true of yours, except with golden threads."

He helped her to sit, and the strange field around them shimmered before fading to nothing. The others approached them with caution.

"It's all right," Murel started to explain. "Jess, Madyan...you must heal Nifolhad. Mitra and Kardia have given you gifts. The desert must join forces with Queen Aghna and King Ranulf and rid your realm of Diarmait and his influence." She tilted her chin and looked out past the opening to the lake, as if listening to some voice. "A part of Be'alu now resides in Diarmait, feeding him and giving him power."

"Won't Be'alu try to stop us?" Sefrina asked.

"He can't. He's part of me now. If I try to purge him before he is healed, he'll simply find another vessel to fill, and the cycle will continue. Perhaps not in our lifetime, but again. For years, he imprisoned the Wind God and Kardia. Now, it is his time for penance."

"Murel, you can't!" Jesper forbade.

"It is the only way to heal him," Murel explained. "All this time, we were wrong about the prophecy. The part about one saved by four never referred to Madyan. The one needing saving was always Be'alu."

"Then we're not the fifth couple in the prophecy," Madyan deduced.

"Murel," Sefrina called out from where she still held her grandfather.

Tomas supported Murel as he led her carefully to where the old man had collapsed, though now held in his granddaughter's arms. There was a commotion behind them, and the elders filed into the chamber.

"He wishes to tell you something," Sefrina explained.

"There isn't much time," the old man wheezed through his pain before his eyes fluttered closed. His chest hitched and shuddered with each effort to draw breath.

Murel took Tomas's hand and knelt down. "The one who did this to you is still within me. But if you trust me, I can help with the pain."

Sefrina nodded for her grandfather, and Murel set her hand over his heart. The gift she received from Mitra, the ability to heal, was strengthened by the Wind God's power that still resided in Tomas. Her palm warmed, and a soft glow emanated from her fingers. Sefrina's grandfather opened his eyes, and his chest fell and rose with less effort.

She sensed Be'alu's curiosity. *You did this. You caused this man's pain. He is dying because of you.* Be'alu retreated.

Tomas carefully lifted Sefrina's grandfather from the floor and carried him to the bed.

"Can you heal him?" Sefrina asked.

"I'm sorry," Murel said.

"Don't worry, Seffi," he soothed. "I'm at peace with it being my time. But you need to show them the error of their ways."

"It's all right. We know that we were wrong about the prophecy," Tomas told him. "About the one being saved by the four."

Sefrina's grandfather shook his head as Murel pulled a blanket up over his frail body and ruined shoulder. Palinah stepped forward with a soft cloth to wipe the blood from the old man's mouth. "Your prophecy is missing a line. And some of what you translated is wrong."

"But you said it had to do with the five realms, Papi. Not six."

"Maybe I was wrong as well. Sefrina, you must take them to the peak. Show them the stones. What is written upon them is important. I know it is. And I believe that it is the original prophecy, not some watered-down-by-time prose."

"But it's runic," Palinah countered. "No one alive can read it."

Sefrina's grandfather grinned and pointed at Tomas and Murel. "But what resides in the two of them can."

# CHAPTER TWENTY-ONE

# Homeward

*The Kaldemer Sea, Northern Coast of Whitmarsh, Aurelia*

"Something troubling you?" Tomas asked softly as he came up behind Murel, where she leaned on the railing of the vessel that carried them home, though not to Floresta, nor even Pheldhain. He wrapped his arms around her, enveloping her in his thick, fur-lined cape. Murel turned to accept the kiss she knew would be waiting for her. Her bondmate. A connection stronger than even marriage vows, yet they took the latter all the same when Captain Grieg offered to perform the rites.

Five months ago, when they finally were free to leave the Fyrost Desert, they had traveled directly to Vynfyr, the western port city where they met with Queen Aghna and King Ranulf. There, they'd discovered that Captain Grieg had sailed to Nifolhad to seek them out and bring them home. *Moon Caster* had made port in Vynfyr while Grieg had used his network of contacts in the hope of hearing some hint of their whereabouts.

Word had been sent to him to ready the ship whilst Murel and Tomas met with Aghna and Ranulf and relayed everything that had transpired in the Fyrost. Almost everything. Of the stowaways who shared a space in their hearts, they said nothing. And though Aghna and Ranulf were queen and king, it was to Murel and Tomas that an odd sort of deference was made.

They hadn't made their exodus from the desert alone. Madyan had sent a contingent of Fyrjian warriors with them, including Sefrina who would offer an alliance. Murel smiled, remembering how Sefrina's name and long list of honorifics were announced to the queen and king, along with the important addition of Fyrjian ambassador to Aurelia, for her journey would take her far from her desert home.

Together, they had shared what they knew of Diarmait, and Ranulf had confirmed that rumors of his resurgence were running the length and breadth of the realm.

"I was thinking about Jesper," she revealed.

"He is in good company with Madyan, and has found his place, and with it, peace. "

"I know. But I miss him." They were quiet for a few moments, staring at Whitmarsh's forested coastline. "And of how we are going to explain to our king and queen that we are now both Aurelian and Fyrjian."

"Our dual allegiance was not a choice we made. We'll find a way to make them understand. But what about you? How is the beast this morning?" Tomas asked her, using his nickname for Be'alu.

"Sleeping. And our gusting god?" Murel asked, referring to Wind. She turned around so that she could wrap her arms around her husband's waist.

"Quiet, but available. Do you recall Grieg's reaction when he first saw us?"

"It's hard to forget...he was going to run me through with his sword but fell to his knees when you stepped forward. He didn't trust me until I healed one of the crew with my glowing green hands." Murel laughed now, but it had been a tense moment explaining to Grieg how Tomas had come to have part of a deity residing in him, and Murel, what could only be described as a demon. More confounding to all was that she also possessed a gift from Mitra, allowing her to heal injuries, and so a piece of the Sky Goddess herself. Of Grieg's and the crew's discretion, they had absolute faith. Southron Islers would never betray anyone linked to their goddess.

"I've been considering what our captain told us of the Fanm and how she converses with Sky. What I have with Wind is different. I feel tethered to him—he's here"—Tomas patted his heart—"but not here." He touched his brow.

Murel searched for the telltale flecks of gold in his irises. "Brown and beautiful," she observed.

"And your monster?" he asked, cocking his head to look into her eyes from a different angle.

"Behaving. We have an understanding about when and where he should surface. Be'alu has become...respectful." At the mention of his name, she felt him stir and knew tiny black filaments would deepen the already dark blue of her eyes.

"There he is," Tomas observed. At the same time, his eyes were shot with gold.

"Interesting," she said, tamping down Be'alu. "I suppose he is not complaining. I still feel his rage, but there is something else that is itching him...a curiosity that is slowly eating away at the anger. He's impatient to be off this ship—this world is alien to him, for all he has known for so long is the desert. He's eager to see the forests and lands that I promised." She looked up at the sails that billowed loosely above them—since sailing past Cathmara, *Moon Caster* seemed to be crawling through mud and not the icy waves. Her progress was so slow that even now, fat snowflakes drifted lazily onto the ship's deck.

"Perhaps we can speed the journey along," Tomas said. He closed his eyes, and when he opened them, the normally rich brown hue flashed golden, and he winked at her as the breeze gusted and the sails billowed with the force of it. *Moon Caster* rushed forward. Tomas took her arm and escorted her to the captain's quarters, where they would dine together.

• • •

Murel leaned back, staring up at the pines whose spires grew so tall they could almost kiss the clouds. A week ago, they'd anchored the *Moon Caster* in a hidden inlet tucked against the cliffs of Black Pine Island. It had been the dead of night when they'd arrived, and they'd waited until the following evening to take a skiff to the mainland, the northern coast of Kings Glen. With their Fyrjian mounts and their strange Nifolhadian garb, they'd been cautious and had avoided the sleepy fishing village, instead veering southwest and into the foothills that skirted the border of Whitmarsh. Grieg and the crew would wait a week, provisioning their stores with fresh water from the island and whatever game they could hunt.

Murel took a deep breath and held it, savoring the crisp winter air and the smell of pine sap. She had agreed with Tomas regarding the circuitous route and traveling only with him and Sefrina—avoiding people in her current state wasn't merely prudent, it was necessary for their safety. With the thought, she felt Be'alu stir. She hadn't let him free yet, giving herself over to him as she had with Mitra, for she was unsure if he would relinquish his hold on her. But she fed him with peaceful moments such as this, and she filled her senses with the beauty around her. It was having an effect, for he was no longer a mass of roiling impatience in her heart.

The soft scrunch of snow as something drew near had her turning. A doe stared curiously at her with its long-lashed eyes, sniffing the air with its wet nose. The deer took a dainty step closer, then its ears twitched in the direction of where their group had made camp. Someone was approaching. Except for the snow, they would have done so silently. Murel could never get used to how her friends could be so stealthy, for it was a skill she'd never mastered. But unlike the others, Tomas was unable to come at her unawares—the connection between them was too strong. But this wasn't Tomas who was joining her.

Sefrina emerged from between two tall pines. She stopped upon noticing the deer, no doubt the regret in her eyes was for forgetting her bow. Unperturbed, the doe meandered away.

Sefrina had never experienced a winter with snow, and Murel smiled at her wide-eyed wonder as she gawped at the white blanket. "Come sit with me," Murel invited, patting the thick rug she'd spread out over the snow.

"Tomas asked me to come find you," Sefrina explained, sitting beside her. "He is laying in wood stores for this evening—he said that it'll be colder tonight, even inside the hunter's lodging that we found." She scooped up some snow in her gloved hand. "It gets cold in the Fyrost, especially in the higher elevations, but I could never have imagined this." She puffed out her breath, entranced by the white fog.

"There are places in Aurelia that grow even colder. Places where, if you draw in breath through your nose, your nostrils freeze closed, and tears crystalize pearl-like on your eyelashes. One such place is in the Cathmaran state of Deighlei—its lands are made up of a massive ice plain, and the snow never thaws in some areas, even in high summer. Claire and Trian can take you one day if you wish to see it. Cathmara has a wild nature, much like its people."

"I should like to meet one," Sefrina stated, shaking the snow off her hand.

"I suppose we should return. We'll need to bed down the horses."

"Already done. We wedged pine boughs in the gaps in the lean-to. With the horse blankets, they should be snug enough."

Murel knew without looking that Tomas neared. And when he strode into the clearing, Sefrina rose. "I'll see you both later."

Tomas sat next to Murel as Sefrina disappeared into the trees and after a moment, asked, "Are you cold?"

"His rage keeps me warm," she said after a moment. "It's constant."

"Then maybe it's time to let a little of Be'alu out."

"I'm afraid to. What if he hurts someone?"

"If you wanted to try, being here in this wilderness of trees is perhaps the safest spot. I can help you to control him."

"We had Mitra and Kardia as well." She let a little of her fears free when she spoke. "When I was trapped in my own mind, it was worse than that day at the beach in Pheldhain. In Kardia, there was nothing but agonizing pain and my own screaming to keep me company. I almost didn't come back. Be'alu was...is...incredibly strong."

"Yet here you sit, in control of him. What is stopping him from taking over? What changed?"

"I did. I ceased desiring his demise and began trying to heal him."

"Then it seems that Be'alu wants that as well. He told you about what he gave to Diarmait, so he must trust you, if that's possible."

Murel tilted her chin, gazing up into the trees that Be'alu viewed as his children. "I let him see my memories of places like this. Even now, before you sat down, I was feeding him with the scents and sounds of the forest." She remembered how she'd given herself over, giving Mitra the opportunity to experience her desert. "You're right, of course. I'm going to have to let him out."

"But not today. Let's get inside where it's warm," he said, pulling her up with him. "The conies are roasting. And Sefrina made some kind of mashed root that she brought back with her. She called it a dust tuber and told me to give the scraps to the horses."

Murel laughed. "Now we know what to call it."

"I don't know. Stinky sour feet root had a nice ring to it. Perhaps it'll taste better when seasoned and cooked...more like mud and less like dirt." He leaned forward and kissed Murel lightly on the lips.

"I miss you," she said. "I miss this."

"Me, too," he admitted. "Not touching you. Not making love with you. I know you're frustrated with me, and I'm sorry that I—"

Murel pressed her fingers to his lips. "Don't be sorry. What we have together, what we are and become when we love one another...I would not share that with anyone."

"But..."

"No buts."

He touched his forehead to hers. "Then, if the weather permits, we'll try giving Be'alu some freedom tomorrow."

She smiled and took his hand to trudge back through the trees. "You'll make sure the weather is amenable, right?"

"Don't you know it," he confirmed. As they came into view of the lodge, the aroma of roasted rabbit wafted over to them, and something else, something exotic. "Let's hope cooked dust tubers taste as delicious as it smells."

. . .

Tomas knelt in front of her, one hand holding the band inked on her arm, the other set gently over her heart. Murel's hands were likewise positioned on him. Between them, white clouds of mist formed with each of their exhalations.

Next to where they knelt, they had built a campfire, and the flames warmed her even as the cold seeped through the thick rug and into her knees. It had snowed whilst they slept, and the muffled silence of the forest in the early morning was serene. Golden light flashed in Tomas's eyes, and a gust of wind whistled through the lofty branches overhead, sending a brief rain of snow upon them. The burning logs sizzled and hissed, but after a brief expulsion of steam, burned merrily on.

The previous night, Murel had tried communing with Be'alu. Whether he understood or even deigned to listen, she had no idea. But she explained a little of what she planned to do, warning him of the consequences should he decide to fight against returning to the shadows of her mind.

"Ready?" Tomas asked.

Murel nodded. She felt Be'alu stir, as if he were a snake adjusting its coils. *Are you ready, Be'alu?* she silently queried. She showed him her memory of how it felt to be Mitra when she'd set her eyes upon her desert. "We promised you that you would see your children," Murel said, this time aloud, and steeled herself as the suffocating blackness oozed into her senses, overtaking everything that was her. Except this time, she was truly tethered to Tomas, his hands anchoring her to the fore. He would not allow her to be dragged into the dark, hidden place where pain reigned.

"What is this?" she—rather, Be'alu—demanded. "It is brighter than even the sun on the desert."

*Do you have no recollection of snow?*

"Snow," he repeated. "It's cold."

*You are not looking, Be'alu.*

. . .

Tomas's heart recoiled, watching Murel's eyes, whites and irises, turn oily black as she gave herself over to Be'alu. Immediately, he knew this was different from the time she was possessed in the temple. Be'alu's voice was hers, though it carried with it an unearthly tone. He was conversing with himself, or rather, with Murel.

"Where should I look? Upon one of my captors?" He shifted his focus off Tomas and upward, into the dark green canopy.

As Tomas watched, the expression on Murel's face filled with something akin to both sadness and joy.

"You did not lie. They are so beautiful. Are there many places like this in this realm?"

"Thousands," Tomas replied.

"I did not expect you to fulfill your promise, nor the Wind God to keep his." Above them, the trees swayed in the breeze. Be'alu gave his attention back to Tomas. "Your woman grows weary, for she did not answer. Can you sense her?"

"I can," Tomas affirmed. "And she is strong, but it is time for you to step back into the shadows."

"I will, soon. But I will speak with your companion first."

"Next time," Tomas ground out, needing to see the indigo of Murel's eyes once again.

"Let me," Be'alu insisted.

"If you hurt her, you will be ripped from existence. I'll make sure of it." Tomas closed his eyes, and when he opened them, a golden light spread out, creating a cocooning sphere over where they knelt. Unlike Murel's experience, when the Wind God possessed him, they shared Tomas's senses. Black mist swirled and eddied around them.

"Why did you help me?" Be'alu demanded. "I betrayed your sister for my own needs. I trapped you for centuries. On the vessel, you sensed my frustration and impatience to see this place, to see if the men and women of this time can speak the truth, and you filled their sails."

"Can't you sense it from Murel? Their lives compared to ours are brief."

"She said that last night. Life is too short. But I am not like you and your sister. I was once like them. Do you know what I am now?"

"You are the spirit of the man you once were. And when you were stripped of everything, laid bare, all that was left was your lust for power and need for revenge from seeing your children destroyed. But I only carried them away. They are here, and in Nifolhad, though not as abundant. Here, in this young realm, they thrive."

"I am tired," Be'alu revealed. "I do not belong here or anywhere. My time in the world should have ended long ago."

"This is truth."

Be'alu stared around them, pausing his study of the forest. "They are very pure, aren't they? Not like Diarmait. Even if I wanted to taint them, I could not. They would rather sacrifice themselves."

"Truth, again."

"She is asking me to yield. She could make me, with his help. But she is asking. I don't want to return to her mind."

"Do you know what that means?" the Wind God said through Tomas.

"My existence will cease."

"Only as you know it. You will become something else, for nothing is ever truly gone."

"Will she be there? Does she still live, my Goddess of the Forests?"

"Could these trees exist without her? Listen, and you can hear her voice in the very air in this forest. In all the forests. And she will let you rest in her arms if you so desire."

"I do," Be'alu said. "Tell this one who made good on her promise, this Murel, that I leave her a gift. Tell her not to be afraid of it. She can trust it, as I trust her enough to control it."

"What is this gift?" The question carried more of Tomas's tone than the Wind God.

"The best of me, a gift that will manifest as she regains her center—her mind is still at war with itself. The worst of what I was resides in Diarmait. Murel will need my boon to heal him, as she healed me." Be'alu took a deep breath, stared up into the snow-weighted branches of the pines, and gave a soft smile. "I am ready."

Through the Wind God's eyes, Tomas saw the orb surrounding them swell. The golden light and dark mist swirled and eddied until entwined together, filling the clearing and lifting up and into the air. Gusts of wind spiraled around them, carrying the light and the dark above the trees where it expanded until nothing of either essence remained.

Murel slumped forward and into Tomas's chest. He caught her, feeling the wild beat of her heart.

"He's gone," she breathed. She lifted her chin, and taking Tomas's strong jaw in her hands, she kissed him long and hard. She pulled back, and seeing his return gaze, she flushed pink.

Tomas's eyes, still golden, stared back. "You truly are as pure of heart as Be'alu said. Though it was not your intent, thank you for sharing your passion with me. It is one of many layers of love between you and Tomas."

"What happened? Be'alu...he's gone."

"Better that I let Tomas explain."

. . .

## Mount Kanta, Nifolhad

Diarmait surveyed what remained of his assets. No lords of worth to captain his forces. Once Phelan died, those who remained switched allegiances to his niece, Queen Aghna. A handful of his bastard children had followed him to Mount Kanta, of whom Danold was the most useful. Mirra was at least legitimate, having been born to one of his many wives.

She'd been acting as his chatelaine, though very little staff remained for her to govern. He stared at the room that held his coffers, amazed that he'd retained as much coin as he had. He would need more to bolster his army with sell-swords.

A tentative rap sounded, and Diarmait closed the door to his riches, sealing the panel that hid the room behind it. "Enter."

Danold came in. "Sire, an envoy awaits in the hall."

"Kill them," he ordered. "I will not treat with my niece and her upstart prince."

"The envoy is not from Queen Aghna and King Ranulf, m'lord. But from the Southron Isles. They say their queen wishes to form an alliance."

"Queen? Queen of smugglers and pirates, more like."

"They say they bring a great gift, m'lord."

"Make them wait in the hall. And tell Mirra that she is to attend me immediately."

"Yes, m'lord."

Diarmait threw off his robe and—naked as the day he was born—strode to the tall reflecting glass in his chamber. His skin was clear of sores and infection; more, it had been rejuvenated. His entire physique was that of a man of thirty years. A rap on the door signaled Mirra's arrival, and he bade her enter. If she was shocked by his nudity, she hid it well. "You remind me more and more of Roger. He was the more calculating of my two sons."

"A compliment indeed, m'lord," she replied dutifully.

"I have decided to meet this ragtag envoy in my full regalia. Make yourself useful and help me to dress."

"As you command, sire..."

"If you have something more to say, then speak up," he ordered.

"The envoy..." She helped him into his clothing and raiment. "They are not what one would expect from the Southron Isles, m'lord. They are adhering to proper protocols, and their appearance...they do not look like smugglers and pirates."

"If you are going to eavesdrop, you should not use my exact words back to me. Now tell me what you sensed about them."

"Pardon, m'lord, I only repeated what Danold related to me. As for the Islers, they came with little expectations. Word must have reached them of your former incapacity. But care should still be taken, for their confidence is not false bravado."

"You are to accompany me, Daughter," Diarmait ordered. "Listen, but do not speak. Let us see what these ruffians offer."

"'Tis a great honor, my liege."

# CHAPTER TWENTY-TWO

# A Meeting of Minds

## Stolweg, Aurelia

"'Tis breathtaking—ordered fields and pastures, wild forests to the west, and those austere mountains to the north. The lake—it's so calm compared to the mighty Stolweg River," Murel admired, appraising the lush basin below them. They had arrived before dawn, Tomas having said he wanted her first view of Stolweg Keep to be the moment when the sunrise flushed its way down the stones from ramparts to roots. He'd spread out a blanket on the dew-touched grass, giving them a private moment before riding to the keep to meet the others in their group.

Months ago, she and he had briefed King Godwin and Queen Juliana on what they had discovered, then spent the winter at court. The first few weeks of celebrations, banquets, and the usual trappings of high court, felt alien to them. Sefrina, still there, quickly became a favorite, thanks to her dry wit. The proud Fyrjian had been enthralled by the pomp and circumstance.

But for her and Tomas, it seemed as if life at Kings Glen had continued forward while they'd been irrevocably changed. As winter marched on, they participated less and less in the daily festivities, preferring their own company or sojourning to the library, where they transposed the scrupulous notes Murel had taken.

A gust of spring-tinged air kicked up around them, freeing the pink petals from a nearby cherry tree. Tomas wrapped his arm around her shoulder, enrobing her in the warmth of his cloak, and they watched the magical fluttering swirl around them. The patterns were too elegant and purposeful to have been caused by a random breath of weather.

"Wherever we travel, flower petals shower down upon us." Murel smiled and tucked herself closer to Tomas. "I find the beauty of these gifts soothing."

"Then I'm glad," Tomas said, kissing the top of her head.

She didn't need to explain how turbulent her mind was; he could sense it. Their time in Kings Glen had been difficult for her. She'd confessed to him of wanting to scream at the frivolity at court, knowing that greater, more powerful forces were waking. She hadn't, but Queen Juliana was an observant woman. Without demanding an explanation, she tacitly agreed to allow Murel and Tomas to slowly withdraw until the weather permitted them to travel.

"The first time I laid eyes on Stolweg Keep," Tomas reminisced, "I was with Lark, Warin, Trian, Ailwen, and Lord Baldric. I remember asking Lark if he believed Lord Roger would be hanged for treason, and I was worried that Anna would be caught up in his crimes. I was so green. And now..."

Murel turned to him—his eyes revealed the ages of time, eyes like her own. For though not even thirty years old, the desert had made them as timeless as itself. She felt the call of the Fyrost even now. She always would—Tomas, too.

"We have so many years to grow old together," she whispered to Tomas, knowing that, like Fyrjians, the years of their lives would surpass a normal human's lifespan. "Decades to discover new things about one another, to watch our future children grow, and their children after that."

"I was thinking of other things at this moment. Like how you are more beautiful than the sun as it kisses the castle's parapets. And speaking of kisses..." He leaned in, unraveling her senses as he trailed his lips down her neck.

They spent but a little time divesting themselves of clothing. Falling back against the blanket, Tomas covered her with his gloriously naked body. She felt him, long and hard and ready, nestled in the vee of her legs, and when she spread her knees wider, needing him inside her, he shook his head.

"Not yet, my love," he murmured between kisses applied to the crease between her breasts. "Not until I've had my fill of you."

It was scandalous, Murel thought, making love in the open, where any errant god or goddess might observe them. But when Tomas drew her nipple into his mouth and sucked her, everything felt right in the world. She moaned as he pulled her deep into his mouth and then took his time laving the bud he'd drawn out. His tongue lashed at her other breast next, and she speared her fingers into the pure-white frost of his blond curls.

He nipped and licked his way down her body, and as gentle as the petals that floated about them, he swirled his tongue and teased her with a rhythm that shot sweet yearning straight to her core. When his lips closed around her nexus, he began strumming his fingers against her wet seam and hummed his appreciation at finding her ready.

Murel cried out her want, her need to be filled, and when he lifted his face and drew up her body, she put her hand on his chest. "I want you inside me while the world awakens."

He growled and brought himself to her opening. Then he surged, filling her completely. Once seated, he rocked forward, slowly withdrawing, and then lunging again, in a powerful dance that left her craving even more.

She met his thrusts, further sealing their bodies together with each powerful surge. She was ready to come apart, but he wasn't finished. Propped on one elbow, he possessed her breasts, kneading and massaging her in time with the pumping of his hips. She gasped, urging him deeper with her heels.

"Tomas," she moaned, and he kissed her, long and passionately.

Hips still pumping, he reached lower to tease her where their bodies were joined. And after his thrusts grew frenzied, he surged one last time, taking Murel with him as he tipped over the edge. Before them, the sun illuminated the sparkling granite of the distant keep. They collapsed in a heap on the blanket, lazily rearranging themselves to stare up into the morning sky as soft pink petals rained down around them in perfect, widening circles. Tomas pulled his cloak over them as Murel tucked herself into his side.

"We missed the sunrise," she managed, twirling a finger at a flower petal as it fell upon them.

"We can come back here every morning, if you like."

"That's all right. I'm looking forward to a bed." She rolled on her side to study his profile.

"I've enjoyed this part of our journey, just you and me."

She settled her cheek on the crook of his shoulder. "Maybe it comes from having had other voices in our heads. We never had a chance to talk about it, but what would you like to do when this is over? I could live anywhere as long as I am by your side."

"I feel the same," he said, kissing the tip of her nose. "The king mentioned Ragallach to me, but it's so far from Pheldhain and Floresta."

"But nearer to Nifolhad, and somehow, that feels right." She sat up and reached for her chemise, pulling it on. "We don't have to decide yet. Let's enjoy being itinerants for a while longer."

Tomas shrugged into his shirt, and then grabbed his breeches, poking first one foot, then the other, through the pant legs. As Murel lifted her hips from the blanket, pulling up her breeches, Tomas did the same. They dropped their bums back down at the same time and turned to each other to laugh. "A bed, a private bathing area...and Doreen's cooking."

"Are her pasties as good as everyone claims?" Murel asked, pulling on her boots and lacing them up.

"Better," Tomas said of Stolweg Keep's famous cook. "I would like to see what she can make of the dust tubers that Sefrina packed for us. Now, that would be something." He stood and held out his hand to her. A few paces off, their horses munched on the spring greens growing near the trees that edged the hill.

"Are there any left?"

"A couple dozen. The rind keeps them remarkably well preserved."

"It's the dirt crust," Murel said, and they chuckled. She gazed off toward the keep. "I suppose it's time."

They got up and folded the blanket, kissing as they brought the corners together. After she secured it to one of the horses, Tomas boosted her into her saddle, then mounted his Chevlain steed. Murel rode her favorite gelding from Kings Glen, on loan to her from the queen. Their Fyrjian mounts followed behind on leads. Tomas pulled up next to her, lifted her hand, and kissed her knuckles. Then they nudged their horses forward and over the crest of the hill. The slope was gentle, and they set their mounts into a canter, directing them to the causeway at the mill crossing.

• • •

Tomas held Murel's hand as they followed the sound of children's laughter, making their way to the great hall. It had been years since Tomas had been at Stolweg, and he took in the changes to the formerly forbidding space. The dark tapestries had been replaced with thick damasks, and the table that had been set upon the platform for the lord and lady had been lowered to the main floor. In fact, the dais was completely gone. Long tables with benches filled one section of the room. And a roaring fire filled the hearth, chasing away the damp chill from the spring morning. Comfortable furniture had been pushed before it for people to sit and rest and warm themselves.

A young girl with raven-black curls chased a little boy carrying a wooden sword, and a large, rather shaggy hound bounded after them. "They've grown," Tomas said to Murel, "but I'm guessing that those are Lark and Anna's children."

Nearby, Claire's youngest was tugging on her mother's skirt. Trian transferred their new babe to Claire's arms, and then whisked up his boy, tossing him in the air and catching him as his son giggled with joy. Claire looked up and was the first to notice their arrival, giving them a warm smile. Trian turned and waved, as did his firstborn.

From a side door, Anna bustled into the hall, carrying a tray laden with food. She was followed by two women also carrying trays. "That will be Grainne and Doreen," Tomas whispered to Murel. "She must have heard your wish, for those are pasties piled on her tray."

Lark followed a moment later, carrying jugs of either cider or beer in one hand. As his son ran past him, he plucked the wooden practice sword from his grip and handed it to his much-relieved daughter. His son pouted, but Lark gave him a stern look, arching his eyebrow.

"Sorry, Cella," the boy said to his sister.

"It's okay, Hughie," she relented, after leveling him with the same expression their father had given. "You'll get a practice sword soon. You need to grow a couple more inches first."

Grainne clapped her hands and called to the children. "Come along now. Celeste. Hugh. We set up a picnic in the courtyard for you."

"Where's George?" Hughie asked.

"With my little Hannah in the courtyard. I hear Will is letting them chase the chickens," Grainne answered. She offered to take Claire's baby.

"No need. Sarah's on her way," Claire explained, and a moment later, Sarah skipped into the hall.

Grainne shooed the children out the side door, and Doreen and Sarah, carrying Claire's baby, followed her.

Tomas kissed Murel's hand. *Ready?*

She nodded.

They joined their friends, and Tomas looked around. "We thought Warin and Anwyl would be here."

"We are," the couple said in unison as they entered the hall.

"It must be a special occasion," Warin added. "Doreen made pasties." He gave Murel a hug, then clapped Tomas on the back.

"It's good to see you, Tomas. And welcome to Stolweg, Murel," Anna greeted next, embracing them. "I would say that I'm glad you both made it back, but I had it on good authority that you would. And that authority was Claire, of course. The pasties are best when warm, so we should eat before Lark and Warin finish off the platter."

"I heard that," Warin called out jovially—there were two or three already piled on his plate and a half-consumed pasty in his hand.

"They're all acting—"

"As if nothing happened over the last year," Tomas finished for Murel when Anna stepped away. They stared at their friends for a moment.

"Anna wasn't joking," Trian said when he and Claire came to greet them. "Those pasties will be as good as gone. It's really good to see you, Tomas," he added, giving him a hardy slap on his arm. He narrowed his eyes. "Here I assumed you would return stones lighter from your trek across the desert, and you stand before us healthier than ever. Murel, you must be good for him." Then he noticed her hair, and Tomas's. "I'm looking forward to hearing your story."

"Go save them some pasties, Trian," Claire suggested. "The watch alerted us to your arrival hours ago, so we believed a good meal and some normalcy would be the best welcome we could give you." She tilted her chin in thoughtful contemplation. "From your expressions, perhaps it is too much."

"It's lovely, Claire," Murel insisted. "It's only that we were gone for so long, and we've been back for months, and…"

"It's as if we are still not home," Tomas finished for her.

"Perhaps, like your love for one another once was, home is still something you both need to discover," Claire suggested. "But you are among friends now—I take that back—you're among family. If you're hungry, grab some food. And if you would rather, you can first take some time to bathe and rest."

"I've been dreaming of trying Doreen's pasties," Murel admitted.

"Excellent," Claire said, looping her arms through theirs and taking them to the impromptu banquet. "Anna put you in the East Chamber. Your belongings have already been sent there."

"Isn't that the Armory?" Tomas asked.

"Not anymore," Anna answered. "We relocated all the weaponry to the original armory. It's much larger, and with more soldiers here, we needed the additional space. Claire and Trian have the North Chamber—so Trian can wake up and look toward Cathmara. And Anwyl and Warin are in the West Chamber. We moved the herbarium, as well."

"Built an entirely new building to house Anna's collection," Lark added, motioning everyone to sit. He narrowed his eyes. "Warin, you're being unusually quiet."

Murel's cousin swallowed, and then nervously cleared his throat. "I, uh… Say, what happened to your hair, Coz?"

"Warin!" Anwyl scolded. "I bet you were the envy at court, Murel. I remember how the ladies all wanted hair like Madyan's. They used dyes to disastrous effect. Who was it who lost her hair?"

"Lady Ellen," Warin provided. "Last I heard, it grew back, but as gray as a muddy day in Ragallach."

"Unlike something else which can't grow back if chopped off," Murel stated pointedly. "Castration? Really, Warin?"

"Castration!" Lark cried.

Tomas explained about the oaths Warin had secured from the noblemen at court.

"That's terrible! Why would you do such a thing?" Anwyl decried.

"It's all right," Murel interjected, rescuing her cousin from their affronted friends.

"I was wrong to do it, Murel. And I'm sorry," Warin apologized. "My sole intent was to protect you from the likes of men like...like...well, me. I never stopped to think about how it might make you feel. Something I was often guilty of back in those days." He gazed lovingly at Anwyl, and her scowl disappeared. "I hope you and Tomas can forgive me."

"Warin," Tomas began, "if there is one thing we've learned in the last couple years, it's that it's useless to hold anger and grudges. Life is too short. Of course, we forgive you."

Claire smiled at them both, nodding to Murel's white-frosted tresses. "Nifolhad left its mark on both of us," she remarked, referencing the beautiful ink covering her own body.

"Not only our hair," Murel stated, pulling up her sleeve and showing them the band around her arm.

"Our?" Anwyl asked. "Did the Artists mark you as well, Tomas?"

He pulled up his sleeve to show them his right bicep. He rotated his upper arm, revealing the full design and unintentionally flexing his muscles. The three ladies turned to Murel next with similar private smiles on their lips, and Murel grinned. Warin and Lark rolled their eyes.

But Trian laughed. "You're putting us all to shame, Tomas. Fatherhood has softened some of our hard edges."

"Speak for yourself," Warin retorted. "We haven't even begun our family yet."

"About that..." Anwyl started.

Warin whipped his head toward his wife. She nodded. "I was going to tell you last night, but we arrived so late, and you wanted to test out the...never mind," she finished, recalling that there was an audience.

Congratulations were shouted from all sides. "Now we'll have two reasons to celebrate on the equinox," Anna exclaimed. "A new baby on the way and your union, of course."

Tomas took Murel's hand as she smiled and thanked Anna for planning the fête, but privately, he felt her thoughts intertwine with his. *We're among friends here. They share this quest with us.*

"A celebration on the equinox sounds lovely, Anna."

As before, no one seemed to sense that he and Murel were somehow apart from everyone else, and then he caught Claire's eye. Each of them had gone through some ordeal in their lives, suffered some loss at the hands of others, but they had all survived, thanks to their trust in one another. Claire smiled and gave them a slight nod. These were friends who understood that something greater than themselves existed.

"As much as we want to hear everything as soon as possible, your journey has been a long one. Why don't you take a few hours to bathe and rest? We'll convene in the library before our evening meal," Anna suggested, bringing everyone back to the task at hand.

"Yes," Tomas said, rising from the bench and lending his hand to Murel. He began to lead the way to the East Chamber but stopped. "You haven't moved your library, have you?"

Lark grinned. "Not yet."

* * *

It was late afternoon when they made their way to the library. Earlier, fresh water had been delivered to the East Chamber, and she and Tomas had soaked for what seemed like forever, sharing the large basin. Oils, soaps, and soft drying cloths had been laid out. She'd buffed most of the moisture from her hair but hadn't enough time to properly plait it, and it hung over her shoulder in a loose braid, accentuating the strands of white against the dark underlayers.

They were the last to arrive, and Murel smiled, remembering the reason. Tomas grinned back at her. But upon entering the room, Murel couldn't help feeling the agitation that she'd experienced earlier creep back up. These were her friends, but why did she feel that they could never understand what she'd gone through? Tomas, sensing her disquiet again, took her hand in his and kissed her knuckles. He soothed her heart, and she'd somehow forgotten since returning to Aurelia that she could draw strength from him. So, she sat, facing the others, while he poured them each a glass of wine, handing it to her and sitting beside her.

Warin gave her an encouraging nod, keeping a lock on his characteristically glib tongue—the casual group they'd banqueted with in the great hall had been replaced by three couples intent on hearing every detail of their journey.

"Everything began in Naca'an." Murel then told them about the first attack and how she came to be marked. She spared not a single detail—even telling them about the exotic spices she'd smelled on *Moon Caster*—and related how they'd been attacked on the dock and how she'd nearly been killed by the assailants in the alley.

"And you were the only one who was injured," Trian asked, "in both incidents?"

"Ronan was also hurt," Tomas explained. "He was knocked out when the pallet broke free."

"And he was recovering, then grew ill again, complaining that he was forgetting things?" Claire asked.

"Yes," Murel replied, wondering why it was important.

"What happened after you were attacked in the alley, Tomas? When you, Jesper, and Ronan managed to save Murel."

"That's not exactly correct," Tomas answered, surprising her. "Ronan was not with us. Only Jesper, and then Sefrina, with her fellow Umbren."

"Did Ronan ever say what happened to him?" Trian asked.

"No," Tomas said. "When we woke, Jesper told us he had already set sail back to Aurelia. But we're getting ahead of the story now."

Murel sat forward and recounted, "We never determined who the exact culprits were. Process of elimination pointed toward Diarmait's supporters."

"He's the most likely culprit," Anna agreed. "His hatred of Claire and me, and Anwyl, is well documented."

Tomas explained how they came to be marked, and how it connected them. How they were able to draw strength for one another.

"But it's more," Murel said with a soft smile. "We're bondmates."

"You mean they marked you, and suddenly, you're married?" Anna exclaimed.

"Yes…no. It's more, actually," Tomas replied, "but I know what you're thinking. This wasn't forced on us—though we reacted as if it had been at first. Later, we came to understand that the Artists could not have marked us in the way that they did if we were not already in love. And in binding us together, our union is stronger than any wedding rite or handfasting—we did both, by the way. I don't know how to explain it, but we're…connected."

"That's so sweet," Princess Anwyl said.

Murel shared a look with him. They were still learning what it meant to be bondmates, and much of it was private. She changed the subject and spoke to them about Jesper being the Rottu and being hunted by the storm. And how she and Tomas were drugged and abandoned by Sefrina.

"Hunted?" Lark asked. "As in, the storm was sentient? How did you survive it?"

"It was our connection and the runes on our arms that saved us," Murel stated. "We gained entrance into Mitra's temple." She then explained who Mitra was and how she traveled the desert with them.

"A goddess lived within you," Anwyl said. "How is that possible?"

"She is that part of the Sky Goddess who can take corporeal form—forgive me, if she's listening—but lesser than Sky. It has to do with being a vessel and open to being filled by her spirit. This hair was her doing—she said it was a gift." Murel hadn't missed the concerned look Warin passed to Anwyl when she'd asked for Mitra's forgiveness.

Claire steepled her fingers. "So, Madyan should have been the one to be filled by Mitra, and Jesper as the Rottu, he was for Kardia."

"They got there in the end," Tomas added, after Murel tried explaining what happened inside the mountain with Be'alu and the Wind God. "Jesper and Madyan; Mitra and Kardia."

"And you left Jesper in Nifolhad?" Warin asked.

The question was innocent enough, but six pairs of eyes waited for her answer, and Murel couldn't help but bristle. "Jess finally has some peace, Warin."

"He found love," Tomas added. "And with Madyan, of all people. Show them the maps that you drew of the Southron Isles, Murel."

"I've sailed with Grieg for years," Warin said after she spread out the rolled parchment. "I never conceived of there being so many islands." He started making notes.

"Can I see your marks again?" Anwyl asked, and they obliged. "Sylvan…and Mitra graced you with the gift of healing."

"Yes," Murel answered, and then regarded Claire. "There's Umbren here as well, and though I am not a warrior, Tomas lends me strength."

"You said the Mitra and Kardia were like shadows. Be'alu, too, by the sounds of it," Trian offered. "It makes sense that you would be marked as both a healer and a shadow."

"You're a shadow healer," Anwyl stated sagely, reminding them that she had one of the brightest minds in the Known Realms, even though her statements could sometimes sound young and naïve.

Murel had never thought of it that way, but it was true. "There is one more thing," she added. "But first, we might need something stronger than wine."

While Lark poured apple brandy from Meramont, Murel spread out the pages of rubbings they'd taken from the mountain. Everyone gathered around the table.

"These are ancient and…Fyrjian?" Anwyl wondered aloud. "They predate anything I've ever seen in Sophiana."

Tomas pointed to one of the figures. "This one is on my arm; it is called the rod. And that cup-looking one on Murel is the chalice. They are inscribed at the very top of Mount Kardia," Tomas explained. "In a crown of stones carved from the peak of the mountain itself."

"Like a henge," Anna stated, and Murel nodded. "Many of these match the carvings in the stones in our valley to the south."

"Another mystery to solve, for no one alive can read these," Warin noted, pouring over the first page.

"Er, we can," Tomas said, surprising everyone.

"But how?" Warin demanded.

"Because," Tomas said carefully, "as Marlita and the Fanm are able to commune with Sky, I can commune with Wind. And the runes represent his story. He himself etched the stones and then flung them across the known realms. It is why the symbols are the same here in Stolweg."

"Our henge is from Nifolhad," Anna said, and sat down.

"Carved from the very crown at the acme of Mount Kardia in the Fyrost Desert," Murel said.

"There are other henges in Aurelia," Trian pointed out.

"Warin and I have visited them," Anwyl stated. "None are so old as the henge here. And etched runes exist nowhere else...at least that we know of." She paced. "If the story is true, and the Wind God—Wind, as you call him— saved Be'alu's brethren, sending them to be the first people of Aurelia, it would make sense that they would erect monuments to their gods and goddesses."

"What do they say?" Warin asked.

Murel opened up one of her journals. "We all know the prophecy by heart. Does it bear repeating?" she asked, and everyone shook their heads.

"Thanks to the Fenrhi, our prophecy is missing a few ingredients," Tomas revealed. "Before I start, you have to understand that the intent of the prophecy is as how Wind translated it to me. Our version imposes our rules of phrasing to what was translated, and over the centuries, the original meaning was distorted. The early scholars broke up the words in the translations, and the Fenrhi assigned these divisions, creating their caste system. Duty, shield, truth, and healing. According to Wind, no one idea can exist without the other."

Murel slid the journal toward the others. "You must forget about the Fenrhi castes and see the prophecy through fresh eyes. There are five realms: sky and everything in it; then water with its seas, rivers, and lakes...even snow and rain; earth, or the mountains, hills, and plains; fauna is next and is comprised of all animals, including you and me; and finally, flora, with its trees and plants, even mold. These five realms work together to balance life and death. And the old gods and goddesses ruled them, beginning with Sky, as her domain covered everything."

"Are you saying there are deities for mountains and lakes and flowers in addition to Sky and Wind and Forest?" Warin asked. "And...do you believe in these...these...deities?"

"What if we do, Coz?" Murel shot back.

"Warin is concerned for you," Claire offered. "He only—"

"Believing in something is not the same as worshipping it," Murel interrupted, staring at Warin, as if he had called her loyalty into question.

Tomas set his hand over hers. He cleared his throat. "Yes," Tomas said, answering Warin's original query. "There are many...entities. Just because they are forgotten does not mean they stopped existing." He directed the conversation back to the sheets before them.

"The prophecy isn't so much as wrong as it is incomplete," Murel started.

> *"Duty and shield to cast out blind obeisance*
> *Truth and healing be a warrior's protection..."*

"And this new line—" Tomas interjected.

> *"All working in harmony to bring back that which is lost."*

"Claire's markings are the closest to what the ideal should be," Murel added. "We must all work in harmony. The next line holds the most critical error. 'One saved by four' referred to the quest set to Tomas and me. It does not refer to Madyan being the fifth and being saved by the fourth couple."

"Wind explained that the lines do not occur in any order...no 'this happens first, then this next,'" Tomas went on.

"It took four of you to save one," Anwyl said, understanding coming to her features. "You saved Wind."

"Not Wind, though he was freed," Tomas said. "We saved Be'alu. Wind and I, with help from Mitra and Kardia."

"You saved Be'alu?" Anna challenged. "When you already knew that Diarmait's evil can be traced to him? He is the monster who set this all in motion."

"Because for life to exist, everything must be in harmony," Claire explained. "The good in this world. And the bad. The rest of the prophecy, 'five control the sixth.' How does that differ?"

"It means that for harmony to exist, we must find one more couple to succeed. For only five are needed for life," Tomas stated. "But...it was prophesied that a sixth couple would rise to try to control the five realms.

Instead of '*Five control the sixth,*' it should be '*Five unite to stand for life; the sixth commands death.*'"

"*But first and last, there will be blood,*" Murel finished. "Wind said that she, the Sky Goddess, is the first and the last—her absence has thrown the five realms into discord. And we can all understand the blood part."

The room fell silent as they each contemplated the task ahead. It was Anna who finally rallied. "Do we all agree that the sixth is most likely Fanm Larenne, and she controls death, or the Sky Goddess?" Everyone nodded. "Then our next step is obvious: we must find the fifth couple."

"But where do we start the search?" Claire asked.

"Warin and I have an idea," Anwyl answered.

"Does it have anything to do with why you were so interested in Ronan?" Murel guessed, and Warin nodded. "He's being influenced by someone, isn't he?"

"A rogue Kena from the Fenrhi, though I don't believe she was behind the attacks. Her name is Vala," Anwyl provided. "And she helped us to escape Prince Bowen. I watched as she sailed away on *The Salt Wife*. She controlled Captain Juna—he's from the Southron Isles and so is his crew. When the storm hit that destroyed Bowen's ship, *The Salt Wife* sailed due east. It hasn't been seen since."

"Ronan—if he's being controlled by Vala—probably had her stowed away in his cabin," Warin added.

"To what end?" Tomas asked.

"She's in hiding," Anwyl answered. "She's wanted by the Fenrhi, by Queen Aghna, and probably Diarmait. And she was smart enough to steer clear of Fanm Larenne."

"And don't forget," Warin added. "Juna and his crew, like Grieg, would be killed if they returned to the Isles. Vala needs information and protection. Ronan is in a position to give her both."

"What do you see, Claire?" Murel asked. "Can you tell us if Ronan and Vala are the fifth couple?"

"I wish it were that easy. I've never met Ronan, or Vala, for that matter. I have no idea what their futures hold for them."

"Then we'll have to try to remedy that," Warin stated. "Except for his trip to Naca'an, Ronan has become a recluse. He doesn't venture from Meramont, but one event may draw him out."

"The Royal Tribute Day," Murel guessed. "And Vala would not want to miss that. The next tribute day is over a year from now. What do we do until then?"

"I have at least a thousand questions for you both," Anwyl stated with a grin. "Enough to last months, if you are willing to be interrogated by me. The Fyrjians and their lore are topics that have always intrigued me. As you know, I am Queen Aghna's ambassador—Warin and I must tour Aurelia again. Would you join us?"

"We've been asked to consider residing permanently in Ragallach," Tomas revealed.

"I'm so sorry!" Warin blurted out.

"Warin!" Anwyl, Anna, and Claire censured at the same time, while Trian and Lark chuckled.

"It's all right," Murel said. "I don't know how to explain this, but we are connected to the Fyrost Desert now. And nowhere else in Aurelia are we so close to Nifolhad."

"And don't forget your love of sheep," Tomas stated, patting her hand. "Ragallach has the best wool in the known realms."

Everyone stared at her, and she and Tomas burst out laughing.

"Sorry," Tomas added. "I thought we could all use a little levity. Blood and death and all that."

"Your delivery was impeccable, as always," Warin saluted.

"When do you start your tour?" Murel asked.

"This is our first stop," Anwyl replied. "We leave for Whitmarsh in two weeks. Then Cathmara and Ragallach in the summer, and south to Morland and Sterland in the fall. We'll spend the winter in Pheldhain, visiting the southernmost smallholds, then the rest next spring. We'll then return to Kings Glen for the Royal Tribute Day around the autumnal equinox. Claire and Trian are coming with us as far as Cathmara to see his family. Lady Caroline will be there with Cordhin."

Murel shared a quick look with Tomas. Neither wanted to venture south and closer to the Isles. The King's offer of Ragallach was quickly becoming the perfect solution.

"Ragallach," Lark wondered aloud. "Ailwen will be happy to be relieved of that duty; he's written that his mother has finally called him home to Calí. Ragallach couldn't ask for a better lord and lady."

"We'll join you," Tomas answered for them both. "At least until Ragallach."

"This is a good time to break before supper," Anna declared. "We have a few things planned for the next couple of weeks, including a hunt and a visit to the springs."

"Springs?" Anwyl asked, following her from the library with the others.

"Hot springs," Anna expounded. "Trian found them, actually. Very restorative. Lark and I have even visited them in the winter."

Claire lingered behind. "Can I speak with you both? Privately."

Murel closed the door to the library, and she and Tomas sat back down.

"There are very few people in this world who I cannot read. Trian is one, and to some extent, your brother. I knew before you left Aurelia that you and Tomas were the fourth couple. I saw your love and knew that you would return safely to our shores. But now, I see nothing."

*Should we tell her?*

Tomas nodded.

"That's because we are different people than who we were before."

"Are you able to silently communicate with each other?"

Murel nodded. "If you can't read us, how did you know?"

"Trian pointed it out to me earlier."

"He's always been the most observant of all of us," Tomas noted.

"Each of us has been changed by this prophecy," Claire began. "We all have a former life, one that we had to survive in order to flourish later. My time in Nifolhad took what was innate inside me and made it flower and grow. Had I stayed in Aurelia, I would have never known that of which I'm capable. Can you tell me how you are different? And I don't need to use my sight to know that you are angry, Murel."

"Can you blame me? We didn't ask for any of this," Murel stated. "Sure, we accept it, because, to do otherwise…well, it was a choice between life and

death. What happened to us, to me, it was painful beyond words, and—"
She paused. "It's not your fault. I'm sorry."

Claire took her hand. "No need to apologize. Ever. The rest of us...we've had more time than you to come to terms with what fate had thrust upon us. But with the sharing of our stories, and over time, our pain and heartache became more bearable. I was once under the control of the Kena Caste, and they manipulated me into forgetting who I was. But I can't imagine what it must've been like to give yourself over to Mitra, to lose control of yourself. I am glad that you are free of her now, free of being possessed—what is it?" Claire asked when Murel flinched. "Is she still with you?"

Tomas squeezed her hand. "It would be easier to simply show her."

Murel sighed.

"You must swear to only reveal this if lives are at imminent risk." When Claire agreed, Tomas gave her an encouraging nod. "Go ahead."

Murel closed her eyes, then opened them and lifted her gaze to Claire. Their friend gasped. Murel blinked again, knowing the black tendrils that had filled her eyes would recede. "We told you that we saved Be'alu. But it was..."

"When we separated Kardia and the Wind God from the storm," Tomas said, taking over the telling. "We explained how Be'alu tried to kill Madyan when he sensed that Mitra transferred to her. The void left Murel vulnerable—she was an empty vessel, and she had her gifts from Mitra that Be'alu could manipulate."

"Be'alu took me," Murel said steadily. "In every way you can conceive. He ripped into all my memories, tore through my heart as if he wanted to rend my soul from existence. I killed...he killed a man. Then, he...used me to...we hurt Tomas." She lifted Tomas's hand to her heart. "If it hadn't been for you and the others... Claire, it's bad enough to be aware of your very essence, but it is a whole new level of hell to be helpless against another entity trying to destroy it. I did the one thing I could: I hid. From Be'alu's evil and the unbearable pain."

"In the end, the only way to defeat Be'alu without destroying Murel was to heal him," Tomas said. "We could not allow him to escape, so Murel was forced to carry him within her."

"Is he still with you?" Claire asked.

"No. He's found peace. Wind forgave him for trapping him in the storm. We proved to him that his children survived the Sky Goddess and that the Forest Goddess, in her own way, still exists here, in Aurelia. We healed him," Murel finished.

"*You* healed him," Tomas amended. "And together, we released him."

"But your eyes?"

"A gift of some sort, according to Be'alu," Murel provided. "Though I do not yet know its import."

Claire leaned back where she sat.

"We didn't tell the king and queen," Murel said. "Only you know."

"And every Fyrjian," Tomas added dryly.

Claire smiled at that. "I guarantee that they will never tell a soul." She then pinned Tomas with a piercing gaze. "And you, Tomas?"

"Me?"

"Your connection to the Wind God is stronger than simply communing with him."

"Why do you say that?" Murel asked, suddenly wary.

"His eyes flashed with gold when you showed me what remains of Be'alu." She looked back and forth between them. "Will you set Wind free?"

"I don't hold him, not like the Fanm holds Sky. He chooses to anchor himself to me. And before our quest is over, we are going to need him. His sister will be angry when she is liberated from the Southron Isles."

"Thank you for trusting me," Claire said.

"But…" Murel prompted. "You wish to share this with Trian, don't you?"

"No, that's not it," Claire stated. "Although I would like his insight."

Tomas shrugged, as if leaving it up to Murel. "All right," she said. "What else is it, then?"

"I was wondering," Claire asked, "could I try something with you?"

"That depends on what you ask."

"When you showed me your markings, I was instantly aware of the runes woven into the designs. Drawn to them, if you will. I can only describe it as some force surged through me. Do you mind showing them again? I would like to touch them." She pushed up her sleeves first, revealing the tendrils and vining lines on her arms.

Murel and Tomas did the same, and Claire reached out to touch the bands. She gasped, pulling away, and they all stared in wonder at her arms. The moss-green and sooty-charcoal designs moved on her skin as if being stirred by a gentle breeze, and the amber pattern of the honeycomb glowed and pulsed. "Your eyes have changed," she said. "Both of you!"

A soft breeze wafted through the room, bringing with it a fluttering of flower petals and the scents of a sea that was leagues away from Stolweg Keep. "So many unexpected surprises in this realm," Tomas, or rather, Wind stated, reaching for Claire's arm to study the designs. "Why have you called us, Daughter?"

Murel touched Tomas's chin, drawing his face to hers. "Daughter?"

The door to the library flew open, and a gust of wind brought more flower petals. Trian rushed in, followed by Anna, Lark, Warin, and Anwyl.

Tomas stood, and Wind made him seem impossibly taller. He smiled upon them. "You are all my children, descendants of Kardia and Mitra, gathered together for—two are missing..." He regarded Murel. "Now I understand Be'alu's gift."

"Where is he?" Claire asked. "And is Tomas all right?"

"Tomas permits me to share this form. He sees and hears and feels what I do. He is very much here."

"It's true," Murel stated, and the others in the room stared at her eyes.

"Do not fear for Murel—it is she who speaks, not Be'alu. What you are witnessing is drawn forth due to my connection with him. But Be'alu will never again be more than a shadow. His spirit is busy rediscovering his love for the Forest Goddess. It is she who sent these flower petals, courtesy of her sister."

"They are here, in Aurelia?" Claire asked.

"Of course," Wind said. "As are all of us who tend to the five realms. Unlike me, and my sister, they have always existed here. Who do you think gave you each your gifts?"

# Epilogue

## Ragallach, Aurelia

Tomas smiled at the orchard mistress, Jilleann, and her daughter. Coming back to Ragallach had been like coming home. He'd spent years in the far northwest territory and had learned to appreciate the stoic people who populated the long strip of land that ran down a third of the western coast of Aurelia. They were a hardy people, and slow to trust outsiders. After years of being under the thumb of Lord Roger and his men, the abused Ragallachans had every reason to mistrust Tomas and Murel.

He and Murel had officially accepted the king's offer to govern the territory and were appointed its permanent lord and lady. Word had been sent to Ailwen that his temporary posting to Ragallach would end upon their arrival, freeing him to return to his home on the island smallhold of Calí. From there, he would begin his new mission, watching the comings and goings of his neighbor, none other than Lord Ronan of Meramont. He hadn't envied Ailwen and his impending reunion with his estranged mother, but even Ailwen had concurred that it was time to mend the rift between them.

Tomas had been surprised, however, at how welcoming the people of Ragallach had been. Though he'd been gone from the territory for over two years, they remembered him and opened their arms to their new lord and lady. The transformation didn't end with Ragallach's people, either. He stared at the pijala orchard with pride. "You've done amazing work here, Jilleann. I've seen the trees in Pheldhain and in Meramont, but here, your trees have outpaced them in growth."

"They do love our narrow band of earth," Ragallach's orchard mistress explained, nodding to include her daughter in the conversation. "But I have to admit that we've never seen so many blossoms as there are this spring."

A soft breeze gusted along the cliff, pulling the buttery-yellow petals from the branches, causing them to spiral around Jilleann, before swirling around her daughter like a halo. "I told you, Mama," the twelve-year-old, Hina, whispered. "They came back."

Jilleann looked worriedly at Tomas. "Pay her no mind, m'lord."

"Nonsense," Tomas soothed. "Your daughter is correct."

Jilleann's mouth dropped. "But…"

"Lady Murel and I would enjoy hearing Ragallach's lore. You'll find that we may be able to add a little to your histories."

"See," Hina said. "Lord Tomas and his lady brought them back!"

Tomas smiled at the girl and plucked a few flower petals from her hair. "What if I told you that they never truly left?" He winked. "Speaking of my lady, I find myself missing her." He took his leave of the mother and daughter team and went in search of Murel.

He knew where he would find her. It was their favorite place in Ragallach. A sheltered dip along the cliffs, where a grove of coastal willow trees flourished—though everything in Ragallach, from bark to beast, was suddenly thriving. The secluded spot was also the westernmost point in all of Aurelia. Nowhere else in the realm was the distance to Nifolhad so short. He took the moss-covered path through the thick patch of trees, coming up to the flat boulders where Murel was waiting for him.

She turned to greet him, smiling and holding out her hand for him to sit beside her on the weatherworn boulder that was just a touch too regular in shape to be naturally occurring. If that weren't enough of a clue, it was the same granite that topped Mount Kardia and, though they were nearly eroded, were etched with runes. Once he was settled, she leaned against him, resting her head on his shoulder. "How are Jilleann and Hina?" she asked, as they gazed out at the sparkling Western Sea.

"Aware that our presence has opened the doors to our unconventional friends." He chuckled. "The rest of this realm perceives Ragallach to be a near-barren territory, home to only sheep and pijala trees. But the old ways run deeper here than even in Cathmara."

"I'm not surprised," Murel stated. "This morning, when Silva was showing me the storerooms, a tapestry fell and unrolled before us. It depicted a spring festival."

"Did our friendly housekeeper have anything to say?"

"No, but she was a mite enthusiastic when I asked her to have it cleaned so that we might replace some of the more dour tapestries that were installed when Lord Roger was here. According to Silva, there is one for each season. They were hidden when Roger ordered them burned."

A comfortable silence grew, and for a while, they simply enjoyed the spectacular view before them, watching as the sea terns competed with the osprey, wheeling in the sky before diving into the waves at the base of the cliff to pluck out unwary fish.

"We made the right choice, Tomas," Murel finally said. "This place feels..."

"Like home."

Beside him, she nodded. An osprey lifted away with a silvery fish flapping in its talons. Instead of flying to its nest, it flew toward Murel and Tomas, landing on the boulder next to them. Neither he nor Murel were surprised when it stared at them, then crouched to take flight once more, leaving behind the freshly caught fish.

"That's the third one today," Murel said, pointing to a lumpy sack at her feet. "Welcome gifts."

"I've been thinking about Be'alu's boon," Tomas started. "He was a human who married a goddess and had children with her. Something about him was different...special...a man able to see the gods and goddesses, to live with them. Perhaps this ability is part of what he gave you. And if it is, it stands to reason that our part in this strange odyssey will involve not just Sky and Wind, but their brethren as well."

"As long as I have you by my side, Tomas." She tilted her chin and leaned forward to kiss him. A mere second before their lips met, she pulled away. "Thank you. You're a fine hunter, but three fish is enough for us. Besides, you probably have a family to feed."

The osprey had come back, and Tomas laughed as the raptor cocked its head at its catch, then lifted away with it grasped in its talons. He turned back to Murel and told her about the pijala tree blossoms and Hina. "We might need to set some boundaries, or I'll never get to kiss my wife."

"Then I'll have to do it for you, my heart," Murel stated, planting a kiss upon his lips, one that quickly grew passionate.

And as Tomas drew her closer, and she wrapped her arms around him, everything felt right in their life. Tomorrow's troubles would wait—for now, peace was to be found in each other's embrace.

...

## Acerto Island, Meramont, Aurelia

"Are you sneaking out on me again?" Ronan dazedly mumbled. He sat up on his bed and rubbed the sleep from his eyes. "You could stay and break your fast with me. Meet my mother."

As she shrugged into her shirt, he grabbed the hem and pulled her toward him. She allowed herself to tumble forward and into his arms. "Stay," he suggested again.

"I mustn't, my dear," Vala replied. "Though it will be difficult to leave you, looking as delectable as you always do in the morning."

"Difficult for me as well," he purred, drawing her attention to his aroused state. "Please stay," he begged this time, and then leaned down to kiss her.

Vala lost herself in the feel of his lips, and when he rolled them so that she was on her back and he hovered above her, she gave in. He made love to her, slowly and tenderly, until their passions were sated. After, he wrapped her in his arms, tucking her against him as if fearful she would leave.

As much as she wanted to give him that which he desired—what she desired, as well—she couldn't. For Ronan truly did not want her. It was all a lie. And Vala, having fallen for him, would rather live the lie than be rejected. "Sleep some more, my love," she soothed, imbuing her voice with the power of the Kena. Moments later, his breath evened.

She dressed, slipped from his chamber before anyone woke, and made her way to the harbor where her cabin awaited her aboard *The Fish Wife*. Juna had left the gangplank down for her return. She skipped lightly up the incline, then jumped down, landing like a cat on the deck. Her captain stood before her.

"Don't look at me like that, Juna," Vala said, and yawned. "The sun has not even risen, and I need to get some sleep."

"How am I looking at you?"

"Like you are judging me."

"You're a fair enough judge of your own character, Vala. You don't need me to arbitrate your actions. Besides, a woman has the right to take what pleasure she can, whenever she desires it. But she should not abuse her power over men."

"You think Ronan will not care for me if I free him."

"What I think is that you will never know that answer until you do," Juna replied. "When you freed me and our crew, did we reject you? The opposite, in fact. We swore our fealty. What could it hurt, to ease Ronan from your thrall? If he rejects you, then he is not worthy of your regard. Besides, there are other places we could go. We could request asylum from King Godwin."

"You know that they would demand some payment in kind. Information I would not readily give. And what about you? Could you betray your brethren? Could you share the secrets of the Southron Isles with the Aurelians? Secrets you have only hinted at to me?"

"I would not be betraying my people if my words could speed the removal of Fanm Larenne. I would be helping to liberate them. And you are making excuses."

This, Vala knew, was what ate at her friend. He and his crew had fled the Southron Isles, leaving behind their friends and families. These last few years in Meramont, Vala had stalled for time. She was comfortable here. The last thing she wanted was to be involved in some war between the realms, but it was inevitable. She would have to take a side, and Juna and his crew would follow her.

Vala smoothed her tunic. "I'll worry about choosing allies tomorrow. Today, I need to sleep." As she stepped away, a soft breeze gusted around her, one carrying a shower of flower petals. She lifted her arms as it swirled around her, bringing with it a scent she'd forgotten: home. She tilted her head and closed her eyes, and on the breeze that ruffled her hair, she could just make out the tinkling notes of wind chimes.

She opened her eyes, wondering if she had imagined it, but all around her were flower petals. And her friend Juna stood there, smiling at her.

"Was that your goddess?" she asked, half-afraid, for she had once witnessed the deity's terrible power.

"Not mine," Juna said. "That was something else entirely. And whether you wish it or not, the choice has been made for you."

The End.

# ACKNOWLEDGEMENTS

Writing the Heart & Hand series is a battle between following an outline and being dragged away from it as my characters force me to write their stories as they see fit—at least it feels that way. *The Shadow Healer* was no exception. Even its title proclaimed itself before I had a chance to conceive of Mitra, Kardia, and Be'alu.

*Merci mille fois* to Nat at KaNaXa for her amazing cover art. She designed Murel's and Tomas's cover a half year before their story was even finished, capturing their love and strength perfectly, and providing me with visual inspiration.
I would like to thank both Kay Copeland and Cindy Ray Hale for once again helping me to catch my typos and punctuation missteps.

As the dedication notes, I am so grateful to my readers. I hope you find yourself transported to the Known Realms when you read my stories. And if you haven't already guessed from the epilogue, book five of the Heart & Hand series is in the works.

ABOUT THE AUTHOR

From San Diego, where I met my Montanan husband, to San Francisco, where I married him, to Chicago, where the twins were born, this Michigander wanderer-at-heart settled once and for all in Northern Virginia. Here, I continue to write, work, and play.

For exclusive content such as deleted chapters—"Strawberries" and "Belly Button" to name two—visit my website at www.nekelleher.com to subscribe to my newsletter.

# OTHER BOOKS IN THE SERIES

*Wild Lavender*
*The Queen's Dance*
*The Naked Moon*
Coming Soon: Book Five